SAFETY OF WAR

ROB BENVIE

SAFETY OF WAR

COACH HOUSE BOOKS

first edition

Published with the assistance of the Canada Council for the Arts and the Ontario Arts Council. The publisher also acknowledges the assistance of the Government of Canada through the Book Publishing Industry Development Program and the Government of Ontario through the Ontario Book Publishing Tax Credit Program.

LIBRARY AND ARCHIVES CANADA CATALOGUING IN PUBLICATION

Benvie, Tigre, 1975-
    Safety of war / Rob Benvie.

ISBN 1-55245-143-7

    I. Title.

PS8603.E58S34 2004   C813'.6   C2004-905572-0

As if out of a dream: gnashed teeth and fistfuls of tank-tracked mud. Shoulders of gleaming stars, chests like continents. Landscapes, snow-coated stretches. Reclining desert dunes, where terrain proves harsh and dust infiltrates all nooks. Dust in boot soles. War. Panels of skin pasted against crumbles of brick. Blood in toilets. Soldiers and ox carts. The reek of sweat against plastic, or canvas. A soundtrack swelling as opening credits roll, foreshadowing doom and apocalypse and chaos and love and disappointment. Digits tiptoeing steadily from 0:00:00. A sudden impact, then caramel spilled over Umbro shorts: a Dairy Queen Peanut Buster Parfait, engraved in memory's stone. Trauma shuffled into slogans. Faces of proud men in lines, pixels. Helicopters splitting clouds. Gassy columns rising through drooping vines and charred branches. Smoke. Faces. A child, staring out at a boundless ocean, wondering where eternity is. The yellow eyes of a demon who breathes flame and sings in voices like howitzers. Cityscapes assailed by lightning. Speed in circuits, metal machines, cataclysmic whorls. Cities crumbling as champions sweat. Heroes in the throes of rapture, sinless. Heroes spitting and sweating. Mouths screaming, fangs tearing, howling. The battle rages. Hero as unbridled force, pounding justice into the world. Hero as harbinger of doom. Hero as geography. Hero as cartography. Bravery. Honour. Bloodthirst. Flaming cities, cartoons of panic. Heroes sneering at valour, their noses aimed at grease-slick metal and the cleaning of carbines. Oceans, storms, beer. Vast tracts of grassland, littered with land mines and fragments of bodies. Hit PAUSE, freeze-framing death's sweeping grandeur. The hero's strong jaw. Image as the greater ideal. Heroism as hope, as passion, as breakfast. Freeze the march of integrity's corrosion. Years of sacrifice stagger and wobble. Shell casings lie in puddles of gore and excrement. Heroes, fighting and loving, dying with grace and unshakeable valour. Noble champions. Fathers, weeping.

I

Yes. November was cold, and December was colder, but January – it is the coldest cruellest hardest yet.

Trapped in winter's descent, everything slows. The city hunkers down, all routes and fissures clotted. Huge bulwarks of dirty snow ridge sidewalks, rising out of collapses of greyish wetness. Branches waver with the clinging weight of ice, ready to splinter and fail.

This day is a blip of static, an echo, a point on the graph of fluttering time.

Look: David, our hero, gazes at and into the frozen city.

This day is nervous and shaky and skeptical, even before it begins. There is no forgiveness in the assault of sub-zero temperature, no mercy hurrying against the first stabs of the morning sun, no ecstasy in the sudden freeze of hair still shower-wet or in the noxious gulps of bus exhaust. And there is certainly no forgiveness in the elevator as David ascends the innards of Tower 2, up to the sixteenth floor like a gurgle rising in the building's swallowing throat, his only companion in this skyward venture the squat little woman who commands the coffee cart on its morning route through the duohexagonal floors of Tower 2 and its twin, Tower 1; there is no tenderness in her squiggled scowl as she sells him a varnished blueberry scone and a cup of coffee, no glory as she sniffs politely to the tinkle of change plopped in her palm, saying *have a good one*. She departs at the twelfth.

David continues elevatoring, then exits through parting doors, striding unquestioningly through the hallway's bending elbows to a large pine door. He enters; this is the reception area of the office where he works.

Naoko, the vigilant and birdish receptionist, headset framing her head's narrow point, looks up from her computer keyboard.

'Morning, David,' she says.

'Morning,' he says.

This is how they greet one another, with cheery formality. At the end of the day he will depart, and she will say to him in the same tonality *see ya tomorrow David*, and he will say *see ya tomorrow*.

He continues through reception, past Naoko's bunker of fax and computer and file cabinet, past the leather couches and the coffee table fanning *Newsweek* and *Digital Marketing Monthly* and *Advertising Age*, down the hall past the conference room. He casts a quick glance inside to find several of his co-workers seated around the large table, their faces in coffee mugs or hunched over binders, printouts, newspapers.

David nods. He is nodded to.

This corridor leads him to an adjoining corridor, which in turn brings him to an opening, an expanse of room compartmented by desks segregated at perpendicular angles by alleys of space and a long table armed with a paper cutter and a dry-mounter. The room is cast in stark light by an enormous window lining the opposite wall, gaping out at the city spread below.

David's desk is in the far corner. There it is: a fine desk, adequate in breadth, solid in mass and satisfactory in height. Atop it sit ready the necessities of his daily work: pens and Post-it pads and paper clips and floppies and labels, the three-hole punch and keyboard and mouse, today's shuffle of memos in hard copy. A large pad of yellow legal paper ravaged with absent squiggles and jottings. A photocopy of an ad the agency ran last week. A small day calendar, as of yet unflipped, still dreaming of yesterday. And there is the computer, its screen facing his empty chair, waiting to be roused from its slumbers.

Like David, the computer is slow in the morning.

David sits and sips at the rim of his steaming cup. He blinks. He nibbles scone.

Shannon, AKA the Shan-Man, lumbers into the room, his pocked face buried in an oversized printout. He droops into his chair, inspecting the print with displeased eyes. 'Hey,' he croaks.

'Hey,' David says.

At another desk sits Owen, he of shaved head and pimply neck and Discman, submerged in mouse manipulations, attentions fixed on screen, his morning litre of Mountain Dew at hand.

'Heyo,' Owen says.

'Hey,' David says.

David switches on his computer. Its re-entrance into life is the rising whirr of its hard drive and the electric spack of powering up, the perky assertion of its duties. Icons assemble on the screen.

A Post-it note affixed to his desk asks *are we communicatORS or communicatERS?*

Shannon calls across the room to Owen, inquiring about something technical, a hardware issue. The two production designers communicate primarily through sequences of sarcastic jibes and expletives, their enormous monitors hiding them away like fortress keeps.

David consults his inbox. Most mornings he avoids these memos and forms for as long as possible. Example: CR #00-3737 – its lined regions bear the hasty slashes of Helen's handwriting. Helen, Senior Account Manager: assertive and threatening. Helen, who decrees the fate of all the copy David produces. Her writing dictates a dissatisfaction with his offerings for the upcoming Children's Telethon; in clenched pen strokes, scrawled points: *place emphasis on the particularity   special gala   charitable event patrons encouraged to do their part.* She remarks on demographics, pinpoints the target. Accentuate: the client, the hotel management, has other special events and promotions yet to come. Associate associate *associate* – invigorate with bubbly bold-text screeches.

Lydia, the chirpy young Junior Accounts Manager, enters the room prying apart the lid of a mini-sized coffee, a stack of papers tucked under her arm.

'Morning, men,' she says, unloading the stack onto Shannon's desk – redos and rewrites and reconsiders. Shannon yeeps at the height.

Lydia's unblemished blondeness lingers, fluorescent lights framing her golden dome, her careful coffee sips. This is her strategy: to hover, feigning casual interest in the backroom's goings-on, making idle chit-chat, when, as an envoy of the accounts department, she is actually concerned only with adherence to deadlines and the satisfaction of her Junior Managerial agenda.

She says to David, 'We have a thing we need to go over today. Maybe after lunch. It'll only take a sec.'

'Oh,' he says, 'right. Okay.'

'What's your schedule like today, is it hectic?'

'Moderately,' he lies.

'If you're swamped.'

'Not really. I could … '

'Well. After lunch. If you could just come by before end of day. Let's say one.'

'Okay. Sure.'

Exit Lydia. In her wake, only the incessant wheeze of the Canon printer persists.

David gets to work. Writing the words and rewriting the words. Making them fit.

There is a menu, or the emergent inklings of a menu's layout. This laser output presents a poorly scanned digital montage: a lobster atop a raft of romaine, a bucket of ribs, an overflowing pint of beer, shining breakfast platters, a toppling salad bar – all situated against the pixelated rendering of a sunset bleeding across some twinkling bay.

David draws unenthusiastic air into his lungs.

Shannon: 'Appalling.'

David peers over his monitor. 'This?'

'This photo. Look at the waffles, the stack of waffles. The whole thing.'

David shrugs.

'Look at it,' Shannon implores. 'Look at how shitty that is. I would not eat that buttery hunk of crud. Would you eat that? Based on that shot? I told them we needed to hire outside. Get a real photographer, with lights, with a modicum of know-how. Not just Jeff with the digital piling stuff on his desk and *zap*. Look at that. Did you see the clubhouse?'

'No.'

'Jeff just plopped the sandwich on his desk and shot it with the Fuji. I said to him, Jeff, the pros, they use lights and angles and glycerin and everything to make it look presentable. They fancy it up. You know … they make it look at least edible. They don't just – *Agh*.'

David nods polite agreement. The Shan-Man thrives on complaints, complaints often valid but equally as often excessive. He savours the agency's idiocy, his sense of superiority feeding on malfunction, on technical glitches.

'How am I supposed to do anything with that?' Shannon moans. 'I can't do fuck all. All the Photoshopping in the world won't make that hunk of turd gleam. And when it goes for approval and the client kicks up a stink, who will get blamed?'

A pause, for effect.

'I will be blamed. Fucking *agh*.'

Owen hoists his emptied Mountain Dew and whips it across the room at the wastebasket by Shannon's feet. The plastic bottle careens off the corner of Shannon's desk and lands neatly in the trash.

'Heyo!' Owen cries triumphantly.

The list of food items for which David has been instructed to concoct a revised, more detailed menu is dishearteningly long. David reads about the Seafood Hoagie, the Pesto Chicken Basket, the Florentines and Benedicts, the Stouts and Pales and Bitters. The Skins and Melts.

Seafood Hoagie.

He grimaces as thoughts turn to lunch. He could hit the food court at Scotia Square, pursue falafel, the crunchy pickled turnip. Or the cabbage soup at the Hungarian restaurant. Or a Whopper at the Burger King where the secretaries from the phone company go. But that cabbage soup – that cabbage soup is unbelievable.

He pries open his thesaurus and locates a listing for *delicious*. Then, for exactly fourteen seconds, he thinks about the word *nectareous*. Then, for eighteen seconds, *ambrosial*.

After surrendering to the safety of *mouth-watering*, he checks his e-mail. For an instant the computer labours, then reveals three new messages: a memo from Naoko reminding everyone to have their new online time sheets filled out by *10:30 and no later*, a billing statement from his bank that he quickly deletes, and:

> Good Day Leo!
> Here is your daily horoscope, courtesy of serious-
> horoscopes.net:

Leo (July 21–August 21): Times will be tough, but persevere and you'll get through it! Be ready for the unexpected, and lingering questions will become more clear. Meanwhile, try and get a good night's sleep!

David begins plugging account numbers and dates and hourly tallies into the online database. He types *00-1666 Acker Motors Group* and the date, consults a time sheet messy with his own scribbled memos outlining the week's activities, performs some quick mental calculations, then in the column marked *Total Hours* he enters 4.5.

Compiling his hours makes him tense. Tense, yes, because it's all lies. It's sheer bullshit. He is hanging precariously on to this job, sustaining the illusion that he is doing good work, hard work, honest work, *any* work. Because he is not working. He is doing very little. He tightens the occasional sentence, corrects spelling, feigning the appearance of one engrossed in serious reflection and care. But he is not actually *doing* anything. He is a link in a futile, meandering chain. He fades, remains scarce. Flipping through pages, checking e-mail, toeing a meagre line. Allowing time to slip in lumbering compartments, like trucks over potholed overpasses, like cheeseburgers clumped in the stomach's pit – time moderating even as it hastens, passing in flickers of misaligned frames. Every day promptly at quarter to nine, he comes and pretends to work – and days roll on, weeks disappear, months filed into a database, and a year expires like a whim, until, in a brutal thump, he is here: circling figures, fixed in time yet slippery, lost but motionless.

David has learned to appear busy.

He enters into the database *Seaco Foods* and assigns a date. Again, he consults his notes and finds he has invented three hours of imaginary work on this account – he enters 2.75 to be thrifty. In actuality, the Seaco job probably took twenty minutes for him to write up, edit, rethink and print for his supervisor Deb's once-over and approval. Twenty minutes of semi-conscious activity, slicing and dicing text, following the established pattern, the artifice, the sleight of words.

Tightening things up.

His only cunning is maintenance of the charade. He's a faker, a diversionist, a fraud, a sham.

The thesaurus suggests *charlatan* or, pushing it, *mountebank*.

David turns to the window. From this elevated perch he can view all of Halifax's meagre downtown. The cluttered city below, just beyond the glass, down there. *Look*: the assumptive pokes of office towers infiltrating morning sky, spiralling concourses beneath; parkades like impossible concrete sandwiches; trucks tearing through traffic, bullying aside spatterings of pedestrians hurrying through slush; cars surging through congested streets, windshield wipers thwapping; the brilliant lights and unbrilliant lights and extinguished lights and dotted paths of lights. Morning's churn of motivations, its skirmish of quantities. His city, its citizens – today, here.

The end is nigh.

Perhaps, apocalypse: we will perish by fire, by suffocation, plague. Perhaps by grinding metal, starvation, pestilence of speed-wracked ambition. Perhaps a rain of brimstone and cinders will scour the earth and ravage the earth. Perhaps. Annihilation. The act of some rogue usurper, the wield of technology run amok. Biological warfare. Huge swooping end, past prophecies coming horribly true, the earth's death murmur, the winding down of the whole program. Frogs. Blight. Waste. War, famine, et cetera. Rain of slag. Perhaps.

Below, beneath him, it all fits so perfectly together, so seamlessly, this illusion. Beneath the veneer of order: ruin and devastation, hellfire, the end of everything. Doomsday. He is above it all, and of it all.

David cracks his knuckles. Then he rotates his forearms and finds a satisfying *crck* there too.

Lunch.

Moving down the pedway toward the mall with others temporarily freed from their offices, David pauses to again watch traffic swirling below. Rain batters down, rendering the accumulating snow an icy sludge. At bus stops, discouraged masses gather. Everything is bleak.

He presses a palm against the glass. The glass is temperatureless.

Then – he is in line at Ray's Falafel with the lunching hordes, ordering Special #3, nodding as the smallish woman behind the counter informs him *no kibbi*, David opting instead for #2, chicken shish taouk with mechouia. Around him the mall and its inhabitants merge into incomprehensibility, burbling and gulping forked squiggles of pasta and fistfuls of molten brownies into its collective gullet, poking at palmed organizers, dabbing at lips with serviettes before hastening back to offices, to desks, to spreadsheets.

David takes his tray to a corner table and buries himself in food and a discarded *Sports Illustrated*. The chicken globs, the cayenne tingles. On the magazine's cover, Tiger Woods smiles elfishly, winningly.

But David is thinking of other things.

He thinks: *try and get a good night's sleep!*

Loneliness is a hard pinch, biting into the pit of the neck and the base of the skull. Time becomes a chasm: waves crashing in a dull roar, layers of force pushing down into the yawning throat of the drowned under-everything.

Here is the hand of hope. Grasp it as it beckons. Learn its contours. Define the range. Persuade elements. Mediate factors. Run a worn finger along the inner ridge of the hand of hope. Form strategies corresponding to the narrow slice of hope. Devise a systemized method for dampening your innermost pain.

Our hero, David, is searching for something but he does not know what it is. He is searching. He is perpetually uneasy. His scope is narrow. He seeks a way, something to which he can adhere. He longs. He waits, for *something*. This absence, which he knows as intimately as the slump of his own mirrored cheeks, is an ache amplified in daily trials. It is pain. It is longing. Scarcity, flailing. It is a force.

David wobbles amidst mirrored fountains in the mall's khaki light. He waits in line at a bank machine, then checks his account balance. His heart sinks; the fettering freight of debt remains a losing battle. And armaments of retaliation are low in supply.

Sometimes you want to just admit defeat.

Then, out of the surrounding garble, he hears his name.

David. A girl's voice. He jolts as if stricken. The mall is a blur, a rodeo.

Wheeling around, he hears his name again: *Daviiid.*

It's Lisa. Suddenly. Of course. *Yes.* His young cousin Lisa, exploding from the bustle, draped in a baby-blue raincoat, brandishing an enormous green umbrella adorned with polka dots, her toothy smile jutting through the murk.

This Lisa, who is lovely. Lisa. Lustrous Lisa. Lisa. Dream of Lisa. You imagine a halo, a halo of oiled brass, or gold, or platinum – something gleaming, encircling her perfect dome.

Seventeen years old.

'Oh,' David says. 'Lisa. Hi.'

She approaches. Hair, hanging damp. Raincoat, slick.

'What're you up to, dude?' she says, grinning.

'Just, you know. Lunch. Ray's.'

He gestures feebly, indicating the tables, the counters, the scene. Lisa nods. She stares at him, head cocked to one side. Her eyes are glassy, narrowed into something resembling playfulness, or scorn. David realizes she is very stoned.

Lisa. David is helpless in her midst.

'What are you … What's going on with you today?' he says.

'You know, farting around. I just bought this amazing umbrella. Do you like it?'

'Wow.'

'You like?'

'I do. It's tremendous.'

'I agree. *Tremendous.* I'd open it up and give you the whole show, but you know. Bad luck inside. I'm sure you understand.'

David nods. 'Yes.'

'But I really like it. I take pride in it. It makes a statement.'

'Definitely.'

'I'm not sure what kind of statement exactly. But you think it makes a statement?'

'It's pretty bold … but in the end, you know, as long as it keeps you dry.'

Under her raincoat she wears a red V-neck sweater, exposing a generous peek of neck. In the cradle of her collarbone, David spies a glob of water, a sparkling pearl, trickling against skin. Skin crease-less, mellifluous, like butter left out to soften. Like cream cheese.

Perhaps we will perish in floods of sweet flooding floods.

'So, you have to go back to work,' Lisa says.

'Back to the office. Back to the grind.'

'Zut. I thought maybe we could play together this aft.'

They walk. The mall roils and echoes around them.

'Aren't you supposed to be in school?' David asks.

Lisa sputters laughter. 'I suppose I wasn't in the right *mind frame* for the relentless grind, not today. You know.'

'Sure. Not like I'm … '

'I called the secretary and told her I had *crippling* PMS.'

Another round of giggles. Lisa: joyful, free.

'Where are you headed now?' David asks.

She wavers. 'I wish you could hang out. We could go shopping for sneakers. We could find you some hot new kicks. I told Dad I needed new soccer cleats.'

'Soccer. It's winter.'

'As if Dad would figure that far, dear comrade. But credit card he nonetheless allows. So fun for us to have. But I see you are committed to your work. No time to fool around with your poor dejected cousin. I can respect that.'

She wipes her nose.

'Sorry,' David says. 'Such is the way it is.'

'Okey-doke.'

They halt at the pedway's entrance. Lisa's hair hangs like unmarred wheat, its rain-wet ends tickling her shoulders. David fights an impulse to grasp these shoulders and draw them close, to hold her tightly in his reach and keep her, unsquirming, unexposed. Just to hold her, to hide her away. Keep her from being ruined by the terrible world beyond. To hold. To hide. Just that. If even if for a moment, screens will draw back to reveal glory hidden beyond. Columns of light will blow sky-high, strobing cities with sudden splendour, bleeding hope across asphalt, unclogging wild beauty and wonder.

Lydia said to see her by one. And the Acker Motors thirty-second radio spot is deadlined for 3:30. Jim said *urgent*. And when Jim says urgent, sometimes he actually means urgent.

'See you later,' David says.

'My parents are having one of their things this weekend.'

'Um.'

'You know. The thing Mom and Dad have every year around their anniversary, where all of their friends come to celebrate the everlasting glory of their love. It's totally abhorrent, but sometimes there can be laughs to be had. You've been before.'

He remembers. 'Right.'

'They'd be tickled if you came. It's been a while. They talk about you now and then.'

'They *talk* about me?'

Horrors. Jo-Beth and Gary, his mother's sister and her husband, are brutal. They'd run him down. His shiftlessness. His lack of motivation. His dishevelment. They'd tear him apart, even *in absentia*. The sneering. The pity.

Lisa: 'I'll tell them you're coming. Show up five-ish Saturday. There'll be gallons of booze and everything, you know. They go all out. Dad'll open up the wine cellar. He gets ripped and sings Elton John.'

'Elton. Really.'

She smiles. 'I had a dream about you two nights ago. I had a dream that you and I were sitting on our back deck. It was night-time, in the winter, and there was snow on the ground. The pool cover was on. We were watching stars fall out of the sky. Like a meteor shower.'

She pauses. David feels his lungs heavy in his chest.

'Are you a vegetarian?' Lisa asks.

'No.'

'Then show up Saturday and we'll get the barbecue going and freak out on hot dogs. Screw winter. Do you like sauerkraut?'

'Love it.'

'Then we can make my dream come true. If you don't show up, I swear I'll be miserable. I'll be crushed. You'll crush my dreams.'

'Then I suppose I must.'

'Yes. You must.'

White overcast light beams through a glass section of roof, hyperactivating the freckles twinkling across her nose.

Lisa. His cousin, seventeen years old. She oozes peril.

They bid each other farewell with a flubbed high-five, and David returns to the office. The pedways issue him back into the awaiting monotony. He glides over the gun-grey city, streets crammed with cardboard hotels, plastic cafés, edifices of stone, glistening mortar. Look at this place, the city, where he lives and works. Gridded like a toaster waffle. This is his city, his turf, everything hidden and washed out and lonely.

He has lived here his whole life. But he doesn't recognize it at all.

This battle is to be waged in the gymnasium, in the weight room, in the pool. Four times a week, maybe three, David systematically suffers the treadmill, the Lifecycle, the AbRoller, the StepMill – an extensive arsenal of gruelling torture devices. He curls, executes reps, contracts and releases and lifts and pulls and shoves and strides. He feels fans waft coolness on his drenched skin. He sweats, and others around him sweat. Broad-chested ogres bench-pressing titanic weights, wide-thighed blondes fiddling with headphones on StairMasters.

David considers his own reflection in the gym's ubiquitous mirrors – sweaty and huffing and red-faced – and he is discouraged. The sag of pectorals. The stripe of cellulite. The pastiness. Discouragement.

The battle is in cardio and kilos and sick unrealistic aims – battle against the self, against other selves, the place of the self among other selves. They all strain. Sucking up and out. Battles rage, culminating in the drowsy recline of the post-workout ritual and the gratifying punishment of steam. Here, in the steam room.

David slouches on the wooden bench, a damp towel his only garb. His face gushes a steady flow of sweat. He needs to clip his toenails. He needs to trim his nose hair. He needs to do something about all this extra French toast softening his waist and stomach and butt. He needs to improve. Maintain. Shear. Chisel. Punish. Edit.

His head swims.

Thick atmospheres obscure the fuzzy figures surrounding, towelled men wearing flip-flops, smearing shaving gel across their chins, sighing. In exercise, in purpose, you find cessation of other concerns. No one laughs and no one weeps. The battle is to be waged against the self, within the self. The spoils of labour are retraction and release. Steam.

Time is stalled, freeze-framed. The moment is a VCR PAUSE. Men sit and bathe in close vapours. Heads swim.

Then, showered and shaven, he is on the sidewalk. His limbs ache stiff aches. Cars *sssh* over slushed streets. Streetlights ignite as the city curls into its nocturnal ebb. David passes the Public Gardens, seasonally closed, where behind wrought-iron gates ice obscures flowering shrubs and vines, pausing running streams.

The ducks converge in loose assembly near the fence, shivering against the cold. They have not flown south; their wings are clipped. When he approaches, leaning through a grate, they waddle close with curiosity and suspicion. Regardless of how often he visits the ducks, winter spring summer autumn, they never learn to trust him as a friend. They remain skeptical of his friendly approach, his plea. But he persists, pursuing their favour, their waddling whims. The grace of their black-bead eyes, the sleek arc of their proud heads. The ducks, with their pride, and their helplessness – they seem honest, but still suspicious and standoffish, even as they flock for handouts.

'Hi, ducks,' he says quietly, almost whispered.

A duck says *hey Davey*, or, perhaps, *quack*.

At the corner he encounters an unexpected commotion in progress: the street is flooded with a raucous mob, expanding out of shades and darkness. Waves of bodies, marching. David freezes. Among the swarm there is heated chanting, pickets hoisted. Voices hollering into bullhorns. Hands clapping. Feet stomping. Thumps thumping in time. Occasional whoops. A demonstration. The oncoming street, David sees, is closed off by emergency-orange barricades. Police cruisers, officers observing, speaking into walkie-talkies. A sign, held aloft by a beefy darkish kid, reads UNITED AGAINST THE CORPORATE STRANGLEHOLD. He spits and bellows, his glasses twinkling under scattered slices of light, his mouth tufting cold breath. From unseen amplification, a bullhorn squawks *enough is enough*. Voices vow resistance to an array of causes – to INJUSTICE, to IMPERIAL-IST AGGRESSION.

The sound of the mob is an indistinct rumble and squeal, machinery toiling in self-perpetuation. A triad of girls in heavy coats and mittens looms up behind David, chanting with arms linked; he tries to skirt their advance, instead finding himself caught in the tide, into the relentless thick of marching bodies.

Coming to the next intersection, the march reaches an impasse. Further barricades are in place, with a pair of police vans curtailing the march's progress. There are boos. A police siren bloops sharply in warning. The shouting swells; the mood shifts from irked to irate. David tries to duck and circle around, to disentangle himself from the mob, but the crunch of bodies presses too closely. A bullhorn says *we won't let our future be thwarted by corporate profiteers.* Light from a restaurant's neon sign frames a policeman's broad-chested silhouette in eerie purple light. Someone screams *come on* in David's ear. Bodies mash together. The protester's voice in the bullhorn, louder: *these imprudent violations serve as admonitory* something something something. He is crammed immovably in. His lungs begin to seize, losing power, shrivelling. His throat gets tight. His vision becomes hazy.

A woman's voice: *defend the innocent.*

There is a push from the rear; several stumble. David feels a sharp blow to the small of his back, scarcely registering its force. His body grows cold and numb. The cops assert their blockade. His mind screams alarm. His head swims.

David pries apart fissures of bodies with his arms, then gradually manages to stumble left into a clearing. He leans against a brick wall for support, and gradually his breath begins to return. Struggling along the crowd's periphery, he tries to shirk the escalation by passing the police blockade, but there he finds another mob gathering, rabble from the demonstration pressing against the barricade, alarmed and outraged. More police vans arrive. More blooping sirens.

A shout: *fuck the poh-leece.*

David burrows desperately back in the direction he had come, finding refuge in the shelter of a pharmacy's doorway. Around him: a morass of activity, squeals and shouts ringing, engines revving. Squeezing up to a barricade, David is met by a bulky policeman.

'I need to get out of here,' he tries.

His plea goes unacknowledged.

More shrieks from within the mob. Strange laughter echoing through the street. More bullhorned outcry. David's heart hammers and his mind executes nonsensical patterns of panic.

The policeman says, 'Stand *back*.'

David stands back.

Then, look, over the crest of the surging crowd: a bottle thrown, sailing in a slow arc, pinwheeling over the heads of the demonstrators, labelled in bold yellow and orange, capped in red and gold: Fruitopia. Captured by gravity, it dangles defiant in air, catching a wisp of light as it plummets earthward.

Snared in David's vision, this bottle becomes something else entirely. The bottle is deliverance, weaponry. Fruitopia as first-strike initiative. The intermediate-range missile. The H-bomb, the Scud, its mortal freight unchambered unto an unsuspecting suburb. In slow frames, bombs drop in punishing trajectory, initiating fresh disaster. Glass and violence. The threat of something unretractable. Doomsday: the end is nigh.

As we accumulate, we simultaneously separate – chaff from wheat, lowly from high. Here are the patterns. Power invites tragedy, hardheadedness invites assimilation, or ruin. The fierce general bows to the agreeability of the times. The road bends to the tread of tanks. Desert denizens forsake livelihoods for the quashing of dictatorial rule. A king waves aside prophecy with pride's dismissal. We shake hands with our future killers and make merry with evil. The son reckons with his inheritance in stunted steps. He assumes the wreckage, the waste, the awkwardness, the haste, the limpness, the deceit. The progression. The dubious legacy. Son begets father. Patterns drenched in subjectivity. The time frame. The laziness. Son slays father, son begets son, son becomes father, son slays father.

The Father. *Yes*. Above all else, despite everything – The Father. The memories of The Father. The moustache, the trimness. The smell of The Father: Noxzema and tobacco and mouthwash. The musty sweatshirts of The Father; he wore sweatshirts while folding ties. Time with The Father, and time without The Father. And time with The Father, yet still *without* The Father. Phases of having. Phantasmic proximity. The vacuum of his absence. The cracking of his beers. The steaks, balanced by TV tray, on his lap. The newspaper-reading of The Father. The nervous chortle of The Father, no longer stuttering in hallways and living rooms. The jangling of change, or keys, or change and keys, in The Father's pants pockets. The Father, wraithlike, skulking on the periphery. The pallid cheeks of The Father.

The apartment of The Father. The yellow-tinged ceiling of the apartment. The stifling atmosphere of the apartment, late in the afternoon. The blankness of The Father. The farewell of The Father, or, rather, the absence of a farewell. The gradual emaciation of The Father. The extended exit of The Father. The silence of The Father.

The bottle finds a target, striking an unsuspecting officer in the side of his unhelmeted forehead. He reels back, his face spewing blood.

The mob erupts. A phalanx of police surges forward, clubs raised; the melee crashes back in response, while another tide of protesters disperses. Tear-gas canisters erupt. David is again swept into motion by gathered impulse, flailing, scrambling to flee. Pandemonium prevails; elbows fly.

A few of the more animated agitators fall behind to be pummelled by police. A dreadlocked kid in a hooded sweatshirt falls in slow motion to a torrent of blows, his cries and flailing arms no defence against his attackers. It is amazing how many blows – and these are not tempered blows, but blows delivered with zero restraint – are required to demolish the head. The skull is strong. The skull is resilient. Dreadlocks turn ruddy under truncheons.

Night has now achieved its full dark bloat, the utility-orange cast of streetlights turned hazy, bluish gas staining the street with caustic vapours. Through rising fumes the city is remade as a battleground, everything lagging and watery. David watches – there is something powerful and dark generated in the murk, phantoms and zombies walking among men, hints of history in nethers. Something is happening.

In the distance, speakers from a restaurant sing *baby hold on to me whatever will be will be*.

A group of punks has commandeered a nearby bus shelter, dangling from its sides while randomly kicking and swiping at passersby. A skinny kid in snowboard pants and a balaclava teeters, brandishing a pair of Colt 45 bottles, one in each fist. He waves them over his head like he's conducting symphonies, shrieking *muthafucka*. He casts the bottles earthward.

Geysers of glass. A woman cries in outrage, or pain. Wails against the night.

David feels something detonate in his face. He cries out. There is a whirlwind of pain. Shock. He drops to his knees, then further down.

The world goes flat, terribly flat, then black.

When he stops throwing up, David says, 'I'm really sorry.'

The doctor pats him lightly on the back. 'No worries.'

David falls back in bed and wipes his mouth with the back of his wrist.

'A reaction to the anesthetic, perhaps,' the doctor says. 'And shock. The body seizes up against trauma. Your body is in a state of alarm. You'll be all right for now.'

'I … I think so.'

'Good to hear. Good to hear. I'll call a nurse to clean up that yuckiness.'

Exit Doctor.

Lean back. Stare at the ceiling. The ceiling is flat. The ceiling is a photocopy of a ceiling. The lights are artificial solar splinters. The flaws in the ceiling, the panels dotted with holes. The ceiling is a hack's rendering of a ceiling. The ceiling is a display wedding cake, unspongey and undelicious. Styrofoam. The ceiling is not sympathetic. The room smells of – The room is absent of smell, except for David's vomit, which smells foul. The room is quiet, except for the hum of equipment and voices from other rooms, which are loud. The room is not quiet.

David's temple and left cheek are numb, yet hinting with tingles.

He is not entirely confident this is not a dream. It could be a dream. But dreams are fluid and shifting, while nothing here shifts. It's all flat.

A nurse enters with a mop and pail. She is disarmingly small. 'Got a little sick on the floor, hm? No problemo. Wouldn't be a hospital if people didn't get sick, would it?'

David really really *really* doesn't feel like faking a laugh to that.

He fakes a laugh: 'Ha.'

The nurse mops. David concentrates on the ceiling, the emptiness of the lights.

'We'll be keeping you here overnight, I'm afraid,' she says. 'We have to keep an eye on you, pardon the pun. *Ha*. But overall we're not finding any spread of nerve damage. So as long as you listen to the doc you'll be back in action in no time. You'll just have to be careful. We'll be setting up appointments for you with an ocular therapist. But you won't be in hospital too long.'

David grunts. He is cold.

The nurse leans over him and peers intently at his face. She frowns. 'Still feeling any pain?'

'Not really. My face is mostly numb.'

'That makes sense. We'll be giving you enough Tylenol and gauze to tie you over. Did the nurse at the desk get your info?'

'I. Um. I don't think so. I think I was unconscious ... '

'Oh. Well, we can do that now. I have your chart.'

She questions him. Name. Age. Date of Birth. Allergies. Medical History. Et cetera.

'Someone you'd like noted as an Emergency Contact. A relative, a spouse ... the person to be contacted, if anything should ever happen.'

Think. 'Like my parents or my mother or someone.'

'Sure. Your mother's name.'

'Uh ... she's sort of unavailable.'

'I'm sorry?'

'I just think she wouldn't exactly be the most helpful person to contact. She lives ... abroad, and she's not, exactly, in this sort of ... '

'Perfectly fine. Your father, perhaps?'

'Deceased.'

'What's that now?'

'Dead.'

'Ah. Right. Sorry.'

Flat sympathy. Flat clipboard. Flat room, flat walls, flat medical paraphernalia. Flat tubes and flat windows. Flat diagram of the flat human anatomy, hanging flatly.

'Anyone you can think of. Anyone who you'd consider responsible.'

David touches the thick wad of bandage on his face.

'Um,' he says, 'I'm not really what sure what's happened ... '

'What *happened* to you?'

'I think I blacked out for a while there. I have a tendency to faint. It's a recurrent … I don't really remember.'

'What's the last thing you remember?'

He thinks. 'Was I shot?'

The nurse snorts. '*Shot*? Gosh, no. You were hit by a shard of glass. In that demonstration downtown. Somebody smashed a bottle. You got glass in the eye.'

'In the *eye*?'

The bandage is bulky, heavily packed. A weighty growth sitting on his face.

'I'm surprised you don't remember. You were quite lucid when the ambulance brought you in. You were saying something about returning videotapes. Or something like that.'

'Videotapes?'

'Something about videos. You were very composed. Nary a tremble.'

Nary.

Hours creep. In this sanitized bunker, time's passage is undetectable. There is no window, no moon, no stars; there is, however, a television mounted on the wall opposite his bed. David watches *48 Hours*: tired-eyed Lesley Stahl shakes her head, perplexed in inquisition.

A trickle of pus dribbles from his eye. It is warm, pudding-like. David feels nauseous again, but convinces his stomach not to lurch. His body's facilities feel remote and out of his control. Cushioned in self-pity, his head's ache throbs and dwindles to strange dreams. He dreams of past seasons, of birds, ducks fleeing terrestrial shackles for freer horizons. Ducks gliding across the hazy topography of sleep.

Flat flat sleep.

Dream of the beach. Beigeish sands, infirm under nubby toes. The sky a parfait of vanilla and grey and Pepsi blue. Perspective is tipsy. *Whoosh* – a steamroller of swelling frequency, then an immediate ebb: tides. Craggy boulders line the outer periphery, pounded into misshapen sandstone husks. Swimsuited bodies lie slain along the beach's stretch. Aunts, hoary neighbours, picnickers, cottage neighbours basking, all incorporated. A youthful summer retained in dream, scraps shredded with associations. Everything is shifting and relative, floating above the slathering of buttery lotions and capping of beer bottles and thumbing of paperback corners, drifting toward the rushing ocean. Breakers are coming down hard, cyclical bursts leaving silt streaked with wet traces. Dive like a manic dolphin through the crashing spray. Drive into the wave, ride its crest until, upended, you are cast back ashore. Spit. Pant. Collect gritty sand under your toenails, in your scalp, in your navel's pit, in the crevice of your butt. Bathe in pebbled foam. Nearby an adult voice calls out. Gaze into the distance. Conjure fantasies of riding adrift in the sea, floating off to foreign lands. To Africa. To Antarctica. Envision stadium-sized squids patrolling the ocean's floor, squids with huge wrinkled eyes gawking up from darkened depths. Think of sharks. The freedom of limitless ocean. The immeasurable. You enter the sea not as conqueror but as co-conspirator, wading through froth, buoyant with pulsing waves. Rough waters impede your stroke – and yet, you persist. Breathe steadily. Maintain a pace. Let waves persuade you up and down. Somewhere, way back, your mother might be glancing up over her *Chatelaine*, scanning the shoreline. And you are not there. No, her son has fled for wilder worlds, forsaken this world's playpen for the chop of the sea. A buccaneer, set sail. But there is the increasing barrier of pressure. Escalating weariness. Waves come raging. The horizon in glimpses, unmarred and pale. Surging whitecaps break in your face. You lose grip, on direction, on *up*. Twist in the overpower of waves. Vie, struggle. Weight crashes down, and now you are underwater and without air. Your eyes open to a misty emerald smog. There is a tugging, torso's twist, and the understanding: you are *going under*. Panic rises. Something hard slams against your coccyx – rock or tide or squid – in an attack of bright pain. There is a bursting sensation. You flail for up. Something hammers on your chest and grinds you into the rocky floor. Casting you ass over eyeballs. Helplessness assumes full command. A young life, a doomed way. A fistful of years against the fury, the brine and the scum and the inviting darkness. Watery demise. But – despite the crush, you find a brace in the floor, you manage footing, and somehow your face emerges from the lapping waves. You cough and suck at air. The sun's full arsenal showers upon your face. Unthreatening shallow waters surround. Your heart pounds as you wade back ashore, the waves' rise and plummet now calm. This is something unexplainable – this fleeting, or half-imagined, encounter with mortal threat. Details, moments in peril, as momentous as genocides. Perhaps we will perish in trivialities. Reassume the beach to resume the sunburning afternoon. The dream is not the peril, the dream is the disappointment melting into stomach growl and a need to urinate. Goodbye, Antarctica. Exit the beach with a flutter over sand and a sidestep through years, a skim over losses, waking *waking up*.

In the night David is woken by a nurse attending his wound's dressing. She dabs at his eye's under-region with a soft swab, inspecting whatever mess waits underneath. David hasn't yet investigated his wound, and hasn't asked to. The nurse's nasal breath brushes lightly against his forehead. He struggles to keep still, maintaining pretended sleep.

When she leaves his bedside, David relaxes. The bedsheets are crispy, like crusted Kleenexes, the bed an unforgiving torture rack. The door of his room is left ajar, allowing a constant scuffle of feet and slivered light to invade the room. Even the simplest comfort is unimaginable.

The doctor has said there could be operations, possibilities. Techniques and treatments. But the reality remains: his left eye has been damaged very badly, nearly destroyed, by the edge of bottle which neatly speared it. Nerves severed. Tendons detached. In the bag there is a medical eyepatch to be placed over the bandage, which is to be replaced daily. The doctor said there are other options beyond this medical patch, a whole catalogue of styles and devices. David imagines this particular market must be an extremely specialized one. Cripple fashion: Gucci crutches, Armani prosthetics. Snappy logoed dressings. Snazzy wounds.

If he is lucky, the doctor told him, *extremely lucky and open to experimentation*, one day he might again see out of his left eye.

In the wheelchair he is Franklin Roosevelt, overexposed in newsreels, iconic in spastic frame speeds. He is Christopher Reeve, Stephen Hawking, Dr. Strangelove. He is an evil genius, an arch-enemy, a criminal mastermind, complete with eyepatch and wheelchair. He is plotting global domination, cackling as his plan unfolds.

A stocky male nurse steers David's wheelchair down the hospital hallway. They pass doorways, tributaries of bodied stretchers, ceiling-high piles of dingy linen. David is still groggy. In his lap are pill bottles and dressing materials and a scrawled prescription. In his throat is a salty heap of humiliation. The nurse wheels him through the labyrinth of corridors and observation rooms and waiting areas and stretcher bays. There are charts pinned to every available space. Everybody appears insipid and gaunt. Everything is sterile. Flat.

He does his best to not weep. FDR would not weep. He would assure in firm but gentle tones. This is David's own New Deal: itchy semi-blindness.

They reach the main door. The door revolves. Outside is a jolt – it is early morning, and the sun is sharp. Intermittent snow falls earthward in lazy static. Everything, traffic and corners, is distant and close. Near and far. Nowhere. Blurred. The x-axis fails to meet the y-axis. Or the z. No depth through dead eyes.

'Someone coming?' the nurse asks.

'Taxi ... '

They wait, watching ambulances zip in and out of the emergency parking. David wipes his nose and barely feels the pressure on his face. How could this have happened. His horoscope hadn't anticipated this.

The taxi issues him through the starkness, this city of chances and unlucky breaks. Scarecrows with rubicund faces wave their arms and shout at buses; legions of men in suits patrol sidewalks, uttering damnations into cellphones; square-shaped mothers push strollers, shopping carts, wheelchairs. This is a city of rejects and would-bes. An unbounded architecture of failure. David receives these visions, halfway and skewed.

The taxi driver *hgcks* a cough and turns up the radio. It's the same song that played last night, in the confusion and clamour: *baby hold on to me   whatever will be will be.*

Eddie Money.

Someday all of this will be just a paragraph in history, an anecdotal passage. The travails of time. *Yes*. Hugeness in towers and technologies. All of this will be gone. Raise glasses to the triumphant spirit. Salute. And David – his story, his sad tale, will be only a brief file in the ever-expanding cabinet of time. A moment, a blink. Forgotten. Temporary.

But. How did this.

How.

If only. So many. But what if. Lisa. But the eye. *Eye fucking eye.* She smiles. If only I and the eye and the smile. But there are so many. Jim never said. Jim's jawline, like what, vulture beak. *Rewrite.* Her sparkling eye *damn eye* and the doctor scratching his chin, but if the eye was only, and the gym was only, but *fucking eye stings like* but Jim and the whole office, a good night's sleep, and her neck, and her mouth.

It's late. David is at home, queasy with painkillers and drink, growing concerned that his eye has acquired infection. It itches. See him cracking yet another beer, watching television with one eye. Infomercials: lawn-care demonstrations. See him isolated. See him alone in his apartment, his bomb shelter, awaiting apocalypse.

Perhaps we will eventually be extinguished in our own idle decline. We will become the signals we pursue, only blips and bleeps and the chatter of transmission. We will be instant and eternal.

What if only this, nothing but this. *What if nothing but the itch.*

Boosting himself from the couch, he teeters, uncertain, an unsteadily staked flagpole. Half-blind. Nothing: the only worse thing would be – *if only*. The little things that. The only way it could be worse – nothing. All he has ever wanted was to journey an epic journey. To affect and be affected. To dream dreams.

Last November, after the dust of The Father's funeral settled, David's mother had insisted on whisking him away to her home in Spain. *To put some distance*, she said. David supplied little resistance. He hadn't seen his mother in eight years, so her participation after The Father's passing had been unforeseen and odd; David wasn't even sure how she learned the news. But, regardless: bam, she had arrived, wailing and gesticulating, assaulting him with an outpouring of concern. He was at her mercy.

As they taxied back from the cemetery, she told David he *simply needed to have a degree of faith in the ways of God*. David said he didn't even know who God was, how could he trust someone he didn't even know? But his mother just sighed and patted him gently on the forearm, her eyes misty and disengaged.

So he had flown back to Spain with her and her husband, Darren. Darren, with his jowls and vessely complexion and Irish brogue. Darren and his doctorate degrees. David tried his best to reserve judgment of Darren.

Put some distance. He couldn't say no. Not to her.

David's mother: a juggernaut of emotions.

Of all Barcelona's strangenesses, the mopeds were some of the most amazing. Seated on the balcony with his arms dangling over the rail, David would peer out at the narrow passages between huddled buildings, gazing down at bobbing heads, the parts of hair, the thin Spanish women in skin-hugging dresses, the burly chests of men peeking from loose collars, at the fat old grandmothers airing laundry, sheets flying like flags down the street. At mid-evening the plazas would flood with people, and he'd sit awestruck at the TelePizza delivery guys weaving through the tight crowds on their mopeds, free of caution. Delivering pizzas – this was amazing. In Barcelona David was constantly ill at ease, but in his anxiety he was enthralled. The lisping language. The unfamiliarity. The vigour of the hazy sun, high in the highest heights of a cloudless shield.

Here he spent afternoons lazing in the Parc de la Ciutadella, drinking Fink Brau under quivering leaves, listening to their coded rustle while waving away pigeons. He felt plunged into a reassuring blankness. Here his thoughts did not lean to the consequences of The Father's self-immolation. Forget about the monotony. Forget about nooses. His thoughts led nowhere. He felt shaken. His past had been conveniently removed. Barcelona, a bath of breezy unexperience, enwreathing him like a glob of cool gel.

It was empty and good.

David travelled waterfronts, sucking aqueous air as yachts and sharp-hulled schooners filled the marina. Small men, shirtless, hailed one another. The congregation of small craft forming an unbroken wharf of wealth and overtanned flesh. The water rippled out into unimaginable distances, a straight sheet of unmarred blue.

Down the beach, in the shade of an overhanging walkway, groups of men sought shelter from the sun's steady blaze. The men lay on tattered mattresses in the shade, smoking, drinking Coca-Cola, playing cards. They wore undershirts and stubble and worn-out shoes. Sun-cooked complexions. Many of the men seemed ruined – all appeared weary.

David stood at a distance, watching and chewing gum, wondering. Two men playing checkers mumbled to one another; they looked like fathers. Most of the men looked like they were, or once had been, fathers. Their weathered forms – stout, thick bodies wrapped in tough hide, clenched jaws – were those of fathers. The Father's body had been trim and narrow, yet, with time, displayed deterioration. He lagged like an aging stag, acquiring new tics and unsightly habits. Twitches. The jangling of the keys. The clearing of the throat that substituted for laughter. The men on the beach were addicts and schizophrenics, damaged artifacts – the first line of souls, perhaps, sacrificed in impending judgment. Perhaps we will perish in self-saturation and alienation. Perhaps we will recline passively into a dreamlike abyss. There will be walls built and lines drawn and status granted, tickets drawn for salvation's cloudy advent.

This place was good as any to be Ground Zero for the final reckoning. Perhaps the Hard Rock Café, just a brief scamper up the beach, would prove the first stem of impending ruin.

The restaurants. The glimmering lights. David couldn't get used to the unsystematic catacombs of streets and alleyways. Nothing was orderly. Home was traffic clots and teeming streets pitting man against bus, crowds against corners; here all was squirm and coil and cobblestoned mazes, indistinguishable doorways, mystifying crooks.

His mother had begun inserting the word *if* into discussion of David's return back home.

At dinner Darren grinned, hastily ordering carafes of wine. David stared blearily into the hazy candlelight, sipping at his glass, trying to wrap his mind around the squirmy situation.

Darren said *David   I perceive you to be a touch nihilistic   or misanthropic.*

David's mother said *Europe provokes intelligent thought and freedom of mind   back in Canada you're so restricted from discovering the purity of your spirit   don't you feel a weight   a burden lifted.*

She said to him *these are precious days.*

David could only nod in agreement as he gazed into the candle, fork-sifting the remnants of his paella, wondering what meagre part of her mind bothered to confront the facts. The Father's suicide. The impulse behind the action. The tying of the noose. The securing of the noose. What was her take on that? The stepping up on the ottoman. The fitting of the noose around the neck. The tightening of the noose. The final sighs. The last tastes of the apartment's air. How does she imagine these last desperate gulps? Whatever treat his eyes found in their final scan: a section of wall, a pane of strewn light, a TV screen. Kicking away the ottoman, his feet dangling, his neck *crcck*ing, his throat clamped shut, did he have regrets, doubts? And what would David's mother, here espousing the *underappreciated delights of the Ribera del Duero reds*, find in these hypothetical doubts? This imagined purity of spirit – where to go from here?

Darren, still grinning, said *I can see your mother's dreaminess in you David   you both see life as one endless fantasy.*

Enough.

He runs an unsure index along the television's surface, tenderly strokes its screen, its possibility. How it naturally accompanies the stereo amp, the face of the CD player. All these machines he has purchased on credit and account overdraft amid careening economic shufflings, delving into phantom finance – he appreciates them in light pats, languishing in their smoothness and purpose. Machines. Adore the machines.

Along the narrow shelf behind the TV are videotapes. Movies. And atop the stereo there are more videos, rented tapes yet unwatched, their cases banded blue-white and yellow-lettered.

At the top of the pile is *Patton*. Its cover bears the noble image of General George Patton, as portrayed by George C. Scott, in poised salute before a limitless span of red and white and blue, stars and stripes. David considers this general. He considers this entertainment. He considers bed and possible rest. Outside his apartment, in the world, there could be battles storming, allegiances tested, virtues affirmed.

A critically acclaimed film that won a total of eight 1970 Academy Awards   PATTON is a riveting portrait of one of the 20th Century's greatest military geniuses.

Realities grasped by remote control, rewinding, pausing. Frames of film collaborate into mythologies, like slogans from schemes of language. Heroes of imagination. Villains of sleepless nights.

His head swims.

David pries apart the dual case for *Patton* and inserts the first tape into the VCR. The tape is in rough shape; its digestion is poor and wobbly. There is a laboured instant of snow, but nevertheless it rolls: black screen, FBI warnings, 20th Century Fox logos, trumpets.

All sequence is plot, every moment a balance of tension. Everything is up for action.

A hall. A flag. Patton at the flag.

Movie.

'First of all,' Jim says, 'we have to discuss *concept*. What constitutes a concept. Because, in the end, that is the kernel of all that we do. It all generates from an initial established concept.'

The words plod familiarly from his lips: *Initial. Established. Concept.* His beakish nose gleams in the polished sparkle of the boardroom. He continues.

'Definition of a concept. A concept is what?'

He pauses. His query seeks no reply.

'What we have is the intention of communication. The success of our work is defined by the effectiveness of such communication. It's a one-way channel. We are not engaged in discourse. What we are engaged in is taking pains to draw, and sustain, attention to the product or service involved in this communication. The benefits of said product or service or brand. What are the key selling points of this product or service or brand? Are we targeting loyal customers and reminding them of their loyalty? Or drawing new, curious, consumers? Or are we out to draw attention from the competition? What is the targeted demographic? These are all, obviously, factors. Every single smidgen of information we can base our process on, these are all key. We have statistics. We have focus groups. As you see with the empty milk cartons before you, our market research is comprehensive. We have these retards in here looking at milk cartons and spilling everywhere. Thumbs up thumbs down on the new point-five-percent container. What do they say? I don't know. But the point is that the data is all there, accumulated and processed to be heaved at the client. And yet they look at this stuff and they fall asleep. I'm at these meetings. These people are bored. And if these asswipes are *bored* – just imagine the general public. Therefore, the need for a lure. A brand. A logo. A *concept*. See what I mean. We all know this. Do I need to remind you? I need to go to these meetings confident that I can calm the client's every little pesky concern. These people own factories and deal with unions and fuck knows what else. Dean Whittle from Whittle Foods, what does he do all day? Plays golf and talks on the phone. That's it. That's all the son of a bee knows. But when I go into a meeting with him and we finally finish yapping about his vacation to Nuevo Vallarta and get around to talking biz, I can't at this point be feeling the least bit unsure of what I'm doing. I need to be able to say, "Dean, I know how to get the public buying Whittle SuperTaters and keep them buying Whittle SuperTaters." And he'll say, "Well jeepers, Jim, last quarter earnings were down nineteen percent and you're proposing doing the same old shit we did last year with the Blast into the Taste of Summer bullshit, which didn't work in the first place and didn't even really make any sense?" He'll look at me like I'm a turd. And in many ways, at that point, I will actually *be* a turd. Unless I can retaliate with something absolutely phenomenal. Something that not only possesses a distinct vision in its own right, but also makes Dean Whittle himself feel like a superstar. He needs to be struck by lightning. He needs to have the plan reaffirmed in his mind in a *light-second*. Do you know how quick that is? That's *quick*. That's like a thousand fucking miles an hour. I have to be right there, presenting him with what. That's right: a *concept*. So, to define our terms. A concept is a system of communication, both to the public and, more importantly, to the client. Despite how it seems, we are not hired by the public. We are hired by the client. Client, priority. Public, not the priority. Our own personal moods and tastes: *definitely not a priority*. I cannot stress this enough. Money goes in, concepts come out, money comes in. Occasionally a client needs a gentle nudge in the right direction. That's my job, and Lydia's job. *It is not your job*. Your job is to develop the concept. We cannot stray from this pursuit. The Labatt thing, that was good. It was strong. Keep thinking stuff like that. The Boulder Springs thing, that was not strong. That was shit. I accept much of the blame. I failed to read Eric and his cronies correctly, and this misreading was then filtered down to you guys and ended up on a billboard over Kempt Road for six weeks. Well, live and learn. Just make sure you learn. Stay true to the concept, but not *too* true. These people, these managers and CEOs, they are the ficklest bunch of motherfucks you could ever meet. They change their mind in a flash. In a light-second. Therein lies the need for a gentle nudge. But that is *my* job. Remember. You stick with the concept. Develop concepts. Think beyond. Be proactive. Be *pro-proactive*. I'm serious. Don't smirk, Jeff. I'm exhausted. We're all exhausted. I had a sangria at lunch and I can barely stand up. But I have a two o'clock at Yeege and I've got to stay perky. Stay focused. Read the CRs. Brainstorm with Deb. She knows what I mean. I'm so exhausted.'

All the while, not looking at them. Looking at his hands, his briefcase, the table. Finally he eyes each of the staff, one by one, stopping on David.

'What the hell is on your face?'

'Eyepatch.'

'What are you, a pirate now?'

Chuckles all around.

David: 'I kind of had an accident … '

'Aye aye, matey,' Jim says.

'I got caught in the middle of something … '

'*Arrr!*' Jim growls, squinting.

Owen joins in. 'Shiver me timbers!'

'It's actually sort of … serious … '

Jim: 'Well, then we'd best be sailing the seven seas for booty of ye olde golden pearls! We'll swab the deck and walk the plank, matey!'

Fateful circumstance, riddled with regret: it was just over a year now when David had applied to the agency. A bygone era, prehistoric – things were different then. Yes, those were desperate times: bills scattered in the doorway, heart-sinking tallies on ATM slips, alarming credit-card notices. Yes, he could barely afford laundry. Yes, he had to quit the gym and disconnect the cable and cut out sandwiches from the expensive deli. Times had been grim. Sneakers bore sad holes. But at least he had been self-propelled. He had been authentic. Now he lives in perpetual resignation, accepting everything as part of a miserable inventory, of squandered time.

Commerce trumps greatness. Finance prompts enlistment.

When David stepped into Jim's office that June afternoon, he immediately knew this was a man he could never respect. He could endure his grasping at tangents and coddle his delusions, but would never respect him. They shook hands. Jim, Senior Vice-President, offered David a seat. David took the seat. Outside the corner office's enormous window, the view expanded into a voluminous sweep of the harbour, dotted with bobbing buoys and the steady wade of container ships headed further into the basin's elbow. It was a spectacular view. Jim sat rubbing his temple with an index, taking pains to assume the air of one engaged in deep difficult thought. David did his best to maintain composure; after all, it was a relatively well-paying position. Jim produced David's resumé, adorned with a dense confusion of red ink scrawls. David craned his neck and attempted to decode the markings, but the scribbled handwriting was impossible to decipher. Jim asked about *experience*. David muttered a disjointed stream of noise about university papers and writing movie reviews for websites. Jim asked if he was going to *get all postmodern and shit* and David nervously answered *I sure hope not.*

The wordsmith, seeker of *le mot juste.* The simplicity of lies.

Jim leaned back in his chair, folded his arms behind his head, stretched the cords of his neck to work out some kink, and said *what I'm wondering is* – a heavy troubled sigh, the sigh of the reclining warrior, the captain of industry – *are you prepared to work your ass off?*

And David had pledged that *yes,* he most certainly was, declaring his craving for challenge, that he was fascinated by the fast-paced marketing world, that he possessed keen judgment of when to buckle down and go solo versus when to solicit the assistance of others, to be a team player. He professed a hunger for dynamic language, for the assembly of words. Nothing he loved more than learning.

See: the easy flow, the aplomb, the effortlessness.

Jim: *for most of us as you can see* – indicating his own pressed Dockers, his unstained unwrinkled blue shirt – *dress is corporate casual but we let our creative guys get a little funky.*

So David was hired to write ad copy. The first day he had sat at his desk staring out the window, doing nothing and feeling useless.

The day crept by. At five he was told by Naoko to fill out a tax form and his first time sheet. He did so, concocting an account of *reviewing materials and performing administrative duties.*

Time sheets. Every day from then on: time sheets.

We let our creative guys get a little funky.

On his second day Jeff, he of spiky-blonde Astroturf hair, whose job seemed to consist primarily of circulating raunchy e-mails and organizing hockey pools, asked David to write brief bios of everyone in the agency and all regional branches, for a brochure to be assembled that week. These people numbered over a hundred. David balked, suspecting this to be a joke, a prank on the new guy. But no. It was not a joke. David asked for phone numbers. The phone numbers were produced. He set to work, interviewing, compiling, slaving over polished paragraphs. By week's end he had gotten only halfway through the list and had to write Jeff a sheepish e-mail begging more time. He was sorry, really sorry. But Jeff never brought it up and the pamphlet never emerged. David then realized that there were to be unreasonable expectations and miserable tasks in this job, a consistent dumping of menial duties and busywork. An endless cycle of interoffice redundancy.

And Jim. In Jim lies the furthest dearth of – something. Jim's life is one endless brunch meeting. He leads the troops down an unsteady slope of fax confirmations into a shrouded valley of deadlines. Jim glowers at David with suspicion.

David is in the copy room. He is running an ad for Acker Motors through the mighty Canon photocopier. The copier hums subsonic frequencies, whirring with a robotic flutter. David places the page on the copier's glass and closes the cover. He punches buttons, calls up the ZOOM screen, sets it to 150%. He presses the large green GO button.

Here it goes. The reproduction.

David touches a finger to his eyepatch and presses lightly on the gauze underneath, finding a light, satisfying twinge of pain. Like picking at a scab, like revisiting shadowy memories: the reaffirmation of pain. Battle scars, relics of combat.

The copied page is ejected. It is warm. He inspects it for quality. The enlarging process has altered, roughened, made the newsprint grainier. The Pontiac Sunfire Mid-Level Coupe 1SB, slightly less discernible.

Lifeless. Flat.

David opens the cover, removes the original and replaces it with the enlarged copy. He sets the ZOOM setting to 135% and presses GO.

The copy of the copy. A blotchy sidebar.

He copies this.

Stranger, blurrier. Copy, again.

This is the progression of days, of weeks. This is his flat world. Copied. Rendered and regurgitated. A weak reproduction. He does a third. A fourth. A fifth, even. Deeper, blurrier. With repetition, the image deteriorates into fuzzy dots.

Helen enters the copy room, wafting floral perfumes.

'Whatcha doing?' she asks.

'Making copies,' David answers.

She looks at his eyepatch and laughs. 'Aye aye, cap'n!'

By afternoon the heavens have delivered their displeasure unto the city, a remorseless scourge of blustering snow and whirling winds beating against the window.

David sits at his desk and, with his one good eye, watches as the city disappears into white.

The loss of his left eye has robbed him of depth perception. At the hospital the doctor had asked him *do you work in a field where you are required to maintain a high level of dexterity   such as operating mechanical equipment   or are you an active player of sports   such as racquetball?*

This is almost funny.

Nevertheless, the truth is alarming and odd. He finds himself grasping haplessly at doorknobs, clutching at air, questioning his reach, losing balance at corners. Everything is simply *there*, without context of distance or size. Columbus's trumping of naysayers had been reversed: the world was indeed flat. The city, from this sixteenth-floor view, is rendered merely a map, flattened, without scale as guide. The office is a curtain. The buildings are shoeboxes; the cars are ticks.

Snow veils all. Cars lie paralyzed in streets, hoods sunk in mountainous banks. Pedestrians stagger in the storm. David watches helplessly as his bus, packed solid with bodies, passes in a cold white spray. Admitting defeat, he treads bitterly uphill toward home. Monotony into deadness, enervating; all you can hope for is to sink into the wetness, to submit to the swirl, to drift away.

Perhaps this world will slowly slide into an endless Ice Age. Oceans will freeze, cities usurped by stadium-sized glaciers, streets buried in an impenetrable crust of ice, the world compacted with dry freeze, finally hardened into a glorious sparkling humanless crystal.

The apartment invites him, dependably, warmly. He shucks his bag, his coat, his snow-ruined shoes. The eyepatch is bumpy with gathered ice flecks, now melting in cold drips. He retrieves fresh gauze from the bathroom, puts the patch aside and rebuilds the bandage.

Again: light pressure, the reassurance of pain.

He sinks into his recliner and presses PLAY on the TV remote. All day his consciousness has been occupied with Patton. Wanting *Patton*. The fictionalization. The man. The gruffness.

Last night, watching the movie, his mind had caught fire. Flee these ignoble times for 1945, 1970, to the Kasserine Pass, to Hollywood. To bloodshed. Stand firm against the abyss of desert plains. Maintain composure against washed-out cinematic history. What foe does filmic Patton, the actor George C. Scott, encounter in the Mesopotamia of his mind? Panzers – strive to discern the nuances of the fearsome Desert Fox, Rommel at El Guettar. Patton hugged the wide open like a lover, finding in its voracious opportunity a kaleidoscope of possible blood-flingings. Patton thrived on wounds; The general-poet wrote *through the turmoil of ages midst the pomp and toils of war have I fought and strove and perished countless times among the stars.* Quiver at Patton's rage, his revulsion at a young soldier's cowardice, slapping him upside the head. David, snotty and nine years old, sat on the front stairs as The Father crouched before him, lacing up his hockey skates. David wept. VCR-Patton waves a gloved hand – David's cheeks suffered humiliated tears. Nostrils heavy with sweaty pads. The Father scowled, bent and silent; this was the last time he would pander to such pussy-ass behaviour.

If time is a sieve, then let it separate the mud of the Czechoslovakian front from the present to which it clings. Free childhood's tears from scathing salts. Let the shrouded figures prowling sad memories be replaced by august heroes, titans, in the petty receipts confirmed by lesser men.

Jo-Beth and Gary's house sits plunked in the bend of a tree-sheltered cul-de-sac, a stately stronghold nestled in a neighbourhood of similar strongholds. Cars and SUVs sit in the driveway and up and down the street. Sun twinkles through a pair of large elms framing the house's gaping maw of punctuative shrubbery.

David knocks. The door flings open: the beaming face of Lisa. Lisa, in a green turtleneck and a jean skirt, hair dangling behind perked ears.

'David,' she cries. 'You came.'

Meekly: 'I did.'

She tilts her head with concern. 'You're ... What's ... '

It's the eyepatch, this violation of his face hiding a gruesomer wound beneath.

'I had an accident. This is this, it's an eyepatch ... '

'Yes. I see it's an eyepatch. Very evil genius–mad scientist, yeah yeah. Come in. It's freezing out.'

She guides him into the foyer, removes his coat and hangs it, then leads him by the hand into the house. There is mingling, dimmed lights, a blazing hearth. Coziness abounds. Sweatered men in groups – some glance at David as he enters. He offers a general smile, unaimed.

Perhaps we will gather on Apocalypse's eve and reminisce, grinning happily at our accomplishment with fond tidings as the final hour encroaches.

Lisa hands him a large glass of wine. He expresses gratitude.

Lisa: 'Are you hungry? Are you thirsty? There's all this ... '

She waves at a vast range of hors d'oeuvres, miniature sandwiches, cauliflower florets partnered by dips. Trays of Camembert and saltines, knives poised for pâtés.

'That's all right.'

'Come *on*. You're not hungry? We have casserole.'

'I had this microwave lasagna a few hours ago that pretty much annihilated my appetite.'

'Oh *god*. What were you thinking?'

Lisa yanks him by the sleeve and forces him to sample the smoked salmon, piling the oily slices atop a soda cracker and cramming it all into his mouth, then assembling a mountainous heap for herself. She regards him and the room with weird glee, unfoiled humour – utterly unafraid.

They proceed into the dining room, which for the occasion has been converted into a makeshift buffet. David greets cousins, aunts, kinfolk twice removed, thrice removed. From another room David hears bellowing, satisfied laughter, unmistakably his uncle Gary's. It spikes a chill into David's bones.

Lisa thrusts a plate upon him and, against his protests, begins to slop casserole. They are together, the two of them. Everything else falls pale. She giggles; they are allies, cohorts, together against everyone.

Lisa: 'Pepper?'

Seventeen. She is seventeen. Sparkling with adolescence. Picture her winking at horny boys in chemistry lab, spurning their clumsy advances. Disappearing on the weekends into the foxholes of a frathouse bash. Demurely straw-sucking a milkshake, dangling a shopping bag by a finger. She is seventeen and ageless.

She wipes a globule from her mouth with a serviette. Her eyes dance.

'I'm so fucking glad you came,' she says.

David starts to say something about not hanging around too long, but before he can, Gary emerges from the den. His dark brow. His bourbon glass, waved. His jaw, locked in a fierce grin, always ready to cackle: *heh heh hcck hcck*.

'Dave Davey David,' he says. 'Oh my christ. It's been quite a. Wow.'

He extends a meaty palm. David allows his hand to be wrenched.

Gary leers and inspects David's face, the eyepatch and bandaging. 'What the hell is going on with *this* thing?'

'I had an accident,' David says. 'It's really not that big a deal.'

Gary crinkles his face in tipsy amusement.

'Dammit, David. *Damn. It.* But at least you finally got rid of those retarded sideburns.'

'Oh. Yeah. Streamlined for the new year.'

'Thank god for all of us, eh.' Gary cackles, glancing at Lisa, at David, at his glass, into some obscure zone of his own understanding.

'I had to twist his arm into coming,' Lisa says, looking away.

David: 'Mm.'

Gary shakes his head and sips at his glass. Today he is immersed in his role as the mellow entertainer. Tender of the fire, filler of cups. Overseer of tidy times. The proffering of this manor and his self-made grandeur. His life is a comfy crewneck sweater.

Lisa can't even look at him.

Gary: 'So. What you up to these days, Davey? Any fortuitous prospects on the horizon?'

'Uh, I don't know,' David says. 'We'll see.'

'Landed yourself a job of any sort yet?'

'Actually, I'm working at an agency downtown.'

'An *agency*.'

'An advertising agency.'

'Really. Fascinating.' Gary turns to Lisa, tells her: 'He's come a long way, this kid. Humping his way through the whole system. It's tough to be alone, right, Dave? It's tough to be swept aside in the march of time. But if he can keep his head out of his ass, he might just pull it off.'

'I don't know if that's exactly it … ' Lisa says, her eyes on her plate.

'I'm sure it's not,' Gary says. 'But survival is measured in lots of different ways. In some cases it's having a life like ours, with all these things and security and the nice car and the driveway. People do it in their own ways, kids. We're all trapped in the same iceberg. And at the end of the day we all wipe our asses with same single-ply. The globe only spins in one direction.'

His grin wobbles, as if only just now realizing something. David forks the casserole.

'I want to show David the addition,' Lisa says.

'Sounds good,' Gary says distractedly. He has many hours of hosting still ahead; he whacks David on the arm and gazes into a nearby salad.

Orange strokes of reclining sun seep through windows as afternoon dwindles to evening. The party grows thick and noisy. Swiping the bottle of wine she's been glugging, Lisa leads David downstairs to a dim basement. Thick carpet blankets the floor and photos line the walls: here is Lisa, a smaller Lisa, posed next to a ten-speed with Jenny, her sister, David's other, more aloof cousin. Here are Gary and Jo-Beth on their wedding day, the young couple beaming triumphantly through a span of years.

A huge trophy presides over the mantle. David sets down his glass and reads its inscription, proclaiming Gary CHAMPION 1988 Atlantic Fisheries Open Golf Tournament.

Lisa produces an odd flat-handled object and hands it to David. A paddle.

'Ping-pong,' she says.

With this, he is led down a chilly stone-floored hallway, through a glass sliding door into a broad sunroom, its picture windows now dark. She snaps on a light.

Here it is: the ping-pong table. She takes position at one end of the table, David in unwilling opposition, the room sparingly lit.

'I will now proceed to destroy your ass,' she declares.

'I don't really know how to play,' David tries, but Lisa is already readying her strike. Her expression intensifies as she palms a small white ball, rolling it through her fingers. She gives it a quick bounce against the table – *pak* – then delivers it blazing over the net. The ball rebounds at a sharp angle, and before unsuspecting David is aware, zips neatly past him.

In half-sight, everything is flat. The ball, the swing, the table, all nothing and nowhere. His paddle flaps at empty air.

'One serving zero,' Lisa announces. 'Ball's by your foot.'

'Nice shot.'

'Semi. You didn't even try. Wake up.'

'Well, I'm having trouble seeing ... and I'm not really ... '

Lisa delivers another ace, tearing easily past him.

'Did you know,' she says as he stoops to retrieve the ball from the carpet, 'that some of the same lawyers who worked for the People's Temple at Jonestown later advised Martin Luther King?'

David blanks.

'Same guys pushing the CIA LSD mind-control tests and the Kennedy probes. There are links. I wonder about Jim Jones, and where he got those killer shades.'

She taps the ping-pong ball against her paddle – *pak pak* – and serves again. David waggles, swings, fails.

Lisa: 'Did you know that soldiers in Sierra Leone were paid on a limb-by-limb basis? Bonuses for amputations.'

She serves. The ball glances off the edge of his paddle, careening backward against the wall behind him; it ricochets and dings him on the back of the skull.

'*Ak.*'

'I had a friend who became a Moonie,' Lisa says. 'She married this guy, some guy from Oregon who she had never even met, in a hockey arena with eight hundred other people. Eight hundred people got married at the same time. Last I heard, she was living up in Nunavut, teaching ceramics to Inuit kids.'

'Nunavut?'

Pow – another devastating serve.

'Five serving zero. Your go,' Lisa says.

Later: they are upstairs, in Lisa's bedroom. Away from watchful eyes.

It had to happen. All tragedy is predetermined, and there is no safety or comfort.

She shuts the door. The roar of the party downstairs is muffled. The room smells like Lisa: soapy. The walls are painted dark violet and the furnishings are sparse, utilitarian. The room is exhaustively organized except for a stack of magazines, several pages torn out and scissored into jagged shapes. The bedcovers are tightly drawn. There is no spilling laundry. It is not the bedroom of a teenager.

Propped against the wall next to her dresser is a long pointed object sheathed in soft tan leather. David reaches for it.

'Don't touch that,' Lisa says.

'What is it?'

Lisa sighs through her nose. 'It's my *wakizashi*.'

'Wacky what?'

She shakes her head. 'It's a sword. A Japanese sword. It's a traditional samurai sword.'

He looks closer. It is indeed a sword.

'Where did you get a ... '

'Off the Internet. Come on. Don't. Come here.'

David stares at the sword. It is long and slender and curved. Its sheath bears hatch marks in leather, inscriptions in Japanese characters.

'What do you need a sword for?' he asks.

No answer. She sits on the floor by the bed and indicates for him to join her. He does, close enough to be available but not so close as to presume. And what could be presumed by this *cousinly* scene. From under the bed Lisa produces something he can't identify: a weird object, made of something glass-like but not glass, bluish and greenish in tinge, with strange rod-like tentacles splayed from its core. Like some sort of robotic lung, a disembowelment. A cloudy glow emits from its interior. It quivers in Lisa's hands.

'*The Exorcist II* was on television the night before last,' she says, cradling the object, which, as David looks closer, resembles a fossilized squid. 'I had never bothered to see it before. It wasn't so hot. There were inaccuracies. But I'm always partial to sequels. Sequels are underdogs. In any case, it was a hellride and a good time.'

She opens a nearby drawer and roots around in it. Squirming in her hands, the object looses a flatulent sound: *pllp*.

It is a squid. A creature, an unshelled snail. An emptied heart.

'Have you seen *Exorcist III*?' David asks.

Lisa, distracted in her rummaging: 'No ... '

'It's iffy too. But I'm sort of a fan of George C. Scott. You should see ... Have you seen *Patton*?'

'I ... a – *ha*.'

She produces a lighter, ignites, then lightly presses it against one of the object's tentacles; the protrusion shrivels like bacon frying, then falls limp. Lisa snuffles at this heat agitation, which gives off a woody odour, then she clasps the lighter shut.

She extends the object to David.

'Hold this,' she says.

He takes it reluctantly, but once the object is in his grip he discovers its feel to be oddly appealing. It is warm; he had expected it to be cold. His fingertips sink into its fleshy mass. Its bulbous glisten is the compression of a taut muscle, a surface softness encasing a firm core. Lisa rummages further in the drawer, raising herself up to look inside. The waist of her sweater rises, exposing a view of her narrow lower back.

David looks at her skin.

The object hums in his palms.

She finds in the drawer a small metal box, which holds a supply of something floral and stalky. Without a word, she takes the object back and begins force-feeding clumps down one of its protuberances. The object then seems to awaken, and by some force begins to suck the powder down, ingesting it, coaxing it deeper into its gut with sentient appetite.

David is uncomfortable.

Lisa again flips the lighter and touches the flame to a tentacle. The squid-thing dilates with thick fumes. Lisa keeps the flame applied to the tube's mouth for about five uninterrupted seconds as the object's gelatinous innards expand, bloated with smoke.

'Puff?' she offers.

The object, smoke-fat, trembles in her palms, membraned like stirred glue.

'You go ahead.'

Lisa clears her throat and places her lips against the tube.

Lips. Lisa's lips, curled like parentheses. They encircle the tube; David watches in mute awe as the object grasps back, emitting a sound like a quiet whinny. Its rubbery rims respond to provocation: wobbling, then paroxysmal with chundered smoke. Its ridges expand beyond Lisa's expectant mouth, opening like the widening mouth of a fish. Finally, it re-exerts its discharge upward, joining Lisa's face with a sagged puddle of pinkish, rank smoke.

Lisa closes her eyes, then after a prolonged moment, exhales. Her eyes are black canvas. Her mouth hangs open.

'Take a go,' she says.

The object quakes in balloony jiggles. Pumped with future, aligned with release.

Right now she is so close. Her denimed leg brushes against David's. She looks at him with anticipation, expectation, extending the object. Lisa, lustrous. Lisa, beloved. Somewhere, elsewhere, in the unhigh undrunk dinnertime-blabbering judging background, there are restrictions and demands. Everywhere else, reason rules and time trudges without joy. But here, there is Lisa and her smoke-seeking lips, her foggy eyes. She is nowhere but here. She is young. She hints at truth. She sings without sound, beautiful against belief.

It is the absolute best way for a girl to be.

As his lips meet the tube, he detects suction from within, accompanied by a faint whine. But he does not shy. His lips are drawn into it, around it. Its skin seals itself around his mouth, adhering firmly. Suddenly it quivers and expels smoke into his throat, down into his lungs – the force is so direct, he doesn't even have a choice whether to inhale.

Instantly his mind is awhirl.

Mental jungles. Storms. Flags flying, regions segregated in maps, soaring stars. Medals. Bodies. General Patton and his interminable cigar-puffing. His arms, folded across his brawny chest. Chests like tanks, broad workmanlike necks. Dialogue: *I won't have cowards here with these brave men.*

Before. After. Intermediary.

This moment, here. Cavernous.

Whewf.

Lisa says, 'Hits you hard, hm?'

'Yeah … pretty significant … '

Look at them sitting on the floor. The squid-bong gets passed back and forth several times. David loses track of time. Of location. Identity. He wonders what it is they're smoking. The issue of zombie manipulators. Droppings from schizophrenic phoenixes. Demon flesh, gristle stuck in its jaws. Monsters racing over snow, leaving bloody tracks. Look at him: grinning and grimacing. Fear is pleasure, riding the spine in spasms.

Lisa sags against him, resting her golden head on his clenched shoulder. Look at her delicate paw, gently stroking his cheek. Look at them languishing in the stalled moment.

So quiet: 'David.'

'Yuh.'

'Can you imagine … *anything* … better than this?'

Winter: a ravage of wet air and wet wind and wet cold. Sidewalks vanish under slush and lawns go lost. Clouds empty their frozen dandruff on the unwitting as the barometer stalls, and everything slows. Cars skid past stop signs, their tenuous handling thwarted. Bodies bow and buckle under whooping currents. Squadrons of snowploughs advance on the streets.

Perhaps we will be buried under the freeze of years, the tireless plod of auto-annulment.

David is standing at his bedroom window, naked but for his Hanes briefs, rubbing sleep's grit from his cheek. He gazes out at the mounting blizzard, wishing he never had to venture outside again.

Everything is oppressive. Every resigned breath brings fresh dread, as he waits for something, not knowing what it is.

The eye screams to be scratched, torn out of his skull.

The phone rings. He finds it and thumbs TALK.

It's Naoko. 'Are you listening to the radio?'

He reaches into the back of his briefs and scratches one cheek of his ass. The cheek is cold. 'No.'

'Well, don't bother coming in. The roads are awful and it looks like they're bound to get worse.'

'Okay.' *Then why are you at the office*, he thinks to ask, but doesn't.

'See you on Monday, then.'

He puts down the phone. The weekend comes early. Freedom. He stands in his underwear. He opens his palm and cups his butt cheek, squeezes hard. This feels good. He does it a few more times, then heads back to bed.

In his last years, The Father had been but a mere shadow of his self. A glimmer of former presence. Skeletal. With grim world-weariness, drink, divorce, he'd undergone a steady decline from the hoohah of the pressing world. Flaking between sales positions, getting canned for absenteeism, finally settling in as Assistant Manager at a home repair supplies warehouse. David's father was in his late fifties; his immediate superior was twenty-four. And yet he remained.

Picture The Father straining to smile while dolefully clipboard-checking stocks of flex conduit and circuit breakers and duct insulation under the watchful eye of some pimply kid. A fate unbefitting even the coldest of hearts.

Fathers. Fathers enduring rugged distances. Fathers testing knots. Fathers manning barbecues. Fathers grappling sons in ways that are not assaults but hugs. Fathers calling for butter at breakfast in ways that do not prey upon their sons' insecurity. Fathers who are not villains.

There had been long nights in David's youth where The Father's rage had brimmed so evidently behind his strained exterior that David worried the friction would catch a spark and burn down the house. He was a man of jumbled torments – he rarely spoke. He had been known, when well-beered at picnics or informal functions, to rip off a callous huff, but never prolonged dialogue.

Eons ago: David's eleventh-birthday sleepover. He and a few kids from his soccer team, in rowdy prepubescent revelry, gorging on pizza and playing Nintendo and watching rented videos of not only *American Ninja* and *Ninja III: The Domination* but also *Gymkata*, all in the same sitting, the downstairs den of David's suburban home transformed into a battlefield of boyish goofery. David's mother twice appeared at the stairs to request a charity of volume as the boys practiced ninja moves atop a deftly constructed arena of inter-zipped sleeping bags; at both junctures David emerged to answer his mother's patient pleas, perspiring with excitement, sugar-giddy, saying *guys let's just keep it down a bit Mom's gotta sleep*; because Mom at this point was enduring woes of migraine, woes at this point still merely burdensome rather than the gushing agonies they later became, and the guys consented to ghetto blaster's MUTE and a return to the quietly blooping bliss of Nintendo. Until, in the night's wee hours, the boys still in a Chips Ahoy! and Pepsi–fuelled mania, somebody suggested a venture outside. A sneaking out. So sneaking they went, exercising excruciating restraint as they tiptoed out through the basement door, single file through the laundry room and into the garage, David imploring his teammates to *shh*, out the back door into the warm summer night. Like thieves, like *ninjas*. Practicing the stealth of an assassin.

The night was emancipation. Imagine their blissful camaraderie as they scurried up the backyard's brief incline, rounded the bend of the house, hurried through a tangle of bushes – the street's glow beckoning – and then, just as the ninjas rounded the house and gathered at lawn's edge, a car roared into the driveway, headlights training across their shocked faces. They froze in their tracks. In the car a bulky figure, indistinguishable in shadow, manned the wheel, while another man slid out of the shotgun seat. This man was heart-wrenchingly recognizable. The Father. Witness the weaving shamble of the drunken Father. Witness the amused fury in his leering perusal of these boys standing on his lawn. Look at these boys, so pumped up and hyper, most in sweatpants and jammies. Witness the thwarting of their glee. Witness the reeling of The Father, soused, driven home from the bar by some stranger. Witness the bleary stare. Witness the raising of the finger and a garbled reprimand, in front of all the guys. So: back to the house. On the stairs' landing, The Father glared down at him. The Father's thick moustache was the axis of his rage at the failure of the son to meet expectations, and how the son's abuse of the leeway he has been given betrays the fact that he is *not to be trusted ever*, and that the son is an *ungrateful asshead*, and is he even *listening to me are you listening to me are you listening to me*. And then come the pokes. This is The Father's secret weapon, his H-bomb, his lightsabre, his ninja bo staff. It is his Sherman tank: the poke to the centre of the sternum. Despite untargeted eyes, he jabs with surgical precision, driving home each word: *Are. You. Listening. To. Me.* The slurred words of The Father. The alcoholic stink of The Father. David sensed that this assault, these words and pokes, were not even necessarily meant for him; that maybe they were for some unseen adversary – they are pokes against everything. All of this is not real. The drunken Father is not real. Bawling like a baby as your Father rags you out with words that don't even make fucking sense: this is not real. And yet, tomorrow, the old man will be outwardly equable. Hungover, night spent on the couch. The Father will dither in the kitchen, frying bacon and scrambling eggs, and the guys from the team will undergo a half-hearted interrogation of the team's prospects, the stats and the league, and David will wait with mounting agitation for the expected ragging-out over last night's antics. But it won't come. *No.* This is how it happened. His adaptation of authority, this teetering man. Toast will be toasted and the day will continue as any other. Nothing proven or achieved.

Now it's all hackneyed plotline, disposable sets, props barely held together, scripted battles, forgotten characters. It's all illusion, story as history.

None of this is real.

Relentless snow pounds all day, into night. But there is the shelter of houses, furnaces and fireplaces, insulation. Inside homes, televisions. Entertainments.

The world's bisected flatness is puffed to life, inflated, made new by the steady whirr of the VCR.

Patton stretches into hours. Its finale begs rewinding, and so he rewinds and replays, over and over. During the day such repetition destroys his soul; tonight it proves his salvation. There are no tugged heartstrings in *Patton*, no melancholy or spare mirth. No love scenes. There is primarily one single man occupying the frame, but we do not *know* him; there are no voice-overs, no internal monologues, no confessions. No shame in his conquest. No desire for redemption or apology for his massacres. There is no cleansing of the blood and guts.

With the fourth viewing, David realizes: there are no women in the world of *Patton*.

George C. Scott played General Buck Turgidson in *Dr. Strangelove*. He played Mussolini on television. He played cops and doctors and priests. He refused an Oscar. Wore medals. Died of a ruptured abdominal aortic aneurysm. Shot at fighter planes. Wept soldierly tears.

Enter a zone of tested heroism, screaming bombers, camels, maps bearing numerous tacks. Tacks on maps of Northern Africa, of the shores of Sicily. Storm all the way to Hitler's backyard and *kick him square in the ass*. Watching, you sleep the unsleeping dream. No time sheets, no photocopies. The windows are coated with ice. Today, tonight, you can be unworried. You can grasp the ivory handle of a cathode-ray-tube remote-control bayonet Colt 45 bottle and thrust it into the soft belly of a Nazi Jim Father Hun. Blood and guts. Speak in the gravelly voice of a hero uncontained.

This man is not a trembler. David sinks into the refuge of him, bathes himself in the woozy comforts of the man. But it is not the man, nor the actor who portrays the man. It is the ideal of the man, and the portrayal of this ideal – so simple, so stark, so pure. It is the brute force. It is the gleaming buckles and the shining nose. It is the time lost in the saga. This man is not a kitten.

The Father listened closely to weather reports. Retreat, no. Crank the volume. Snow paralyzing the city. The sun over the pyramids. Heroism. Wounds. Where are all the teammates now? Nobody ever won a war by dying for *his* country – he won it by making the other poor dumb bastard die for his country. Life is passing. The proud forehead of the General. The yawn of years to come, the years that have passed. Everything is deception and veneer. The insubordination. The slapping. Soldiers falling under heavy shelling. The time sheets, always, the time sheets. The hawk-like sneer of Jim. Nothing ever the fault of one man; everything is attributed to the collective. The tanks creep over unquestioning countryside. Seas sparkle. Snow like dust from a forgotten age. The rigours of the VCR, undying in the turning of tape. The passage of time, solidifying the weight of a life, a proud life. This man is a lovesick fool, his mistress the battlefield. The glory. Set your place in history. Try to become. Drink the wine of history. Be a man. Finally, last goodbyes. The clinking beer bottles. The heroes of unknown zones. Where The Father lies.

It is nearly midnight when the phone rings. The outside world invades.

David blinks and awakes: his good eye's vision is glassy from uninterrupted staring at the screen. He rises, stiff-necked, from the chair.

The phone: 'Hello?'

On the other end there is a long sigh, then: 'Hello … David?'

Lisa. It's Lisa.

He clears his throat: *kah*. 'Lisa. Um. How's it going.'

'Iffy. I don't know.'

Her words come slowly, uneasily.

'What are you doing?' she says.

'Oh. Just watching a movie.'

'That … sounds nice. Is it good … '

Like she's talking in her sleep.

'Are you okay?' David asks. 'You sound a bit funny.'

'I'm okay … a bit gooey, I suppose. I took a few Percodans and drank a bottle of Pims … just taking it easy … '

His throat clenches. Tonight, Lisa. Of all times, the perfect worst time. She's located him, here, in the swirls of nothingness.

On the television screen a measureless Algerian plain is trapped in PAUSE.

'Are you at home?'

'I'm in the kitchen. Just cracking a brewsky.'

'Jeesh, Lisa. Are your folks there?'

He can hear the capping of a bottle, then a hard glug.

'Lisa.'

'David David.'

'Are your parents home?'

'No no no. They're up at Wentworth skiing. Dad had to try out his new … you know, what do you call them … *skis*. They hit the road. They're off. Is it still snowing?'

'Are you alone?'

A long pause. He can hear her curse to herself, some fuss, but the sound is distant and muffled.

'Lisa?'

Clk. The line goes dead.

His breath is slow in returning. Is there cause for. Lisa in the midst of. Drunken stoned lustrous Lisa, with her narrow neck and alien bong and creaselessness. Alone in that house. David rings *69, gets her number and calls back. The phone rings once, then the voice mail picks up. Jo-Beth: *hi there   you've reached* –

He hangs up.

His apartment is queasily silent. In one hand there is the telephone, in the other the remote control. Thumbs waver over TALK and PAUSE – these are the options.

Back to the Algerian front and the safety of war. Back to the war.

Ring.

'David … *hi.*'

'Lisa. Jeesh.'

'What?'

'Oh, I was just … nothing. I was kind of worried there.'

'I went out … for a *cigarette*. I told you that.'

'No, you didn't.'

'I'm sure I did … So what are you doing now?'

'Talking to you.'

'No, before … I called … '

'I said. Watching a movie.'

'A *pornographic* movie?' she snickers.

He tries to laugh in return, but it comes as a nervy hiccup. Lisa: seventeen, but she careens with force beyond years.

'Why are you at home alone watching pornographic movies, David?'

'I'm not … '

'Because there are such deeper experiences than that. You could be playing in the snow with me … we could go out in the snow … it's so pretty, we could be out there in the snow. I love the way it falls … it's like passing away, sort of like science … '

'Science?'

Yes. They could be diving through piled banks of powder, swimming through sharp wintry air, holding mittened hands as the city fades to backdrop. Strolling through the night, laughing against the cold. Like snow riding the crest of a hill, blowing through alleys, veering through labyrinths of ice and concrete.

Yes. No.

Lisa: 'Don't you think the snow is pretty?'

She sounds like she's losing consciousness. 'Lisa,' David says, 'this is not good.'

'If it's not good … '

Silence, a breath.

'David.'

'I'm here.'

'Do you like sushi?'

'Yes.'

'We went for sushi one time, right?'

'I took you to that sushi bar with the big tissue-paper fish. Remember the big eel and the big crab?'

'The *crab* … ?'

'There were those cartoony characters for all the seafood. It was this lame thing. You kept saying how *gratuitous* it was. There was an eel and a crab and a bunch of others. A yellowfish. A tuna fish.'

'I remember. Gratuitous. Your hair was wet.'

He is standing in front of the television, in the middle of the room, shuddering to the meter of her words, words which mimic the shape of her mouth, her agile curious lips.

'You know what?' she says.

'What.'

'I think nothing … nothing is better than this.'

'Maybe.'

'No. *Nothing* is better than right now. Nothing gets better than this. Nothing improves … We're basking in the, it's like a carousel … spinning … '

The phone feels like a mile-thick condom.

No. No. *No.* He crams down so many thoughts.

Lisa: 'Why are you at home … watching pornos?'

'I'm not watching pornos. I'm watching *Patton*.'

'Patting. Poor David. At home, patting himself. David, do you have a girlfriend?'

'A *girlfriend*? No, I … you know. The lone wolf. It's the … you know … the plight of the … you know.'

'No reprieve for gentlemen of … '

'No rest for the wicked.'

'Never.'

'Never.'

Lisa sighs. 'I had a boyfriend. He was a fucking champ.'

'So what happened.'

'Couldn't keep his ... *ass* in line ... so I cut him loose.'

'Uh.'

'I think I'm going to go now.'

He can hear strange noises, rummaging. He pictures her in her violet bedroom, draped in strange smoke.

'Are you sure you're going to be all right?' he says.

'I'll be *fine* ... '

'I have my reservations, you know, about you being there by yourself, getting all ... '

'Oh?' she snorts. 'And are you going to come here and keep me company? Will you come hold my hand? Are you going to ... cast out my demons? Are you going to come here?'

No. He is not. He *can't*, and she knows it. There is a line he cannot cross.

'Are you coming to be with me?'

The Algerian desert. The humming refrigerator. The buzz of the vandalized eye. The flatness. He says nothing.

'Then this conversation is over ... isn't it?' she says.

'Lisa.'

'Bye. Fuck you.'

Clk.

Moments later. *Ring.*

'Lisa.'

Her voice is faint. 'David.'

'I think I should come over. You don't sound well.'

'No ... '

She is just a girl. A child. Hear her breathe.

'David ... '

'Yes.'

'What are you doing?'

'Still watching the movie.'

'Oh.'

There is silence, until he begins to think she's fallen asleep. Then: 'Do you know the *Necronomicon?*'

'The neck ... wha?'

'This book, the *Necronomicon*. The testimony of the Mad Arab. I have it here on my lap. I just need to smoke a bowl and read one sentence and I'm gone. You should read it.'

'Okay.'

'*The wolves carry my name in their midnight speeches and that quiet subtle voice is summoning me from afar and a voice much closer will shout into my ear with unholy impatience the weight of my soul will decide its final resting place.*'

Her reading is slow and slurry and laboured, her voice a tremble. But somehow she commands the words like a sniper commands his scope. David is transfixed.

She coughs, then continues. '*Time is short and mankind does not know or understand the evil that awaits it from every side from every open gate from every broken barrier from every mindless acolyte at the altars of madness.* Do you know what this means?'

'I don't think I get it.'

'David, don't you see? Because just being alive ... we're in peril ... but if we die, we open up new avenues ... '

Pause.

David: 'We're in peril?'

'The most difficult way for a samurai to commit *seppuku* is called *jumonji giri*. You cut across your belly, then cut straight up the ... centre.'

'What.'

'Up the centre. Entrails. Honour through suicide.'

'What.'

'You make a cross. Like a *jyuu*. A Japanese ten.'

Another long pause. She is thinking.

'David.'

'Yes.'

Lazily, drifting: 'What happened to your father?'

What happened. 'He ... Why?'

'Where did he go? What did he do?'

'Oh jeesh, Lisa. You know.'

'I remember, he was a … jumpy guy. Must run in the family. He was a bleak dude.'

'Hm.'

'He couldn't sit still.'

Barriers and breaking points. Trenches burrowed, figures knelt, sizzling heights. The battle will be waged in shrugs, strained communication.

'I think … it's time to go,' she says.

'That's what you said before.'

'No … I mean it … I'm really … '

She's fading, drowsier and drowsier.

'Are you sure you're okay?' he asks.

'Yeah … '

'Okay.'

'Good night, David.'

'Good night, Lisa.'

'David.'

'Yeah?'

'I wish you were here.'

He cannot speak.

'I wish … I've been wishing about … you know … how just before … '

There is a sound, a rumple, and the line goes silent. David waits a moment, says her name, louder, waits, then hangs up.

Clk.

Victory and defeat. For every victor, a fallen enemy, a vanquished foe. Scars run deep, like tank tracks tearing through passive earth or villages left in cinders. Irreversible wounds. After the final credits roll, and the story's majesty has concluded, there are questions. In battle everything is ambiguous. Snow blankets corpses lying in fields. Winds whistle fanfares against rattling windows. Battalions retreat, mopping up messes. Crack a beer. Drink generously, because this ceasefire is only a respite. The silence is temporary.

Thursday.

Eric, the recording engineer, pinches an drop of gingko biloba into his cranberry juice, then knocks back the glass. He taps keys on his console and speaks into the talkback mic: 'Oak Orchard Golf Club. Thirty seconds. Take eight.'

He sits back in his chair, quaking with lungy hacks. He is suffering a touch of flu and thus is cranky. David pretends not to notice as he sits quietly at the back of the control room. He hates sitting in on these radio recording sessions; he serves no purpose, but must maintain the illusion of vigilance, of work. The tedium is necessary.

Right now he thinks about lunch. He thinks about Whoppers.

In the studio's main room, the voice-over dude, Randolph, wears headphones and speaks into the mic. Through control-room speakers: *membership has its privileges   experience the pinnacle of luxury in our distinguished clubhouse   sample the delicious fare from the Nineteenth Hole Bistro Bar.* He expounds, in an economy of phrase and time, upon the myriad virtues of the club, the complex and challenging majesty of the newly restructured fairways and resodded greens, the friendliness and competence of the staff, the peerless all-encompassing wonder of the Oak Orchard Golf Club, just off Route 117, in twenty-eight seconds, with leeway. This script – refined and trimmed and re-edited and clarified and final-approved – is originally David's, but in appeasing the whims of Roland Humbe, Jr., President of Oak Orchard, any subtlety or humour or flow has been drained in favour of superfluous information. All rhythm chucked, all grace abolished, by decree of Humbe and his lickspittle staff.

David has learned that this work is not his in which to feel pride. It is but clay, clay with which morons shape replicas of their own hollow idiocy.

Randolph finishes his run-through. Eric swivels in his chair and looks to David.

'That's probably fine,' David says. 'He should do the fifteen-second one too.'

Eric honks his nose and instructs Randolph to move on to the next script. Through the speakers David hears Randolph, a local stand-up and notorious old beerhound, emit a long and fizzy fart. Then he delivers the fifteen-second spot, a truncated translation of the same script, in his seasoned radio voice: expressive to the point of silliness, snappy, rip-roaring.

With take's end, Eric again spins in his chair.

'That's probably fine,' David says. 'Maybe he should emphasize the thing about the sumptuous whatever a bit more. Humbe mentioned that specifically. Really drive it home.'

Eric sighs and relays this to Randolph through the talkback mic.

'Oak Orchards, fifteen-second spot, take two.'

It's all a *game*.

David lingers while Eric burns a CD of the session. The studio is one of the least engaging places David has ever been, all spare surfaces and acoustic panelling. He can't wait to get out of here.

'You guys should fuck using Randy for all these spots,' Eric says.

'You think?'

'He's tired. He *sucks*.'

'It's not my decision. I just sit in. My responsibilities are next to nil … '

'Well, tell whoever it is that does decide that their boy Randolph sucks, and they should get new people. And this is coming from me, and I don't at all care about any of this diarrhea.'

'Okay.'

'I just push the buttons. I just chop it up and put it back together. I'm not the chief turd with the waxy sheen.'

Apparently Eric has turned a shade bitter, recording and mixing high-fidelity tedium, editing together radio spots all day every day – this is the same downward spiral David rides. If he stays with his job for much longer, there is the threat of complete meltdown. Even the most easily satisfied mind grows restless with such drudgery.

Eric: 'MNG is really trouncing you as far as radio is concerned. They at least budget their things semi-realistically. You guys cut corners and I get testy phone calls from what's-her-face.'

'Helen.'

'Right, Helen. She called me after that last thing and spazzed out on me for like ten minutes. I explained that the numbers you guys listed were totally unrealistic. And yet she still didn't get it. She was inconvincible.'

'As I told you, I have no say in that area.'

Eric: 'You should use this chick I have coming in next, Sarah Promise. Great voice. Very commanding, very crisp, very versatile. A bit of a strange duck, but worth considering.'

'Really.'

'Very adaptable. She does cartoons mostly. She does Tianna.'

David begins to wonder whether he'll have time to get lunch before heading back to the office. He thinks of cheeseburgers. Onion rings.

'Tianna,' he says.

'You know, Princess Tianna. *Princess Tianna and the Guardians of the Gilded Flame.* It's that show on the cartoon channel with the warrior princesses and the thing with the sea and the gold armour and shit. It's fairly massive.'

'I'm not familiar.'

'Well, Sarah is Tianna, and she's a pro. She does it all. You should get her.'

'As I say, it's not really my call.'

'She should be doing this golf-club bullcrud.'

'All *right.* I get it.'

Eric shrugs and ejects the finished CD. He leads David back out into the hallway. As they arrive at the elevator, a woman steps out.

This woman: face hidden by enormous blue-tinted sunglasses, a dense tumble of blonde-brown curls, lips exploding from her face like a wound. She wears a long burgundy coat buttoned up to a fur collar, high-heeled leather boots. Eric greets her. She stops.

Eric: 'Right. David, this is Sarah Promise. The one-take wonder.'

She nods ungenerously.

'David could hook you up with some work,' Eric says. 'Lots of radio work.'

'Eric … ' David says.

Beyond Sarah Promise's harsh exterior, there hides something else, an instantly detectable suspicious something. She removes her sunglasses to reveal dark crescents of green and red; she looks like she hasn't slept in days.

These eyes scour him, razing him. David is immediately uneasy.

'What are we doing today?' she asks. 'The Big Brothers Sisters whatever thing?'

Eric: 'Yeah.'

'Fucking A.'

This woman. Sarah Promise. She is a panther licking ebony paws, a snake in a thicket, throbbing with danger. Menace. Everything about her is immediate and scathing. David catches her confusion of scents: spearmint gum and hairspray and cigarettes.

Self-consciously, he touches fingers to his eyepatch.

'Do you work with Helen McMillan?' Sarah Promise asks.

'Yeah, she's the … '

'She's a major hag. To be honest, she's a brainless cunt. One time she called me at home at six in the morning to bitch about … I forget what it was, a car thing … '

Her words drift. She may be drunk.

Eric: 'David, you should sit in. Listen to Sarah work. Kickass mic technique.'

Whoppers. Onion rings.

'I suppose I can kick around, if you want me to.'

Eric turns to Sarah Promise. 'It's a joy recording you, compared to all the painful crap I have to sit through. Like this guy Randolph David keeps bringing in. This guy just *sucks*.'

'Jeesh, Eric,' David says, 'how many times do I have to say he's not my … '

'This guy Randolph is one of those old-school chumps who does that whole *I'm calling from inside a refrigerator thing*, you know what I mean.'

Neither David nor Sarah Promise react.

'Well. I guess that's just a thing I made up myself,' Eric says, squeezing a wettish nostril with a Kleenex, heading back to the studio.

David resumes his position on the couch, almost knocking over a small cactus on a coffee table. With his impaired sight, distances remain treacherous.

Sarah Promise is at the mic. 'Is this the script?' she asks.

'What number does it say at the top?' Eric asks through the talkback.

'Eight point two.'

'That's it. I have a note here to *keep it quick* and *not too Sally Struthers*. Interpret that however.'

'Check.'

The twiddling of knobs. The adjustment of levels. Sarah Promise: *one two one two   tch tch   check.*

David leafs through a magazine plucked from the pile before him. But he is riveted.

Check check   mwa mwa mwa.

'Sounds good,' Eric tells her, then swivels around to David, dabbing at his dripping nose. 'Told you she's a pro.'

David nods. Eric begins to record.

Sarah Promise reads from the script. Through the glass partition David can see her eyes dance across the page, processing the words. She begins: *Big Brothers Big Sisters needs used clothing and household items* and continues, forming sentences in placid tones.

But what David hears leak forth is not the words on the page – no, it is something else; it is thunder and havoc, tarry syrup, coarse shavings of chalk, friction and distress. Her voice is a force. Syllables crackle like flung sparks: *David   I see you and you are unwanted   you are a defect   you violate the codex   your bastard soul affronts these burning fields   my fanged deliverance   am I not a Philistine and ye a servant of Saul   battle me   you will fall to me in battle like sheared wheat   it takes not only brains but guts to win wars   a man with guts but no brains   or brains but no guts he is only half a soldier   the battle will be long and hard and you will travel great distances   you will sob in the emptiness of dark valleys   and ultimately you will be defeated   you will be torn*

asunder   you will tremble   your loins will burn   you will suffer
you will defy me and fall   David   David   you will fall.

She finishes the script and asks Eric how it was. Eric tells her it
was A-OK.

David looks at Sarah Promise through the glass partition,
trying to understand. But she is as flat and dimensionless as everything else.

'I think that'll be fine,' Eric says. 'I'll check for glitches.'

As he plays the spot back, David tries to refocus on the magazine on his lap. His mind reels with threats and roars. Sarah
Promise. Promises. Promises of defeat.

The corner outside the radio building is a flood of afternoon light
and swirling activity. Traffic, road construction, dozers heaving
rubble. David stands sniffling in the cold, dreading the return to his
office.

Then Sarah Promise is next to him. 'You're headed back downtown.'

'Uh.'

She places her sunglasses back on her forehead and produces a
pack of Avantis from her purse and lights up. 'I'll drive you.'

And then they are in her Volvo wagon, weaving through traffic.
Her resolute command of the vehicle is striking: hands firm but
relaxed on the wheel, attention focused on the road, briskly accelerating and decelerating.

On the radio, Elton John sings *there's plenty like me to be found*
mongrels who ain't got a penny   sniffing for tidbits like you on the
ground.

'So,' David attempts, 'have you been doing voice work for long?'

No reply. Never do her eyes deviate from the road.

David tries again. 'How long has it been that ... '

'Look,' she cuts in, 'I never talk while I drive.'

'Oh. Sure. No sweat.'

He turns to the window, gazing out at the flat streets shifting by.

Perhaps hurricane-wielding armies of destruction will come
hurtling out of the horizon, the sun spearing their ominous

shadows. Fighter planes, Valkyries, flying saucers, delivering wrath from above, from the stratosphere of the doomed future. From the sky.

Tower 2 pokes audaciously upward, flipping off the heavens, its tiled face of windows bracketed in mortar, its columned body hurtling up to an apex of splintered light. Sarah Promise eases the Volvo into the parking lot and brakes at the entrance.

'Here,' she says, shifting from D to P.

Beyond the windshield is the wiped slate of the city. And they are packed here together, nothing but upholstery and radio and glass to house them. Sarah Promise gives off bizarre radiation, like the sterile breath of a microwave oven. Something unidentifiable, unchronological, yet specific to this moment.

This moment – there is an urgency.

Sarah Promise turns to face him. 'Your birthday's when.'

'Mine? August.'

A glimmer of a smile, some factual ingestion. She seems pleased. 'Virgo. Like me.'

'Not Virgo. Leo.'

Sarah Promise shifts in her seat, hoisting her sunglasses atop her curly head, unbuckling her seatbelt to twist fully.

'Would you say you are a passionate person? Do you yearn to be freed?'

David tries to devise a response, but it appears she doesn't expect one. Her hand rises from the gearshift and falls on the back of his neck. He almost jumps. 'It's *David*, right?'

'Yep.'

'So. What happened with this eye?'

'Oh. I got caught in the middle of something … '

Her hand remains on his neck, not squeezing, only maintaining contact.

Sarah: 'Can I ask you a question that might perhaps be taken as something it's not meant to imply, or might be unanswerable?'

David braces. 'Shoot.'

'David … are you interested in chaos?'

He has nothing. 'I'm not sure I really understand the, uh, question.'

Her hand crawls up his neck. Its palm is hard, like a semi-ripe peach, but equipped with narrow exploring fingers. Spider-like: they move around his throat, over his Adam's apple. David swallows instinctively. She moves toward him. Her fingers find his chin, then ride upward along the ridge of his jaw, back again to the base of his ears – wispy touch tickles the lobe, a shiver icepicks his spine – then arrive at his bandaged eye. The gauze and dressing. He is trapped in her sights, unable to move.

In a whisper: 'Does it still hurt?'

'Yes. Always.'

A lag, a thought, and then she lurches forward, and her mouth engulfs David's.

The city combusts in hellfire.

The radio, barely audible, calmly sings: *we're gonna make it a night like it used to be when our hearts were young and our souls were free.*

Free.

On his last night in Barcelona, David had returned to the beach. The sky was peppered with stars. His lungs devoured the air. It was the air, he later decided, that made Barcelona so unique in his memory. The air was druggy, oceanic.

The next day he would fly back home.

Someone once said *no man is happy but by comparison*, and someone else said *it is not enough to be happy it is also necessary that others not be*, but in that fleeting moment, David was distinctly aware of the possibility of happiness, though just beyond his reach. It was out in the ocean, hidden in the swelling waves, whispering in another coded language. It was real, but unavailable – even there, away from everything.

Back at his mother's apartment, his feet gritting sand and his head light, he entered to find his mother knelt on the kitchen floor, working against a spill of red wine as Glenn Gould filled the rooms with peppy piano plinkings. Darren was in the living room trying to read *El Mundo*, offering aloud the occasional item in crude translation. On David's entrance, his mother looked up, her face glazed in a film of sweat. Her hair was dishevelled, her glasses slipping down her nose. She met him with a questioning look. She was, doubtlessly, beautiful.

A duration of time passes. Sarah Promise retreats, wiping her mouth with the back of her hand.

David feels ill. He struggles to regather his surroundings. At the parking lot's boundary, a trio of seagulls attacks an overspilling bin, tearing to shreds a discarded pizza crust.

His head swims.

'Thanks for the ride,' he says weakly.

Sarah Promise grunts as if nothing has happened: *buh*. And, for a moment, David suspects that nothing actually has. But *no* – this has happened. His pants feel tight. Sarah Promise inspects her face in the rear-view.

Waving a limp goodbye, he hurries from the car into the cold day, hurrying to the tower's safety. Behind him, he hears the Volvo pull away.

Strangeness. Unremitting channels of strangeness. Streams of indecipherable data.

Movies as an anchor. Anchoring against what. Deep-seated loneliness, regret, doubt. The chasm of The Father – The Father can now be understood only as a vacancy. Perhaps, as a spider's cephalothorax aches with sperm, like a whelmed Frisbee seeks an inhabitable yaw, like the native functions of heavy machines implore the plunder of track, our hero simply seeks a truer way.

Perhaps.

Playing and replaying films of battles, wars: *All Quiet on the Western Front. The Longest Day. The Glory Brigade. Run Silent Run Deep. The Bridge on the River Kwai.* The repetition is not merely a segment of the plan, it is the very grit of the plan itself. It is the embrace of futility. It is the luck of unluckiness. It is the fetishization of the abyss. Darren would say *you know David those who thrive on whining and complaining they'll always be busy but they'll never be happy.*

These are imprints of predecessors. Fathers and stepfathers. Photocopiers, photocopying photocopies.

> Good day Leo!
> Here is your daily horoscope, courtesy of serioushoroscopes.net:
>
> Leo (July 21–August 21): Several factors will come together this week to effect a change of surroundings. Now might be a good time to think about getting away from it all!

There are forms to be addressed and proofs to approve and the need to reorganize his files, but he finds himself unable to muster the energy. Coffee only furthers his unease.

On his desk sits the disc from the Oak Orchard radio spot, Sarah Promise's voice held within. It is unlabelled. That voice like a chameleon's hide. He has postponed passing it on to the account execs. He wants to listen to it right now, but he needs privacy. To be alone with the voice.

He peels a Post-it from its small pad and pens a note: *chameleonal? chameleonic?* Then he asks Shannon if there's still a CD player in the boardroom.

'There's that miserable Samsung piece of poop that I keep telling them is unfit to be playing anything on, let alone for clients,' Shannon says. 'I sent Jeff those sites with all that choice cut-cost gear, but he didn't even acknowledge the … '

'But there is one,' David interrupts, 'in the boardroom.'

Shannon: 'It should still be there, unless they moved it for some inane … '

David is already gone. The boardroom is typically free this early in the day. Empty muffin liners and coffee cups litter the conference table. He seeks and locates the CD player on a shelf, inserts the disc. PLAY.

The voice. The grit of scuzz against silver. It makes his bowels unsteady and his mouth dry. It is the voice of death and memories. Secret chambers of the heart. Sarah Promise. The promise of ruin. The crumble of a colossus. Mouth of immeasurable cosmos. Mouth of heat and tongue of nimble fury. A mouth that has met his own. Sarah Promise, tramping over fields littered with burnt bodies. Sarah Promise is Rommel to Lisa's Patton, or to David's watching of *Patton*. Sarah Promise is a fanged eagle to Lisa's reclining flower. The trenched countryside of France. The capture of Paris. Sarah Promise is the Battle of the Bulge.

No.

He grasps at equations, formulae, yet none come. But a battle is certainly underway, somehow and somewhere, between forces commanding destiny's shallow spaces. *No bastard ever won a war by dying for his country*, George C. Scott proclaims in *Patton*'s opening scenes, and the words echo in the minds of a hundred offscreen GIs. The question of sacrifice is not a question but a command barked over bursting shells. *He won it by making the other poor dumb bastard die for his country.* Every day of work is a battle – battle against himself and battle against the cold structure of a cold world based on cold cash. Every day he fantasizes about quitting, and every day he comes and stands blank against Jim and his sneering cronies, with their fetching blouses and tasteful ties and their narrow-rimmed glasses, without question.

Those goddamn glasses.

In the hallway he is met by Jim and Perky Ashley. Perky Ashley is carrying a huge box filled with different-coloured milk cartons.

'Focus group!' she cries, near exploding.

Jim glances at David. In his hands he carries a plate of freshly microwaved burritos.

'Well, good morning, Jolly Captain One-Eye,' he says.

Fuck you fuck you fuck you flashes through David's mind; for an anxious second, he thinks he may have actually said it aloud. But Jim and Perky Ashley continue past him unaffected, and the moment passes.

Only two more hours until lunch.

But his lunch hour is taken up at the optometry clinic. David is laid horizontal under a halogen light, inhaling the doctor's fishy breath as his damaged eye is inspected with a magnifying lens.

'Nasty accident,' the doctor says.

'Mm.'

'Pain?'

'Yes.'

'Itching?'

'Yes. And I keep losing my balance and bumping into things.'

'That'll happen. Can I ask how?'

'I got caught in the middle of something.'

'I'd say. Boy oh boy. Severed. Mangled. Anyone spoken to you about reconstructive surgery?'

'Um. No.'

'Well. I don't know. It's hard to say.'

'What is?'

The doctor retreats and falls back into his chair.

'Whether or not we'll have to resort to an evisceration. I'm going to have to refer you to an oculist.'

'Oh.'

'But I have to say, there are numerous options emerging in the area of prostheses. It's a fascinating field. Some of the designs they come up with are awe-inspiring. My daughter-in-law is studying ophthalmology down in Tucson.'

The halogen lamp glares down with disapproval.

'We keep in touch, of course. It's so easy these days with e-mail. She sends me these funny jokes, you know how they spread around those funny lists and things. Sometimes I just sit back and laugh. It's good to laugh, it keeps you young. Keeps the heart pumping and the mind clear. They say laughter is the best medicine. Well, I'm a doctor and, as far as metabolically and such, I'll say it's true. Having a positive attitude is the key. You bet. Stress will turn a healthy heart into a dried-up husk. All these people today with their cellular phones and their hand-held computers, I have to wonder. It all seems so darn self-involved. No one ever thinks anymore, they just spend spend spend. Some of these women my wife plays bridge with, all they do is chatter on about their stock profiles and what's on sale at Banana Republic and *blah blah blah*. It's not a fit way to live. Sometimes I sit back and I wonder, what if things had been different? We're always riding that edge, you know, between what's reality and what's just horse dung. Where we stand in relation, if you understand what I'm getting at. If you don't, boy oh boy, you will. You'll find out. Oh, you will, you stupid kid. You think this eye hurts, wait until you see what's coming. You'll see. Yes you will, damn you. Goddamn you, you son of a bitch.'

David dawdles through downtown streets on his way back to the office. There is work to be done, scraps of copy to finalize, but his co-workers will be too preoccupied with the month-end focus group to notice any absence. So he basks in the killing of time, losing himself in the confusion. Forward-rushing streams of people, surges and currents and resistance, enormous in smallness, fruitless in progress, accelerated and jittery with perpetual coffee buzz.

On a whim, he stops at a bookstore, a dingy corner shop that sells mostly lottery tickets and cigarettes, but houses a few sad racks of plastic-sealed comics and battered hardcovers. He scans the shelves, baffled by names and titles. These days he reads only in hopes of distraction — found sections of discarded newspapers, magazines thieved from work, snippets on a screen. Books have become strangers.

In the biography section he discovers a book titled *Last Days of Patton*, by someone named Ladislas Farago, who, David learns by reading its jacket blurb, also wrote *Patton: Ordeal and Triumph*. David recognizes this title; it appears in the opening credits to *Patton*. Based upon. Inspired by. Its cover displays a colourful photograph of Patton, his eyes crinkled, his chest surging, a huge collision of medals adorning his chest. David opens to page 21 and reads *On November 11 1944 when George S. Patton, Jr., turned fifty-nine he was confronted by a vexing paradox.* Two Xs in the phrase *vexing paradox.* File this away as potentially useful in a jingle, a slogan. X-X: *ecks ocks.* Here is the General, whose defeats over the Axis forces were grand and staunch, the man who confounded and inspired military historians.

But this is not *Patton*, the pasty-faced figure who visits David's dreams. This figure is too real, too lost in times of yore. He returns the book to the rack.

On a shelf in the occult section, another cover stands out, a black and white illustration of figures in profile, shirtless demigods, encountering a naked man rising from some gloomy depth, shedding the grave, and in scarlet lettering: *Greek and Roman Necromancy.* This book apparently presents *ghosts zombies the earliest vampires evocators sorcerers shamans Persian magi Chaldaeans Egyptians Roman emperors and witches from Circe to Medea.* Another dark cover stands out: *Forbidden Rites: A Necromancer's Manual of the Fifteenth Century.* David pulls this from the shelf and learns about the Munich Handbook of Necromancy: Codex Latinus Monacensis 849. There are spells and divinatory experiments, a table of purposes: *for causing a person to lose his senses for arousing a woman's love for obtaining a castle for obtaining a horse for obtaining information by gazing at a bone for resuscitating a dead person for finding something in sleep.* Think of ghostly figures in stinging neon-lit vapours, a street of phantoms. Opening avenues.

No. These too are untruths. Artifice. The dead lie cozy in their graves, squirming only in legacy. There are laws, fundamentals. There are incontrovertible facts. He closes the book.

Eventually returning to his desk, David finds his phone's message light insistently blinking. From behind a mountain of computer hardware, Shannon tells him, 'You had calls.'

'*Yeew hed caulz,*' Owen mimics, also hidden behind his huge monitor.

'What?' Shannon says. 'How is that funny? Tell me how that is at all in the slightest way funny.'

Owen, singing: 'Gimme all your loving, all your hugs and kisses too!'

David checks his messages.

Doot.

'David. This is Sarah Promise. From the other day. I'm just watching this shit with these farmers and agriculture guys on C-Span, and I don't know if you have a TV where you are, but if you can check this out, you have to. My mind is being blown. I got your number from Eric at the station. The purpose for calling is that I demand you take me for hamburgers tonight. I need protein. I need iron. Women in my family face risk of iron deficiency and it is imperative that I address this need. So, the Midtown, tonight, let's say seven-thirty. If you're not there I'll assume we will never see each other again. The television is blowing my mind.'

Clk.

Sarah Promise. Her creaky unlubricated voice. Artificially accelerated. Prolonging syllables, halting in pauses: druggy *g*s and wondering *vs.* Bl*ooo*wwwing. Imperativ*vvv*e.

Next message.

Hello this is FlixMaster Video calling with a reminder that you have several seven-day rentals overdue. Please drop by your nearest FlixMaster location to settle your overdue fees today. Thank you.

End of message.

In a flat world, relation and proportion are put in a choke hold by density, structure, solidity. Every minor element is detonated, and the enormity of chaos is diminished to a trifle. The world is an aquarium of bumping matter. A skyscraper swats a fly. Granules of sand pulverize an office tower. Things accelerate and decelerate.

The Midtown is just a few minutes from the office. Dingy windows, onion smells, beery atmosphere. The sign in the window boasts LIVVER & ONION $4.99 12 oz. DRAFT $1.99 and OPEN til 1pm NITELY.

They need someone new writing their copy, David thinks.

The tavern is smoky and thick with noise, but he immediately pinpoints Sarah Promise, seated at the bar. Her toppling blonde locks. Fierce lips gripping a cigarette. A leg half-bared by a twist of skirt. Propped on a stool with a half-empty glass in her hand, she watches a wrestling match on a nearby screen. The beer slopes in the glass. Her leg slopes against the stool. The bar stinks.

'It's the David,' she says, grinning as he approaches.

He sits and wrings his hands. 'Crappy weather.'

'If you say so.'

They sit, her watching wrestlers, him watching her.

A waiter appears. Sarah Promise tells him, 'We'll have two loaded Cheeseburger Platters and a pitcher of Clancy's. Plus another glass.'

Her eyes fall on David. She smokes with force, her mouth attacking the cigarette, exhaling in a sustained *taah*.

'This Taoist prostitute that I know, an acquaintance of my dear friend Ike Hamdaber, she has an enlightened understanding of her physical needs. I try to heed her advice, with a philosophy of obeying the body's impulses to keep it satisfied. Balance and communication. Congress with the inner beast. When I'm tired I sleep and when I'm hungry I nosh. I've trained myself to live outside schedules.'

'Must make it hard to, you know, hold down a job.'

'*Hmf*,' she scoffs. 'I make enough doing these cartoons, I needn't sweat it over finances. My lifestyle adjusts to itself.'

'Eric from the studio said something about this Warrior Queen or something.'

There is an outburst of groans and a weak bleed of applause from the bar as, on the screen, the ref counts out an oily-chested contender.

'Yep,' she says, 'I do Tianna. It's easy, it's just this squeal – *like this*.'

Suddenly. The voice of someone larger, deadly. A voice that machetes. A heroine. '*Such is the power – the mighty power of PRINCESS TIANNA – Guardian of the Gilded Flame!*'

David is floored.

'It's pretty brazen. A lot of subtext. You hear sick interpretations. You should see the fan mail. People send panties.'

David, incredulous: 'Panties to a cartoon?'

'Panties to a cartoon. One of the other characters I do is Bink, a big funny whale. Even the whale gets horny letters. It's the Internet. People get worked up and write horny e-mails to a cartoon whale.'

'But not panties to the whale.'

The waiter arrives with a gigantic vessel of beer and two glasses. Sarah pours deftly, leaving a narrow thread of foam.

'Truth be told,' she says, 'a lot of the time they just cut and paste dialogue from old episodes and put it in the new shows. Kids don't mind. Kids crave repetition. The show just copies all that Japanese high-tech digital shit. It's all catchphrases and garbage. But it's big.'

'Big with the kids.'

'Kids have sway.'

'It's fascinating.'

Sarah Promise crushes out her cigarette. 'What I am is a dancing monkey. I'm a puppeteer. No, even less: I'm a puppet. I'm a trained doofus ready to mimic and chuckle and announce. My actual talent is of zero consequence to these de-testicled idiots. Give me a voice.'

David sips his beer.

'Come on,' she says, 'give me a voice. Give me a voice to do. Describe a voice, I'll do it.'

She looks at him. Challenging.

'What?'

'Say it. Bring it on. Use your imagination.'

Dangerous thoughts emerge.

'Could you do, uh … '

'Name it.'

'A girl. A spaced-out … girl.'

'What, like some crack baby?'

'No no no. More like a … troubled teen. A girl. Not a completely … you know, a girl with, um, issues. Like a young girl who is sort of too smart for her own good … '

'I don't think I get it. Elucidate.'

'You know the type. The teenage girl with *privilege* – the cute one, troubled at the core. Like the perfect girl who secretly reads … Nietzsche, or Céline, or has, you know. Dark issues.'

'She's cutting up her arms.'

'Yes. Well, no. Not that, she's more of … she's hiding some- thing. You know, the kid who you worry about, but you secretly have feelings for.'

'I have *feelings* for her?'

'Or … imagine as if you were looking at this young girl, and thinking – '

But the waiter swoops in – *here ya go* – with two plates, each bearing an enormous burger and a mountainous heap of french fries and cole slaw. David is suddenly hungry; with his first bite a huge clot of greasy ketchup spurts onto his shirt and collar.

'Oop,' he says through a full mouth, trying to dab the mess away with a napkin.

Sarah Promise fork-spears a clump of fries. 'What again is this girl you're conjuring up?'

'Forget it,' he says. 'Just a stupid thing.'

'No. Who is she? Is she pretty? No … she's terribly homely. She's escaping something horrible.'

'No, I don't … '

'She's the scarred product of a broken home.'

'I don't know about scarred.'

'It's on your pant leg too.'

She gestures to his thigh. There is a puddle of ketchup there. He tries to mop it away with his napkin. 'I'm making a disgusting mess over here.'

'*What're you up to, dude?*'

The mouth transmitting these words is Sarah Promise's, but the voice is Lisa's. *What're you up to dude.* Lisa's lazy slide between syllables. The mashing together of buttery sound. It emits from Sarah Promise's mouth as if a receiver is embedded, transmitting directly from Lisa's vocal cords. David blinks. He can hear his eyelids blink. He can hear the veins in his eyes throb with pressure. His palms begin to sweat.

Dude.

Sarah Promise drains her beer. She dribbles out the pitcher's remainder into David's half-full glass, then waves over the bartender.

'Another one,' she says.

Chaos, Sarah Promise later tries to explain, is *less about physics and more about digestion*. There is, she confesses, little she understands about chaos in the mathematical scientific sense. Strange attractors and unstable aperiodic behaviours – all this seems to make sense, as far as she takes it. The ideas are thorny in coming, but she can, eventually, get it. At its root it's not so tough. The technicalities don't completely resonate, but what she can grasp, ultimately, is *nuance*. The gravity of a flicker. The heaviness of a light touch. David nods, drinking her words like a narcotic milkshake. She continues: chaos isn't just math, and it isn't sheer confusion. It's the reorganization into disorganization, the reformation of everything. Perspective, obsession. *Chaos*. It's surrendering sequence. It is the flare of dawn torn into dusk. Chaos, she says, isn't about judging the world unflavourful or insufficient, it is embracing this insufficiency and the glory of lack. Sarah Promise slurps her beer and projects her confusing radiance and says *David has anyone else ever tried to convince you of Chaos?* And David says *no just you.* Just you.

Only in the dark does she fully reveal her Promise. They are in his apartment, in his bedroom, in his bed. They are unclothed. David's head swims; it is the vertigo of breached time, of suddenness, the shock of things happening in hurried stages. Her body is soft and her breath is boozy. Her mouth gnaws at his cheekbones. Her hands grasp his neck. Her weight presses down, on his pelvis, on his ribcage. She swings her head back and produces a sound like a slowed-down hiccup. In the dim light his vision traces the contour of her hips. Like the topography of the Atlas Mountains, like the desolation of Antarctica. Treacherous inclines, radical dips. She breathes heavily. The sheets are musty; she casts them aside with a flip of her foot. The Promise of Sarah Promise: brimming with wondrous nothing. This is the sweetness of the abyss. There is a cigarette burning on the bedside table; David can't recall it being lit. Her fingers and palms curl into fists, jackhammers of pleasure, and he can't deny that Sarah Promise's promise is persuasion. They are here and nowhere. They are suspended in foggy focus. The cigarette is a filter and a dying cinder. Its burn is history. History is a series of triumphs and engagements. History writ on soiled sheets. Sarah Promise flops over and guides him atop. History is lost to us. We know great conquerors through depictions in film. Actors hoisting legacies, posed as statues. The recycling of great stories. How many movies have been made about Billy the Kid. Joan of Arc. JFK. Heroic inheritances. Fathers to sons. How many ways can we tell a story, frame a shot, script a plot? Dive into mythologies. Myths as parodies. Lifetimes as fables. We crave juicy myths and lore. David's pace is too eager, too greedy. He must regress, retreat, regather his powers. Sarah Promise provokes him further, but he must take pause. He clenches his jaw and forces respite. The re-establishment of a fortified front. Patton became Rommel, defeating him by poring over the Nazi's own tank-warfare stratagem. Or so the film claims. The Father surrendered after a lifelong battle – through this act, did the hero find deliverance? Warfare is the grand nullification, precursor to oblivion. A certain end is edging forward. But. Sarah Promise is a sunfire of coming glory. Promise. Forward. Here. The curvature. The glory.

Later, there is silence. David doesn't know what he has done.

He heads to the bathroom, uses the toilet, then pauses at the mirror. He considers his bare self – the self-administered punishment of the gym has produced little result. Consider the deterioration, the misshaping. His face is saggy and pouchy, his chest droops, his frame is contourless. Look at how little these ab-rollings and bar-dippings and treadmill-trampings have wrought. Look at this wreck. The mangled face. It has all been for naught.

He flushes the toilet and splashes water on his lips. He feels caught in something dangerous.

Just as he flips off the bathroom light, the phone rings. He answers.

'David.'

The voice is slight, very not-quite-there.

'Lisa?'

'It's me.'

'What ... what's going on?'

She offers no answer, but he can hear her breath. 'Look. It's really late.'

'You never ... '

'Yeah?'

'You never showed any ... '

Her words trail out to sniffles, then she asks, 'Does it ever bother you ... that our ancestors owned slaves?'

'What?'

'Don't you ever think about how our family, our ancestry ... We don't have a *culture*. We don't have a past ... nothing to be proud of except, what. The combustion engine. It's all fat white guys with whips ... '

'Lisa ... '

'You think death ... you think it's the end. But ... it *isn't*. The book I told you ... the *Necronomicon*. You can raise demons. You can walk the forbidden realms. You can find the ... the Gate of Nanna. Ishtar ... destroyer of the hostile hordes ... all of the names of the ... demons. It's not over, David. Abdul Alhazred even says *I have raised demons and the dead.*'

From the other room, David hears Sarah Promise cough. Or fart.

Lisa: 'I'm already away. I'm leaving.'

He says, 'Lisa, this ... I'm sorry ... '

'Oh. Do you have a ... girl there?'

'No. *No.* Come on.'

'David.'

'Please. Come on.'

'I have a gun.'

What. 'You don't have a gun.'

'I do so have a gun. Fuck you. Fuck you.'

'Oh, for the … Come on.'

'I have a gun.'

'Lisa. Come *on*. Please.'

The darkness is the quietness. More than anything, David wants to understand, and be understood by, Lisa – Lisa of his longing, cooing in his ear, teasing – but the perpetual frustration and shame is killing him. Now more than ever, his eye throbs, its flesh pulsing with unappeasable itch.

'Do you really have a gun?' he asks.

'No.'

'Good.'

'I don't. Sorry.'

'Good. Now you should hit the pit.'

'I should what the what?'

David rubs fingers into his temples, the corners of his eye sockets, yearning for the cessation of his eye's tingle.

'Go to bed. It's a thing my father used to say. *Time to hit the pit.* It used to drive me bonkers.'

'Oh. I have my knife, though. The samurai say … you have to actually … put yourself *on top of the knife* to … be fully … '

He is too tired for this.

'Lisa. Come on. I wish … I want you to get a good night's sleep.'

'This *wakizashi* is so sharp. I could slice you into a million pieces.'

'Come on. What are you trying to. I'm sitting here being … and you're … '

Silence.

'*Lisa.*'

'Mm.'

'I'm going back to bed now. Time to hit it.'

'Hit the pit,' she says.

'Right. It's late and I have to get up in the morning. Call me tomorrow. Okay?'

'Yes.'

His head is achy and spent. 'Call me.'

'Yes.'

'You'll call me. Tomorrow.'

So quiet: 'Yes … '

'Tomorrow.'

Clk. No farewell.

With sleep come dreams. Dream of water. Dream of fog rising on water, dense mists wafting over slow grey waves. Dream of fighting fog. Dream of depth in ripples. Dream of concrete plains like oceans, rivers like highways, skies like forests. Dream of dreams coming true. Dream of lives yet to be lived. Dream of a distant pinprick, a beacon, a pulsing light visible through the murk. Head for the light. Head for hope.

This day of work progresses as emptily as any day previous. Scones and e-mails, stunted discussions, vapid brain-storm sessions. Prolonged gazes out the window. Jim paces the office, hands jammed into pockets, hawkishly eyeing the story-board Owen is assembling atop a light table. They discuss the toxi-city of the adhesives used to mount presentations onto cardboard. Jim makes a joke of a slightly graphic nature. Jim slaps his forehead. Jim bears the weight of the world on his shoulders.

Sarah Promise's presence lingers: on skin, on lips, in ears.

The hurt of David's slashed eye only accretes. He repeatedly presses lightly on the patch, but that indulgent reassurance of pain, that tingle, is no longer pleasing.

His weekly horoscope had said *several opportunities will come together this week to effect a change of surroundings now might be a good time to think about getting away from it all!*

Armed and ready, steeled for disaster. The future is coming.

Today, David thinks as he types out the revised copy for the Donaldson Office Furniture Annex direct-mail brochure. *Today I will quit.*

Weyerhaeuser First Choice Premium Multi-Use Paper, as low as $8.23 a ream.

Somewhere in last night's strange unfolding, Sarah Promise had said to him *so you're the one who fills the world with so many words.* Yes, this is his mandate: to produce the clutter, to put a fine point on crap. To describe the vacuous void of a photocopied world. Homer had his Trojan War – David, similarly blind, has the Global ObusForme Multi-Tilt Chair. He is the scribe of overextended commerce.

Today. It has to be today.

Jim crosses the room to hover near David's desk, his mouth poised and eyes squinted, as if about to say something but unable to express it.

'How's it going?' David attempts.

Jim frowns. 'It goes. With great difficulty.'

David nods. Jim departs.

Apparently, Patton was dyslexic. Would he, in his crusty assessment, have been able to get through *this elegant mahogany desk exudes an air of distinction and style guaranteed to impress express your individuality with one of eight custom colours and finishes* without waving away such dreck with a flip of his gloved hand?

When George C. Scott, assuming the role of Patton, reclines on the couch and presses meaty fingers against the ridge of his gleaming nose, he exudes an air of unimpeachable confidence, grave brooding. This is, in many respects, the air for which Jim aims, and misses.

David faxes off some documents, then visits the kitchenette for a glass of water. He senses a headache's initial inklings. His stomach suffers familiar anxiety gurgles. His breath is heavy. His throat is tight and his lips are dry.

The office's soundtrack is the mousy scamper of keyboard taps, voices murmuring behind closed doors, an occasional sneeze.

He will knock politely on Jim's door. He will stand steadfast before Jim and deliver his notice. He will be firm but courteous. He will hear out whatever response Jim might supply, and then he will leave, and soon enough he will not be here anymore, and he will feel a great relief, and he will never return, and he will be freed. He will rise from Tower 1, spread his arms like wings, and enter the Valhalla of self-expunged warriors. Honourably discharged. Unshackled and free.

The word he has abused most in his tenure is *dazzling*. Second – that would have been *mouth-watering*.

David is on his way to Jim's office when the lights go out. In the other room he hears Shannon wail *mother son of a*.

The power is out.

Helen emerges from her office. 'You gotta be kidding me.'

David shrugs. Helen huffs briskly past. He can hear others shuffling in their offices, swearing, confused.

Eventually they all congregate in the creative department. Lifeless overcast light fills the room as, deprived of work's fuel, the staff become sullen and remote. David sits at his desk and chews on a pencil. Lydia, the nubile and tanned Junior Accounts Manager, assumes a roost atop the supplies table, clacking gum while thumbing absently through a magazine. Her tanned thighs, slipping past a hiked hem, aim their luminescence squarely at David. Shannon is trying to fix a broken stapler. Owen is listening to his Discman. Others gawk out the window.

As he tries his hardest to not stare further up Lydia's skirt, a realization – so obvious and brutal that he almost falls out of his chair – suddenly strikes David: *these people actually want to do this*. They are not just biding time until some unspecific greater opportunity reveals itself, enduring this theatre of dullness in the meantime; they are anxiously waiting to go back to these jobs they ungrudgingly attend. They are striving wholeheartedly. They are awaiting refreshed electricity so they can return to their jobs, their conference calls and routines and photocopies. Lydia: she sits, radiating conscientious vibrations. They all do: Jeff wringing his hands and discussing hockey tickets slid his way by a client; Perky Ashley, tearing apart a carrot muffin as she listens to Creative Supervisor Deb bemoan the difficulty of finding a good plumber. All of them. Even Owen, listening to death metal as he clips his fingernails into his garbage can, usually hungover or suspiciously pupil-bloated, even he digs into his work with his own imitation of dedication. Everybody wants to be here. The squat little woman who commands the coffee cart. Naoko, whose job is simply to corral everyone. All of them thrive by affirming their designated roles. Their jobs are their lives. No – their jobs are their *lifelines*.

Incredible.

David chews on his pencil and debates writing a note of resignation. There is a yellow legal pad before him. Several pens. All the makings of a monumental repudiation; finally his work in unobjectionable verbosity could be of use. He remembers the advice supplied to him when he was hired: the secret is to say everything twice, as simply as possible. Be direct. Be vehement. Employ a balance of two, three max, well-composed phrases to create a complete mental image. Bequeath no extra intelligence to the reader.

No. Stay pert and exact. Be flowery but brief. *Dumb it down.* People don't read words, they see words. If they encounter a daunting block of text, their eyes rove. If a sentence deviates from its propulsion, or is polygamous in subject or tense, people are jarred from their morning McMuffin, and they are lost. If a passage reads like the concoction of some specialist, some hack, rather than emanating directly from the welcoming heart of the corporate identity itself, then the very process renders itself moot. The consumer mind, though simple, is still able to discern this, and will be lost. *You do not want to lose people.* You must move from one word to the next like a dog sniffs along a sidewalk. This is the aim. This is what David was taught. Jim advised *don't confuse poop with shit it's a totally different ballgame,* and when David asked what that meant exactly, Jim rubbed his nose and said *I don't know must I always have a point.* On a few occasions David tried to argue for responsible writing, raising objections at crude grammar, saying *we don't have to be pedantic we can be conversational but we can't end a banner heading with* of. No justifiable excuse for a preposition so gratuitous. You can't run a commercial that thousands will see with the claim *It's the Discount You're Dreaming Of.* Similarly, Helen had once brought him a CR supplementing the Rapscallion's Roost Pub and Grill catchphrase *This Taste You're Wanting!* And David had pleaded, as diplomatically as possible, that they might consider a rewording. With this recommendation he'd chuckled jovially, because he really didn't care or regard it personally. Helen had not chuckled.

He'd assumed his co-workers all headed home, escaping to spouses or adoring pooches, relief in lives despite the dogged processing of deadlines and client-coddling. Enduring long days to collect a paycheque, knowing other, better, things should be in store.

But now he sees. People work and they live. People have tasks and they perform these tasks. It's a galactic scheme to which he has never been privy.

It's all a game. He plays one game and they play another. Both, just as ridiculous.

Deb says to Perky Ashley, 'I think the power's out in the whole building. Both towers.'

'Think it's the temperature? It's been cold.'

'Oh, I don't think so. The grid is down or something.'

Perky Ashley turns to David. 'Don't you know about this sort of thing?'

'Me? No ... '

'Oh.' She cocks her head. 'I thought you were the one who was all knowledgeable in electricity and circuits and stuff.'

'Not me.'

'Oh.'

They mull around the room for an eternity. Then Jim comes charging into the room waving some document, even more possessed than usual. He paces back and forth in front of the hulking Canon printer, discharging an indiscernible barrage of incoherent whispers. Everyone stiffens, preparing for the outburst.

Finally he stops pacing and says, 'Okay, everyone. Listen up.'

They do so. Somehow, Jim's eyes manage to explore every millimetre of the room without once making contact with any single individual.

'There needs to be a discussion regarding DynaSport. I got a call from Glen Mucks over there and he was very aloof. Where once he was very warm, very welcoming, very *tender* to me – today, just this morning, he was aloof. His words bore no kindness. He was not excited to hear from me. He made excuses, and he pretty much hung up on me. Cut me off. Glen fucking Muck Fuck Mucks from DynaSport Sporting Goods Warehouse treated me with as much respect as you'd give a crackhead who wants to walk your dog. Just a week ago we were arguing over who's picking up our three-hundred-dollar tab at the Press Gang. He nearly drank me under the table. He told me this joke about a porcupine and a Paki that I can't repeat here. We were the best of friends. Now he's hanging up on me and his bitch secretary's lying to me that he's at lunch. So I'm sitting there, a bit confused, a bit *perplexed*, wondering why such a dear chum of mine would be so rude. I thought to myself, what has changed between then and now? What circumstances have occurred to effect such a turn for the worse? Then it dawned on me. Of course, it's the Sidle Up to Spring sales event. This is it. This week the radio spots hit the air. The flyers went in the mail. The ads went to the papers. The Sidle Up campaign, which we laboured on, which all of us ... '

Indicating all present.

' ... worked very hard on. We did. We put all we had into it and created a proposal that was solid. The DynaSport account is a valuable account. Mucks has *scads* of cash ready to be tossed around. We needed this baby. So we put together this very impressive proposal. We did countless mock-ups. We stayed here that night until ten o'clock and finished that mock-up. It looked like a million bucks. Like a million of Glen Mucks's fucking bucks. So we went with it. We went with the Sidle Up to Spring sales event and Mucks wholeheartedly dug it. He was keen. So today, I wondered, what made him change his mind? And then it clicked. Of course. The S. That stupid S. I knew that that S in the new logo was too pointy. I knew it looked too much like a lightning bolt. I knew it. I said it to myself a thousand times: *too pointy*. Mucks saw it. I saw it but *goddamn*. The S. The S was too pointy. I knew it. I *saw* it.'

His hands wringing, his neck taut.

'I've been in this game for twenty years. Twenty arduous years. Twenty years of toil and foolishness and bullshit. And in the end it all comes down to Glen fucking Mucks, that fucking cocksucker ... '

Jim's body crumples and he begins to sob. No one hurries to help him; they are all transfixed.

Through his tears, Jim looks around.

'Why aren't any of you people *working*? Why are you all just sitting around? I can't believe ... '

'Power's out,' Deb says. 'Everything's shut down.'

Jim wipes his nose with his palm and clears his throat. 'The power's out?'

Owen pats his dormant monitor as demonstration. Everything is quiet. No phones ring.

'Well, then,' Jim says, inspecting a swipe of snot, 'we might as well call it a day.'

An hour later, David is running. His feet flap against the treadmill like the metered slapping of some taut buttock. His forehead drips. His arms dig into the pace, rhythmic, in and out, striding. Alongside, others mirror his motions. They run. David adjusts the tread-mill's incline, climbing a simulated crest. In this he toils. In this he sweats. Despite this confrontation of his body's faculties, he feels removed from his legs and feet. His body is foreign, distant. He is not here. The world is flat. Hurrying among men. Racing toward unattainable finales. It is the 1950s. The 1940s. There is heat in squirming ether. Uphill. Up. Up. The treadmill's keypad is like the controls of an airplane. A dirigible. Gliding through clouds in the 1930s. Breathing plumes of smoke, rising uphill, ascending through a weird miasma of lobsters glistening in their pots and heaping platefuls of french fries and mouth-watering delicacies from our grill. Come try a bucket of ribs today. Flanks of seared flesh. Flanks in the clouds. Japanese swords cutting incisions in the firmament. Uphill. Faster. He sees licking jaws, halved bodies. Legs no legs no arms. Distant and nowhere. Moving up. He is King David, anointed with drops of aftershave and beer. Moving. Into skies over and behind. Beyond mountains of angry burning clouds. Where. *Up*.

And then he is in a chair.

'Sir?'

No. He is not himself. He is the unknown soldier, dogtagless, stretchered.

'Is your name David? We checked your card. Your name is David?'

He opens his usable eye and discovers an office, a door, a man crouched before him. The man is wearing shorts and a sweatshirt and holding David's gym membership card.

'Yes,' David says.

'Do you know where you are?'

'The desert.'

'No ... '

'At the gym.'

'Right.'

'I blacked out.'

'Yes. How are you feeling?'

David shifts in the chair. 'Fantastic.'

'Do you know what happened? You're wearing an eyepatch. Do you have a condition?'

David sits up. He begins to regain clarity. He'd lost his balance, that was all. Balance and awareness. He fell in the hurtling midst, dove into the velocity. He challenged the mire and lost the grasp. Fell into chaos.

He stands. He does not teeter; he stands firm. 'I need to take a shower.'

The man in the shorts steps back. 'You sure?'

'One hundred percent.'

'I'm a bit concerned. Maybe we should call a paramedic.'

'No,' David says, leaving. There is focus. 'I have to go. I'm fine. I just need a shower and a steam.'

'Oh, I wouldn't recommend you using the steam room if you're experiencing lightheadedness.'

But. No. His head is not light. His head is *heavy*.

The recording studio is on the third floor of an unassuming warehouse next to an enormous used-car dealership – an unbreaking ocean of minivans and sedans extends into the waning horizon.

Even before he finds the control room, David is aware of the voice: Sarah Promise's voice. Her voice travels down the hallway, amplified in a direct auditory assault. His knees turn gelatinous.

The voice says *if we don't hurry   these spikes will cut us to ribbons*.

David enters with caution. The room is dark and cool; he feels like he's crashing a funeral. The spectacled engineer is hunched over an enormous mixing board, staring at a computer screen.

'Can I *help* you?' he asks.

'I'm just here for Sarah,' David says.

The engineer gestures to the glass window, the room beyond. 'We're in the middle of a take.'

'I … I can wait.'

The engineer sighs and brusquely indicates a seat at the back of the room.

Sarah Promise is barely discernible through the studio's gloom: her wild head of hair is reined in by a pair of headphones and her face hides in shadows. Speakers bleed forth her voice; under its pressure, he again questions his hold on any certainty. Beyond this room, beyond this day, beyond all that presses from outside. The voice defies all. The voice is an avenue, truth and deceit sandwiched together.

It says: *I've never seen the oracle this upset before   the situation must be worse than I imagined.*

Her voice appears in spiky waveforms across the computer screen. The visualization of sonic mayhem. The prize of his dreams.

Where is the Bronze Key   without the Bronze Key we'll never be able to enter the tower.

It's nonsense, cartoon dialogue, but the actual words are of little consequence. It is the viscosity, the implied ache, the bone-quaking penetration of sound that delivers them. The horrible freedom. Screams echoing across canyons of milk chocolate. The unfolding of clouded apocalypse. The *k*s clack with percussive finality; the *b*s bubble freely.

'That's the finish of that section,' the engineer tells her.

Sarah, through the monitors: 'Then that's finally the end.'

She tears off her headphones and barges into the control room, lighting a cigarette. Her smoke wafts, golden by sparse track lighting. She raises her eyebrows at the engineer, then looks and finds David. He offers his best smile. Her eyes are weary.

'Sounded good,' he tries.

'Oh. You're here.'

Despite everything he thinks he may have learned about Sarah Promise, the closer he gets, the further she fades from understanding. The deeper you look, the more mysteries emerge.

She heads to her coat, laid out across a chair, and digs in its pockets to retrieve a small scoopish object and a baggie containing a fair measure of cocaine. She scoops a portion and sniffs it up her right nostril, rubs her eyes, then sucks another portion into her left. She does this without performance, as a chore.

'You spoke with Ray,' she says to the engineer.

'Ray. Yeah. He said *Tianna* was being renewed. Fourteen more episodes, starting in March.'

She nods. 'Then I guess we'll be discussing my contract. That polesmoker. Most definitely a smoker of pole.'

'Do you think you can take fourteen more episodes of this? Because I don't know if I can.'

'Yeah, well. Perseverance.'

'When is this on, this show?' David says, rising. 'I'd love to check this crazy stuff out.'

Silence. Sarah Promise looks at him like a speck clinging to her sleeve.

'Don't bother,' the engineer says, filling in a track sheet with a Sharpie. 'No one watches it but pant-shitting gimps from Germany.'

Sarah Promise snuffles up another wad of coke. David watches as her eyes morph from dim to puddled. A bead of sweat forms on her forehead.

He asks her, 'Do you want to go … get a drink or something? Are you hungry?'

She glares knives at him. Her aura, acerbic.

'Eat. With you.'

Her face disappears in puffs of smoke.

'I don't even know who you are.'

His horoscope suggested *a change in surroundings*.

A change. Try to imagine the bliss of the migrant, the gypsy, the hobo. Every day a new place of rest. Not this dreary routine, day in day out, returning home to the same tired bed, with the same bored load on your mind. *No* – imagine sleeping under fresh stars, sleeping the slumbers of the roving soul, waking to days not yet emptied of possibility.

Stand again before the mirror. Peel back eyepatch and the gauze affixed beneath, expose the mangled eye. Grimace at the mess. The socket is raw and red and ruined, like the inner flesh of a defrosted pork chop. He gingerly touches the lower ridge, the lid, to find an immediate needle of pain. The flesh is almost bound together, almost sealed; there is little of the actual eyeball exposed. The doctor insisted upon the permanence; the word was *evisceration*. There is no hope. His vision is bisected. The flaw is permanent. No see, no more.

David has a sudden urge to tear away the ruined skin and pry the eyeball right out of his skull. Maybe that would stop the persistent hot itch nagging from within. Exorcise the fucking *itch*.

But no. He cups a splash of water in his palms and slurps. He reapplies the gauze and replaces the patch.

Returning to the living room, he finds the cordless phone next to his new Technics stereo receiver, still in the box.

You have two new messages.

A guttural, ape-like, sound. A huff of air. David begins to identify this sound: weeping. A man's weeping. Mechanical sobs: *gah gah guh guh*. Then, through the bray of tears, words form: *it's Gary David you better phone gah gahdamn David you phone us now now now.*

Gary. This is not a man who weeps.

Now. Then: *clk*.

The voice mail offers him options of erasing or saving. David balks; neither seems suitable. So he saves.

Hello, the next message says, *this is FlixMaster Video calling again regarding*

David severs this communication. Erase.

Speaking of which. He assumes the power of the remote, switches on the television. He encounters some sort of game show, something making cartoons out of the heads of politicians found on dollar bills. Switch. Talk shows. Switch.

PLAY.

And there is Patton, and there is *Patton*, still resting in the VCR. He wonders what might happen – will FlixMaster stormtroopers hire rogue mercenaries? Will they come storming up the stairs seeking the rented tapes, waving bazookas and lobbing smoke bombs, demanding hasty and unquestioning surrender? Are these men of honour? No. They are men of Clooney and Caramilk and Redenbacher and Pfeiffer and Disney; they are unimpressive foes, and thus will not be treated with the respect Patton offered Rommel when he toiled into the wee hours of that dark night, studying the German's own strategies of warfare by lamplight before the next day's advance. When these minimum-wage lackeys come to wage war on his video delinquency, David will react as

Patton reacted when those dirty Hun bastards came barrelling over the encampment at Tunis in Northern Africa; he will fire pistols into the air and offer every ounce of opposition he can summon. He'll *fight*. And when Gary and Jim and the doctors and studio engineers who oppose him line up their guns of shame to paint him as a failure, conspiring to castrate and defame him – *he will resist*. Just as Patton – there on the screen – makes mincemeat of Nazi tank brigades, David will stand fast.

These are great wars, grim hours.

He dials Gary's number. It rings four times, and he is about to hang up when there is an answer.

'H-Hello … '

'Gary?'

'Yeh.'

'It's David. You called … '

A long silence, a weighty sigh – a sigh of not knowing how to begin. But then Gary explains, breaking down into tears, voicing unprecedented sounds, strange innovations in grief. It was the *knives*, he explains through spits and sobs. The knives she cherished. Her knives and swords. Never knowing the reasons for the knives and swords. They had always expressed concern. What she would do. *Why*. Now they knew. Her stomach. There was blood everywhere. She turned herself inside out. She had plunged the knife into her stomach and turned herself inside out. Lisa. Why. Her dead drained face when they found her, lying there. Dead. Lisa's face, white as bone. An expression of shock. She looked *surprised*. Stabbed herself in the stomach and twisted. *Seppuku* – David knew it right away. Honour through suicide. The repentance for disgrace. Surprised by death. *David*. David. Gary repeats his name like a mantra, grasping for a foothold. *David*. It was you. It was you, David.

The phone is hot in David's hand.

'She left a note.'

'A … note … '

'She left a note. I have it here. There's flecks of blood on this, this … it. The blood sprayed. The blood *sprayed* … '

Hold your position. Do not retreat. Don't let the enemy smell your fear.

'What did ... what did the note say?'

'It said *Ask David*. That's all. *Ask. David.*'

The room is lost. The apartment is lost. He is sitting in a muddy trench with his uncle Gary, their cheeks smeared with mud and their rifles cocked. Rats nibble at their bootlaces. Shells burst overhead. Karl Malden yells orders above the cacophony of mortar.

'Ask me what.'

'*Ask David*. That's it.'

In the distance, thunderous mortar. The sky, azure and fierce. The battle is heavy and long. Casualties are piled atop grassy peaks, compressed into a river of suffering.

Gary: 'So I'm asking you.'

'But.'

'I'm asking. She said ask. I'm asking.'

'But. I don't know ... '

'I'm asking you, David. She turned herself *inside fucking out*. So I'm asking you, you piece of shit. I'm asking you, David. I'm asking you. I'm asking you. I'm asking you, you piece of shit. I'm asking. I'm asking. I'm *asking*.'

Lifetimes spent chasing unforeseeable goals. Absence that groans like an unstitched wound, a longing persisting for so long its origin flees memory. The solitary soldier, paralyzed, becomes one with the razed plains, the smouldering heaps. Immobile and limp. A verse from an unsung song.

Unhappiness is a cancer on a tumour; unhappiness feeds on unhappiness. People wallow. People survive on wallowing. The city continues to churn. Dawn fires up.

With renewed pulse, things begin to take shape.

Early in the morning, the phone rings. David, our hero, hides buried under the weight of covers.

Dream of turbid harbours, dim views. Dream of uncertain navigations.

Phone. Night-harassing light screams at the window. The phone insists.

Phone. Phone.

No.

Dream of sky still in night's chambers, fevered with stars. Cottony hazes between logos and trademarks. Powdery constellations. Purple, uneasy purple, in the heavens, where destinies are interpreted in brief sputters. Purple like heat, heat without flame. Words form dreams. Dreams create screens. The stars operate.

Dream of stars fidgeting around the anchored moon.

This nothing. Here in the now. Now there is. Nothing but.

Phone. Phone.

Finally, he answers.

Sarah Promise: she asks if he's been considering Chaos.

Not really. Maybe.

She asks if he'd like to go for a while. With her. She says there may be a way to resolve his yearnings. A place.

Now might be a good time to think about getting away from it all!

Nothing is harsher than the blunt sick reality. Of it all.

He says: *okay   where.*

II

Unrests of forest along the highway, trees fluttering in a slide show of ashen husks, rising from the earth in daunting columns, trees as edifices, monuments – another landscape, another cityscape, another swell packed into a monotonous grid.

David sits in the shotgun seat of Sarah Promise's car, cradling a Styrofoam cup of coffee. Its heat feels good in his hands. His hands do not fidget. His stomach is not queasy. Miles pass. The city is far behind. They tear past half-built subdivisions and fragmented wetlands, a purgatory of in-between. Highway mesas, armadas of tractor-trailers. A bridge spanning icy floes. Space unfurls around them like the unwrapping of a sandwich; the world is bright with a clouded wash, last night's snowfall draping the land in exhaust-suffused slush.

Displaced and free, escaping from forces that threaten. Moving into waiting possibility. Eluding damage behind. Evading the plunge of the blade. They speed past muddy shores trembling against brief rivers, truck-stop signs in fitted letters: SALT 5.99 6lb BAG SANDWICH'S DIESEL. Signs with dormant lights demarcating warehouses and truckyards. JOHN DEERE. HOME DEPOT.

Against all expectations, time moves on. A slow trudging stream, backward into memory. Memories are dispelled shells left scattered in the wake of combat. Memories are casualties, or reprimands, golden decrees. The world – watch as it fades. The selectivity of memory is the lowliness of the condemned, the losers who perish in battle, those who die without splendour.

Perhaps the battle is to be waged in transit, in restlessness.

Sarah Promise handles the steering wheel with steely confidence. She is still a fragment of a question. A silhouette with dull edges.

They have been driving for hours in silence. David grows bored.

'Radio?' he suggests, reaching for the knob.

'Doesn't work.'

He withdraws his hand. 'So … how far now?'

'Not far.'

'Not far any minute now, or not far we'll get there this week?'

She looks at him. 'You're attempting to start a conversation.'

'Right. I know the rule. No talking.'

'Oh, you can talk. Talk all you want, my dear. Just don't expect me to listen.'

David sniffs. Trees. Gravel pits. A muddy patch. More trees. Towers, electric lines strung like veins. Train tracks snowy over 4x4 trails.

'Nothing to say anyway,' he says, sinking further into his seat.

It was snowing that day too, steadily and mercilessly. Almost a year ago now. The roads were impossible; nevertheless, David ventured forth. It was The Father's birthday, and David had obliged himself to take the old man to lunch. The occasion filled David's guts with a squeeze of dread, but there was to be no candyassing about it – the thing would occur. David waited forty-five minutes for the taxi to make its way through the whitening streets, and on arrival, the fat lip-licking cabbie had said *you don't want to be going anywhere in this*, indicating the snow and wind and bluster. David responded with silence, not uttering a sound until they pulled up to The Father's grim apartment building, and even then he had said only *take it easy*, handing the driver a twenty on a fourteen-dollar fare.

David had to practically drag The Father outside, sighing in frustration at his incessant fumbling and stalling. They took the old man's stinky old Taurus; David drove. The Father quietly smoked, flicking ashes out a narrowly parted window.

The lips of The Father were chapped and sore. He picked at them constantly.

They went to a Tex-Mex eatery between a bowling alley and a Zeller's in the nearby mall. Upon entrance it smelt like bad breath and rancid chicken. Nonetheless, they assumed a booth near the window and accepted ice water. As they scanned oversized laminated menus, the world outside endured a pelting of wetness. The

Father dabbed at his lips with a serviette. They sat in silence until David instigated a discussion of the potential merits of the chicken quesadillas. The Father read the word *chimichanga* with unfamiliarity, then said no more. David coughed a few times. The Father lit a cigarette and David had to remind him the place was non-smoking; The Father looked like he had been punched in the groin. The Father's hands: worn, dry, constantly moving. His eyes: always roving. The Father sipped his water every twelve seconds – David found himself counting. David asked if he was still running. The Father offered something about a bum knee. David nodded okay. Their waitress arrived to take orders – her face was an adolescent catastrophe of pimples and makeup, her frame a pudgy sink of chub. The Father ordered baked haddock with fries and a Pepsi. David ordered a cheeseburger with a side salad and a pint of Smithwick's. The Father said *oh then I'll have one of those too.* The waitress asked if he still wanted the Pepsi. The Father didn't answer. David spoke up, telling her: *um no you can cancel the pop I guess.* As she departed they again fell into thick silence. For lack of better topic David found himself commenting on the waitress's beleaguered complexion, her acne-ravaged cheeks and forehead. The potential for scarring. He continued against The Father's stony silence.

I had a pretty rough go of it too if you remember, David said, *I had these sores on my back and neck that became these huge welts.* He understood how the waitress must feel, the shame of one's face. Young David's own complexion had been a minefield of hellish outbreaks. Soreness, volcanoes of pus. Popping, picking. He had employed countless pore-cleansers and scrubs, Dermaclear and Clearasil and Neutrogena, until a dermatologist-prescribed Accutane regimen finally transformed his face from spurting disaster to a healthful hide.

The Father once caught him delicately dabbing cream on these facial eructations, snarling *what are you some kind of fifty-fifty.*

Fifty-fifty: one of many pet cryptic terms.

When their food arrived, The Father engaged his haddock with chilly trepidation. There was nothing in his actions that didn't radiate foreboding and suspicion; that was his way. Even his forking of the fish was a negative act. He speared a wedge of lemon and raised it for scrutiny, asking *am I supposed to eat this* and David hadn't answered, digging into his burger, until many seconds had passed and he looked up to find The Father still mystified by the lemon, this aberration, and David snapped *you don't eat it you squeeze it on your fish or you get rid of it*. The Father blinked and set it aside. Immediately David felt a wave of regret. This was what they had come to: this man, whose rule once overshadowed all else like a dirigible of authority, had become an object of sorrow. Pity. His hangovers and depressive spells had sentenced him to a life locked away on his own. Years of bouncing around: AA, countless jobs in countless offices amounting to countless pink slips, the gradual retreat. He couldn't adhere himself to anything; he was simply unable to meet expectations.

And yet David couldn't allow The Father to disappear, not completely. Even if the tired old man desired it, David couldn't stand idly by and let it happen. There was an inkling of something in there, somewhere. A morsel of a possibility. Perhaps.

Even so, despite every attempt, despite the lemon and the beer and the taxi and the serviettes and the stabs at straightforwardness – in the end, David failed. They had finished the birthday lunch in silence, the snow pummelling the earth without lenience, the clouds raging against the paved plateaus of the vanishing parking lot. The possibility went unrealized. It all drifted away. The cars. The city. The world.

David looks out through the window's condensation, depthless fog made distinct with a bored finger's autograph. With only one eye to rely on he possesses nothing, nothing but trickling outlines. Nothing further, blank – like the hyperaccelerated passage of frames in the clunky ViewMaster he'd obsessed over as a kid, its miniaturized yet spectacular 3-D views of landscapes or movie scenes or cartoons. As a boy, David treasured most his ViewMaster slide for the movie *Superman*, visiting it again and again for its glories of flight, red-white-blue insignia, towering strength. But beyond Metropolis there was a void. It was cinema, facade and nothing else. Even in the slide for *The Wizard of Oz*, with its vivid trippy fields and sparkling yellow brick, there was nothing real beyond the swirling fantastic. As true experience, it was empty.

Now everything is that way: distant, at arm's length. Cardboard and semi-fictional. The doctor had said *boy oh boy*.

Gravel. Snow. Mud. Farms. Cows in a field, heads lowered.

A change in surroundings.

How has he ended up. Why has everyone abandoned.

Photocopies of photocopies. *Ask David.*

Perhaps we will perish in a perpetual retread of our own mistakes. Death by rote, by repetition, by recycled time. Perhaps death will be merely a revisitation of the demons who haunted us on earth – on the pavement, the grass, the grime, the carpets. To walk eternal battlegrounds, slouching through a mess of limbs.

It was horror, late in the afternoon. The apartment was furnished with a ridiculous menagerie of mismatched chairs and end tables and drapes, all yellowed with cigarette age and sagging with years of ass weight. This tired room where The Father mulled over the resolve of his last days, and drew his conclusion. The furniture had been rescued from the sale of the family cottage and had sat in storage until The Father moved into this sad little place. Coffee mugs – HITS 101.9, Toronto Maple Leafs, 1987 Inter-Provincial Curling Master Series – and sauce-flecked styrofoam tubs sat piled atop counters and overflowing in the half-kitchen's garbage can. No photographs were displayed. No plants sprang upward. David would drop by the apartment of The Father about once a month – though less frequently, it seemed, in those months leading up to his dark final act – bearing an eight-pack of Moosehead and a bucket of Kentucky Fried Chicken. A Family-Size Bucket, even though the two of them made a pretty meagre family. They would eat and watch TV, rarely speaking. The Father seemed grateful for these visits, for the chicken, but never offered thanks or recognition, never offered to cough up half the costs. His rare interjections would only be occasional protests at unsatisfactory offerings presented on the television, to which he would quietly growl and switch channels. They would sit, the two of them, and drink their beers without conversation.

This was the den The Father inhabited, his days like dusty shards of former efforts. Hunched over the kitchen table, rolling dimes, skimming the paper, biding time. He retreated to this den, escaping the violent incision of inspection. This was his apartment, his unfair territory. Dust coated the towel rack, the windowsills. Always too warm. TV always on, volume just slightly too loud. On the weekends there was football. Through the week there was whatever. Sitcoms.

The Father rarely lowered himself to speak. Better to maintain tight rein. Keep things brief. Strangled. Things were not to be explained, and if too many things were too fully explained to him he would shake his head and rise from his chair to pace; he would jingle his pocket change or blow his nose or suck down one of the five daily cigarettes he allowed himself or begin to unscrew the back panel of a nearby appliance, a radio or a coffee maker maybe – or, in a trademark move, he would pour water from the tap into a glass, blasting water at full throttle to drown out words, then dump the water back out into the sink, refill it again just as noisily, repeating this motion over and over until the subject had been dropped. Or, in later times, when something was introduced into his sphere that he chose not to address, he would simply feign unconsciousness. Conked out. He would close his eyes and fold his arms across his chest and ignore. The Father, impenetrable. The Father, empty.

But. *No.* He was not empty. Inside, his spine was ready to crack with tension. As a young man in photographs, there was wonder to be conjured at the curvature of his jaw, the gusto of the curly-haired chest, a tan lasting through October. There was wonder in attempting to reconcile memories, drawing together clues from the past. Looking back.

Late in the afternoon. Light tilted and twisted through the bedroom window, training across the floor, exposing the neglect within. There was a staleness to the room, a stuffy staleness revealing the shrinking away, the retreat, the reclusion of its only occupant. A pile of soiled laundry burying the chair underneath. The carpet was gritty. The windows had been shut for so long they had to be opened with WD-40.

Languid dust danced in somnolent rays. Detritus in waning sun.

The sun's reclining presence made it all sort of golden, this horror. The gold refractions, the transparency of the dusty air. So: who discovers this. Who walks in. Who carries the bucket of chicken and dangling beer cans, the offering. Who opens the door to enter the stuffiness. Who is it, who does this. Son to The Father.

The old man's cheeks were plump and full, like a puppet's. The cheekbones were plumped rosy with the rope's forced throttle of blood. It was tight. The face was a balloon, engorged and tied, impassive. The man became a broken body. Dangling.

He must have known David was coming. He must have. Who else would be here to find him. Nobody. He knew. He foresaw.

David had clung to the chicken bucket in his hands like a life preserver, trying to remain upright. He could have fainted, given way, but he did not. The stuffiness of the apartment had overpowered him almost more than the body dangling from a well-knotted noose. There was no air. Nothing to breathe. It was a stifle of movement. A gasp, a gag.

Sarah Promise maintains unwavering focus. Her eyes, unavailable behind dark sunglasses, never deviate from the oncoming highway. David realizes he's been dozing, and wakes.

Still moving. Leaving behind. Escape.

Sarah Promise transfers lanes and takes an approaching exit. Over miles and shifts and sleep, he's lost track of where they are, where they've been going, where to find the way back home.

'We're almost there,' she says.

Chaos Farm introduces itself with a pair of oil barrels, ablaze with noxious fire, flanking a gigantic wrought-iron gate. Atop the gate a security camera whizzes and rotates, aiming at them. Sarah Promise honks the horn, and after a moment the gate swings open to let them through.

'Did you pack any weapons, any guns or anything?' Sarah Promise asks David.

Whether or not she is kidding goes unconfirmed. Concentrate, instead, on the introduction of Chaos.

As far as he understands, based on the negligible information Sarah Promise has offered, Chaos Farm is some sort of haven or retreat, a geographic conduit for intangible energies. What these energies actually are, she has offered little explanation of, describing it only as *the one place I've ever felt at home*. The sketchiness of this venture makes him uneasy, but David is powerless against Sarah Promise's persuasion. His only move is submission to the secrecy.

Sarah Promise has spoken of someone named Hamdaber – *Ike Hamdaber*. David guesses this Ike to be the owner or chief resident of Chaos Farm. Sarah Promise utters this name like a favourite curse: lovingly, but hesitantly. Wait until you meet. Save questions until. Ike Hamdaber. Until you meet Ike. What is he getting himself into.

The car eases down a dirt road sheltered by stark pines. David rolls down his window and hoists out his neck to drink the air. The wash of cool air is crisp and clear. A smell of dirt and trees. Like Barcelona – sea breezes whistling through moored yachts in the marina. The freshness pressing against his face. There is electricity in the air, static, *energy*; he senses the fine wisp-hairs on the back of his neck standing alert.

Yet there is also something further detectable, something uncertain and weird lurking in these dense forests, creeping in the boggy shallows. Undulating grey stalks. Dangers in the meadows, murderers in the pastures. Embezzling fawns chomping cigars.

Bears blackmailing owls. Rabbits assaulted in their hutches. Graffiti and contagion in the willows. Forests like ghettoes of threat. Danger concealed in the branches, branches like needle-cysted forearms.

As they mount a brief rise and rounding a bend, the trees give way to a clearing, and there – at the termination of the road's straightaway – is Chaos Farm.

David is struck with an unexpected pang of dread. He wants Sarah Promise to hit the brakes, stop, go no further. This is a bad idea. *Stop*. Turn back. Don't tempt the possibilities. Don't invite strange forces. *Go back*.

But they continue.

As they draw nearer, the farm's layout becomes more apparent. Chaos Farm's buildings are clustered in a semicircle at the crest of a gradual incline. Several smallish cottages, porched bungalows with wiry antennae topping their roofs, barns, a greenhouse, utility sheds – paths and soil beds curled between. But these dwellings are subsidiary to the central building, the largest: the farmhouse, faced with enormous bay windows, its angled peak like a collapsed steeple, the epicentre of Chaos.

From afar, the farm's structure bears the foreboding aspect of a military installation – a bunker, a base, a fort. It looms.

David's disabled vision processes only shape, failing at depth: flat buildings stand flatly atop a flat ridge against the flat sky, bruise-like on snowy fields, like French pastures scoured by Allies in the forward rush for Berlin, where red-splodged bodies lay in snowbanks still clutching the pins of their grenades.

They continue up the drive, his apprehension mounting. Sarah Promise parks near a building adjacent to the farmhouse: an enormous garage, doors shut. The Volvo's cranky rumble hushes. They remain seat-belted, hesitant.

'Seems no one's here yet,' Sarah Promise says.

Indeed, the premises seem vacant. Snow mutes all.

'That light is on,' David notices, gesturing to the farmhouse's front door.

'Oh. Bedel, probably. What time is it?'

He checks. 'Twenty after four.'

'He's probably just getting up. Did you bring boots?'

'Boots. No.'

'Bedel will probably get you out shovelling. And clearing away the icicles on the front roof. Last year someone got conked by one, it was like a frozen sword. They get gigantic. Look.'

She points. David fiddles with his eyepatch.

'Sarah,' he says, 'I wish you'd tell more about. I'm in the dark, a little bit ... '

'*L'il bit*,' she mocks.

'What. What does that mean?'

'You and your sitcom cadence,' she snickers. 'So *conventional*.'

David, defensive: 'You're the one who dubs cartoons.'

She removes her sunglasses to bare icy eyes. 'David. Appreciate what I've done for you. You're about to participate in something significant. Chaos Farm could prove a very meaningful experience. You won't be the same person you were before, and from what I've seen so far, that might not be such a bad thing.'

She lights a cigarette.

'Being a Leo, you are understandably irked about surrendering a degree of control. I understand, and that's perfectly fine. Capitalize on confusion. Confusion is simply a pause in perception, like a hesitant step in several simultaneous directions. You can test the waters. But as you soak it up, be aware of what's happening. It's many somethings. It's the fulfillment of a whole spectrum of somethings. I brought an ounce of this bonkers Himalayan weed. When I smoke it I have orgasms that last half an hour. Something infused from the mountain air, I guess. Altitude and UV rays.'

Her hands drum on the steering wheel, tapping ashes into the dashboard's tray. 'You want explanations.'

'I guess so.'

'*Chaos Farm*, David. Can't you feel it? We are sitting here in the realest of real reality. The realness of reality. Look at your watch.'

'I don't have a watch.'

Sarah Promise picks at her eyebrow. 'Well ... if you had a watch you would probably notice it had stopped. There are tectonic forces converging on this axis, or so Ike claims. This site was chosen after serious deliberation. Not that I'm purporting to interpret or explain or understand anyone's motivations. It's complicated and calculated.'

He doesn't understand. 'I just want to feel that I'm not being … you know … '

'Seduced?'

'No, just … I just want to have a say in my own future.'

She chuckles. 'Now *that's* presumptuous. As if anyone has any say in their future. That's what I'm getting at, David – you have to accept a certain randomness. You have to be able to bend to the caprice of the universe. There is tranquility in disorder. I'm not prepping you for anything you're not already aware of. I'm not freaky-culting you. I'm just trying to help you free yourself.'

She is right in at least one respect – there is no one here except Bedel. Bony and thick-browed, he greets them discourteously, shaking David's hand without cheer.

Music blares from within, guitary refrains: *ain't flinging tears out on the dusty ground   for all my friends out on the burial ground.*

Guitars in echoes.

'I'm assuming you'll be sticking around for a while, Sarah,' Bedel says.

Sarah Promise glances sideways, toward David.

'As long as it takes.'

On the wall near the farmhouse's entrance, there is an enormous diagram framed and mounted: two intersecting swirls, near-symmetrical but faintly distorted, separated by a straight axis. The frame bears a title: *The Lorenz Attractor.* This, Sarah Promise informs David, is a mathematical depiction of a deterministic Chaotic system.

David asks her to explain.

She shrugs. 'Look it up yourself. I don't give a rat's ass about science.'

The farmhouse: abundant with contradiction and wonders. Weird spaces, *feng shui* on speed. Long burrowing passages. Skylights.

Muted colours, beige crème salmon. Strangely textured walls. Sarah Promise tours David through the house. A sequence of Warholian silkscreens depicting tall tabbed cans of Old Milwaukee. An indoor herb garden, immersed in prismed light from a sloping complement of glass. A grand piano in the living room, kaleidoscopic with rhinestones. Many rooms: dormitory-style bedrooms and shelved nooks, parlours and vestibules, a gaming room with shoddy pinball machines and outdated arcade games in their original consoles: Double Dragon and Mike Tyson's Punch-Out!! and 1941. Rugs from a Marrakesh marketeer. Digital consoles regulating humidity in every room. A domed solarium overlooking Chaos Farm's rear fields. Yet, despite these rarified embellishments, most furnishings and appliances are, strangely, of a low-rent Wal-Mart variety: much is fresh and generic, out of the box, lacking memory.

Sarah Promise leads him through a multi-tentacled stretch of narrow hallways, hurrying past partly furnished rooms, alcoves stuffed with packing boxes, half-baths with newspapers spread on newly tiled floors. They stop at a door and Sarah Promise introduces him to a tiny compartment containing only a cot and an uncurtained window. She waves offhandedly at this skimpy slice of space, explaining that these will be his quarters. David had noticed there were countless rooms more spacious and better furnished, seemingly unoccupied. Nevertheless, this is his provided barracks. He drops his bag on a cold rugless floor.

He relents. He has to. *Don't question*: today, nothing is up for debate.

They are standing on the back deck. The wood-slatted deck presents a comprehensive view of the backyard, its hedges and cascading slopes, all blanketed in snow, tumbling to a pebbled ice-chunky beach. A plump sun sinks into the sparkling bay beyond. Heavy hard land, weighed down by winter.

'This view,' David says, squinting his one eye. 'Ridiculous.'

Sarah Promise puffs on an Avanti and says, 'See those seagulls?'

He sees: dark Vs, swooping high away in clouds.

'I empathize with those gulls,' Sarah Promise says.

He turns and faces her. Her eyes meet his through an upsweep of puffed smoke. Sarah Promise, unscowling against the brilliance of the bay and the fading sunset. Cigarette between lips. Shoulders hunched against the chill.

Perhaps we will sink to our ends in the golden raptures of bliss. We will burn in amorous fires, scalding pleasures. Perhaps the truth of our fates will be revealed only in the fitful throes of release. Cadaverous ends.

David leans forward and places a hesitant kiss on Sarah Promise's smoky lips. Her flesh is soft and cold. She offers no objection but does not reciprocate. She considers this kiss as one might consider a pesky mathematical result, an anomaly.

'David,' she says, 'we need to get drunk.'

With a bottle of Tres Mujeres and some frozen juice procured from a kitchen cabinet, Sarah Promise mixes a blender of makeshift margaritas and they return to the back deck. Night uncoils around them, painting the snowy yard in bluish greys and inky blacks. David finds a pair of plastic deck chairs; he shakes the accumulated water from their seats and sets them out. They recline. Sarah Promise grins and swigs generously.

'Things haven't really turned out the … way that I'd imagined they would,' David says.

'You're surprised?'

'I suppose not. In light of being … I imagine that I'll be, with this. I'll be canned. From my job.'

'Job *schmob*. Shed your shackles, David.'

From inside the house he can hear the muffled sound of Bedel's stereo: cracking beats and synthesizer twinklings. David can hear the song's determined vocal, assertive above all competition: *broken ice still melts in the sun and times that are broken can often be one again.*

What does that mean? Often, be *one again*. How. Hall and Oates.

'Look,' Sarah Promise says, indicating the horizon.

'What?'

But he sees: dust-like streaks across the sky's field, little irises of starry light in downward trajectory.

'Meteor shower,' Sarah Promise says.

'Yes.'

'Up in the sky.'

They sit quietly, drinking and watching stars fall, huddled against the cold.

'I was a chronic agoraphobe until I was sixteen,' Sarah Promise says.

'No way.'

'No lie. It was horrible. I was held back in Grade Eleven twice for absenteeism. But I couldn't. I physically could not leave the house. The idea of walking down the street, exposed to all that sky and all that open air and everything, standing up to the huge exposure of it all. Horrible. For a lot of the time I was a slobbering wreck.'

'Jeesh.'

'I didn't leave the house for seven weeks once. That was my longest stretch.'

'Seven weeks. Jeesh.'

'But the terror of the sky, that was the worst thing. Above all, the *hugeness* of it, even through buildings and … just this enormous unstoppable unending bleak thing, everywhere, up above. I would break down and crumple into a fetal position. I almost stumbled in front of a bus once. A very close call.'

'Jeesh.'

It is cold out, but not too cold. The cold is serene. David is drunk. They are drunk together.

'But now … ?'

Sarah Promise waves a hand of dismissal, her mouth busy with her glass, then swallows. 'I'm fine now. This' – indicating the bay, the land, the farm, the wide open space – 'none of this bothers me at all anymore.'

'What cured you?'

'I'm not exactly positive. As far as I can pinpoint, the fears went away just about the same time I lost my virginity to my father's business partner. Frank Skanes. Skanes was the ugliest man I've ever seen: obese, scarred, balding, alcoholic. But for some reason … it was at their corporate New Year's party. I was fifteen. He led me upstairs to the bathroom, hiked up my skirt and did me standing up against the sink. I didn't utter a peep. The next day I felt quite different. It was a new year. From then on I never had fits. I never saw Frank Skanes again either … I think he split town after his wife left him. My god, he was so ugly. I can still picture his face in the mirror, all screwed up and his forehead all sweaty. He reeked like English Leather and stale cookies.'

Sarah Promise lights another cigarette, offers the pack to David. He declines. Chaos Farm surrounds them; things are strange. He thinks of his mother, somewhere, glasses perched on nose, a crossword puzzle under scrutiny. Points are woven together across gaps, drawing pits and valleys and battlefields, where those he knows – those he knew – lie in slumbers and in myth, all in cities or in stasis, starry speckled points connecting memories he can't reclaim. Their identities become phantasms, their voices cease to sound. Memories floating in the ether. Memories collapsing, cyclical, like the sun, like water running down a drain, like Chaos. The disorganization of it all sets the mind reeling. Think of The Father, buried under soil and ice, eternal in disappointment. Think of Lisa.

'I'm perfectly comfortable with the sky now,' Sarah Promise says. 'I rarely feel terrified. I have my freak-outs, but who doesn't?'

David wonders: *are there wolves out here, in the country?*

Late in the night. David lies in the huge bed of Sarah Promise's room, watching the moon lurking outside the window. The moon is unclear, censored by clouds. He is naked. Sarah Promise lies beside him, also naked, face down and quietly snoring, her back fleshy and smooth.

He is slightly ill. The moon is flat. The body beside him is warm, too warm. Sleep is far away. The room gyrates drunkenly.

Something elusive burbles under the surface at Chaos Farm. Sarah Promise had tried to explain, in tipsy grumbles, about how it was a point of concentration where some convergence of powers took place, and that was why it became the thing it is – but she couldn't even make clear what this thing it's supposedly become is. The harder she tried, the fuzzier it became.

But there is definitely *something* here, something not yet fully emergent, something undetermined and potentially menacing. Tension, like a teardrop's tremble on an eyelash. The enemy hides in flowered pastures and gentle flurries. Everything bears potential menace. The vista of the countryside, the crisp air, the smooth hardwood floors under bare feet, Sarah Promise's deft manoeuvres – these are palpable pleasures. But still, there is *something*.

The moon is not a clue.

Suddenly: a sharp unexpected noise, a pained sound ringing from outside. David sits upright, his naked body casting away covers.

'*What was that?*' he whisper-screams.

'Wuh,' Sarah Promise says into her pillow.

Again: a groaning demonic sound. From somewhere nearby, outside, close. Too close. David feels his heart hammer in his throat. '*Sarah.*'

She turns over, eyes still closed, breasts mashed in her arms' crooks.

'I'm asleep. I am asleep.'

'What the … what's that sound?'

And – yes – it sounds again. David stabs the air with an alarmed finger. Drooling zombies, cleaving heads in the woods. Insectoid monsters waging slimy combat in the dark. Trees murdering shrubs. Raccoons sharpening knives. The forest in the dead of night, sculpting doom out of twig and branch.

Perhaps unsuspecting sleepers will be pounced upon in their beds and eaten by slavering beasts.

'*That.* What the fuck is that *sound*?' he whisper-screams again.

Sarah Promise shifts in the bed. 'Moo.'

'What?'

'It's the cows. In the barn. They moo in the night.'

'They moo at night.'

'Yes. They moo. Now let me fucking sleep.'

David lies back down. It does sound remotely like a cow, he supposes – some primordial species of demon cow.

'Why do they moo at night?'

'They have visions. You'll have them too, just wait. Discarnate experience is the core of Chaos.'

With this, she turns away and, in a matter of seconds, regains sleep.

Imagine wonders yet to come. Ignore the muddled past, the shadowed figures. The world is flat. The world is huge. Sleep, eventually – sleep and dream of electric clouds and strange landscapes, of fog, and journeys ahead.

Days gradually become sections, paragraphs appended with footnotes, stricken with edits and splices and snips; days become formulae, data in and result out; days become portholes, or links in flow charts, or units in a downward wobble; days become catalyst, treatment, placebo; days become blankets and towels; days become channels in an incessant program; days become scripts, sour with dialogue and soggy with melodrama, fist-clenched and filthy with emotion over misspent time. Days become weeks. Weeks, years. Days pile up.

Rise to sounds of chatter, plates clinking, fry pans sizzling. Blink against hangover: fierce sunlight washes into the room. Smack dry mouth. Try to piece it together.

David is alone in Sarah's bed. No clock is available to inform him of the hour; there is only dishevelled covers, luggage heaped in a corner, the nagging itch of his eye.

Multiple voices in the next room. A shout of laughter. In the night, others have arrived at Chaos Farm.

Rise slowly. Locate clothes. Buckle, briefly, to a heave of nausea. The sickness of dread and remembering. Hangover of cast magics, nubby desire. Sloppiness. Rise to face vodka residue and misalignment. Boozy, yellow. Breathe heavily. Steady. Try to prepare.

Sarah Promise, in bathrobe, seated at the kitchen table cupping a mug, is the first to notice David's entrance. She glares at him through bloodshot eyes and mussed hair.

'Take heed all,' she announces, 'for David, slumbering boy-child, he who resists the future, enters.'

Hush: all eyes on our hero.

He offers a sheepish wave. 'Morning, all.'

Crisp breakfast sounds, mouths chewing, forks working omelettes. Seated at the table with Sarah Promise are two men, one young, one older. They are being served breakfast by a middle-aged woman who leans on a cane and sips at a teacup.

The denizens of Chaos.

Through an archway he discerns Bedel in the living room, collapsed before an enormous plasma-screen TV, watching a *Digimon* cartoon while dipping saltines into a large vat of baba ghanouj.

The older of the kitchen's two men says, 'There are sausages.'

'Oh … '

His guts aren't ready for such a project. He wants to go back to bed.

'Bacon and eggs,' the man continues. 'Do you want some carrot juice?'

'Oh. Juice would be great.'

'Fresh carrot juice. Detoxify.'

The kitchen is bright and white-cupboarded and busy with reflective surfaces. There are gleaming appliances of chrome and plastic. Here, too, everything is brand new, unscuffed, freshly delivered. Even the air seems sterile in its newness; it's like living in the Sears furniture department.

The man thrusts a tumbler of orange-brown juice upon him. David takes a sip, nodding gratefully, taking the glass with a shaky hand. His entire body is poisoned. His head pulses; his intestines curl and grieve.

Uh oh.

He lurches, trying to settle himself, his hands finding the back of Sarah Promise's chair.

She looks at him. 'You're pale.'

He tries not to swallow. He tries to remember which direction lies the bathroom.

Here. David vomits. He surges and spews. The breakfast table, the floor. Others react: there is much recoiling and revulsion. There is indignation.

David, drooling unforgivable fluids, faints.

Good morning, soldier. Your first day. You're a bit timid, but who isn't, in the beginning? Now, look. You have to ready yourself for the realization that some of us – even maybe *you* – won't be returning home. It's a kick in the pants, but that's the hard truth. I won't hold anything back. At the Carthaginians' fall in 146 BC, I peered down through all that blood-spattered dirt and smouldering ash, all that horseshit, and, analyzing the abyss, I witnessed greatness. Purity. As Carthage burned, women wailed while hacking off their hair for the archers' bowstrings. Meanwhile, we poke at computers. That's the sickness and sadness of this so-called *civilization* we've built for ourselves – sorry men, never required to test their goddamn worth. We've forgotten the magnificence of war. The ultimate test, one man's will against another. Like this map before me, these pins and pricks – vast armies, but in the final analysis it boils down to two men. Patton and Rommel. Me and the Fox, squaring off in the desert. And no matter how many Academy Awards they hand out or Contemporary Cinema Studies seminars they hold, nothing expurgates our triumph. No matter how many times you rewind and freeze-frame and well up teary, you'll never be your own man until you prove yourself in battle.

After he's been provided ice water and laid out on a chesterfield in the solarium, someone graciously mopping up the mess, after Sarah Promise has fled to wash her hair and change her clothes, and somebody sets the percolator into action, and David has muttered sorry a thousand times and initiated an understanding of the squirmy stress of his vicious hangover, he gradually meets the others.

The first is Muzz – *that's right Em You Zee Zee* – the younger of the two men at breakfast. David is horizontal with a damp cloth on his forehead when Muzz sits nearby, introducing himself in a casual drawl. His face is tough-chinned and caramel-shaded, a surfer's complexion. He wears blue jeans and a faded Casio T-shirt revealing sinewy muscles.

'I'm a songwriter,' he tells David, lighting a hand-rolled cigarette.

David, though still shaky, is impressed. 'Do you have a … a band or something?'

'I used have this band called Wax Wax Pilgrim My Pilgrim, back in Oregon. We put out some records. We had a pretty loyal following out there. But you know. Too much Sturm und Drang. Tough times, plenty of. I don't know what sort of thing you have going on, but if I learned anything from being in a band it's that compromise is compromise. *Compromise is compromise.* Sacrificing means *sacrificing.*'

David blinks. His head hammers.

'Life is too short and wonderful to spend it goofing off under auspices of agreeability. You die owning nothing but your past. I have a thirst for experience. I have chasms. We have chasms. You have chasms.'

An impulse: to nab a Post-it and jot down a note: *chasms?*

'I was careless, back there and then,' Muzz says. 'Dark dark times. Way too into the junk. That was part of my compromise, retreating into this condition of drugged – I guess you'd call it *stewing.* I was stewing like a prune. My art was so distant. Distant even from myself. I had to regrasp it. I took my guitar down to the reservoir and chucked it in. My '73 Supro, I chucked it into that muddy crud. I watched that beautiful guitar sink. It bobbed in that shitty water and I felt all the misery in my life converge like this vice clamped around my heart, and it hurt like crazy, but it also shook me out of the comatose fog I was stuck in. The Supro sank. This is a while ago. Six years now. Maybe five.'

'Huh.'

'I was reborn in my Chaos visions. Tonight we'll eat some 'shrooms and I'll sing a few songs. I've got a year's worth of tuneage I'm horny to play. I've realized the need to whittle down the whole concept. No more samplers and racks and doohickeys. I have this two-string banjo-ish sort of thing I picked up at a junk shop in Canastota. It was obviously built with love. I'll haul it out later. Right now I'm thinking minimal, hyper-minimal. Beyond minimal. One or two notes, three max. It's all in the soul of the song. It's in the quiver of my vocal cords. I'm looking for power that isn't in fuzzboxes, it's in the chronology of the performance and the composition. I'm thinking proximity and … pain. Every song is like a solar system with its own rules of gravity and stock market.

If I believe in the song, then just being in this thing – it is. The song exists in singing, in the voice and the plucked string, and nothing else matters – the way I've brushed my hair, how many times I blink ... '

His hands jitter with enthusiasm.

' ... but what I mean is that the song becomes almost like this huge tendril growing out of my head that I barely control. It surpasses its identity. Before it's a song, it's a *possession*.'

He stops and laughs generously, the corners of his eyes crinkling with delight. 'Sorry for prattling. I'm still working things out. Do you like bluegrass?'

David: 'Is that like wheatgrass?'

Bedel enters the solarium, watering plants. Muzz asks if they've met.

'Yeah, we met last night,' David says.

Bedel frowns. 'I don't think so.'

'I came in yesterday afternoon,' David says. 'With Sarah.'

Bedel frowns. 'I really don't think so. Are you sure?'

'You were cranking Hall and Oates.'

'*Hall. Oates.* These names mean nothing to me.'

Bedel stands gawking at David, his mouth pursed, then says, 'I have to go milk Scylla and Astrophil. Later.'

Exit Bedel. Muzz nods. 'The cows.'

'I heard them mooing last night,' David says. 'I never knew cows mooed at night.'

Muzz crushes out his expended cigarette. 'Have you met Wyatt and Samantha?'

The Voights: Wyatt and Samantha. Middle-aged, warm but reserved. Wyatt is red-eyed, spectacled. Samantha – she looks out through a shield of disciplined blackish locks, a weathered face of peering eyes and pale lips. Despite her dependence on a cane, Samantha is evidently far from defenceless; by contrast, Wyatt's posture is thin and weedy, un-tough.

Upon first introduction, their affability is endearing. But after initial introductions have been made, their tone turns investigative.

'You lost your eye,' Wyatt observes.

'Some sort of infection, or contagion,' Samantha speculates.

'Um,' David says, fingering his patch. 'No. Just an accident.'

'What a damn shame,' Wyatt says. 'Was it machine-related? Working in a bindery, maybe.'

Samantha: 'No. A printing press. Our friend Elwood once lopped off an index operating one of those contraptions. He never played the piano again, and Elwood was a renowned pianist. Just terrific. Did it hurt?'

'Well, yes, but it wasn't a printing press … '

'Motorcycle accident,' Wyatt wagers.

'No … '

Samantha: 'Athletics. A javelin. A golf club hurled in frustration.'

Wyatt: 'A genetic defect. Your father or mother, glaucomatous. What a damn *shame*.'

Samantha: 'The insufferable pain. The agonies. I can't even imagine. Elwood approached Bach like Gould in his prime, but more provisional.'

They are sitting at the kitchen table over cups of tea. Muzz is baking cinnamon rolls.

'It was a shard of glass, during this demonstration,' David says. 'It was you know, a glass bottle … '

'Brutal,' Muzz comments, rummaging for a cooling rack.

'A demonstration?' Samantha asks.

'You know. A student demonstration.'

Wyatt: 'And you found yourself sucked into this herd mentality, and you paid the unfortunate price. David, I hope you see how you can't solve problems simply by adhering to an imposed status quo. Pardon the irony, but I hope you see how your lack of vision directly led to the downfall of your actual literal vision, if you follow. In the end, undue haste only leads to an undermining of one's own ambitions.'

Samantha: 'But within that, there is room in which to grow, you know. You have to take a few stabs before you hit the target. I hope you see the gravity of your errors.'

'But I wasn't even really … ' David tries.

Wyatt interrupts. 'My problem with most of today's student movements is this issue of right versus privilege, versus how the basic commodity of knowledge is fissured through education. Students somehow feel that they have some unique privilege of rights sequestered from society. Students fuelled by beer and shouting – they're so *demanding*. They haven't even been whipped and lowered as the rest of us all have, by the guilt and pain and fear and frustration of real life, and yet they propose revamping the rules by which this messy world should be run. They're trying to mobilize a non-existent demobilized population. It's the malaise of spoiled youth. And in my heart I agree, but in practice, David, I can't agree with you. I'm sorry.'

Wyatt rises abruptly and leaves the kitchen.

Samantha tsks. 'He's an extremely principled man, David. You shouldn't irk him so.'

'But. I didn't … '

David looks to Muzz, who is idly fanning the cooling buns with an oven mitt.

'This frosting is completely nauseating, but at the same time completely kickass,' Muzz says.

And it is. They demolish the gooey buns, Muzz and Samantha and David, and then Bedel joins in, and eventually even Wyatt comes sulking back in, slurping a Schweppes. They pig out on sticky buns, delighting in the sweetness. Sarah Promise is nowhere to be found.

Suddenly Chaos Farm seems less an imposition than a possibility, a route to new knowledge. David thinks he's beginning to comprehend the spirit of the whole thing: it's Chaos, it's disjointedness, it's a drawing together with a simultaneous pulling apart; it's neither joy nor dismay, it's a dismissal and a spree; it's like a drugged safety net, an implosion. It's eating sticky buns without caution.

Snowmobiles. In one of the two enormous garages behind the farmhouse there are three Yamaha SRXs, a pair of Arctic Cat Thundercat 1000s and a Polaris 800 XCR. Their hulls are bulky bullets, gleaming in windowed sun.

'There's fifty klicks of cleared trails in the woods,' Muzz says. 'You can really tear around.'

Snowmobiles. David looks at the snowmobiles, then at Muzz. 'I don't know … '

'The speed,' Muzz says. 'Ploughing through that powder. You have to get into it. There's only a few weeks left of snow out here. We'd better take advantage.'

He heads for a shelf bearing a selection of helmets. David is skeptical. 'We can just … take out whatever we want?'

'Hell yeah. That's what they're for. It's Ike's fleet. I go scooting all the time.'

The bravado of Muzz. The marvel of the gleaming snowmobiles, their polished tailpipes and hulls, their musty petrol smell. The apprehension of David. The stomach, still trembling vodka. The head still full of questions.

Muzz extends a helmet to him. 'Decide which of these bad boys you're taking, because we'll need to gas up.'

Speed.

Perhaps we will die in assaults of speed, hurtling through scouring winds with death at every curve.

The forest expands around them, baring teeth of dense trees and rock, its topography haphazard and bumpy. The air is caustic. The eye throbs in the cold, the patch little defence. Muzz is ahead, on the Thundercat. David, on the SRX, is dying with fear. The engine growls between his legs. His hands grip the steering. He is desperately trying to retain focus with his one eye, concentrating on the snaking trail. Distance is arbitrary.

Dive into delirium, speed.

The visions. To be reborn in the visions.

He races forward blindly, the snowmobile's treads skidding out of control on patches of ice, the bumps of the trail ass-pulverizingly turbulent. David's helmet is loose, its visor painfully thwapping his cold-tender cheeks. He tries to anticipate the trail's curves, but through spurting snow all his impaired vision can discern is Muzz's blue parka; this blotch of colour becomes his beacon, against sheets of stark white and the confusion of forest. Muzz glances back through a screen of spray, grinning widely, his enthusiasm unflagging.

Cars. Treadmills. Computers. Snowmobiles. Machines of torture. *Hang. On.*

Cutting over an incline, narrowly dodging a jut of rock half-hidden by snow – *jesus fucking fuck* – then rounding the next bend, David finds Muzz slowing at the ridge of a sudden drop. David attempts to decelerate but brakes too suddenly, fishtailing, almost spinning over the edge. But luck's kindness steadies him, taming the Yamaha's fury. David gasps with relief.

Below them is an impossible countryside: sloping pastures and arterial brooks, patches of dense brush, ambitious peaks, rocky routes winding through hills, the introductory tributary of a huge lake bordered with sparkling ice-covered trees. The land lies electric. Phosphorous. Toxic. Indecipherable data, from the valleys and dangling branches. The natural made mechanical.

Muzz: 'This is it. Most of it.'

This wintry chunk of the world. *Chaos.* In the distance David spots the security fence, nestled in a mob of pines, through which he and Sarah Promise had entered. He follows its arc, and at his fractured vision's furthest reach he spots a trickle of bluish grey rising against the sky: the farmhouse's chimney, tooting smoke to the heavens.

'Ike owns all of it, plus a few klicks past that hill,' Muzz says, pointing toward a hump of land on the horizon.

David shakes his head. 'All of this? But what does he ... how can he ... '

Muzz: 'He does plenty. Commercial enterprise. Fund management. Properties. He'll show up later this week. He'll sort you out.'

Muzz hops back on his snowmobile and revs it up. David reluctantly remounts and follows him back into the thick. They speed further down the trail into a clearing where the press of trees briefly withdraws. To the left is a topple of boulders inclined against further forests; on the right there is a large pond, frozen, shimmering. Cracks streak the water, hints of waters trapped beneath. David eases up on the throttle.

Ducks. Surrounding this pond are ducks, small clumps, gangs. David turns off the engine and dismounts.

A voice: *gwawk*. Answering: *gwaa awk*.

His approach prompts defensive manoeuvres among the flock. Backing off. Ruffled feathers. One mallard, loafing at the pond's periphery, nears with curiosity.

'Hello,' David says, kneeling closer.

Ducks. In afternoon's wane, this duck, this mallard, its head carved smooth. The blinking eye, blacker than black. Eerily unperturbed. Duck as sibyl. Duck as soldier, flock as army. David takes tentative steps forward: one two three. The troops tremble. They are here: the fat and the lean, the striped and mottled.

Muzz appears beside him. 'What's going on?'

David: 'I just needed to look … '

In this wooded hideaway, the ducks congregate. David stands spectator. See them waddling from pond's shore, across precarious ice, their plump hinds shivering. See them gathering in soundless caucus, pecking at granules of dirt set in packed snow. See them hurl bottles and shout curses. See them gather notes and memos, whip off hasty notes in the margins of faxes, chit-chat, flip clipboard sheets.

David watches their slender heads bob and jerk, slapstick quick and zombie slow. Studying their knowing eyes, he feels the same as when devouring frames of video playback. Think of the scene near the beginning of *Patton*, in which Omar Bradley, as portrayed by the nosy actor Karl Malden, surveys the damage following a battle at the Kasserine Pass, troops scattered, nomads scouring, bodies exposed, everything dusty and dead. Think of the scene in which Patton sniffs soil upon which ancient Carthaginians once lay slain, and declares *it was here   their bodies left naked under the sun* – somehow this is the pain of the ducks, the noble steadfastness of the ducks, silence suggesting concealed knowledge spanning decades and fictions. Only the ducks understand these chaotic countrysides. In their mute beaked faces lies secretive wisdom. Like why cows growl in the night. Like why Lisa fell upon the blade. The ducks remind David of Lisa. Economic angles, nothing superfluous. Her glazed eyes, animated by local light. Galaxies of maybes.

Think of The Father, wading into a T-bone like a death-row meal. The Father, fixated on spy novels. Weekends: *NFL on NBC*. The Father, a 49ers fan; alternately, a Packers fan. Given enough leeway and opportunity, one can submit to anything. Anything can intoxicate and paralyze. Think of The Father, mesmerized by flawed caulking.

The forest around him is a temple of quiet cruelty. Ruthless roots jutting through snow, danger in patches, trees conniving. The ducks, shivering snow from feathered hinds, gaze up at cyclopean David, identifying him as yet another lost fool.

By now she would likely be buried, cremated, a processed file.

'The ducks,' Muzz says. 'They don't migrate south.'

'But that's what birds *do*.'

'I know.'

'Snow and ice. It's winter.'

'I know. Strange forces are at work in these woods. There is this sort of … I don't think I'm really the best to explain it, but there are these transient, or contra-transient, voltaic forces here. It's all about this psychic-galvanic experience that Ike maintains – '

'Ike Hamdaber.'

Muzz laughs, his breath in wintry puffs. 'There are reasons why he set up here, in the middle of nothing. It's a bit of a long story.'

A duck jabs its beak at fissures in the pond's surface, the cracking ice.

'They look like they know something we don't.'

Muzz laughs again. 'That's because they do. And we don't.'

By the time they return the snowmobiles to the garage, evening has already slid into night. The farmhouse is buzzing with activity, the preparation of a feast. Dimmed lighting, candles burning. The stereo cranks ABBA. The kitchen wafts ovenly aromas; numerous bottles of wine are readied in the dining room. In the kitchen, David finds Samantha Voight decapitating carrots at the counter, disposing their leafy nobs in the compost.

'David,' she chirps. 'What did you make of the forest?'

'It's dense.'

'It certainly is. It certainly is.'

Samantha's ivory-handled cane is propped against the kitchen table. Ivory – like the handle of Patton's pistol. The handle of the cane is luminous, dimensional. David reaches and touches it for just a second, less.

Yes. Flawless. Pristine.

'We're planning a bit of a hoolie for tonight,' she says. 'We'll all convene and eat and … How are you in the kitchen?'

'Um … not exactly … I usually eat out.'

She nods, whisking eggs.

Later, David is in the bathroom. A magazine rack holds outdated weeklies, Ikea flyers, a few yellowed paperbacks. A spine: *TV Babylon*, by someone named Jeff Rovin. David plucks the book from the rack and turns it over in his hands. On its cover, pictures of seventies television stars: Suzanne Somers, Joan Collins, Farrah Fawcett. The book feels stiff and lifeless in his hands. He opens and randomly reads: *Mackenzie Phillips didn't turn to religion to help her though it probably wouldn't have helped anyway*. He sits on the cold toilet and thumbs through its trashy tales of seventies celebrity gossip, chronicles of sordid abuse and woeful fates, controversies and scandals. Dick Van Dyke hitting the sauce. Schneider and Wopat pulling rank on set. Sal Mineo stabbed. Rod Serling battling networks over script revisions. Sid Caesar, strung out, considering suicide. And on page 192 – *George C. Scott: 'Censored and Outraged.'* Scott, the broken-nosed thespian who became Patton in the face of battle, complaining publicly about battles with producers. Scott, decrying network censorship back in 1963; he had yet to assume the helmet and the binoculars. He is quoted: *those quivering masses waiting for my return can relax and those who hated my guts can relax*. Like the scripted testament of a four-star general dogged by repute. The rats feasting on ankles, in the trenches of Guadalcanal and Verdun and Kandagar. Imagine the gravelly voice, which curls words into bullhorned orders, much like David's guts now untwist, seated on the toilet.

Finding these words, tossed randomly to the zillions in this book idly left lying around, somehow helps assure him all is not lost. He barely walks on the earth. He barely breathes the air. He is a player in a drama, sucked inward and outward. He is a duckling waddling on the turf of Chaos. But he is not lost.

Somebody raps on the bathroom door. 'Hello? Is somebody in there?'

'Just a sec,' he calls.

'Are you okay?'

And David, as clearly and confidently as he can, despite everything, despite his dislocation and mistrust, despite all the pervasive weirdness, despite despite *despite*, his voice clanging in the tiled-floor bathroom, he says:

'Yes.'

The dining room table is adorned with an ornate crystal centrepiece, candles, daisies in vases. The table is tremendous.

And like June bugs circling patio lanterns, the denizens of Chaos converge around the table. They seat themselves with high moods, pleasantries, eagerness. Wine is poured. All carry the appearance of having just woken – they are bears emerging from hibernation. Every year, as winter secedes to spring and the earth sheds its paralytic freeze, they traverse security gates and the shield of woods, led by no inclination but the lure of getaway. They come with suitcases. They come with serious faces and composed dispositions. They arrive in cars.

From unseen speakers ABBA sings: *at Waterloo Napoleon did surrender oh yeah and I have met my destiny in quite a similar way the history book on the shelf is always repeating itself.*

All is cryptic. The angles are fuzzy.

The population has swollen to about ten or eleven. David remains scarce, hovering in the archway, feeling decidedly the outsider. For him, none of this is familiar. Muzz is seated, freshly showered and wearing what seems to be some sort of denim tuxedo. Bedel arrives and immediately switches the stereo to a John Cougar Mellencamp record. He passes David without acknowledgement.

Sarah Promise emerges from the main foyer, accompanied by a beefy man in a dark suit. This man: chubby-cheeked, blinking, bronze-ish – Hawaiian, perhaps. He is dawdling and bloated and unimpressive. But Sarah Promise is stunning. Her formless radiance has been filtered, her hair's disarray compacted, her face's shiftiness calmed. Her frame, draped in a sleek black dress, is repackaged with poise. By candlelight her bladed eyes glint, sunlight on spiderwebs, bright compressions.

In a fleeting assessment of the room, her eyes meet his. He attempts a cool gesture, a raised glass, but in her scope he is transparent, ignored. She assumes a place at the table, whispering something quick into her companion's ear.

Perhaps we will disappear into turgid masses, shadows flailing in societies, the assembled calamity.

Muzz notices him. 'David,' he calls, gesturing, 'park yourself.'

David assumes the seat next to him. Seated immediately opposite is a woman with long straight black hair and a blemished complexion, smoking a bidi cigarette. She stares brazenly; heat flushes into David's cheeks. He ventures a throat-clearing introduction, but before he can, Wyatt requests attention at the table's head. Everyone hushes. Someone kills the music.

'I'll do the official thing,' Wyatt says, 'and welcome all you wonderful people back to Chaos Farm.'

Muzz whoops.

'Tomorrow we'll prepare the farm for the upcoming *projets de la nuit*. We'll shake out the carpets, et cetera. Then the following day Ike will show up, and then the joyful work can begin. But tonight we make merry. Dessert – Samantha, correct me if I'm wrong – will be a choice of apple pan dowdy, polenta pudding with blackberry compote and mascarpone cream, or freshly made pumpkin pie. *Whew*. By jingo, let's eat.'

And in a whirlwind of dishes, an almost obscene abundance of food is spread before them: acres of bread, cilantro crab salad, roasted asparagus and steamed artichokes, scallops in saffron broth, stuffed portobellos, sautéed veal with roasted peppers and anchovy sauce, some sort of weird tortellini with brine-cured olives, a roast leg of lamb dripping thick juices, a mountain of sautéed broccoli rabe, trout grenoblois, Yorkshire pudding, steamed neep, Cornish hen in a honey-clove glaze, roasted yams and broiled salmon and a strange but delicious soup that, Samantha informs David, is made with Chilean ostrich.

'Ostrich,' David says, amazed. 'How do you have all this … pumpkins, in *winter*?'

Samantha smiles and places a basket of chipotle cornbread on the table. 'We get things shipped. Ike has connections in the industry.'

The *industry*. *Connections*. Ike Hamdaber. Ike, who owns whole valleys, devises secret societies in remote forests, wields limitless resources, imports ostrich for soup. Ike, who these people speak of with reverence. Ike, the messianic figurehead. Ike, the tycoon, the despot, the cleric. One begins to suspect that Ike Hamdaber might be a myth – his presence looms too large.

Chatter fills the room. David looks across the table to find the dark-haired woman greedily tearing into a leg of lamb. Her sauce-stained hands tear the meat to shreds in crude autopsy, jabbing bits into her grease-wet mouth, occasional wads of gristle falling onto her plate. All attention on the *meat*, the lamb and the veal and, to a lesser extent, the hen. David watches, boggled; others fail to notice, or respond to, her greedy assault.

Further down the table, Sarah Promise indifferently nibbles on a split of naan. The man at her side murmurs in her ear. She smiles and chews. Her presence remains distant. Unavailable. David senses an irrational pang of headache, or heartache. *No*, he tells himself, but it's too late. Jealousy. Threatened possession.

Sarah Promise's attentions are fickle trajectories, like the ring of a dead telephone. Like the reassurance of pressing a wound. Sarah Promise is definitely a source of pain. Steeply veering pain. Or not. Impossible to say. Her unavailability is her promise. Or the promise, the empty promise, is her availability. Think of love's choreography, of nakedness. David has known her Promise, albeit briefly. If you can swallow this as easily as you swallow olive-oiled parsley-flecked tortellini shells, then maybe you can survive in the heartless world with zero scruples. Write a Post-it note: *scruple-less*. You can stand as a man among men. You can be a shroud and a slave. You can salute and perform.

'This veal is a triumph,' the Hawaiian man declares. 'An unabashed triumph.'

'How about we crack open another bottle,' Sarah Promise suggests.

Quietly, David asks Muzz who the man is. His name, Muzz says, is Paul Hirota. Heir to a fair-sized stationery fortune. Chess grand-master, ranked thirty-third. A *real sharp character*, Muzz says.

The meat-eating woman discards a hunk of polished bones and moves on to a fresh piece of lamb. Her attentions are unflagging, possessed. She looks up and catches David staring. She extends a hand to be shaken. 'I'm Gwendolyn,' she says.

David takes her hand; it is moist and greasy.

'David,' he says.

Gwendolyn gazes into his eyes, then down at his hands. 'Are you at all knowledgeable in palmistry?'

'Uh, not … '

'Ever have a reading?'

'Never.'

'Uncharted territory,' she says. 'Enticing.'

'You should let her have a go at your mitts,' Muzz says.

'It's Samudrik Shastra science,' Gwendolyn says. 'The Ocean of Knowledge. The well runs deep. This moment, here, this is all just a speck on a meteor. You'll see. I'll do your hand lines.'

Her eyes reflect a whispering mania. 'Look here,' she says, taking his hand between hers. 'This line is the Girdle of Venus. As you can see, yours is fragmented but clear. I read this as indicating an oversensitivity. One tends to brood and overexamine. You transfer your doubts and fears onto something, or someone, else.'

David's palms are standard, unworked. The soft hands of a typist. He withdraws. 'No no no. That's not me.'

Muzz clanks a fork. 'Duders. Listen to Gwen. She knows what she's doing.'

But David keeps his palms in reserve. Caution must be maintained, especially in Chaos.

As the meal progresses, the atmosphere at the table becomes less a casual congregation and more an addled caucus. A man at the end of the table, whose presence David hadn't noted until now, honks his nose into a napkin. He has a stern crewcut and an athletic build, an audacious ridge of chest swelling from a wide-collared tennis shirt. David then becomes aware of his face: misshapen and strangely textured, as if having suffered serious burns. His eyes sag in pockets among rivulets of misshapen flesh and discolouration. David tries not to stare. Best not to pity the piteous.

Next to him is a woman with thick dark glasses and a squashed piggy nose. The two are engaged in low conversation. Both appear perturbed, or apprehensive.

Muzz catches David looking. 'Hector and Roslyn. They're from San Diego.'

David nods. 'That's a trek. To come all this way.'

'It's worth it. Wait and see. Shit will happen.'

Muzz: grinning, chewing.

He had imagined, perhaps foolishly, that he might claim Sarah Promise as his own. But as the evening collapses, wine overtaking order, decorum failing, it becomes less and less likely. Something connects Paul Hirota and Sarah Promise. While David sits alone and disconsolate on the living room couch, watching the candelabra melt into failing light and nursing the last of a million glasses of wine, he watches her exit on Hirota's fleshy arm, mumbling into his armpit, loping with a drunken lean.

She doesn't say goodnight.

David downs the remainder of his glass. His head swims.

Succumb to twilight whims, here in the plunge. Slumped amidst the ramshackle decor of Chaos, envision amber throws of light as the slain, icons as martyrs, sacrifices unmade. David is the vanquisher of marauding invaders, guardian of the defenceless, foe of ogres. Conductor of noble trumpets. Orchestras. Trumpets ricocheting over the Tunisian deserts and into the air, like the calls of prehistoric birds.

Bed. Shabby blankets. The descent.

David's dreams navigate canyons trenching neon landscapes, lightning-bolt shreds, ultraviolet shades. Stripes of yellow and purple columned in unreachable distance. Rigid and symmetrical, sizzling yet lifeless. Dream colours changing and threatening, hot cold hot, territories widening in the whizzing spectrum, ferocious in their unchecked energy, metastasizing in the emerging dreamsky. Boundless in the dreaming mind's eye, the sky burns white and unflecked, spreading like an enormous fan of feathers. Dream of the sky: the thing you reach for and can never hold. Yet even this purest purity invites tarnish – in stained greys and wounded reds, the sky begins to bleed, tainted like clear solution introduced to a toxic agent. An irrevocable corruption. The sky reinvents itself as a bluster of fire. Dream of a sky on fire. The stratosphere combusts as sacrifice to time misspent, forging grandeur from absence. In its flames are voices, faces: the faces of men, tired men wilting under pressure. Men sniffing nervously and yelling over the din of their own lethargy. Dream of men with heroic aspirations. Dream of the faces of exhausted fathers, their mouths flaming in history's wake, billowing over sons. Lie fearful in dreams.

David opens his eyes. Shudders resonate in his arms and legs, then subside. Sleep proves difficult, but eventually it comes.

Outside, in a starless night, the cows begin to moo.

It would be better to forget. But he can't, not completely. The bleep of messages. Mail, Visa bills screaming threats. Debt. His credit cards are maxed and stressed. They send notices. The notices remain unopened, like critical questions withheld.

Ask David. Gary, seated in his glorious house's main foyer, violently running weathered hands through his thinning scalp.

Hector and Roslyn of San Diego tend to the Farm's livestock, collecting eggs, milking the cows, scheduling feedings. But David has noticed little regularity to these chores. The Farm operates with little obvious order or structure.

He stands in the barn, watching as Roslyn pats the cows and rustles their hay beds. She tells David that it often seems that Chaos Farm is less a farm than a zoo. She winks. This wink is disconcerting.

The future is in frames. Patton growled *this individuality thing is a load of crap*. At Chaos Farm there is so much idiosyncrasy and free self-determination that individuality becomes a moot invention. Everybody is equally lacking, all lost and found.

In the morning, David switched on his Braun electric nose-hair trimmer and green sparks flew from its vibrating blade. There are untamable energies in these countrysides. Things happen. Days at Chaos Farm flow in segments, morning afternoon night. Rise to unbridled sun, sleep under chaperone of controlled luminescence.

The Farm's coop is jam-packed with chickens and cows, but the eggs he ate for breakfast came from a carton, and his coffee was artificially whitened. Gwendolyn mentions that Ike has an aversion to unpasteurized dairy and any foodstuffs without some sort of seal of approval.

Ike Ike Ike. His name is spoken with reverence. They say Ike will arrive tomorrow. Ike, a name like reassurance, like the secret mangle under Chaos Farm's bloody bandage.

His eye is beginning to feel weird.

Over spaghettini and cognac in the farmhouse's solarium, Muzz explains the circumstances leading to his own arrival at Chaos Farm.

'I was impetuous as a young guy. I was a real Christer. I guess it's just a side effect of having big ambitions. I had big plans for my life. Like, here's my shot, this one gleaming available hunk of time, this life, so what's it going to be? I wanted glory, or fame, or whatever. Impossible heights. But this self-scrutiny and introspection led only to a sort of hyper-awareness of myself, and a propensity for self-destruction. You know?'

'Sure.'

'In Portland I was working as night watchman at the Forestry Museum, which was an insane drag, dusting off the fake raccoons and shit. But there's where I first met Lyle. Lyle. *Man.* When it comes to Lyle I can't even. Lyle comped me my first fix, then sold me my second. Lyle was a mandolin player for this weird bluegrass band around town, they sort of had this little community that would follow them from show to show ... he was the most amazing charismatic handsome guy. If I've ever, like ... if there was a man I could, you know, *love*, it was I guess it was Lyle ... '

Muzz's eyes glaze over. He begins to sing a wistful minor-key melody: '*My name's just a murmur on the breeze   our souls only transparencies   nothing binds a heart to which it heeds   nothing steels a scythe to its misdeeds ... *'

Pause. Sigh.

'That's from a song Lyle wrote, called "My Life Is a Shambles." I'm not completely sure what it is he's getting at exactly, but I think it's the most beautiful song I've ever heard. He never got it down on tape properly. Fucking shame. I guess the way Lyle intended the song was too ambiguous or heavy or delicate to get right, somehow. Lyle had an amazing voice. It was this bellowing wonder.'

Muzz shakes his head.

'Anyway, Lyle got me into the thing, the drugs, and once I'd peeked into that abyss I was gone. Just a taste of that hell was all I needed. We sat in his apartment listening to old Ike and Tina records and shot up day and night. I was the skinniest stinkiest piece of crud imaginable, but in my heart I felt – I genuinely felt this – that I was somehow accomplishing something. I don't know. I try to remember what my motivations were then, because I want to understand what exactly I was thinking. But whatever it was, it's lost now. I remember throwing a mailbox through a jewellery-store window. I poked my arm right through the shards of glass – my hands had these cuts these awful slices – I reached in and yanked out a bunch of necklaces and bracelets. That image stuck with me for years: reaching through blades of glass and coming up with a fistful of gold. Of course, an hour later I was hawking that gold, but somehow that memory has achieved a sort of sturdiness in my mind. It's like diving into a tidal wave and ... I don't know. But it sticks with you, you know?'

David nods. Fistfuls of gold.

'Eventually things got so bad that I developed these massive infected cysts on my arms. They grew and got horrible. Then the abscesses started to itch really badly and actually developed a kind of stench. My skin was rotting off my bones. Not so cool. One night it got really bad. I thought I was going blind, I was so destroyed. When I went to the emergency room they tried to put me away in some institution or something. I can hardly blame them, I was in hysterics and singing "Surfin' Bird" at the top of my lungs. You know that *bird bird bird bird is the word* stuff, that's prime material when you're freaking out that hard. Man oh man. I was so paranoid I escaped from the hospital. It was raining, I remember. Raining that hard West Coast rain, it's this rain coming down in this barrage, like this complete hopeless rain. That night it was unreal. In seconds my shirt was soaked to my skin. So here I am, at the end of my rope, lost and sick and scared and wet. My arms hacked to shit.

'I guess I fell into the street, because next I know this taxi driver – he was Haitian or something, he was very very small – is helping me up out of a puddle and into the back seat of his cab. This driver, this small small man, he sticks with me now. His face was shiny and sort of rectangle-shaped. I fell in the back of that cab and puked. And my little driver friend, my mini rescuer, he didn't complain. For some reason this little rectangular angel took pity. He asked me where I needed to go, and, somehow, through the froth and drool and puke, I guess I must have given him Lyle's address. It was a Wednesday – I know that because every fourth Wednesday Lyle received some sort of compensation cheque, some sort of allowance related to his father. His father had been an ambassador or diplomat or something; he had been driving his just-off-the-lot Mercedes and was hit by a driver for Purolator or FedEx or one of the courier companies and father and car had been completely obliterated. Lyle got these monthly cheques from the settlement every fourth Wednesday, so Wednesday meant money, and money meant supplies.

'My little West Indian or Haitian saviour must have brought me to Lyle's while I lay in the back throwing up over and over and over, because the next thing I recall was sitting on the couch in Lyle's room, hours later. And what happened was, well, not to get too grisly about it all, but Lyle died that night. He OD'd. He bought outside our sources and ended up with bad shit, cut with strychnine or something. Lucky for me, I was at the hospital while Lyle … Lyle just wanted to stay high forever, why wouldn't he? He never found a way of expressing his sadness on a scale that befit its depth. I came home to carpet stains and an empty apartment, and when I tried to sleep the next night on the pull-out in his apartment, there was an absence that was like love. Lovesickness is a variable thing. The way it kills without obvious symptoms. But, okay. I sat in the apartment for the whole afternoon, smoking cigarettes in my bare feet. I rubbed my bare feet on the dingy carpet of his life. He died alone in cardiac arrest. I loved that motherfuck. Despite how thoughtlessly he used me, or I used him, there was love there. And still, I rummaged through his drawers and rifled through everything, the cupboards and mess, to see if any of that Wednesday skag was left behind. This is how I desecrated.'

Muzz: blunt, pained. He is trying. He picks at his pasta. He is elsewhere, remembering, retrieving.

'The next day I was rebuilt. The thing that was *me* … the situation or portion of the overall that was me, this thing was refreshed and … changed. Irreversibly. I woke up and wanted to spit hellfire. I was so prepared to just *defy*. Physically, I felt exhausted. There was this searing agony in my upper back and neck, this poisoned inflexibility. My point is that I was at a loss. You know what I mean.'

David: 'Yes.'

'After that I coasted. Three years of hopping trains, hitching, couch-surfing. I was pretty disillusioned and fucked up.'

Folding and refolding his legs.

'How did you find about Chaos Farm?' David asks Muzz.

'It was a combination of things,' Muzz says after consideration. 'But if I boil it down … I first heard about it at a Husky in southern Alberta. It was the middle of the night and insane outside, the wind was like something biblical, so to escape I holed up in this truck stop. My layover in Spokane had turned into a week in Kamloops. I was heading east and trying to get as quickly – My head was unclear. I was distraught. These were not good times. But where was I … '

'The Husky,' David reminds.

'Right. So I'm slouched over something, eggs, when this person sits down. This older guy with a sort of leathery drinker's face: *plomp*. He sits down at the table across from me. The guy was pretty filthy. Sort of garbagey-smelling. He had that look of being into some kind of long-term badness. Eyes struggling to adjust, black teeth, you know. I think he might have been huffing, or just so drunk for so long he finally lost his shit. His hands were stained this weird copper colour. He just sat there staring at me. I couldn't tell whether he was going to try and roll me or what. But I was ravenous, so I just said hi and kept on with my breakfast. Eventually he starts pulling out these little crumpled slips of paper, five or six little papers in his shirt pocket, all dirty and frayed. He fanned them out on the table and started trying to explain something, but it was just *glaah glaah glah*. More like gurgles than words. I could barely understand. He kept shaking his head and laughing, or crying, or both. He was showing me these papers, especially this one that turned out to be a crumpled picture of a young girl. He was trying to explain about a car crash or something, that this girl, whoever she was, had maybe been in a car crash. It was impossible to understand. He kept gobbledygooking something over and over that I think was *paralyzed*, but it might have been *paradise*. He was incoherent. The picture was this coiffed little girl, a classic cutie in a pink sweater and a barrette. The guy said *dringin and drifin izza sin   itza sin*. My translation was *drinking and driving is a sin*. I thought maybe he was the guilty driver. Maybe. Or the father of. Who could tell. When this thing had happened, or whether it did at all, was open to speculation. He was that fucked up. I couldn't unscramble the transmission. But I caught his drift, in a general sense. The stink he gave off was the stink of remorse, that was understood. He was at the end of his rope, and I knew how he felt. We sat in the booth while I sopped up the rest of my breakfast, and all the while that sad little picture lay there on the table, all wrinkled and worn. Next to it he'd dropped another scrap which caught my eye. The man kept gurgling as I checked it out.'

He's remembering.

'It was a folded note paper with a diagram. The same diagram … You must have seen it, over by the front door.'

David: 'The swirly thing.'

'Yep. It was a copy of Lorenz's model. The chaotic system. Not like I knew that then.'

Muzz gazes out the window at the meadow beyond. He scopes out the separated land like it has answers, solutions to his woe. David decides that Muzz is different. He's one of the good. And yet, despite his ease and cool grace, his kind eyes betray a trace of distance, a trace of longing still for those dark times. Lack of resolution.

'Self-pity is a miserable state,' Muzz says. 'It's the opposite of living. Self-pity is hiding from hard truth you already know. On the other side of the diagram was a phone number. I swiped it without the guy noticing. In retrospect I probably shouldn't have been so hasty. I should have bought him a sandwich. But I wasn't so clear-headed at the time.

'Anyhoo. Long story short, I eventually called that number and got Samantha, and she contacted Ike, and Ike brought me. Without even knowing me, he footed the bill for me to fly east to Chaos Farm. He saw the need. He saved my life. Things have been pretty steady since. I come here every year for a few months. When I'm not here I'm on tour. I'm working with a theatre troupe in Brewer on a musical play about the life of Errol Flynn. He was Lyle's idol, so I like to think of it as a bit of a tribute. I work in Florida, supervising orange-pickers. Guatemalans. I log hours and crack whips. Figurative whips, that is. Couple times a year I'm in Maui surfing. When there are waves. I keep hopes. I subsist.'

Outside: snow-blanketed meadows, outward-sprawling landscape, the glittering bay. Broad-winged birds tear across Chaos's scope.

Eagles, maybe.

Muzz finishes his plate, slurping down the last forkful. He leans back in his chair and drinks down his glass with satisfaction. Outside, unassuming snow starts to fall, wafts on light currents, drifts downward like plummeting statistics. Clots of moisture gather on the sill.

'Nice,' Muzz says.

Perhaps we will perish in pitiless retread of the past, reliving the abortion of our individual paths, dying in repetition. Perhaps the end of the world has already happened, thousands of times, and the ground on which we walk is simply debris from catastrophe.

Fifteen, sixteen, maybe. Dark pubescence, epoch of oily youth. Era of pimples and perspiration. One of a thousand nights, late autumn, wandering among spectral suburbs. Boys and, importantly, girls. But *tonight*: you discover a breach in the fence encircling the wooded reservoir near your school. Usually bone dry, tonight it gushes with athletic waters. Protected by cover of night, nothing confines you. The ground is damp, sloping down into a gloomy mire. There is excitement. There are cigarettes, giggles, hands crammed in pockets, hash balled into turdish pebbles. Focus: the girl for whom you privately pine. Take pains to maintain balance. Restrain. Measure words. Do not shake fists at unseen enemies. The air is brisk; nothing exists but joyful temporary adultlessness. She sits by your side, by the reservoir's strange piping dotted with slimy leaf-gatherings, as you share the last bottle of Ten Penny. The park surrounds, nocturnal and alive. Headlights flicker at the reservoir's opposite end, staccato blips, far and segmented. And there is contact, a difficult meeting of mouths. A moment forever preserved; no one ages, no one fades. A smush of faces. Let the moon above be the photo flash that captures your inelegance for endless replay. And later: you lope home through winding crescents and courts, touring this neighbourhood as a conqueror.

But every victory has its cost: returning home you find lights burning. Despairingly, you head downstairs to the den, finding – *of course* – The Father, bent over before the TV, ass waggling in air. Ghostly static fills the screen. The Father is trying to program the new VCR, its workings requiring manual tuning to each VHF and UHF band by tiny finger-punishing dials. And The Father is very drunk; it is, after all, Friday, Fridays ritually being his heaviest drinking nights, a punishing orgy of beers at home and later at the Copper Penny. The Father looks up from the old Hitachi machine and notices you witnessing his struggle. He coughs nervously and swigs from a nearby can. He instructs you to *come here and help   don't just sit*. You approach. The Father gapes, his eyes like manholes. He focuses on something within you which only he sees. You seat yourself on the floor beside him and try to redeem the mess he's made, the coaxial cables and manuals and remotes. The Father says *stupid not co-operating no co-operation*. He rubs his moustache and says *never buy Japanese*. You say *jeesh Dad   you reek*. This is how your night dwindles: simple triumph erased in The Father's mumbles, listening to him burp and cough until he says something about you raking leaves in the morning before stumbling upstairs to pass out on the couch. The Father as agent of the unimpressive, lackey to self-condemnation. The Father as a colossal drag. The Father as disappointment.

Muzz: *here's my shot   this one gleaming available hunk of time   this life   so what's it going to be.*

David is living in the past. The future seems so far away.

There is so much room at Chaos Farm, and yet no unwilling share of space. Hallways, terraces, limitless nooks and alcoves, basement chambers; the farmhouse and its orbiting sheds and cottages all comprise a labyrinthine inward webwork of dwelling where one can easily get lost. Wander the halls. Laze on cheap furniture. Gaze upon unspoiled textures.

David wanders out to the barn where Roslyn is milking the cows, Scylla and Astrophil. Gazing into the forlorn brown suns of Astrophil's eyes, he is overcome with dread. The cows are not optimistic. They know their odds are stacked.

Roslyn asks if he'd like to try his hand at an udder. *No thanks*, he obliges, wiping snow from his sleeves.

Hanging in the stables, above the cows in their stalls, an enormous sign made of oak is bolted to the wall. In blocky letters burnt into the wood, it reads: HUMILITY BEFORE THE SLAUGHTER.

There are hints of connections, intertextual connections, here. Discovery seems possible and near.

In the kitchen David finds Gwendolyn, a huge shank of beef set before her. She sits tearing at flesh with her hands, inspecting it, nibbling, discarding pieces. She tears it to ribbons with an approach equally hideous and erotic.

'Still snowing,' he says.

She looks up, dazed, barely registering. Pinkish juice on her chin. The room, bloated with saucy smells.

'Yuh,' she grunts.

She wears appetite like wounds, like damage. Her eyes are tired in their sockets, her greedy lips sorrowful. David thinks of what to say, what gesture befits, but comes up empty.

Once, David had been ambling through crowded sidewalks, heading downtown for sushi, his Wednesday routine, when, passing the Oxford Theatre on Quinpool, he'd spotted Lisa among a throng of girls. A glimpse: her face beaming under the marquee's intemperate light, cast upward in a laugh, joyful. His heart galloped. He tried to pass undetected, but she stepped into his path and snared him. *David.* They had talked chit-chattedly, and he had mentioned his destination. Maybe, she'd suggested, he'd want someone to tag along. Her eyes had radiated delight; her hair was bundled back in a careless ponytail, allowing her neck to emerge emboldened. When was this – last year, before things became so perplexing. Lisa had clutched his arm tightly as they walked, leaving her friends behind. Even through his windbreaker her touch had been generous. She was so young, so sad – only now can he fathom how sad. Surrounded by the crush of friends and the allures of popcorn and burgers. Lisa in her haste. No one knew.

Lisa, breathing druggy breath into the phone: *we're basking in the sun   it's like a carousel   spinning.*

But he still doesn't understand.

When I was a kid   when we used to go on trips   Disney World the year Epcot Center opened   Orlando   whenever we'd take a plane   we'd be at the gate   waiting   I'm nervous   flying sickness Mom prying open a pack of Gravol   Dad   he'd have to be first in line   the second our seat was announced   yanking us by our sleeves stupidly irrationally   possessed   first in line   and after landing the second the seat belt light went out   shoving his way   pressing forward   first in the aisle   no matter what. David, here, now, thinks: *how could this make any sense   slaving   to achieve what   at the front of every line just to wait around longer   pointless   hurrying to prove what   why.*

The compulsions of the mind. Hangings. Swords. Queues. Rewinding tape. Fear. The sun behind Epcot's Geosphere burned like a tortured mind.

Two casualties, Lisa and The Father. *He was a bleak dude,* she said. Bleak – the battle is fought in mailboxes, in parking lots, in ATMs, in dim recollections of failure. Casualties clipped from the day's paper and magneted to the refrigerator. Missed climaxes. They were those left unnominated, undecorated. Some American revolutionary – *who?* – professed regret that he had but one life to give for his country. George C. Scott as General George S. Patton, Jr., had gazed upon smouldering ruins where fresh young recruits had fought brutally for hours in a territorially inconsequential bloodbath, and, against celluloid and chronology and edit, had confessed: *I love it   God help me I love it   I love it more than my life.*

Perhaps this is how The Father and Lisa now dance together somewhere in an uncomfortable embrace, like unfamiliar relatives squished together at a wedding for the amusement of cooing aunts. This is their shared lot. Perhaps they exist only as casualties, the cherished fallen, dying for their survivors' expectations of grandeur. Like Lyle dying for Muzz. Suppose there is a reason, a higher whatever, brokering deals.

No. *Fuck that.* David rejects this. The ducks would disagree with a ruffle of feathers. Fuck it. All of it. Lisa and The Father aren't together. Not the grumpy old man, not with her. They don't step aside, just to make way for David's slogging pace.

Things aren't that way.

The battle isn't over.

Snow swirls into the evening.

Adjacent to the living room's stone fireplace is the television, a technological behemoth of broadband receiver and fifty-inch plasma screen, nauseating woofers and iridescent tweeters. It is a beaming testament to the marvels of fidelity and resolution. Peer into its depths. Behold the universe unfolding, the speakers growling like cosmic rotors. Images more real than real. An internal decoder nabs chunked data eddying in the ether, taming it and reshuffling it into infinite entertainments.

They are gathered around a weather report. Ike is flying in tomorrow from Morocco, and there are concerns over unfavourable conditions. On the screen graphics depict a low-pressure system rolling over the coast, a rotating white blotch, its tendrils like the swirling Lorenz Model: Chaos curled, graphed but random, inward-seeking. High winds and flurries tearing north. An infinity of topography buried in stormy fractals.

Bedel mans the remote, punching buttons, scrolling through menus. Muzz lies on the floor, focused on a photo book titled *Outhouses of Appalachia*. Joints are passed around the room and glasses are filled from a hefty bottle of Krug. David sits seated on the couch, sipping from a Minute Maid juice box. Next to him, Samantha sketches with a nub of graphite. Her hands work feverishly. David sneaks a glance at her drawing; it's a rough and shadowy rendering of a circle of seated figures, men and women around a strange box, from which smoke and something vaguely humanoid rise.

Her figures are faceless.

The TV erupts with commercials. Jingles bellow. Gulping faces, animated smileys, tidal waves of moisturizers, trucks like rhinos conquering hills. Suns novaing into logos, heralding better somehows.

David's mind rolls through its own channels, its own retrieval of files, his confused resignation. He is losing full recall of where he's come from, what he's done. His eye feels strange. This morning he'd peeled back the patch to discover new soreness in its folds, the skin an upsetting pink that revolted under his touch. He worries about infection. Irreparable damage.

He wonders where Sarah Promise has gone: retreating to her room, to the basement, to the opulent vacuum of these weightless rooms. To Hirota's cottage and his flabby arms. He doesn't want to want her. And yet this sheer want has dug itself into his thoughts. This pain rivals the throb of his eye. Its undirected pain. Anxieties, compounding.

Channels flutter by.

'You're going too fast,' Muzz complains.

In distracted reflection, David jolts from his reverie when the TV suddenly flashes an instantly recognizable image. He orders Bedel to stop flicking.

It's the chin, the eyes, the thrusted chest. A salute. Moroccan soldiers, sporting proud and noble colours, on parade. Drums pounding. Kaleidoscopic batons twirling. Elephants. Scott as Patton, his pallor grey yet erupting with cinematic glory.

Muzz: 'What is this?'

David sits upright, his thoughts clearing. *Yes.* Broad shoulders. The unerring precision of his vision. The General: the light, the defender. Like a kernel of order in Chaos, reminding him of nights at home, buried in sofa and beer, against snow.

'I've seen this,' Bedel says. 'It's about World War Two, it's that one with the guy standing in front of the flag. The George Patton movie.'

'Yes,' David peeps.

TV-Patton says *it's a combination of the Bible and Hollywood.*

Bedel scoffs. 'This is such dreck. This whole glorification. Please. I laugh at this shit movie.'

'You don't like it,' David says.

'I *despise* it. Making murder into hee-haw hilarity, trying to pretend that war is some kind of … test of mettle. It's propaganda.'

'It's not propaganda,' David says.

Bedel stares angrily at David. A strange prolonged moment passes, then he shakes his head. 'Who *are* you? Nobody wants you around. Why don't you just go the hell home?'

David stares at his hands.

Look at him, staring at his hands.

There is a collective decision to go cross-country skiing. Wyatt and Bedel and Muzz and Gwendolyn and Hector and Roslyn don enormous snowsuits and barge outside, clapping mittens, rustling Gore-Tex. Samantha tells David she would love to frolic in the snow but is prevented by her leg.

Sarah Promise emerges from the hallway, her eyes glassy and her face flushed. She passes through the living room and sits on the couch next to David. General Bradley points to a map of Italy, explaining the army's impending movement. Sicily is a scuffed boot, the entry point. Sarah lights a cigarette. David sucks up the last dribbles from his juice box.

Paul Hirota waits by the door. His thick face does not beam with the others' glee; he glares knives across the room at David, who tries to remain fixed on the screen. Hirota: unfriendly, pudgy, potentially dangerous. A small diamond stud in his left earlobe. A sinister goatee.

'I'm heading,' he announces.

'Fine,' Sarah Promise says, looking at David.

'You coming?'

She flicks an ash. 'I want to see who wins this war.'

Pause. Hirota storms out.

Perhaps we will shrivel into nothingness by scorn and wrath. Perhaps we will implode in the throes of our self-immolation. Perhaps woe will sculpt the shape of our deaths.

Patton in the snow, leading the troops in a hellbent surge toward Berlin.

'You want to get high?' Sarah Promise asks him.

'Um. Maybe ... '

'I'll be back.'

While she hurries away, David concentrates on the movie. It plays, reveals, reminds. You attach meanings to its flow, redesigning its scenes as guideposts; you decipher its plot and character and stitch them into your being, the current of your days. Movie as support system. Movie as suicide note.

Sarah Promise returns. She kneels and places a small jewellery case on the floor, along with a small leather bag. Out of the bag comes an object, a pipe-ish stomach-like thing – David is taken aback. It is identical to the thing Lisa had in her bedroom, glowing with the same internal radiation, wormy life stirring in its bowl.

'I've seen one of those before.'

Sarah Promise opens the jewellery box to retrieve a vial of a beigeish powder, a folded sheet of tinfoil and a small ladle. She scoops up a sizeable portion of the powder into the ladle and plops it onto the sheet, then heats it from underneath. The powder begins to dissipate and liquefy.

'Paul's not a warm individual,' she says. 'He's a vicious person. He owns a huge paper and packaging conglomerate – he's a very wealthy individual. And because of it he's gained enemies. He's ruthless. I've seen people literally tremble in his presence. His world is private jets with black guys in white military uniforms greeting you in countries you've never heard of. I think the reason he loves me so much is that I don't fear him. That's not to say that *you* shouldn't fear him. You probably should. But there's a link between Paul and me that's beyond fear. I feel I've loved him my whole life, even before I knew him. But at the same time I loathe him. Ours is a love that goes beyond. It's a seeking thing, like … like a parasite in some bloodstream, like this bloodstream is some-how the world and this love is like a parasite in it, and we're just two simple … um, molecules … '

The concoction readied, she crams it into the squiddy stomach and takes a hit. She exhales; her eyelids flutter rapidly. Heavy fumes crawl upward. She prepares another hit and places it in David's hands. Its weight jiggles with dark life, hungry for toxic release.

Lisa's face would clench, wresting smoke from the alien lung. Her shoulders would heave.

David places his mouth around the tube. Sarah Promise applies flame, and he engages its pressure. *Pow*: the brain buckles. The drug blazes in David's eyes, his ears, in the cords of his neck. Lightness overtakes.

He feels undefeatable; he feels dead.

The two lounge against the couch. They face one another. They are close, the distance between indeterminate. Inches. Football fields. Universes. He breathes; she leans forward, closes her eyes and lets residual smoky plumes kiss her pale face.

'David,' she says, 'have you ever been in love?'

A multitude of replies scroll through his mind. *Love*. Certainly he has felt love, or at least lovesickness. Love has been approached, mulled over, investigated. Love has wormed through the tubes of fluorescent lights overhead and dangled precariously; love has commanded elevators and heated up leftovers. Love has scarred and branded. He has fretted over love. He has steered through its dank chambers. But to say that he has been *in* love – he hesitates.

Instead. He finds himself telling a story, his words slow via addled facilities. A story about Barcelona. A story about remorse. How he had to *put some distance*. He talks of the mysteries of the nocturnal city, of hurrying in the midst of beautiful Spanish women. And he tells of a chance meeting at a café. She had identified his accent or recognized the book he was reading or some detail that brought them together. Soon they were walking. The woman was stunning; David was enchanted. This is his story. He describes to Sarah Promise their time together, he and the woman: strolling through the park under evening's reclining sun, dining late at night tucked away in the back of a candlelit restaurant, a kiss stolen under an awning while waiting out a sunshower. Her small but quaint apartment, rented from a kind old woman who spoke no English but served him soup as he waited for his darling to dress for their evening out. They are dancing in a nightclub, clinking glasses, whispering in museums with linked arms, watching boats laze across the afternoon horizon. He is winding a tress of her long dark hair between his fingers, letting the strands slip absently from his grasp to her delicate bared shoulder. Her eyes were brown and her body was petite and her laughter was the gleeful song of a giddy bird. David says *she was everything I ever dreamt of   but in the end I knew it wasn't going to last*.

These words creep from his mouth like sickly sweet syrup. It's a tragic gush.

And, of course, it's all lies. The whole thing. Bullshit.

David continues to recount details of his fictional love, how growing tensions with his mother drove him back home, and how his lover wept. A promise never to forget, her refusal to take an address or number: by such access she would always be tempted and rueful. An embrace, and on their last night together, making love until daybreak, chickadees in trees cooing tunes of ill-fated love. Love and loss.

If he had a word for this lie, the word would be *feckless*. As in feeble, pointless. Post-it this and slap it somewhere. This would be marginalia, texty sectors. Search references, explore semantic gymnastics, as days waft away. Picture David, son of routine, at his desk, gazing beyond monitor and photocopier and the blunt futility of work, down into the city. The city below is a punchline without set-up. From this lofty perch, its dimensions are measured in blocks and tosses, skylines. Sink further into its bowels, into alleys and crevices. Deeper: spans in stains, plastic flapping on breezes, mounds of discarded butts. Deeper: granules of disappointment, flecks of blood, ants, vermin. Deeper still: subatomic. Depth burns in re-entry, measurement becomes moot, impossible; the more precise the blade, the narrower the cuts.

Through a mouthful of shrimp, Darren had deemed it futile to claim actual measurement of pretty much anything. He said: as posed by some physicist in the question 'How Long Is the Coastline of Britain?' the coastline served as a model for infinity, the relative universe. I.e., if you measure by one scale, one yardstick, you come to a numerical conclusion; but decrease the unit by which you measure – metre, centimetre, millimetre – and your result will vary, gathering decimals with each boost in resolution. Accuracy can be magnified to the infinite, and the coastline, with its erratic measure, is therefore ungraphable. *Infinity like beauty is subjective*, Darren had proclaimed, smacking satisfied lips. And in David's mind Barcelona was consumed in flames. Let the city burn.

Everyone lies. David lies. Charades and inventions and ruses. Fallacious work hours. Apocryphal loves. With Sarah Promise, he attempts to communicate. But transmission falters, goes garbled. Impossible. *Feckless.*

Sarah Promise buries her head in his chest, arms holding him tightly. This – this is nothing like love. Not even falsified love.

'Memory has its price,' she says.

Her hand encircles his wrist and squeezes.

To think such a tangle of limbs and parts could be so – *galactic*. Kingdoms have risen and crumpled by lusty weight. Lives of conquest. Warfare merely this: application of pressure and measure of rhythm, offering and taking. Grasping at regions of flesh. Narrowing. Dropping drawers. Making moves.

Sarah Promise shrieks instructions that sound almost angry.

But she will not be his to keep. She rises from the bed, her unclothed body silhouetted by a window's bleed – night skies clear over Chaos – and begins to dress. David asks *where*. She says she has to. But where. Why go. Stay here. With me.

Sarah I want you to stay.

At bed's foot, with folded arms parcelling her bare breasts, she reaches and lightly touches his eyepatch. David grimaces. Her hand retracts.

Sarah Promise parts her lips and speaks hushed sounds, but what David hears is the sound of holocaust. Sarah Promise speaks the unsaid. A subsonic roar, a grinding sound, wind hysterical: *David defiler against you the dead will rise caverns will close but I have appraised your lands and deemed you the undead.*

Her voice crackles and detonates. Cannons. The collapse of rainbows. A sudden cleavage, flesh blistering, a final *thud*. Sarah Promise's eyes widen, then shut.

Goodnight: the call of war.

Tonight Sarah Promise sleeps with Paul Hirota, her true false love, while David lies alone. He will dream of smouldering battlefields, ammunition, expense of lives. Battles will rage in sleep's gritted cavities. Skulls will be split. *Against you the dead will rise.* There will be mayhem and carnage. Tonight and forever.

Morning spreads huge over the countryside, its arena peppered with dusty cloud streaks, ridges of whiteness smudged into blue. Birds wing figures, dipping and soaring without apprehension. New grass pokes through the lawn's encompassing white glaze. The air smacks of rebirth, renewal.

David sits in the solarium, propping his feet up on an ottoman, spine reclined, gulping blender-fresh carrot juice as he finishes a chapter in *TV Babylon* covering Robert Blake's woeful career. Between garish purple covers, the book offers various testaments to television's vicious industry, its anecdotal hypothesis that even the most hardy of souls shall be tainted by the lures of profit and fame. They booze, they carouse, they whine, they fail. Cameras roll and click.

Tony Randall is the perfect example of a TV star who manages to stay on the pleasanter side of the fine line between being a pompous eccentric and being a bastard.

Today he is up before everyone. He thumbs down a page's corner and closes the book. A tingle of warmth and comfort ripples through his joints. He cracks his knuckles. He feels good.

Here. This morning.

Visits to the duck pond have become David's personal regimen, replacing the sweating and stacking and steaming of the gym's discipline by chugging via Yamaha down through foresty paths, into their midst. By the pond, the ducks express agitation. They ruffle wings, quack perturbed quacks, dart frenetically between positions, gathering and disuniting, assembling and splintering. The ducks peer at the frozen pond beneath their webby feet. They shudder with something resembling dismay.

How helpless, ruled so severely by the elements, waiting helplessly for spring to shatter the thaw. Like the anonymous eel of workers filing through the pedways into offices, off to lunch, off to minivans, off to portioned lives. Think of Jim, inspecting catered hot plates at the client hospitality Super Bowl buffet, sniffing at halibut brochettes. Jim, praising the actor Antonio Banderas. Jim, memorizing a clipboarded pitch. Jim remarking *I never met a woman who didn't titter with a little prodding.* Many times David – in sustained moments of loathing for his co-workers – had imagined them as some insectile colony toiling together as a factory manufacturing futility. All drones, with David the lowliest among them. Work: foray of the subjugated, the tarry crude of imagination's dearth. David: another envoy of the slow sucking parasitism of proliferation, the packaging of contemptible informations. This was a life, this *is* a life, someone leads. A life of steady rigours. A life of plopping ass on cushioned seats, adjusting weights, grasping handlebars, drawing handles to chest. Repeat. Inhale exhale, release. Regrasp. Exert. Run distanceless races.

This is a life David can no longer lead. And with day's gradual rise out of its vague gradient smear, with crows on the lawn cawing with riveted beaks, he steels himself for the coming day. He has to regain control, and stand firm against what may happen. Because these are chaotic times.

An uproar is stirring. Wyatt and Samantha, still bathrobed, are buzzing intercoms and rapping on doors, raising a general ruckus. Bedel frantically tidies while Gwendolyn mans the kitchen, baking challah and folding omelettes. Muzz, in unshaven disarray, tries to straighten the living room into presentability. Even Paul Hirota, disinclined toward early rising, nonetheless participates.

Wyatt informs David that Ike Hamdaber is about to arrive, even now passing through the security gate.

There is excitement in preparation. All come together, gathering their weird community, but David – he is not truly a member. He is on the periphery, unincorporated, an outsider among expatriates. He heads to the kitchen and rinses out his glass, considers coffee.

'I hope Ike doesn't mind the breakfasty smell,' Samantha says.

Gwendolyn appears with dishtowel in hand. 'He won't mind. He told that story about the grease and the bacon-frying, and how much he loved it as a boy.'

They congregate around the main entrance, wound tight with expectation. There is the rumble of a car pulling up, then – *bak* – a door-slam, another following, and approaching steps.

Perhaps we will exhaust ourselves, striving and failing. We will reach and miss. We will bury our forebears only to live shadowed in imaginary lives, lives devoid of purpose. Swooping ends, death murmurs. Perhaps the mirth of these times is only a ruse devised by some misguided maker, an *un*-maker, a malevolent breed of architect through whom we imperil ourselves to expiry.

The door opens with fire. An abrupt conflagration floods the foyer, sending David reeling. An enormous presence crosses the threshold in a blazing aura of spiky purple and gold, a fractured inferno of colour, spewing shards of light. It gestures, saluting those awaiting its arrival. It is the influx of the future, the past, the wreckage and the ruin and the waste of all.

David's heart jackhammers in his ears; he suppresses a cry.

From near the epicentre of this whirlwind, a voice: '*Terrific.*'

A tall thin man and a young woman stride through the doorway, hauling matching blue leather suitcases. Plumes of smoke rise with every step.

Enter Ike Hamdaber, companion close behind.

David glances around. No one else seems disconcerted by the flames. *No one else sees.*

Wyatt approaches and offers Ike a hand. 'How was your trip?'

'Tedious,' Ike says, giving Wyatt a solid shake. 'It was long and boring and I threw up.'

Muzz: 'Yikes.'

Ike waves a dismissive hand. 'It's over now. Back on *terra firma*. The soil of my heart, Chaos Farm oh Chaos Farm. Is that bacon I smell?'

Despite the awed and enigmatic descriptions, Ike Hamdaber is hardly the grizzled guru David envisioned. Fiftyish and hawknosed, ginger-topped, greying – decidedly average. Conventional. Voice carrying throaty hesitation, sort of Massachusetts. Tall narrow frame, neatly packaged. Turtlenecked. Dockers and

Wallabees. He proceeds, attentions darting. Others follow with respectful distance.

The fires of this arrival now dim. The woman accompanying Ike hangs back. She is red-headed and small, almost camouflaged in her smallness. She lumps their bags in the corner, steps back to consider their placement, scratches her earlobe, then rearranges the bags differently. This seems to satisfy her.

She turns and faces David, still leaning in the archway. 'Oh, hello.'

Dancing sparks frame her head, her face. The unexpected explosion of flame – its source hadn't been Ike. The fires came from *her*.

'Hi,' David tries.

She crosses the room and plants herself close to him. She smells of mint. With slow-motion ease she extends her hand. Cautiously, David takes it into his own, finding it warm and forgiving, like the friendly rubbing-up of an unfamiliar cat. She peers undaunted into his eyes and offers a sideways grin.

'I'm Molly,' she says.

'David.'

The crooked grin expands. There is an azure cosmos in her eyes, singed by searching fires. She gives off the same murmuring pulse he's sensed since arriving at Chaos Farm, that same subliminal hum emanating from the earth and trees and air, the convergence that Xs Chaos on its map. It's in her too.

'Have you been experiencing owls?' she asks.

'Owls?'

'Ike heard reports about a potential overpopulation of owls this season.'

David hasn't seen any. 'I've seen ducks. But no owls.'

Molly nods. 'It might be just be one of Ike's delusions. Lots of very believable things he says are simply conjured in his mind. Like this story he told on the flight here from Morocco, about being subjected as a boy to ongoing psychological torture by an estranged uncle who had spent years in prison for beating his wife. This uncle would get hammered and phone their house when he knew Ike's parents wouldn't answer and unleash these insane tirades to young Ike, accusing his parents of trying to ruin his life.

Being just a kid, Ike was too scared to hang up or rebut. Ike's uncle told him all about jail, about Puerto Rican gangs whose initiation for new inmates was to break off all their front teeth, so when they were forced to suck dick they couldn't bite down. Ike is eleven years old, and his uncle is yelling into the phone *you can't take shit from those can-kickers* and *never trust any cunt who lets you fuck her in the ass.* Talking about beating respect into anyone who treats you wrong.'

'Woah,' David says.

'Ike blathered about this for the whole flight,' Molly continues. 'At least when he wasn't throwing up. This uncle's ongoing weird fixation, getting drunk and forcing Ike to listen. I was quite moved. He seemed so distraught at the recollection. But then he just spaced out, shrugged and said it could have happened. He invents these elaborate stories all the time, but what often happens is that as he's telling these lies, he concocts the details with such flourish he begins to believe them himself. Like this thing with the owls. For some reason he attached himself to this fact of owls. For weeks all he's talked about was how he was going to arrive to find the place torn to shreds by owls. And this was another fabrication. Unbelievable.'

David: 'Uh.'

'But I could never get upset or angry at these inventions. He's not really in control of himself. It's like he always says: *freedom is infinity trapped in whorls of mayhem locked in a matrix of disarray spooned into the cauldron of chaos.*'

'I'm not sure I ... get it ... '

Molly laughs. 'Exactly.'

She starts lugging baggage down the hall. David stands numb, then moves to help. The fires are now mere embers, extinguishing in air, dissipating, leaving him humbled in their wake.

Stand now before the leader, the figurehead, the hope of the tribe, exalted in his return. Observe as he munches bacon on toast, grunting with approval, extending his mug for another hit of vanilla hazelnut coffee. Notice how his shoulders shake with excitement. Be gracious as he strides through his seasonal domicile, inspecting the cupboards, kicking at baseboards, scrutinizing the backyard's grade, nodding with hearty approval. Allow distance as he finds a light switch and spends a few minutes flicking it on off on off on off on off. Be obsequious as he questions Bedel as to the condition of the recently repaired roof, to which Bedel reports having seen no leakage. Stand now before the leader as he pats shoulders and offers greetings, his demeanour pleasant yet distracted, a vexation tainting his economy of words and twittering pointing hands.

There is a bringing of things. A plaster Krishna, skin bright blue and wielding a chariot's wheel. A coat rack carved in the likeness of duelling cobras. A Playstation 2. An enormous cast-iron pot – for lobster suppers, Ike explains. He unpacks books from a jumbo sack, placing them on an expansive bookcase: *Sorcery as Virtual Mechanics. The Book of Kells: Its Function and Audience. Chakras: Energy Centers of Transformation. Liber Null and Psychonaut. The Chaldaean Oracles of Zoroaster. PsyberMagick: Advanced Ideas in Chaos Magick. The Bacchae.* A stack of 1970s MAD magazines. A hefty tome about Aleister Crowley. *The Autobiography of Saint Therese of Lisieux. The Book of Thoth. I, Tina.*

Ike continues indiscriminately through the farmhouse. Others follow dutifully behind, trailing as he looses a slew of comments. *This should be here. Bedel I told you about dust collecting under this. Is this the light fixture as ordered?* His hurried perusal of objects, his focus, his fervour – yes, there are detectable shades of lunacy here.

Kneeling to inspect a loose plumbing joint in an upstairs bathroom, Ike peers between his legs and catches David watching.

'Well,' Ike says. 'A new guy.'

'This is David,' Muzz says. 'Ike, David. David, Ike.'

Ike hops to his feet. 'Are you an only child, David?'

'Mc. Yes.'

'As am I. As am I. And you've been visually impaired like that for how long?'

'Oh, not long … a few weeks … It's not really, sort of … '

Ike leans back and scrutinizes the eye, the patch. His face is rigid, square-jawed. Tight lips drawn around a neat mouth, unslack eyes, narrow forehead.

'Well,' he says, wiping dust from his hands, 'I hope you'll have something to contribute to Chaos Farm. And vice versa. Have you ever been to Marrakesh?'

'No.'

'Tangiers?'

'No. Never to Morocco. Sorry.'

Ike squints. 'You *should* be sorry.'

Muzz pipes in: 'David's in advertising.'

'Really?' Ike says, his face brightening. 'Marketing and such.'

David: 'Well. More on the conceptual side.'

'Intriguing.'

'Oh … not really. It's actually pretty, you know, banal … '

'No need to be synthetically humble,' Ike scoffs. 'Recall scripture: *he that humbleth himself shall be exalted.* But as Nietzsche incisively revised *he that humbleth himself does* wish *to be exalted.* Don't diminish yourself.'

'Okay.'

He peruses a stack of books in a nearby packing crate and opens one to a marked page. 'Listen,' he says. '*There used to be a vacuum in my soul a something I know not what dense as smoke but wisely and religiously I mounted the steps that lead to your altar and you dispelled that gloomy shroud as the wind blows a butterfly.*'

A pause, then he continues: '*In its place you set an extreme coldness a consummate prudence and an implacable logic. With the aid of your invigorating milk my intelligence developed rapidly and assumed immense proportions in the midst of the ravishing illumination that you bestow prodigally upon those who love you with a sincere love.*'

He looks at David. 'This is *Les Chants de Maldoror.* Do you know what it is, what closed the vacuum in the soul?'

'I don't … if you're asking me … '

'It's mathematics. *O austere mathematics I have not forgotten you since your learned teachings sweeter than honey distilled through my heart like refreshing waves.* See?'

'I don't think I get it … '

'It's a calculation. It's extracting theorems from the entrails of chaos. You should read this book. It'll scare the humility out of you. You know what sends shivers up my spine?'

David: 'Um … '

'Halle Berry accepting her Oscar. A few years back, remember? Think about that, David. Think long and hard, my friend. Bone-chilling.'

Exit Ike.

Muzz claps David on the shoulder. 'You want to hit the basement and root out a fresh case of Coronas? I'm parched to my soul.'

To the soul.

In the agency's kitchenette, between the coffee machine and the water cooler, there was a bulletin board where memos and notices were posted. Most often the space exhibited hockey scores and cartoon strips – *Dilbert* and *Calvin and Hobbes* being favourites – but there was also a weekly scrap of paper tacked up by Claudine, who filled in for Naoko on Fridays. As far as David could glean, Claudine was a believer of nonspecific faiths, a devotee of thinking often lumped together as *Spirituality*. So these scraps would be photocopies or clippings from a variety of sources, familiar quotations or aphorisms attributed to varied doctrines, inoffensive metaphysical ponderings lifted from self-help guides, nothing too obtuse or interpretative. David spent much time lounging in the kitchenette in ongoing efforts of appearing busy; he'd rinse cups or peruse memos, saying hello to guys in Accounts who still didn't know his name.

Hey buddy   how's it going chief   wassup homeslice   howdy there guy.

He had become increasingly fascinated by these daily wisdoms, these kernels of knowledge scissored from their original context into packaged doses of personal enrichment and/or inspiration. Thus David was instructed to *do unto others as you would have others do unto you* and he was reassured that *blessed are you who weep now   for you will laugh*. One morning, as he scraped hardened cheddar from a dish with an SOS pad, he was met by this tacked note: *He whose heart is set upon goodness will dislike no one – Confucius*. And one morning he discovered a columned list: THE SEVEN DEADLY SINS. David scrolled down the list, the words pronounced in his head by an androgynous voice like the robotic whirr of a laundry dryer. Pride and Envy and Gluttony and

Lust and Covetousness and Anger and Sloth. And for each of the list's indiscretions he gauged himself, sizing his own worth against these standards, these unroaring aims – and his personal sins proved plenty. In the checklist of wickedness he stood judged a Sinner. Even a shirker of doctrine like him could be chilled by this classification. Sins. Transgressions. Failings. Yes – all and every. He had returned to his desk and consulted online databases. Opinions abounded. Along with the Deadly Sins he discovered the Seven Heavenly Virtues: Faith and Hope and Charity and Fortitude and Justice and Temperance and Prudence. And he read of the Seven Contrary Virtues: Humility and Kindness and Abstinence and Chastity and Patience and Liberality and Diligence. He read of Gandhi's recipes for doom: Wealth without Work and Pleasure without Conscience and Science without Humanity and Knowledge without Character and Politics without Principle and Commerce without Morality and Worship without Sacrifice. Virtues. Checklists. David sat in silence as around him office equipment hummed white-noise medleys. He sniffed and considered his own damnation. All of this was his, all this neglect, all this corruption and trifling iniquity. The Virtues were alien recipes. Doomsday was nigh. He was unquestionably a sinner; there was surely a cancer in his being, yet by none of these damning scalpels could he duly prescribe the necessary surgery on his soul. This was no simple diagnosis. His sin was a mishmash of *all* these tenets. His was a Modern Sin, the sin of waste; call this Emptiness. The empty heart isn't one without fury; that would mean Serenity. Nor is it the heart's satisfaction; that would be Success. The truth, David decided as he clicked his way through the afternoon's time sheets and e-mails, is that Emptiness is a crime against one's own self, a suicide glorified as bored trial. None can maintain seclusion from the truth lodged within the icy caverns of Sin. No heart is so faint. Yet the list that challenged David, which troubles him still, could be, perhaps, a false directive; for Envy and Sloth and Wrath, et cetera, are not crimes against the greater good, but crimes against one's self, a bankruptcy of one's own being, and should be so regarded. It is only the self that sins unto itself. Breathing venom into your veins and rendering brittle your cerebral cortex; your self-failing will be your deliverance. Dodge these Sins. Take the reins, the ivory-handled pistol. Define heroism in less than a word. Grunt for the past. Flex sins like biceps. Devour the future.

With Ike's arrival, the general conduct changes. David is reminded of young Christmases or Easters, when the house would be lifted out of its usual drudgery to alight itself with the preparation of a feast, a party, the prospect of a roomful of visitors. Surfaces would be cleaned. Squares would be baked. His mother would vacuum briskly and prepare crockery and fill the fridge with Cokes and beers and wine coolers – elevating the house, by transformation, by improvement, into its own ideal.

This is how Chaos Farm reinvigorates itself today. Languor gives way to vigour. There is a motivation, a force. This is suddenly not a holiday, a tea party, a lakeside wahoo. There is business. Everyone is preparing for the advent of greatness, a whipping-into-shape, expecting something greater to occur. Here.

While Muzz instructs David on the proper technique of splitting fire logs in the back shed – *observe the grain   the rough   the ring* – he and Molly try to explain the reasons Ike first laid roots here. What this greater aim is. Chaos may be a retreat, but it's no holiday. More like a laboratory, maybe. A contained, yet free, environment for the execution of exercises. Procedures. Ike himself suffers from a coalescent range of mental conditions, traumas, insomnia, phobias, compulsions. Dysfunction. Though most of the time he manages to keep it together, the demons so vocal in his mind remain unquelled. Even with wealth and untold resources, access to teams of psychoanalysts and therapists and parapsychological healers and shamans and soothsayers and a copious array of advice furnishers. None is of any comfort. Woe persists. And he is not alone in his nightmares.

Since Muzz first came he has seen much, he claims. Weirdness has gone down. Roofs have crumbled. The walls have menstruated. Ghosts mowing the lawn. He's seen gravity flip.

Here: there is a hidden life in the slope of the land and the burrow of the soil. Feel it in your heart, in your groin. Others felt it: Muzz has heard of a movement headed by Rinzai Buddhists – others say Santerian priests from Brazil – who, by some combination of decisions now unknown, located this bucolic location on a map of North America in the early eighties and pinpointed the site. There were cartographical measurements. Pioneers pioneering. Consultation amongst seers. Futures beckoning. Somehow, this land was significant. It held inner power. A secret life.

Muzz has seen readings leap off meters, spiking levels: purities and impurities, aluminum levels, magnetisms, thicknesses, the wet air lashes, bearing mysterious ingredients. Elements united. By whatever measure, Monks or Martians or Mentalists deemed Chaos to be an epicentre of influences.

At some point someone gazed upon the mud-clumped cliffs and verdant meadows and decided *yes this is it.*

Of Ike's eventual discovery of Chaos, both Molly and Muzz are fuzzy. No one knows anything except that Ike's fortunes allowed easy purchase. In the kitchen now: Muzz and David down the last of the carrot juice, and Molly loads film into her twin-reflex Hasselblad, and Roslyn loads the dishwasher, and out in the backyard Ike inspects hedges, and others skitter about, and the sun breaks through an overcast white sheet, at last, to tan the countryside.

David is in his room counting clean socks, matching pairs on the bedsheet.

Then: *ahem.*

He turns to discover Gwendolyn at the door, chewing her hair with a quizzical look.

'You know,' she says, 'you shouldn't be so reserved.'

David is semi-preoccupied with argyles, woolies. 'Reserved?'

'To the whole thing. You make yourself inaccessible to community. Together, we commonly heal. In sharing we learn. By hiding we steal.'

Gwendolyn's body is too svelte, too lean. Her chin and cheeks, blistered. She is too satiated, too swollen, licking her lips after polishing off a roast's remains.

'There's a thing Ike said once … I think it was from the Bible. And when Ike quotes scripture you know it's somewhat legit. *Many waters cannot quench love neither can the floods drown it.*'

David looks up. Gwendolyn smiles a satisfied kooky smile.

'Song of Solomon,' she says. 'The horny stuff.'

'I see.'

'Ike and I met in Colorado eight years ago. We share an interest in numerology. I can advise you about it if you'd like. Give me your birth date and we can … Is there some paper and a pen?'

'That's okay … ' David says.

'No, really. Your birthday shapes your life path, from which any … '

'I'd really rather not.'

Gwendolyn frowns. 'See. That's what I mean. Negativity with every word. You have to be more receptive.'

'No … I'm receptive.'

'You're difficult.'

The socks. Wadding the socks. Piling the wadded socks.

'I'm not.'

'You are. I hate to be the one telling you. We don't know one another that well.'

This is pressure, almost work-like. Schedules. Departmental. And as the Chaos Farmers unite for another gluttonous meal, David feels even more of an outsider, a lame-ass – particularly with Ike, holding court at the table's head, babbling ceaselessly about this afternoon's Lakers game. *Appalling.* The gangly fumbling. Hands like a spastic baboon. Nothing in the back court. Ike, spitting potatoes and chugging wine, detailing recent travels along the Nile with Egyptian systems programmers. Describing the Pyramids through fractal geometry. The erosion. Days sick in bed after eating disagreeable grilled pigeon. Wyatt suggesting a recent article about Mayan astronomy. Discussion of a rare species of red-eyed eagle that patrols the Northwest and lays poisonous eggs. Sarah Promise hogging the wine jug. Hirota adjusting cuffs. Ike saying *when Molly laid her hands on the sarcophagus the stone began to secrete purple gas.*

David wonders about the relationship between Ike and Molly.

Her: young and cherubic. Him: frantic and fiftyish. She sits quietly, serenely fork-picking an artichoke. Hair hiked over perked ears, havoc hidden in the blinks of her eyes. A girl, a burgeoning woman, a lightning strike of precious beauty.

Like Lisa.

'I had these buffalo wings at the Pizza Hut next to the Giza Pyramids,' Ike says. 'They were just great. Can you make wings like that, Samantha?'

Samantha: 'I'm not sure I'd want to.'

Glasses clink.

Ike: 'Standing in the midst of such permanence, one can't help but be floored. Generations of slaves, with their backs all sweaty and broken by whips. You realize that the shape of the universe is all pliable and bendy. The blocks of pyramids resemble the shape of the universe. You realize you can transcend perspective through design. Those buffalo wings tell unbelievable stories. So spicy.'

Sarah Promise: 'Transcend perspective? As if.'

Wyatt: 'Oh?'

Sarah Promise looks at Hirota, then David. David sits mute.

'We're always at the mercy of perspective,' she says. 'When I was a kid I had a dog who would laugh exactly like Ed McMahon if you fed him enough Alpo. The shape of the universe is unimportant. Fear or no fear, we're all minions to a greater – I want to say *revolt* – in this system we're stuck in. Besides, it's all genetics anyway. The plot is written before we get a chance to fuck with it.'

'That's rather fatalistic,' Roslyn says.

'That's like accusing gravity of being fatalistic. It does what it does. Fear is unquestionable. We are what we are. It's predetermined. I say screw it. Bombs away.'

'That's horrible,' Roslyn says, shaking her head in refusal. 'Our existence is our potential.'

Sarah Promise scoffs. 'Whatever bangs your boner.'

Samantha introduces a whopping tray of steamed mussels, accompanied by a mass of sautéed calamari in a shallow wooden bowl.

Ike: 'I always push for refutation and the blunder of fallacy. I believe in pretence and unproven proof, so yes. Embrace it and swing it. Like Chaos – the examination of impossible result, like meteorology. It's chaotic and therefore impossible to grasp. Waves within ribbons within tangents. A realm where language and suggestion solidify into whatever it solidifies into. Like creating plasma from sing-song. Or building buildings out of metaphor. Innocence and speed and transportation. Like dolphins leaping through sun-prismed waters.'

He pauses to toss back the remainder of his glass.

'I once spent a night reciting incantations with a group of monks in Kulha Kangri. By the sixth or seventh jug of wine an entire congregation of long-billed plovers had assembled on the windowsill. I was sweating through my shirt. One of the fellows, a gent named Xiang, sang every word with this gentle atonal melody that sounded like chimes ringing in a bottomless pit. I'll never forget – I posed a lengthy question about faith and devotion and the possibility of the inner eye beyond the inner eye, and something about the commodities market and other matters relevant to the time. And Xiang's answer, after reflecting for an eternity, was two simple words: *space shuttle*. He sang it. *Spaaace shuuuttle*. I think about those words every night as I lie in bed. As you all know, my night terrors often last weeks. But some nights I sleep well, I sleep like a baby, when I can remember how perfectly and emptily he sang it: *space shuttle*. Those nights I sleep well.'

'That's fucking *beautiful*,' Muzz says.

Ike gazes into his glass.

'Time,' he says, 'is as elusive as the abyss.'

The assembly is wowed. David is not wowed. The Pizza Hut sign glowing on the Pyramids – Patton would smash it with his pistol's ivory butt. The Father would pick skin from his lower lip and swivel his neck. Clouds of disapproval would gather.

Hector, he of disfigured face, asks Ike if he's had any progress in his study of the Witch of Endor.

'Truth be told,' Ike says, 'that path is painted with frustration. The Witch story, from Samuel the First, is a doozy. Debate surrounds Biblical advocacy of necromancy. The diehard didactic argument sees the story as portraying demonic involvement rather than actually *raising the dead*. Saul supposedly enlisted this

Witch of Endor to raise Samuel, whose prophetic military sweeps Saul failed to heed, thereby isolating him from God. Some interpretations see this incarnation of Samuel not as the actual guy himself but as an interfering demon. Satanic spawn masquerading as him, as Samuel.'

Hector: 'How compelling.'

'Sure,' Ike says. 'The hints are there. Depending on how and what you're reading. Saul never directly addresses this revived Samuel – the interpretation is that it's only a creation of his own doubt and mania. A hallucination.'

'A vision,' Sarah Promise says.

Ike smiles at her. 'Exactly.'

David recalls: *the wolves carry my name in their midnight speeches.* Lisa, reading from her creepy texts.

'There's that book … ' he finds himself saying.

Ike looks up from potatoes. 'Ah. The new guy speaks. You're saying what?'

'The – what's it called. The *Necronomicon*. That book that tells how to raise demons. A … friend of mine was sort of keen, she told me that … '

Ike interrupts. 'I'll stop you right there, new guy. The *Necronomicon* is fake. H. P. Lovecraft wrote it to add weight to his own crappy fiction. It was a marketing tool, and a sloppily conceived one at that. But these cretins on these message boards and at conventions still believe in its veracity. It drives me batty. The real stuff is in the ether. It's in the spleen and liver. Lovecraft insults my vexations and my quest. You're just *wrong*.'

David clams up. He is destroyed, severed by his too-ready belief. Imagine Lisa, falsely swayed, her truth marred. Debunked.

Ike: 'And yet, I often wonder. In this godless world, where commerce outweighs devotion and individuality slides under the oppressive grill of materialism, is there still cause, or even desire, for the visitation of such hokey demons? We've gotten so far away from horns and forked tails, but is there still room for demons? Or angels?'

David looks across the table to Molly. She closes her eyes. An aura of consideration, of graceful preparation, gathers within and around her. As if she alone understands. Watching Molly knife her fish is like watching history intersect with the immediate. David sees his own trembling self as a relic from an ancient bygone age, peering into the present. Molly operates on a higher plane than the rest, even Ike. Everyone suffers *something* – but Molly, she has abilities beyond. Fire within. What the others pursue already rests in her grasp. She knows things.

Certainly David has gained awareness of greater, veiled secrets at play at Chaos Farm, but not until Samantha leaves the dining room to return moments later brandishing something enormous and bony in her arms does he become truly afraid of what he has been drawn into.

A giant baboon skull, hollowed and painted electric blue. Inside it are a number of fresh chocolate macaroons, still piping hot.

'This is a new recipe,' she says. 'I only hope it befits the occasion.'

Wyatt tells David of a psychic session he once had that was so successful, so powerful, that the power had gone out in a ten-kilometre radius around the farm. It all rests in the harnessing of the brain's innate powers, Wyatt says. Electricity. Control. Will. Dessert.

Ike poses a question: describe, in one word, the abyss. Question to all in turn, counter-clockwise until the abyss is exhausted.

Muzz plucks out a macaroon. 'Endless.'

He hands the skull to Paul Hirota, who takes a macaroon and says, 'Chasm-like.'

Samantha: 'Briny.'

Hector: 'Innocent.'

Roslyn: 'Spindly.'

Bedel: 'Unfathomable.'

Sarah Promise: 'Clammy.'

Wyatt: 'Miasmic.'

Gwendolyn: 'Charred.'

Ike, slowly, punctuated: '*Kier-ke-gaard.*'

Molly: 'Reverberating.'

Now to David. He feels pressure rising at the table, a tide of forces in their assembled imagination. The dishes lightly trembling. Candlelight wavering. The only image that introduces itself to his immediate impulse is of – *of course* – Scott as Patton, crouched in the dust, inspecting ruins after battle, saying *it was here*. Voices calling him from ancient clashes, swordsmen spilling blood on once-embattled earth.

David: 'Carthaginian.'

Roslyn draws a sharp breath.

'Keep going, *keep going*,' Ike implores.

Muzz: 'Massive.'

Hirota: 'Wrathful.'

Samantha: 'Terminating.'

Hector: 'Fanged.'

Roslyn: 'Fractured.'

Bedel: 'Golden.'

Words, firing like pistons. Faster, heavier, more.

Sarah Promise: 'Never.'

Wyatt: 'Lacklustre.'

Gwendolyn: 'Filleted.'

Ike: 'Labyrinthine.'

Molly: 'War.'

David: 'Lisa.'

Why not?

They are lost in frenzied free association now, barking words in an illogical meandering song, yet somehow managing to create in their sum a working model of some endless dark void: *loveless wanton Texas craterous intercom destruction holocaust aisled minty nomadic spiralling maternal phosphorous terrier blighted sludge Marlboro influenza Sagittarian interrogatory albeit divorce abandoned gulping formatted advertised decrepit flaw chundering top-heavy ferocity …*

David's head swims.

… leviathan hostage tarnished tsunami icepick deathbed spinal sartori sunburned voiceless soiled bleeders laundry acne …

Without warning, a vibration quivers through the table, clinking cutlery. The chandelier rattles. David lurches backward in his seat, but the others, though equally startled, seem to embrace this activity. This is what they've been expecting, what they've been striving for. Something is happening, gestating, changing.

... *comatosequiveringplaguejudasmayhemhavoccarnage haywireblazingslaughterhouse calculus coddled chaos* ...

The tablecloth bursts into flames. All leap from their seats.

'There's an extinguisher in the kitchen,' Bedel cries to Hector, already on his way.

Ike stands transfixed before the blazing table, his air that of a satisfied conqueror. He waves his arms, as if commanding the fires to burn higher, harder. Putrid smoke suffocates the room.

Ike, staring into the flames – finding there, perhaps, the abyss he seeks.

With fire tamed, the gathering disperses. Sarah Promise and Paul Hirota head to their cottage with a bottle of Jim Beam. Muzz retreats to his banjo. Roslyn to the stables. Ike to the master bedroom and *the tortured nightly perusal of my texts*. Others are engaged in various solitary activities, dishes, bed. Any trace of whimsy has been shaken by the fire.

David is again couched in the living room, nursing a can of Holsten Festbock and trying to negotiate the television's perplexing remote. On the screen is Jay Leno, slicing the air with his hand, smacking his other palm, making some humorous observation which sends a comely guest into a gale of uneasy giggles.

Suddenly Molly is close. Here. From where. She sits on the floor in front of him. 'What are you watching?'

'Oh. Nothing. I don't really have much to do, so I'm just. You know. Wasting time ... '

She looks at him, studying his face intently. Smiling that crooked little smile.

'One-eyed David,' she says. 'Drinking his beer.'

David nods self-consciously.

'For if a man rejoice not in his drinking he is mad for in drinking it's possible for this to stand up straight   and then to fondle breasts and to caress well tended locks and there is dancing withal and oblivion of woe. Do you know that?'

'Oblivion of woe. No ... '

'*The Cyclops*,' she says, 'Euripides makes Odysseus into sort of a ding-dong, I think. The Cyclops, on the other hand, I think, comes off as pretty intriguing. He gets plastered and rueful and unpredictably passionate. Blinded.'

She rests on the floor on her knees, leaning near him. David sets down his beer.

'What just happened?' he asks her. 'With the fire.'

Molly shakes her head and smiles. 'Things can happen when you have the right combination of elements. It's difficult … there are forces we have to contend with.'

How can people aim so low. How can strength be so unobtainable. How how *how* – how can a young girl commit *seppuku*. How can visions haunt the half-sighted. How can people speak in assumed tongues. How can flames be the remnants of the gone.

'I don't get it.'

His fingers unconsciously go to his eye, the patch.

'Does it trouble you?' she asks.

The eye. The flatness. The wound. The potential evisceration.

'Oh jeesh,' he says. 'It really really does.'

'How did it happen?'

'I got … sort of … stuck in the middle of something, and there was glass flying, and next thing I knew: *bam*.'

'Blinded.'

'I'm always banging into things. It's really a problem.'

'Because of your vision.'

'Because everything is flat. When I reach out … '

He demonstrates, reaching for his beer.

'You lose stereoscopic perception,' she says.

'Exactly.'

Molly. Her body sinks into a dark green sweatshirt. There is a conduit here, drawing him to her. Something she offers. To be enveloped by her seeing flame, that bursting heat. Molly has capabilities. Hidden powers, access; it gleams in her calm eyes, in her unfailing attentions. All that is artificial in Chaos Farm is real in Molly. All that is temporary in Sarah Promise is permanent in Molly.

Molly comes closer. Her scent is available: clear, tangy, lavenderish.

She says: 'Have you seen the globe?'

The globe sits in the farmhouse's attic, among rafters and dust and trunks and heaps of old linen. Click on a sole bulb: junk, antiques, artifacts of accumulation. An old mannequin, naked in limited light, its torso cracked down one rib. The teeth-like keys of an old de-motored vibraphone. And in the corner, next to a shuttered window, is the globe. It is enormous, at least five feet in diameter, solid oak, cradled in a giant brass swivel. Veins ripple across its seas and nations of olive and ochre, fine etched lines delineating territories, meridians, a detailed rendering of a Spanish galleon sailing its Atlantic.

Molly caresses Asia with her hand. 'I discovered it this afternoon.'

This world is impressive. David brushes an index down the Andes, sliding from crowning Venezuela to macilent Chile. 'How old is this thing? It looks old.'

Molly doesn't know.

'Here's Constantinople,' David says, 'So, what, has to be thirties at least.'

Molly's hand drifts through the Orient, through India and Pakistan, navigating the Himalayas, exploring summits and lowlands. The world at her fingertips.

'I get the impression no one wants me here,' David says.

'That's not true. What about Sarah?'

David doesn't reply.

'She has a powerful voice. I've heard her evoke the voices of the dead. She spoke as a recently hanged serial rapist. She growled like a dog.'

'She uses the voice of my dead cousin.'

'The cousin you loved.'

Skimming the Arctic, smiling her persistent off-kilter smile.

David: 'What makes you say that?'

'She had pain. And you loved her.'

'How are you … why are you saying … '

'Your passions were simple, but ridden with guilt. There was shame. She was young?'

'Yes, seventeen. But *how*.'

'Seventeen. And pretty?'

'Molly. I don't … '

'We all have wounds, David.'

Echoing Muzz: *we all have chasms.*

Molly reaches and touches his eyepatch. Her tiny hand softly brushes his cheek, follows the contour of his chin. He wishes he'd shaved.

'We're all looking to be healed. Ike suffering his torments – his mind constantly battles itself. Muzz still wrestles with addictions. Gwendolyn with her obsessions. Samantha with her spine. We're all looking for relief. We all suffer.'

Yes. We do.

'But,' David says. 'Why are *you* here?'

A glint in her eyes – something changes. Her touch's pressure shifts, probing. She gently pulls back the patch, revealing the gore beneath. Bringing his lack to light. This touch explores, advances, learning this sore and shredded plot. Her hand is offering. Transmitting.

Healing.

To see. To peer into the world and its scenes. To look into frames, the traps of time. Action and Cut.

Recall: a bottle, cast against sidewalk. Daggers of glass. Concrete meeting face. Blackout.

When his eye's powers had been robbed, he hadn't fully believed it. There was lingering faith, denial. Days without depth. The extent of the ruin was slow to grasp.

They say *whether or not we'll have to resort to an evisceration.*

Molly's fingers are columns in a ruined parthenon. They bear time: ages of disappointment and consolation in their prints, their pads like hulking battleships on the horizon, guerillas pouncing from brush, waves of protesters storming city corners, craters on far-flung satellites. They are drills, worming into his face, excavating his skull.

Molly's fingers are soft spongy wisps, seeking.

He sees something like ultraviolet mountain ranges, like scoops of text, fragmented and hot. Something buzzes and hums in the eye's lower fold, instigating new weirdness.

The enemy wants to tell him *fuck you   this world is dead   see no more through this spited eye   live no more through this.*

Sight: the laziest sense.

The burble of Chaos rises. Feet. Ankles. Shins. Thighs. Crotch. Abdomen. Chest. Shoulders. Neck. Tendons. And, up. Into the head. Where.

Molly: reducing, working.

Here he is weak.

Understand and accept this: there are wonders in unexpected places and veiled meanings in scripted legacies. Accept this: *there is nothing beyond what we perceive*, and the dead will not bash away dirt to again walk the earth. File this as truth. Copy it, fax it, catalogue it. Understand the truth. Be steady in your belief. The blind will not see. There will be no hallelujah. There will be no swooping in, no heroism.

But: with Molly's touch, there is a quiver in his eye's wrecked socket. Flesh emergent, springing anew. Nerves in renewal. Do you deny this. No. Do you deny that Molly is the sun, hovering omnisciently over a wooden world tilted in a brass axis. Do you deny that Molly is the giver of light. *No*. You cannot deny this. So. Then. The truth must be reformatted, edited, tightened up, revised in light of newly acquired data.

Everything is putting on weight, gaining girth, inflating. The room expands. The light doubles, trebles. Dimension accumulates. *What is what are you doing to me.*

Recall: just a kid, trapped solo in the back seat on endless rides to the family cottage, with The Father holding a cigarette to the barely parted window, allowing *one and only one pisser stop* for the trip's journey. David would wile away the journey by retreating to window surveillance: passing quarries, green-white signs posting distances, lifeless scenery, furry speed bumps of smushed gophers gazing upward, frozen in disbelief. The world sped by through window as young David tried to capture the space allotted to him, to own it in chunks, direct it like a movie. The trick was to try and shut out all sensation of motion – the motor roaring with velocity rising and stabilizing, the stink of The Father's cigarette, the chatter of AM radio – banishing all information of his seat-belted confines to leave only processes of the visual, with the aim of loosing the motion of the self and the impermanence of this frame to make the blur of speed into solid somethings. He'd mentally reinvent smudged countrysides and subdivisions and paved splatters and offshooting exits and towny patches as captured stills, freeze-framed, and remake this world into a comprehensible array of coloured regions and fractals – like Sarah Promise's impossible voice rendered as graphic waveform on a screen – envisioning the transient world's speedy displacement as something easy and real. What he saw, he'd make understandable in frames. The world gushing by like a cartoon. Escape to the pleasures of packaging. Learn your place by controlling what surrounds you. Frames: like the way the doorway between the den and the kitchen composed a frame around the table where The

Father stood over his newspaper, sweatshirted back to the doorway, home in the middle of the working day due to yet another sacking, his posture betraying crippling defeat, drainage, incapacity, the way his locked image would be forever remembered – *defeated*. Control the man by controlling his form: The Father, thinning, drowsy, inconsequential. Unheroic. Capture the present and sculpt it into memory. Life as a movie, paused on a triumphant brink. Life as vision.

Things emerge. She asks *is it happening* and he says *yes*.

The room is on fire. The room is not on fire. Molly coughs liquefied bronze. *No* – she is revolving around the misery of the globe. All becomes seen. The room is not on fire. The room is packed and stuffy. Here is the globe. Here is Molly, furrowing her brow. And where is the flatness. Where is limitation. The world is becoming. The world is revealed. Now. The eye and its partner. The joint of their shared stem. The process. Exploding. Somewhere someone changes a channel. The possibility of the space. The earth wriggles in its cradle.

Molly withdraws her hand. David stands in disbelief.

Here it is. Revise the truth. His wrecked vision, reimagined with potential.

'You need to look deeper,' Molly says.

David feels wetness in the folds of his eyes. His two eyes, both. There are two.

'You have a challenge ahead,' she says, 'greater than anything you'll find here. I hate to be the one to tell you. And when the moment comes, strike without fear. Strike without hesitation.'

'My eyes.'

'I don't see you as Odysseus. I see you as Telemachus. A diffident son in search of his father.'

'*I can see*,' David huffs.

'Like a Telemachus, you have transformative tests ahead. A battle. It will be important. It will be life or death. And when it happens, you have to be prepared to strike.'

Her comforting crook of smile is still present, but it is different. Everything has changed. Everything is buoyant and full. David tears the eyepatch from his forehead and touches testing fingers to his eye.

This is the treatment of loss. Everything is restored.

'I want you to listen hard to me,' Molly says, clutching his shoulders.

David tries to comply, but the dizzy glee of new sight overpowers his thoughts – *everything yes brand new refocus remake de-evisceration.*

'You fixed me,' he says.

Molly shakes her head. 'You fixed yourself. What's important now is you have to be prepared to face your adversary. You have to meet the tough things and not back down. Forget what you think you know. It's going to happen.'

'I'm just trying to … get the whole … but. Amazing.'

Molly smiles her sad smile. 'Don't be amazed. Just be prepared.'

Look at the moon. The moon at the bedroom window. Look up, at the ungraspable moon, bobbing in the nothingness of space. Look at nothing. Live in the sky. Live in the rotation, the pattern. The moon is a system. The moon is swirled in teargas. Look with clear vision, perfect clarity. Clutching depth. The dead moon, its exhausted soil, its dried shores. The window that leads away. Up. The moon, a porthole in lifeless sky. Chaos sky. Blink new eyes. Here is vision, sight, a night of sky. Look at the moon, its fuzzy light.

They go snowmobiling, Muzz and David, sometimes Ike. Ike exerts. Ike argues theories of Hegelian dialectics no one follows. Ike grows weepy when Hector brings up recent developments in Liberia. Things happen and progress.

David's former life is so long ago. The future seems so far away.

For the most part, David is happy here. He retains his little bedroom. He interacts with the others, he dines and converses and helps dry dishes. Yes, he questions the substantiality of their efforts, this campaign for illumination. But after Molly's restoration of his left eye, he has no doubt that there is something here.

Everything is open, more open than it's ever been. He wanders the meadows and drinks wine and partakes in copious feasts. He allows Samantha to begin a chart of his aura. He stands and gazes upon the bay with eyes wide open, both eyes, and watches as the sizzling sun fuses with water. There is pleasure and knowledge in Chaos. He is convinced.

Late in the night, a kerfuffle rouses the sleeping farmhouse. A horrified yelp from the front door. Lights snap on in rooms. David rises and hurries to the front foyer to discover Roslyn, crouched in her nightie, holding something bloody and odd.

The next day Gwendolyn and Molly spend hours sequestered in Ike's study. Everyone is very cagey about what has occurred.

Gwendolyn's gruesome regressive slip is troubling; she's gone down this road before, they say, and it's never pretty. This was indicative of the old Gwendolyn, the pre-Chaos Gwendolyn, whose morbid obsessions were catastrophic, near-fatal. This caving doesn't bode well. Ike is particularly devastated. Upon seeing the entrails laid in a messy trail from stable to doorstep, snow splattered with viscera, he collapsed into tears. It was Scylla, the cow. Scylla's bull, Charybdis, had passed away from an infection earlier this year; her life since had been lonely. The only other Chaos cow, Astrophil, had proven a disagreeable companion.

Gwendolyn had gotten far inside Scylla before Roslyn had discovered her.

In a former life David might have written: *only the best! everything to your satisfaction! accommodating you since 1996!*

Muzz says he has a new song, about David, and wants to play it for him. David's throat tightens at the idea, but he agrees.

> Here we lie as slaves
> Champions in graves
> Nothing budges us from our ways
> Our hero's young defiance
> Sucked in throaty silence
> Blind and lost in violence
>> Dearest child in Chaos danger
>> Here crawls up our strangest stranger
>> Be prepared to move and struggle
>> Be prepared to be disappointed
> Disappointed in the future
> Disappointed with the future

Each line is punctuated by a searching minor melody plucked by his one-string banjo. Muzz sings softly, with a woeful cadence.

David is stunned. 'That's great,' he says.

Muzz nods. 'Yeah. Well … it's something.'

His eyes betray regret, sadness. He licks his lips and pensively picks strings.

'What does that line mean?' David asks.

'Which?'

'*Disappointed in the future.*'

'And then it says disappointed *with* the future.'

'Yeah. What does that mean?'

Muzz rests the instrument against a chair. 'It's just the way I'm seeing things. It doesn't necessarily mean … I'm just conjecturing. We gather and collect. I ding the tones. The creative act is parallel to actual truth – we just extract and compress.'

'I'm having a hard time with this *actual truth.*'

'No doubt. Who isn't wrestling? But in the grand total we're all in this same complicated situation, so we have to try and learn from one another. All of us. But with you, I sense a heavier significance to your being here. You have something about you that's a bit fucked. As if you're getting ready for something.'

David scratches his forehead. 'What does that line mean, Muzz? To be disappointed about. And disappointed with.'

'I just … I get the sense that things aren't going to play out the way you think they will.'

Muzz's rugged vigour, stout shoulders. His cheeks, bearded hints. David doesn't know what to think.

Quoth Patton: *we are constantly advancing   the only thing we're holding is the enemy   we're gonna hold on to him by the nose   and we're going to kick him in the ass.*

Gwendolyn sits alone at the kitchen table, eating sautéed Brussels sprouts and risotto. She forks grated carrots onto her plate. Her narrow face wants to be loosed, to glisten with happy grease. Her eyes: rifts of loss. The vegetables sit freshly, mournfully, on her plate.

Molly sat with her all day. The two together, locked away. David views from a distance, composing comment. But he's useless.

What did Molly say. What spell did she perform.

Ike is posted by the back door, peering through parted blinds at the back deck and yard. His profile – prominent beak, shaven curves – is sharpened by the invading afternoon brightness. He turns and discovers David close by.

'Oh,' he says, 'it's David.'

David: 'Hey. Hi. Hello.'

Ike assesses him. David is holding a half-empty bag of pretzels, discovered in the back of a cupboard.

'How are you finding yourself today, David?'

'Oh, I don't know … I thought I might take a walk in the woods, go see the ducks … '

'The ducks?'

'The ducks down at the pond. Down the path by the hill.'

'There aren't any ducks down there.'

'Down in that clearing where there's that muddy pond.'

'A muddy pond. I'm unfamiliar.'

'Oh. It's really nice.'

'Right. And ducks are habituating this pond, despite the fact that the forest is as frozen as a Fudgsicle.'

'I know … it's fairly … I thought you'd have known … '

Ike squints. He rotates his narrow grey-templed head in a jerky gesture of disavowal. He asserts his newscasterly mien, trenched with heavy creases. Ike takes a moment of stern consideration, then breaks into a wide smile.

'Maybe I should check out this muddy pond. I'm done with my meditations for today. The sun is on my side. Let's go visit these purported ducks.'

The forest is quieter than quiet. Winter is now slowly and despondently retracting; autumn nears with fresh corruptions. Time is passing.

Ike and David hike the forested path, their conversation scarce. David remains self-consciously reserved. When they arrive at the frozen pond, its busy shimmer, Ike whacks the back of his mittened hand against his forehead. This is new to him. New and unforeseen.

The ducks are more ebullient than on previous visits. They scurry about, shuddering, picking at disobliging ground, greeting one another in quacked code. They seem less doubtful. David feels he's gotten to know them over the course of his visits. The fellas. The family. The team.

'Still here.' Ike says. 'In the cruel cruel winter. This rends my heart.'

He steps down to the pond's rim. He removes his fleece jacket, rests it aside and crouches, gazing intently across the ice. He snaps fingers and sniffs. He makes a long slow sound with teeth and tongue: *tcchh tcchh tcchh*, then a tentative, duck-like attempt: *kwak*.

David watches, transfixed, as Ike kneels on the squashy bank, then lowers to his hands and knees. Slowly, he zeroes in on a brownish mallard that is eyeing him. Everything halts: the breeze in the trees, the shadows training across whitened freeze. The fissures of water below. Everything waits. The duck blinks, light and wary on webbed feet. Ike places his hands on the ground, creeping gingerly forward.

Wak, Ike says. *Gwak gwak*.

The duck is aware. It understands.

Wak.

Watch the duck's eyes. Watch Ike's. Observe: one pair captures another, narrowing.

The duck waddles closer. Closer still. A few of its cronies join in, though apprehensively. Ike offers only sounds, a presence from which to develop contact. Communication: *gwa gwa*. He is manipulating his body's stature, genuflecting before the ducks, simultaneously signalling, rocking almost imperceptibly back and forth. Beckoning without beckoning. Becoming without slouching.

David doesn't budge. He keeps distance, watching.

The duck moves lightly toward Ike, closer, until it takes a seat immediately before him. Unflinching. Qualmless. Ike extends a measured grasp and laces fingers around its lower feathers. The duck says *kwa*. Ike says *gaa*. Something is agreed upon. Ike draws the duck inward to his own body, his arms curling like a receiver protecting a hand-off. The duck's beaded eyes blink.

The remaining flock is mobilized by this embrace. They emerge from bushes, from clustered gatherings, from the pond's outer reaches, arriving with feathered rears bobbing with vigorous waddles. They snuffle snow from beaks and advance in bounces. Ike cradles the duck in his arms, speaking to it in whispered sounds.

Reassuring sounds. Ducks come hopping. They bond to him, this man in khaki pants. Ike squats in a puddle of ducks. Ducks leap and rest on his shoulders, on his bent knees, congregating with happy *quacks* and ruffling wings.

Ike turns to David. There is joy among the flock. There is joy in Ike. David is astounded.

'How … ' he attempts.

Ike's eyes well up, pain disfiguring his face. He looks around at his ducks, then at David.

'David.'

'Yes.'

'They don't know everywhere I've been.'

David: 'No.'

Ike: 'Have you ever killed a man?'

David is at a loss. 'I … '

'Have you committed the sin of murder?'

'Me? No. I've never been in a … '

Ike's lips tremble. He cuddles the duck lovingly, gathers another into his embrace, crouches further to be fully accessed by these birds. He is rapturous.

'I've killed men,' he says. 'I've killed so many men. I've tortured them and deprived them and made marionettes of their entrails. I've drunk their blood. I've stolen their watches. I've rejoiced in death. I've waged wars against hapless uncles. I've borne witness to horrific erasure, the end of existences. I've been a villain … '

Sobbing wildly now. The ducks are inexpressive.

' … I've been a villain. I've murdered. I've killed. Have you killed?'

David has not killed. He's seen killings, slowly and swiftly; he's been party to deaths, sorrowful ends, but never has he himself been executioner. Never has he spilled another's blood. With his own hands.

Ike: 'I carry their ghosts on my shoulders. Every breath I draw is a violation of all that's good and righteous. I am a symptom … I'm a spectre of wrath.'

The sin of Wrath. The sin of Avarice.

He's lying, David thinks.

And yet. The ducks embrace Ike as their own, clustering him as kindred. They peck at his laces and ruffle hinds against his shins, framing him like a discount garland. David keeps a distance, dumbfounded.

Frames in recall. Framed by doorway, The Father: standing over a newspaper fanned on the kitchen table. His chin dropped, licking thumb to pinch pages, flipping, considering the refreshed contents, squinting, moving on. Always wound impossibly tight, resigned to halfhearted yardwork, picking crunchy moths out of a window's gutter, executing vague menial chores in groggy mid-mornings. Like the ducks circling the pond, he flitted nervously, skeptically, paralyzed by some unclotting wound – a gash that wouldn't heal.

The downstairs den has been fastidiously readied for tonight's endeavours. Lights are shaded and dimmed, windows sealed with boards of olive wood. Small torches on brass posts are placed throughout the room, leaking phosphorous emissions. Tapestries of green silk drape the walls. In a large back section of the room the new StainGuard carpet has been torn up to leave the cement floor exposed, where in the centre a large diagram has been spray-painted: a perfect circle, a clock-like ring with twelve points delineated and intersecting lines joining, creating a complex map of triangles and fractals and angles.

The only sound is the polyrhythmic interplay of a clock's tick and the fireplace's crackle.

The twelve arrive, shambling down the stairs in single file – all together, because, as Molly has instructed, they must all share a same visceral experience, the same stimuli, from commencement to completion. They gather into a circle. They are silent.

Last in line is Molly, a shallow copper urn in her arms. She moves to the front of the room, stands before the hearth and surveys the dim room and its occupants. Her crooked smile is absent, her hair is hauled sternly back, her eyes, flickering by firelight, are stony.

No one speaks.

She places the urn on an awaiting tripod and places her hands on its unfastened lid, breathing deeply. Wordlessly, she directs them to sit at the marked points.

They sit.

Molly closes her eyes and flares her nostrils, concentrating. The group settles into position, everyone cautiously quiet, all attention focused on Molly. Her breaths: *hu shu hu shu*. She removes the urn's lid to reveal a small mass of kindling and wax arranged at its mouth, then lights a long wood match and sets it afire, creating a warm contained glow. Then she produces a small vial and dribbles a thick oil over the flame. There is a musky stink.

A prolonged moment quivers.

David shifts uncomfortably on his pillow, seated at four o'clock to Molly's twelve. He worries his stomach will growl through the hushed gathering. He tallies this afternoon's mugs of cowboy coffee – there were many.

Finally, Molly opens her eyes. A semblance of the Molly he recognizes appears. Her knowing smirk.

She says, 'We'll join hands.'

They do so. David offers one clammy mitt to Bedel, the other to Samantha. Ike sits opposite at eleven o'clock, eyes barely parted, his shirt unbuttoned to the middle of his hairy torso. Ike, concentrating, trying desperately to be in the moment, to open himself up to forces, to receive. Waiting for a message to surface, his personal answer.

Molly begins to mumble an almost inaudible incantation. The circle draws tighter. David catches only stray phrases: *this place a place of visitation blood tuo nobore cinctus sum grace this circle undaunted come hither with glee Aie Aaie Elibra Elchim Sadai Pah Adonai this terrestrial province find soil as rich as blood.*

The candlelight flickers.

She executes another sequence of swift breaths, then lets her neck relax and her head drop. Molly is small but not frail. David waits, they all wait, to see what will happen. She raises her head and passes brief eyes over each of them.

'Everyone. Tame your mind's current. Be receptive.'

She brings Ike and Wyatt's hands together before her and links them, extricating herself from the union. Her hands return to the lid of the mysterious urn. Her hands lie still but firm.

'I want you each to envision an absent presence, someone whose departure has affected you. Someone who has left this mortal coil. Anyone. Capture this individual in your mind. Aim less for their image, as in reimagining a photograph or a still image, but more for a sensation particular to the memory. A smell. A resonant emotion. An angle or scene that lingers heavily in your mind. An intimate association.'

Muzz peeps up: 'Anything?'

'Whatever resonates. Just try to create as exact a connection as you can.'

Someone in the circle sniffs heartily; David doesn't catch who. The room seems to be growing darker, sinking inward and upward, seeking the centre: Molly.

'Just think. Recall. Remind yourself. *Retrace*. Be aware. Don't dig, don't strive. Just drift toward this presence. Allow yourself to maintain an equilibrium, a state of stasis. I'll do the rest.'

David registers these orders with a degree of bewilderment. To be here. Allowing himself to be here. Here to reclaim the becalming nature of escape. Before this mayhem there was merely life, simple days.

Retrace.

There were summers dedicated to left midfield position on the district soccer squad. Sporting stripes. Knee pads. Cleats. Earning stains and scrapes. Hazy Sunday mornings, blazing Thursday afternoons. Gruelling drills, windsprints, laps. The smell of mown grass, furious sun searing the back of his neck. Pull forward. Draw back. *Hustle*. This was torture, surely, but the reward was knowing there was at least one nook where he fit in; here, on the squad, gulping Powerade and queuing to execute corner kicks. The boisterous camaraderie. Teamwork. He would leap and sweat and slide-tackle, soaking up that essential nutrient of adolescent survival, the plasma of teenage summers: *belonging*. He dug into the task, obeying plays, dutiful and unlazy. Challenge. Sidestep. Strafe left, right. Joy, but not in the exertion – only a twinge of joy even in possible victory, and defeat was only fleeting embarrassment as the teammates traipsed home sulky and bummed. Joy came not in triumph but in loss – namely, the loss of self through the team.

And yet, there was a particular disgrace embedded in this unbounded glee, because on Thursday's crosstown games, after the whistle's shrill cry and following high-fives and backpack round-ups, waiting on the sidelines would be the man himself, impatiently tapping his watch, cupping a Thermos. The Father, late for Sunday-morning games, arriving groggy and blue-faced, the guys snickering as The Father hawked blackish phlegm and lit a cigarette and croaked in his most hungover grumble *chuck your cleats in the trunk don't get mud on the seats*, practically collapsing into the bricky shade of the nearby school. On drives home from games, 0−3 to the intimidating Timberlea squad maybe, The Father would spend the ride shaking his head in disbelief, barely speaking except to recount certain failures in the game's play, rebuking certain players, praising others, pointing out *that Chinese kid he's got hustle* − *hustle* being the golden commodity of any kid's worth. There would be a critical play-by-play of David's contribution to the game, a running down, a deflation. His poor contribution. Backing off. Slacking. Getting caught unawares. You coulda had 'em but you gave up. I don't think you even *care* about winning. Do you. No frigging *hustle*. Punctuating *hustle* with a poke − the fearsome weapon, the poke.

Retrace.

There was a black-and-white photograph of The Father, a younger version, running the city marathon on a rainy afternoon, his moustache-centred face radiating determination, almost *glowing* with perseverance as his sweatshirt clung soaked to his skin. The face of The Father: defined in fractures of camera flash and torrents of rain, the cold, the odds − all of this found in this picture, this singular exposure displayed in a frame, way back when The Father was still mobile, still motivated, still alive. This photograph sat on a mantle, right next to David's City Division Soccer Championships trophy. Dusted and kept. Advertised in their home.

Retrace: dream of Spain and the glittering balconied city, dream of rapturous worlds − then awake to The Father's beige-carpet apartment, the Stouffer's cartons haphazardly piled by a copper-stained coffee maker that wrenched any roast to crud. Teleport. Flip-flop. Betray the honest grunt of The Father, paralyzed in his chasms. Betray the renewal of his mother. Betray the romance of youth, its valleys and peaks, its rooms and fields of untold possibility; dive headfirst for the ball without fear of volleyed reprisal − David always feared, he never abandoned.

Fear is the way you die. Or: fear is the way you counter death. No. Fear advancing, pushing. Fear: the thunder at the window. Its antonym: *bravery*, the ancient art of sacrifice. Maintain honour. Bleed. Desecrate and dance on the gleaming blade of the old, render it new. Stab. Slay thyself. Gleam forever in young beauty. Die untarnished. *Seppuku*. Sacrificed. Perfect forever.

Seek and ye shall revise.

'Now,' Molly says. 'Now we can regather.'

Bam. David hauls himself out of retread, back into the present. The room, the people. The ritual. An indeterminate duration has passed, with Molly as timekeeper.

'Ike,' she says, 'there's someone you'd like to try to contact.'

All eyes on Ike. Anticipation mounts.

'Oh god,' he says. 'Oh.'

He tilts forward, squeezing Molly's and Gwendolyn's hands. Gwendolyn provides her shoulder as support, but Ike twists away. He wipes his eye with the elbow of his sleeve, blinks laboured blinks, smacks his lips.

'No,' he says. 'Yes. Okay. I'm here. Let's go. Let's just *do it*.'

'Ike,' Molly says, 'you have to tell me. Tell me who you want to speak with.'

'Oh, for the love of ... you know who.'

'You have to say. You have to. Say it.'

'Ma. My Mother. *Ma*. I want to speak with her.'

Molly nods. 'Now, as I continue, you have to concentrate. Say her name to yourself but not aloud. Repeat it in your mind. She's just out of reach. Call to her. Not for us, for yourself. Call through the murk.'

Ike moans while Molly offers more indiscernible mumbles: *by holy rite of Hecate   distressed soul   by flames of Banal   fall unvexed into Chaos   seek attractor and calamity.*

'Ma ... '

'Do you feel it? Do you hear an echoing sound? Is anyone replying to your call?'

Ike: ' ... *Ma* ... she was wearing a blue jacket that had a sort of ... *belt* ... built into it ... nobody said anything about the barbed wire ... '

Is Ike disintegrating before their eyes? Is he flickering away?

'Wait a moment,' Molly says.

She places her hands on the urn's lid as if to open it, but balks. Something isn't right.

David smells, or thinks he smells, something familiar. Faint whiffs. Like gunpowder and aftershave.

'I don't think she's here,' Molly says. 'Someone is here, but I'm sorry. I don't think it's her.'

Ike's head drops.

'But I'm definitely indexing a presence.'

A palpable chill permeates the room. A prickling, a shift. Samantha inhales sharply.

Molly: 'I'm looking at you, David.'

So then everyone is looking at him, judging through the dimness.

David: 'At me?'

'Somebody is calling to you.'

'To me.'

'You.'

'I don't ... Who?'

'Someone from elsewhere. Search yourself. Obey impulses. Listen to your internal receptors.'

Internal receptors. Wait. That stench, fanning from where. Far in the murky gymnasium of the mind. A voice, maybe. A growl, possibly.

'The General,' he says.

Silence.

Ike: '*What?*'

'At least I sort of ... From the movie. I see boots. There's a gun, a pistol. I can make out the bridge of his nose. Just barely, but it's there ... it's just like, when I first saw it, I knew.'

All glare intently, expectantly. Molly says, 'Who is it?'

'From the movie. I think I can see him. I can see his eyes. They're icy. They're like these pits of ice.'

'David.'

'The red and white and blue. I can just make him out in the colours.'

'David.'

None of them understand. They don't *understand*. They haven't stared into the enemy's face and confronted that darkness. The smoke rising from the battlefield. The proximity of death.

None of them have stumbled so blindly for so long, waiting for a beacon.

Molly grips the urn and pushes it closer to the circle's centre. 'Whatever this presence is we've contacted, when I open this we're going to see something. Communication will be direct and consequential. But whatever happens, it is only a reflection of what's occuring in the recipient's own psyche. This being David.'

Keep it shut   keep it shut   shut shut shut   keep it shut.

'Be forewarned. We can still sever this communication. There's still room to retreat.'

Ike is wild. 'No,' he yelps. 'We have to keep going. If we're close, we're not turning back.'

Molly looks back to David.

'I … ' he tries. This is so much. This is too much.

Lisa said *just being alive we're in peril but if we die we open up new avenues.* Sarah Promise would advise him to *shed your shackles.* And the sky still burns, while David remains flaccid and lame.

'Whatever. Open up.'

So.

In the initial instant following the urn's opening, nothing happens – no sudden clamour. The moment halts. All present have mouths clamped, paralyzed.

Then: an orangeish light begins to pulse from the narrowed split, and there is an indistinct sound, heaving murmurs and some type of gaseous vapour begins to seep from the glow, rolling into a thick gungy smoke, spilling heavily onto the floor. It stinks like sulphur. The reek is overwhelming.

Sarah Promise shouts *FUCK*.

Through the haze, it gradually appears. Rising from the urn, hoisted by invisible cables above the circle: a shadowed figure, a complication of angles rising from swirling vapours. Tall. Wide. Something in the shape of a man. Burly. Helmeted. The urn's fuzzy light hums, spotlighting this creature in low fury. Shunning the crypt; unshaped, interpretable; a manifestation of ordeal, risen in phobic gases.

This monster, this *being*, looks down at them all.

'Don't let go of one another,' Molly orders. 'Stay *steady.*'

Shadows give off heat, compressed currents of air. Noise, timbre, the steady unfluctuating hum – the room wavers.

David and the monster make eye contact. Its lips are pursed tight. Its posture is impeccable. Its brow is knitted. Sherman tanks for shoulders, missile silos for arms, legs as fortresses. Its eyes have seen plunging fighters deliver death to thousands, unfortunate klutzes trampled under the treads of their own company's tanks. They have married the spoils of history to the disappointment of a modern age. To these eyes, Chaos Farm is just another hill to conquer.

David almost rises to stand at attention. Salute.

'*Maintain the connection,*' Molly orders.

The general is clad in full uniform, battlefield greens. His posture arches squarely; his gestures are limited and ungenerous, half here, dissoluble, its face defined by lapping light. Look at the medals, the stars, decorations of valour. Stand in awe of this laboured stance, these strenuously polished boots.

'It's fucking *George C. Scott,*' Bedel shrieks.

Ike is paralyzed, his jaw sunken. He appears to be quietly moaning.

Molly, struggling to maintain poise, addresses the creature, shouting something over the hum: *we welcome you to Chaos Farm we offer an open channel,* but is drowned by the heightening din: subsonic, suprasonic. It is in everything, amplified through the connection of their twelve.

'Speak to it,' Molly shouts to David.

David can barely respond. The mind threatens shutdown.

'What ... '

'You're the attractor and the constant. Speak to it.'

What do you say to truth incarnate? By the unrolling of the tape across his old vcr's freaky heads, worlds blossomed between his couched location and the screen. Untold insight. Immeasurable wrath, scorn as fiery haystacks. Bring on the confusion. But now he sits mute under smouldering skies. The face of the end, brewed here in brimstone.

David tries to speak, managing only: ' … I was … '

What do you say?

'This is ridiculous,' Bedel shouts, hysteria in his voice. 'This is a movie.'

But it isn't. This is non-fiction. This is the realization of immense truth, truth weighing heavier and deeper than anything so far. Zombie generals, demon actors, spectres reborn to stalk the earth – this is not ridiculous. This is not fantasy. The General doesn't budge. He hovers ungrounded above the urn.

Ike is convulsive. His face is bruise-purple and he's near-drooling. '*Ma*,' he sobs, '*Ma mama MA.*'

David holds on tight. But against all will, he's compelled toward this apparition. He is here, with the moon shining robustly over forests, snow-coated meadows unravelling for his absorption, ducks toiling in their intemperate domicile. He is here because he has been brought here, and elsewhere there are troubles he hopes to flee. But these are troubles beyond escape. You have to look with both eyes open and perceive the full depth. Situation and place are components of the visual, the task of identification. The General clenches his jaw, creating burrows in this face's rugged terrain, his flesh scarred and spent with razor burn. Looking into this face is to peruse the abyss; nothing there is lovable, only fearful and freakish.

Hang on.

Gaseous matter streams freely over the floor, filling the room. The apparition awaits David's word. Multitudes of options hover and collide. There may be a word, pumped full of connotation and meaning – a word creeping from quivering lips, one word like a hiss, something spat rather than said – to sum up the woe and hardiness of time; importance and resonance loaded into a word like ammo, a prompt charged with potential; a word to wreck cities and lay waste to empires. A word to describe all the terrors, the allure of death, our salacious greed for self-ruin, a word gagging the throat from which it wells in swift poison, a word in a tongue long archaic, scythed, banished. A word. Say it, as a lark. A laugh. Stammer it feebly. Howl it like damnation. Learn it. Say the word. *Say it*. Bring back the dead, accept all possibility. Calm the living with cushions of maybe.

'Speak to it,' Molly again shouts.

' ... I ... can't ... '

But then he does.

Where the heck have you been?

Without parting lips, in a voice like bulldozers ravaging loathing earth, the answer: *at home watching the Niners through the mountain ranges of Algiers and Versailles stumbling through the streets in the city and the country sniffing the snow where the bodies fell falling asleep to infomercials in trenches in court-rooms in streets bearing my crosses pinning medals these kids scoping out want ads.*

And then the creature asks: *But where have you been, chief?*

David hangs his head. *I don't know I've been irresponsible now and then I think I get a step ahead but then three steps back I'm losing ground.*

Bedel is freaking out. 'This is absolute shit,' he yelps, tearing his hands away from the connection.

Molly cries *no*, but it's too late. With Bedel's rupture, the equilibrium is rocked from its base. The shadowed creature begins to shudder, to mutate – the mountainous head shrinks, the proud posture shrivels, the precision of angles softens to a smear. Its pulsing buzz immediately trails to a low whump, only to be replaced by a sudden ear-splitting howl. Listen: its plaintive cry, echoing like plummeting bombs. The sound rises, twisting into a horrific siren, seemingly resounding from all directions, the ceiling, the floor, the mind. The air screams. Deafens.

The image goes fuzzy, static with snow. Poor cable reception.

'*God*,' Wyatt shouts. 'What is that *sound*?'

It says *are you going to fart around the house all day reading frigging comic books.*

Yes. This is The Father, whose battles were waged only against and within himself. He was no champ, no staid warrior swirling in the ether. Faucets and weather reports and informal handshakes – these were his adversaries. David barely recognizes his ruddy complexion and cordy neck, his emaciated build. The Father is not wearing his glasses. The Father, who customarily wore sweaters and GWGs, slippers at nighttime, Timex perpetually, now wears mythology. Jackets of typhoon, golf shirts of dreams. The Father is apparently displeased.

'Don't be afraid,' Molly says, even as she herself inches away.

Roslyn cries out in something between horror and amazement: 'It's all *bloody*.'

Bloody. Look closer: The Father is there, chortling his nervous chortle, jingling change in his pocket. He is there, hovering in and above the circle. But there is also another image, coupled, superimposed, with his appearance. There are drippings.

David almost swears he sees the monster shrug, sort of apologetically.

'Dad ... ' he tries, reaching, his throat stifled to a croak.

But even as it gains clarity, The Father's image recedes, shifting again, leaving only its transparent, ceaseless scream. Behold its gaping maw, its splayed mouth ridged with riven lips, dark gums holding dull-bladed teeth. Witness the nets of spittle intersecting its plates, the sectors of its hungry jaws. Everything else fades, leaving only the greedy mouth.

'Dad.'

This monster isn't The Father. But it *is*. Illusions multiply, superimposed; none of these apparitions are what they seem. The monster squeals like a demonic boar, writhing and shrieking rebellion against the containment of its summoning. Inside its mouth laps a blood-soaked tongue – this mouth would encompass a man, a Volvo, a soccer field. Its rapacious mouth would devour all of Chaos.

'*Close it*,' Wyatt yells at Molly.

She looks to David. For the first time, her face betrays terror. The experiment has spun out of control. The circle is broken; all retreat from the circle and this dripping monster, but – David gleans as his eyes dart from each to the next – none comprehend what they've brought upon themselves.

'*Close it close it*.'

Sensing rising danger, Hector and Roslyn are already hurrying for the stairs. Wyatt helps Samantha hobble away. Sarah Promise remains seated with her palms clamped over her ears, until Hirota hauls her to her feet and they follow the others.

Look to Molly: she's blocked, paralyzed, helpless.

Ike: cowering behind a chair in the corner.

Nothing could tame this freakish thing. Nothing but – David lunges forward and seizes the urn. In a prolonged instant he looks up, lid in hand, and peers directly into the screaming mouth – if, in this moment, it fell upon him to *describe in one word the abyss*, to say and learn the word that crowbars the tomb, that defies all reason, he would now have the answer of answers: *mouth*. Lips fuming, fangs gnashing, a craw coiling into Hell.

These hungry chops yawn for him.

David slaps the urn shut with a sharp *shtack*.

But: the prevailing effect is not what he had predicted; just as the disconnection of the circle's link raised its ire, closing the lid and lopping off its base sends the mouthed ghoul into paroxysms of rage. Its screams reach new levels, baring its razor fangs to fullest extension, and, now freed from the conduit from which it's sprung, rises through sulphuric vapours to stretch itself serpentile to the ceiling's limit. Dark indistinguishable fluid splashes across the circle's ornate diagram.

David's head swims. But Dad. I never knew you could be so. But it's not. It's not really. Its phlegmy trails. Its drooling trails. Why would you. But Dad. But *it's not.* He wants to black out, fall faint, overwhelmed. You want to retreat. Retract. Remove.

Swear it has eyes. Swear it has commanding eyes.

But look: the monster howls and lunges forward, pouncing, toward Bedel.

Why did you. What compelled you to.

No Dad no.

Its fangs find Bedel's flesh. It is an impossibly clean cut, a division without tear or cling, severing the body neatly in two.

The Father had been a champ with a T-bone and a skillet.

Her blood sprayed.

Bedel's halved body drops to the cement.

The mouth lunges further, striking Muzz at his left leg's meatiest flank, managing a solid chomp of thigh. There is an instant gush. Blood, everywhere. Muzz issues a pained scream of indistinct syllables, jerking and kicking it away. The creature thumps against the hearth, dazing itself on impact.

Muzz collapses. David moves to help him, eyeing the monster as it pauses to lap fluid from its lips. They scrutinize one another. Its yellow eyes weep tears of pus. It invites, taunts.

David hears it grumble: *that arsehole referee doesn't know shit from Shinola.*

Molly is at his side, helping support Muzz. Her calm has been shattered; panic grips her.

'What have you *done?*' she cries.

What. Has he done. Muzz claws at David's shirt, his jeans stained dark.

The monster looks around. Many have fled. A heavy globule of saliva dangles from its lips. It looks at Wyatt, who is helping Samantha trudge for the stairs, her bum leg impeding escape.

Its next move is clear.

Get out of here, David tells it.

Just like The Father, always overstaying his welcome.

'Ohmylegmy*leg,*' Muzz moans.

And then, as strangely and unexpectedly as it arrived, it departs. It rears itself in a hunched chimpish crouch, wagging its smeared tongue at him. *Time to hustle. Get a move on.* David swears he sees it wink. Then it launches itself toward an upper basement window, tearing away the boards covering it with one fierce motion, casting the wood aside. It smashes through glass, diving headfirst onto the lawn outside. David hurries across and cranes to look, but the dark has already enveloped the monster's withdrawal. It hurries away into the night, its diminishing screams echoing into oblivion.

'Merciful fate,' Samantha gasps. 'What was that?'

David shuts his eyes. *To be anywhere   anywhere but here.* Pieces of Bedel are scattered on the floor. The room stinks of sulphur and fear. This is Chaos, truly.

'I think it was my father … '

The tail lights of Hector's van shrink into the blackness, red points disappearing into the forested thick. The woods blaze with transport, with shock, with spillage.

There is no excuse for the untold havoc tonight has wreaked. Ike and Molly and Samantha and David are in the kitchen, slurping tea. Somewhere in another room, Gwendolyn weeps relentlessly.

'Where's Sarah?' David asks.

No one replies.

Hector is rushing Muzz to a hospital in the closest town, somewhere west, almost an hour's drive away.

Ike is sitting at the table, staring into his cup, nibbling on Oreos. He hasn't peeped since the incident; he simply munches cookies and sips from a mug that reads *I Got SMASHED in the Bahamas* – the joke is a dent in its side – and pushes his glasses up his nose. He has taken out his contacts.

Bedel had been the caretaker, entrusted to carry on the menial upkeep of the Farm while Ike dallied elsewhere. Bedel, alone through tough winter, attending to the house, readying its rooms. Dusting surfaces soon to be blotted with his own flung blood. Now he is in pieces, collected under a tarp in the back shed.

Ike chews. Oreo after Oreo.

It is getting late. And somewhere out there, a killer, a *beast*, runs free.

Wyatt and Roslyn enter by way of the back door. Wyatt shakes his head. 'It's gone. Made for the highway is my guess. It's quick.'

This, David already knows. It jogged regularly in its younger years.

'We went way too far this time,' Samantha says. Her hands are shaky.

Wyatt nods. 'I think the decision is pretty clear. Something needs to be done about that … *thing* … before others get hurt, or worse. Or it might come back.'

Looking hard at David.

He cringes. 'It's not like I intended … '

Wyatt cuts him off. 'No. But it was you who introduced it. I've been coming to Chaos Farm for almost ten years and all this time, zero incidents. Zero. That sort of evil poop just doesn't belong here. Bedel had a son, dammit. Did you know that? He had a six-year-old son in Chicago. Are you going to get on the phone to call his son?'

No. David is not going to get on the phone.

Molly speaks. 'I can't imagine it'll return. It's free now.'

Roslyn slaps her forehead. 'Free? Why *free*?'

Then Ike stands, unsteadily. All hush.

'David. You are to leave. Right now. You are to go and get rid of this succubus you have unleashed. Wherever it's going, find it and destroy it. Whatever it takes. You created it. Now get rid of it. I'll drive you out to the highway if you want, but you have to leave this moment, because frankly, right now the stink of death is too strong for me to even think.'

The night is unfriendly. The sky over the road out from Chaos is untwinkling.

Ike has the Saturn's heater on HI. The radio is on but low, humbly intoning: *I'm a cowboy and a steel horse I ride.*

David opts not to fiddle. He has been banished.

They pass through the farm's security gates, back out to the highway. 'I'll take you as far as the Shell station,' Ike says, his eyes on the road.

Where will he go. Home. Return phone calls. Videotapes. Ride buses. Fill time sheets. *No* – the faint pinkish stains on his pants point his way. He will fulfill few commands. He will pursue, sniffing the trail. He will finish what's begun. This is his duty – he already senses the monster's taunts echoing in his mind. It has already gained ground. Even now it seeks further flesh to taste.

'Molly sees something in you,' Ike says. 'She believes you're meant for bigger things.'

David: 'Oh, I don't know about … '

'Take that as you will. Right now I couldn't give a shit what happens to you.'

They drive in silence, the radio their buffer. *I've seen a million faces and I've rocked them all.*

The Shell station sits in stark lights and neon: OPEN 24 HRS. Early in the morning and the place is dead. Inside, a fat-faced kid eyeballs them as they pull up, halting near the entrance.

'Here,' he says.

'Ike,' David says, 'I don't know what I'm doing. I don't know where to go.'

Ike is unsympathetic. 'When the time comes, you'll know what to do.'

'I'll know what to do.'

'You'll know. I guaran*fucking*tee you'll know.'

David sighs with something between frustration and humiliation.

'David,' Ike says quietly, deliberately, 'things have opened up. I'd like to say that I don't blame you for what's happened, but I do. All quakes initiate from some epicentre. If you follow my reasoning. That monster, whatever you claim it is – I don't think I want to know – killed a colleague of mine. And Muzz is just barely clinging. I need to be at his side. I need to make what's wrong right. I see teddy bears flexing in the wake. Whatever. You need to be rectifying the damage you have done, starting now. Chaos Farm has no room for those who can't fight their own battles. Chaos Farm is *limited*.'

'But I never claimed ... Sarah implied. She said that it was in the. That being there would be ... '

'Maybe it has. Maybe.'

' ... but it's all backfired. I've never ... My intentions weren't to hurt anyone ... '

All of a sudden, Ike seizes him by the shoulder, clutches a tendon and squeezes hard. '*David*. Haven't you learned anything? Your intentions mean *shit*. Intentions are curses. Hitler had intentions, you know.'

'But. Please, I just. I really don't see what ... what does ... *Hitler* has to do with ... '

'Did you see the hunger in that monster's mouth? Because I certainly did. Is that *your* hunger, David?'

'No ... '

But. His stomach grunts as he spies a rack of Vachon cakes in the store window. Soft, few. Ike releases his hand, leaving a burning ouch in David's shoulder, and lets his forehead fall against the steering wheel.

'I haven't slept a blink in four days,' he groans. 'I'm exhausted. And I've taken enough Valium to stagger a rhino. The last time I remember having a full night's rest was last fall, when I rented out a small apartment in Bucharest and a thug I'd recently fired as my bodyguard broke in, beat the living hell out of me and stole my passport and four grand in traveller's cheques. After I had my broken ribs bandaged up I slept and dreamt of glaciers. The glaciers had faces like the Marx Brothers. Groucho waggled his eyebrows at me coyly, like a pal. That was a good dream.'

'Really.'

'I shit you not. Marx glaciers. Very peaceful, very central.'

'Maybe Molly could help. She seems to be able to ... do things ... '

Ike presses his head harder into the wheel. 'We've had I don't know how many sessions. She suggested heightened social dynamics and prolonged group psychic activity ... lots of un-aloneness, challenges in slim measures. Reminding one of life's zooishness and humanity's specieshood. She prescribed a casual society of induction and deduction. Laughing and eating and lots of pot. She said it would help free me from my reservations, and that soon I wouldn't suffer the anxiety of incorporation. Listen to your anguish. Make it into a motto. Become your wildest expectation. I'd be freed to be a person among persons.'

'But that's what *I* want,' David pleads. 'I want to be freed too ... '

'No,' Ike growls, jerking his head back up. 'There's a murderer in you. I see it. I've seen mongrel fiends chomping at the jugulars of refined men. Predators of all walks. At least I have this capacity. In you there is death. You bring death to the fore. Death to poor poor life. Damn you, David. Damn you.'

Despite the harangue, his face is not angry. His face is the tired smush of an overtaxed source, a well run dry.

'Okay,' David says. 'Okay.'

He unbuckles his seat-belt. The radio offers *forty-five minutes of non-stop rock keeping you up all night.*

Ike stops him. 'Before you go.'

'Mm?'

'Two things. First ... '

Ike reaches across David into the glove compartment. His hand digs through wadded tissues, unfolded maps, a mess of receipts, to produce a object of light russet leather, a black handle protruding.

'A knife,' David says.

'You bet your boots. Take it.'

David accepts it, fingering the bulky handle, turning it in careful hands. He unsheaths it; the blade is sharp, prepped for carving. A knife, a serious knife. Why.

'I'm not so good with this sort of ... ' he starts, then realizes how empty his words sound. How feeble.

'Shut it. Just succeed. Kill it. Then you can whine and complain, if you want.'

David wishes: to be curled in bed, fetal and forgotten, limp against the strifeless strides of a day's work. For once he longs to laze, follow e-mail links, photocopy photocopies, fax faxes, buoyant in nothingness, his strategy for the future influenced only by lunch menus. Somewhere, Jim is flossing his teeth. Teeth full of chocolate.

'Also,' Ike says.

'What.'

'Molly gave me a message. More of a recommendation.'

'Oh.'

Ike mashes his lips together. 'She said *tell David   beware of small enclosed spaces.* That was it.'

'Small enclosed spaces.'

'That's what she said to tell you. The rest I leave to you. But I wouldn't ignore Molly's advice if I were you.'

'No,' David says. 'I won't.'

With that, David exits. The Saturn returns to the nocturnal forgotten, leaving him here, solo at the ridge of nothing. David is tired, very tired, but he doesn't allow himself to waver. He has a mission, a quest. He is a soldier with an assignment. Blood compels. Fortune compels. The enemy hides and attacks. Ahead, the road beckons, taunts. The concrete and tar, the petrol stink, the unshimmering ahead, all of it commands: to *do*, to *go*.

He does; he goes.

III

Victory over the enemy, complete and irrefutable – this is the truth to which we bear witness. The enemy cowers in ruined bunkers, yellow-bellied pissants hugging their sandbags as they sleep their bedwetting Kraut sleep. The lily-hearted enemy. These are not soldiers. These are dogs.

But – *our* boys are brave. They are so goddamn brave that when you watch them clean their rifles you could cry like a girl. United as a proud yoke of silver and camouflage and the heralded beauty of stars and bars, they breakfast with gusto, never looking back at the trembling past. Like a regiment of condors sailing through skies thick with the acrid smoke of bursting shells, like a bison herd crossing virgin plains, like the clockwork precision of the wonders which are our factories producing combs or packets of chewing gum or standard-issue condoms, like the inevitability of our mortal fates – so rise our armies, to melt under African suns, to compose mortar elegies, to wail canticles mourning trenches of pain.

War is dizzy. War is late at night. War thunders in the living rooms of the half-asleep, the semi-alive.

In war there is only the arena of sacrifice, wherein one man's duty is amplified and distorted to appear as one vast wave of rifle-toting figures in fatigues hastening valiantly forward. Our spirited drive reimagines Patton at Messina, Hannibal targeting Rome; but in lieu of tusked steed we have the coach bus, the sport utility vehicle. The quest for glory. The shove of freedom and the vanquishment of despots. The sheer huzzah of it all. In war there is no love and no whipped cream and no fizz and no tweezing and no silk panties; there is no love because war is love, and war is shit, and anyone who says otherwise is a goddamned fucking liar.

This is the waking dream, the dream of a highway uncoiling into night, open and unknowable. The interminable yellow stripe: a guide to deliverance, the tortured route, the hugeness. The weird big empty.

Signs tile the roadside, delineating a highway dotted with the tail lights of semis and rigs, mammoths of transit hauling weighty loads through the dark. The road: winding past darkened towns and neighbourhoods, jutting forth in julienned cement, in possibilities distant and forbidden, the production line of geography coupling and withering, yellowed grassfields and weedy thickets beyond guardrails, plains of rubble pushing up against ramps under the light of more and more road signs violating the dark – everything, the whole fiasco, linked in evanescence. On the highway, the hurtling dream of the road, everything is lifeless and transient. Everything is *in between*.

Travelling, again. Hunting horrors.

This hallucination is a grand and convincing dream. It's like the myth of death – the fantasy that the end is merely the end. That proposition, once a consoling truth, has been dispelled in the opening of a Chaos urn. Now everything is in doubt. And so you can accept the onslaught of these cold days, the colder nights, without certainty to assure your path. The only strategy now is to continue on, to soldier on, and not relent. Never sway from the mission.

Let the cosmos be your guide. Let the pull of your heart persuade you, lead you to your goal.

But can you, confidently, answer the question tugging inside: are you predator, or prey?

His horoscope had foretold *several opportunities will come together to effect a change of surroundings*. That was in another age, under captivity of computer and desk, as he filed away days into nonexistence. Time salvageable by a simple click of mouse: *undo*. Now time, once a valued commodity, is in surplus. Seated at a doughnut shop along the highway as windy day gives way to black night, David leafs through a discarded paper and the horoscope buried in its back pages:

> Leo (July 21–August 21) – You should be ready to 'depend upon the kindness of strangers.' Hesitate and you'll miss needed opportunities. What you've been seeking may be just around the corner.

Yes – he's been depending on the kindness of strangers; he's covered considerable ground in the last few days, hitching rides and hopping buses in an unquestioning stupor, moving as quickly as he can. Spending as little time as necessary in a fixed position. Always pushing. In war, in the pursuit of territory, it is always better to advance than to nestle in, to lay fortifications. So far he has been following his barest instincts, allowing impulse to be his guide, following a dizzying path, trying to pinpoint his direction.

Keep moving, keep going. Keep pursuing. Sniffing along the highway, down countless routes and junctions, down down into dislocation, the wet stink of destruction under his nose. Days have passed, with only a vague but compelling instinct offering any hint of his target. He is wafting on breezes; he is tramping through a minefield under unreined starlight and an Esso sign's sick light; he is sagging on strange curbs drinking a carton of Tropicana; his eyes are searching every crevice for a sign or a signal; he is alone without arms save the blade in his pocket, and his only reference for navigation is a final goal that may be nothing but vivid flashback.

He doesn't want to think too hard about what that goal entails.

All around, greasy batter smells dominate. He is tired and his nose is runny.

David eyes the surrounding tables, occupied mostly by men with ashy teeth and overwrought eyes, coffee-tremoring hands, bellies spilling over buckles betraying years of diner grub. Considerable midsectional heft, the pearish build of overnight drives, the creased faces of caffeination and scant sleep. The challenges of kilometres. Here are truckers, long-haulers, carriers of freight. Men with clear aims.

And here is David, on the margins. Here is where he will stay. No double double coffees with the off-duty nurses and cig-chuffing waitresses. No sunset at shift's completion.

Depend upon the kindness of strangers.

There are vague stories suggesting the gruesome fates befalling those who takes rides with truckers. Crowbars behind seats. A purported network of deviance, plundering the innocence of unsuspecting hitchers. Things sinister behind the corporate logos splashed on broad cargo trailers. Psychos behind windshields. Muzz told a story about a French guy who tried to run him down in his truck when he wouldn't pay for his steak.

But he has no choice. He folds the paper and rises.

He approaches a table of truckers by the window. The grizzled men eye him with dark scrutiny as David hovers awkwardly, asking if anyone's got a spare seat. Just any further up the road. There is silence as the truckers enjoy a moment of superiority.

Then a crewcutted orangutanish man, squeezing an earlobe, asks, 'How far is it going?'

David, uneasily: 'How far does it have?'

'It has as far as it has, skinflint.'

This sends the table into a rollick of hearty guffaws. David suddenly hates them, because they don't know. They don't know the smell of charcoal, which isn't charcoal but sulphur, which isn't actually sulphur at all but brimstone, and they don't know this. He's not even a hundred percent certain he himself knows this. He has visual clues, little else. He has weight to bear; what do they have? Cartons of Mountain Dew and frozen french fries and pain relievers. They have containers of quantities. David has lives in the tissue of his unbleeding scabs.

Another of the men, his body thick and his mouth dappled with doughnut jelly, but nonetheless the easiest-appearing of this gruff crew, speaks up: 'You're putting her how far now?'

'I can't really say. But I would really appreciate … '

The guy eyes him warily. 'You're not some Bible-banger fudgepacker, are you there, skinflint?'

'No banging, no packing. Just needing a ride.'

Another hearty round of chuckles. Guffaws.

The waking dream, the occupation of territory. Heroic spoils. Commanders in the ecstasy of conquest. Tycoons grinning upon boulevards. Jungles, wilderness. Explorers spiking flags, NASA at the moon's crater. Lunar landscapes, asphalt like cooled lava, glacial barrenness, toughness, there are staggering signs staked high in alien earth: U-HAUL and GOODYEAR and EAST SIDE MARIO'S, like flaming flags over paved plains. This is the battlefield of the waking dream, which is less a full dream than a head-nodding nightmare, and an acceptance – present and unswerving – that time can be nullified into logos, into parkades as howling gulfs. An acceptance that every second is a commodity.

'Like the blues?' the truck driver, named Bill, asks.

David blinks into the high-beams of a passing sedan, briefly blinded by refractions in the snow-streaked windshield. 'Sure. Yeah.'

Bill inserts a cassette into the dashboard's player. The recording is raw, distant. Of the past.

'Willie Dixon,' Bill says.

'Mm.'

'His voice has power. You know what I mean? *Power*.'

'Mm.'

Bill sighs through his nose. 'So, where you to, Dave?'

'Um. I'm after someone.'

'Ah. A girl.'

'Uh … no … it's more like … it's my father. Sort of. Not really.'

Bill grunts understanding. 'Oh. Well. That's a toughie. What is it, this Pops you're after is your biological whatever.'

Pause. 'Sort of. Definitely biological.'

'Check.'

Willie Dixon sings *you can't judge a book by looking at its cover*.

'Have you ever woken up,' Bill asks, 'and wondered where a week of your life has gone?'

'Um … '

'I used to be a drunk. I can tell you this. A big bloated drunk. I drank so many people right out of my life, and so many paycheques. I could think of faces, but … no no no. I'd lose days and weeks, back when. It got into me like cancer. Everything became about that *thing*. All the stories you hear about being trapped in a dark place and all that insane bullshit. It's all true. I was there.'

'Jeesh.'

'Darn right, jeesh. Eventually I hit a wall. But it was different than how they usually say. They talk about moments of clarity when the truth and the whole mess is revealed and there's a flash of light and there's a recognition and so on and so forth. That's true too, sort of. I remember, I was holed up in this dingy hotel in Winnipeg, this is almost eight years now. I hadn't done a haul in months, my licence was suspended for a DUI, and I was guzzling like a case and a bottle of Five Star every day. I'm sitting at the bar in the basement, in this place that was the hangout for Indian biker gangs. Most of them were fine enough, but there were a few that always got rowdy and scrappy. There were definitely a few. That whole period is a big blur now. I'd be stumbling down the steps from my room to the bar, so ripped I'm pissing in the hallway and arguing with these loudmouth skanks with their gums all rotted out and these ... '

He pauses while passing a Honda, then eases back into the lane.

'My point being ... anyway. I just had this moment. I'm sitting at that bar and as usual the place is packed in the middle of the afternoon, people parked at the damn video gambling machines, pumping quarters over and over. And I'm sitting there half-conscious when suddenly this little Indian woman with this fat lip and these big-ass glasses starts shrieking this high-pitched shriek because she's hit big numbers on that frigging machine, and this bell goes off, and when I look and see her freaking out – she's almost *in tears* at her pitiful little jackpot – this sort of wave comes over me, rolling up from the floor up my spine, zipping through my whole skeleton. It hit me like a hailstorm. I hopped out of my chair, totally tanked, and sprinted up three flights of stairs to my room and threw myself in the shower with my shirt still on. I just went bananas. I was drunk beyond drunk but it hit me *sharp*. Time stopped. And at that second I knew the truth. It was so so *so* clear. You know what it was?'

David doesn't answer. He waits.

'I just realized. There's no Heaven. There's no Hell. There's no *God*. None of that crud. All my life, I was one of those who just assumed someday I'd get face to face with Lord Jesus Whooziz, and all my troubles would ... pass. Eventually everything would be all right. You say the word *God* and you think. But in that moment, right then, I understood. It was this feeling of complete lonesome emptiness. It overtook me. At that second I knew I was completely on my own. If you understand. I saw through the flashes of light and the clouds and the bleeding fingernails and the curtains. Death was coming like a brick wall, coming fast and coming *hard*. I was killing myself, and I wasn't going to emerge in a fluffy cloud like L'il Jiminy Fuckit floating high above the Earth. I was going to be a hunk of cold flesh in the dirt with the worms and the slime. A pile of ashes. It's easy to talk about these things now, sitting here, but at that second, there in that shitty bar with my nose in a glass and my skin all dried out and my stomach this huge pathetic flabby flap, I understood the reality of my, like ... my *mortality*, just as well as I knew my own frigging ass.'

Outside, the snow is beginning to ease.

'Looking into that hurricane, you'd think most people would want to escape even further. But for me it was the opposite. It was a mind-blowing thing, knowing that at last I had no one to look out for me. Just Billy against the world, nothing else. No second chance. It was up to me to decide how to lead my life. No safety net. No frigging Jesus this God that. I was a corpse on ankles.'

Bill sniffs heavily, his lungs drawing mass. A cheerless breath.

'Lots of truckers are frigging Bible-bangers, did you know that? You ever wonder where those little booklets come from that are always lying around in truck-stop pissers, the ones about how evolution is a conspiracy and everything? Truckers. They get on the e-mail and meet up and have Sunday services in diners. Unbelievable. People are sheep. People are *sheep*.'

Shaking his head in disbelief.

'There's that way we're separated from our mothers and the whole castration issue. The whole complex of how a guy has to overcome those urges, when you want to kill the father. It's the same way people get attached to religion. It's the exact same thing. Because the thing is you don't overcome that need, your weird mother urge, it just adjusts. People are always looking for that reassurance, with drinking and TV and everything. But what they want isn't that approval, not in the end. People don't want to be patted on the head, like here's a good little fuckface, run along now and do your taxes. What they want is to return to that *original* state, in the gulley with the fluid and the shut eyes, where it was safe and calm and you didn't even have to breathe for yourself. You were clean and naked. What is that?'

Again, David refrains.

'That's frigging Heaven. And that's what religion is all about, it's this crybaby thing. When you finally figure it out for yourself, it's so clear and obvious and full of ... You see how people just want mommies and a warm place. And after that everything's different. But what really turns my stomach is when these sexless housewives start yapping about *spirituality*. They think about God, it looks just like Oprah. God in slacks and a turtleneck. I get physically sick when they go on about that whole cozy *start a backyard garden* bull. These zombies with their MasterCards – don't even get me started about that whole self-help frigging ... that sick empty crap, with all that money flying everywhere, it just makes me want to strangle myself.'

Another weighted breath. A thought.

'Sitting at that bar in Winnipeg and staring into those toothless mouths ... a lot of those Indians are totally destroyed from decades of the government screwing them over and all that Catholic priest ass-diddling. It just turns my stomach to even think about how badly things have gone.'

There is a break between songs on the tape, a sluice of soft hiss. The road ahead gradually clears to sharp angles, snowless by headlights.

'Sorry,' Bill says. 'I don't mean to spaz your ear off.'

'No,' David says, 'I hear you. So ... you stopped drinking after that.'

'Just about. I had another spell after, you don't need to know about that. Otherwise, not a drop in almost eight years. That's eight hard years, I won't kid you. It's not easy. I'm a fidgety bastard and I still have trouble sleeping six nights out of seven. Once it gets into you, you can't really get it out. It's how you sit in a chair. It's *everything*. But that moment of finally seeing through the crud of God and Heaven and it all, that is ... I wouldn't trade that for anything. That's the ultimate peace of mind.'

His voice thickens, something caught and throated. 'You probably think I'm a complete jackass.'

'No,' David says, 'I see. People want answers. You found an answer.'

'Exactly. That's exactly it.'

They drive, Willie singing against their silence: *I can heal the sick and even raise the dead and make you little girls talk out of your head.*

On most Sundays and holidays, David's mother and her sister Jo-Beth set off in the family station wagon for church. Fairview United, meekly squished between rival gas stations, was newish and modest. When he was small, David joined the women on these outings. Sunday School, crayoning pages: Moses on a dirty cliff, Jesus in hay-heavy manger, Noah with giraffes. But after a while he began to notice, in the fractured way in which children grasp the strange goings-on between parents, how The Father shunned church. The Father didn't acknowledge or discuss or inquire about church. He expressed no specific irk; he simply never spoke of it. Eventually David followed suit, even though his mother, upon returning from church, always seemed uplifted by the experience, humming the catchier hymns under her breath.

But is she – was she – a *believer*? No recollection of religious fire lingers in his memory. No mention of sin or repentance at the dinner table. God hadn't haunted the house's hallways, the storage closets, the laundry chute. The songs and the sermonizing and the collective spirit, the sombre occasions – this was his mother's devotion to the church. Funerals and weddings and candle-lighting ceremonies. A secretarial for a committee sponsoring Ugandan families. A sense of worth. David's mother, spritzing hairspray, hiking her purse over her shoulder, heading off to answer duty's call.

From time to time, his mother would read to him from a Bible storybook. She would pose questions, testing him: does he remember the story of Jonah? Yes, he would say, Jonah was swallowed by a whale. When Mary and Joseph lost Jesus in Jerusalem, where did they find him? In a church, a synagogue. Where did Samson's strength come from? From his hair, right. She would nod approvingly. It was stories, fables, parables. Characters with goofy names, morals that never seemed to relate to anything. No showers of slag, no wrath. Only heroes and villains.

David would be King of the Jews. A leader of men, a divinely appointed monarch. David would fell the ogre Goliath with ingenuity and a sling. Goliath as General, as Rommel, as the invincible. Goliath shot in the eye with a stone, like Odysseus blinding the Cyclops. Goliath as Stealth Bomber, skimming the cusp of the horizon, sneaky as a wolf. War as history, as a hundred thousand tortured souls groaning at the ridge of the abyss, Judgment Day reiterating itself like the repetition of a blues song.

'Do you believe in God?' Bill asks.

David rubs his temple with his forefinger. 'I don't think so,' he says. 'But I've seen some things lately that, well, they've sort of made me question ... '

'Do tell.'

'It's difficult to explain. I've met people who seem to ... communicate with ... it's really hard to explain.'

Murderous apparitions. Spirits retrieved from death's grip. The healing of a finger's touch. A screech that persists, haunting the recesses of his mind, entrenched into the crust. It is the shrill trumpet of battle. It is the scream of The Father, somewhere out here, luring him. Is it killing. Is it laughing. It moves quickly – where is it headed?

He can't explain these wonders to Bill; he can scarcely rationalize them for himself.

'I really don't know what I'm talking about,' David says, fidgeting in his seat.

The road implores them steadily further. The cab of the truck is warm and the seat is comfortable. He is covering ground. Right now, even if only temporarily, things are all right.

Bill plays more scratchy blues tapes, lonely invocations and wailing harps, as David lolls in proximity of sleep. He gazes out the window at the black view hurtling past: brief towns, deadened suburbs, long stretches of routes pressed against coiling tributaries. Lifeless land spotted with snow, desiccated rivulets, offshoots of withered pavement. The middle of nowhere.

Wait. *There.* On the road's shoulder, he spots a glimmer of motion. He's not sure what, exactly – something moving, running, *galloping,* trying to keep stride with the truck. Something, a silhouette, giving off steam, or smoke. He starts, sitting up in his seat.

'Something wrong?' Bill asks.

'My father … '

Try to focus. He shakes himself alert, to sharpness.

'Your *what?*'

David peers out the window, back. The truck is moving so fast. Trees and boggy ridges line the road's shoulder, hinting at shapes in scarce light. He quickly reformulates what his eyes captured. Maybe. No.

He tries to calm his racing heart. He looks again: whatever it was, it's gone.

'Just a deer,' he says.

'You saw a deer?'

'Yeah. It startled me.'

'Must have been something else. There's no deer on this road this time of year. It must have been something smaller, like a raccoon or a skunk or something. Was it small?'

'Um. Yeah … it was a porcupine. It was just a porcupine moving around. I was … nodding off. Half dreaming, half awake. I thought I saw … '

Bill looks at the dashboard clock. 'It's late. Take it easy. Sleep.'

Yes. *Sleep.* Sleep against the enemy. Rest against wickedness and terror.

At a junction between highway routes, Bill drops David off at a roadside truck stop. Some intuition directs him to go no further north, and right now guesswork remains the only line of attack at his disposal. David smiles genuinely as Bill wrings his hand, bidding him to *stay safe* before roaring away.

This stop houses a muffler shop and a lunch counter, a trio of gas pumps. At this late hour the tables sit mostly vacant but for scattered clusters idling over mugs. David sits in the driver's seat of a racing video game, fiddling with its steering, staring into its pixelated racetrack. A guy in a reflective jacket, a highway worker with slick hair, asks David if he's going to play. David surrenders the wheel.

This hunt is starting to take its toll. Fatigue. Incoherence. His temples throb, uncushioned and unpillowed. He wonders what unbound activity might be transpiring at Chaos Farm at this moment. Dining on some bountiful feast, hacking out philosophies, emptying bottles, mourning the dissipation of time. Tucking their overstimulated selves to bed, their brains molten with heat and smoke. Do they wonder about him, about David, the undesirable who failed to meet standards, who killed Bedel – do they think about him?

And Molly, does she wonder about him?

Hunger gurgles in his stomach. In his wallet he finds a pair of dimes. By the entrance there is an ATM, so he transacts. The swiping of the card, the pressing of buttons, the buoyant familiarity of this common ritual – this most normal of normals, eerily automatic. As the machine spits out twenties, he feels assured that even away from the photocopies and fax machines and messages bleeping on screens, he exists in opposition to the rigid machinery. He is defiant in battle. Even though his chequing account is drained and he has maxed his MasterCard. Even as he orders a cheeseburger and a lemonade from the plump girl at the counter, then sits to consume his purchase.

He is here, in the real world, in the bliss of convention. Ketchup as resource, paper napkin as armament. Unwrapping. Feeding.

And yet, even in this lull, splashes of gore invade. *You created it now get rid of it.* Ike is Jim, the boss. Molly is Lisa, agent to the ethereal plane. David is Bedel, killed, remade. Confusion is association, or metaphor – the way advertisements help you forget the truth. Lies. Slogans. Confusion is the same force that pushes him west, toward Ragnarök, Pandemonium. He's heading toward his title bout. He has to be ready to pounce.

A minivan with skis on a roof rack rolls into the parking lot. David watches as two men emerge, heading for the building. Their sweatshirts brandish beer logos and their wide faces are sunburnt. Their ride is a Caravan, a roomy ride. David decides to hit them up for a lift.

But first, the bathroom. It is standard and stark. Echoing tiles and wsshing water. David uses a urinal, then runs the faucet. He looks at himself in the mirror: stubbled cheeks and blackheaded nose, sunken holes for eyes.

Disappointed in the future   disappointed with the future he whisper-sings to himself.

Then: a rustle, nearby. And intermingling with the familiar antiseptic bathroomy stink: that smoky aftershavey smell. David stiffens. Someone is in the bathroom. Someone. But not just a someone. Something, close. Invisible, instant, a presence. No mere trucker grunting out a squeezer in a stall. Something is here, exuding *wrongness*.

David fakes a cough, the throaty sound ringing coldly against tiles. No sound in reply. He backs away from the sink and glances around, coldness crawling up his back. Holding breath. Waiting, paralyzed. He inches toward the row of stalls, crouching to locate any dangling feet. There are none. But, in the furthest stall, there is a discernible *something*, a lump aside the toilet's stained ceramic that he can't identify. He approaches in measured strides, bracing himself.

Perhaps we will be sprung upon, unsuspectingly attacked, silently slain.

Hesitant: 'Hello.'

He is at the stall's door. The smell of aftershave and beer is over-powering. That smell, soapy and clinical. Noxzema's eucalyptic scour, the piss and ammonia of toilets, stale death.

He pokes the door with a cautious index. The door drifts open.

Sprawled on the toilet is a man with his pants down. Or the remains of a man, caught mid-poop. His stomach has been sliced, split in a J-shaped swerve down the abdomen, his entrails drained into his lap. There is scattered blood, hacked disruptions, smears, congelations. Innards sprayed as if from a hose. There are bite marks and burns, singed portions of flesh. Quadrants of bone. The dead man's eyes are still wide. They are awed. Material flashes –

227

this is the guy with the hair, the man calling dibs on *Cruisin' USA*. This man, no longer a man. A man demoted to mere carcass.

A man who was.

On the wall, framing the body, there is a generous smear of purplish fluid. And in the gunk, hastily daubed in fingers of wrenched blood, letters are formed: *ASK   DAVI*

I'm asking, Gary demanded. *I'm asking. I'm asking.*

David's head swims, his mind lolls. Overcome. His functions threaten failure. Oh woozy. Oh don't go. He stumbles back against a wall, his eyes rolling back in his head. Up up. Fainting. Flanks in the folds. Flanks in the clouds. Airborne. Up up, in a dirigible. Hang-gliding. Over the countryside. The snow. Oh don't. Here we go. The truth, the weight. The whole thing. Staring into the savage jaws of the demon. Oh don't when the. *Hang on.* The tissue of the innocent bystander. Skin in tatters.

Everything about this is far worse than he had imagined. Far far worse.

When you are nowhere, you are transparent. You are merely a signal, transmitted, radiated. You are slogging through hordes, head lowered, moving further and further into unidentifiable space, moving deeper into a begrudging continent, your bearings uncertain. Hopeless day dissolves into hopeless night as you thumb through desolation. Unlandmarked fields lined with electrical posts, filed singly like gravestones. Lightless water towers, abandoned vats. Dotless black sky pissing down, indifferent to your shivering. Motion as strategy, as an attack, a hunt over lands of doughnut boxes and dumpsters with potential danger embedded in every passing pair of headlights. Follow the sun rising over the endless parking lot, morning twinkling off a thousand car hoods, a guardrail a billion kilometres long. Form phrases. Divide days into hours and point-five-hours as time passes through reams of flimsy faxes and cardstock and papers still warm from the printer. Dry your sneakers after shortcutting through a marshy detour. Be invisible and inconspicuous. Be an assassin, a ninja. Be transparent, like smog. No heads turn for you. No communication pinpoints you.

You are adrift, splashing in the wake of a passing semi.

Whoosh.

Further.

The miserable night dragged on, cruel rain pounding down, until David reached an exit promising dining and civilization. Under a Home Hardware awning he shivered, hunched in a sniffing soaked ball of self-pity. Sleep came hard. At sunrise, with abating rain, he wobbled down the road's shoulder until discovering this diner, just opening, advertising ALL DAY B-FAST.

Now he hunches over eggs and toast, his clothes chafing and gritty. He is more tired than he has ever been.

When the time comes, Ike said, *you'll know what to do.* In the days since, David has been pestered by this statement. *What to do.*

The quote seemed so familiar, so blank. And last night, shivering on lonesome road, it finally came to him: the line was from the opening scene of *Patton*, George C. Scott addressing off-camera troops. *Some of you are wondering whether you'll chicken out,* Patton said. The soldiers, unshown, would be fresh recruits, biting back terrified tears. *When you put your hand into a pile of goo that was your best friend's face* – Patton spoke with authority, nodding almost imperceptibly – *you'll know what to do.*

Sanctuary. Early morning. The restaurant is warm and mostly empty. The waitress sets down the bottle of Tabasco he'd asked for. He thanks her and dollops it generously on his scrambled eggs. The eggs are firm and the unbuttered toast is crispy and the coffee is hot and strong. Under the table, he toes off his sopping sneakers to dry his socks.

'Excuse me,' he says to her.

'Mm?'

'Do you know … is there a cheap motel or something nearby?'

She looks at him across the counter, through her cigarette's plume. 'There's a Comfort Inn off Exit 12.'

'Is there anything closer? I'm on foot.'

She crushes her cigarette. She is skeptical, forearms biker-tattooed. 'You walked from the highway?'

He nods. She sneers with interest. 'Really. You're just hitching around, or are you going somewhere?'

'Um. A little of both. I'm on the move.'

She eyes him with curiosity, sizing him up. She is young, twenty maybe, skin pale, complexion of a heavy smoker and poor eater, blackened bangs hacked straight, the rest yanked back in a utilitarian braid. Her figure is wide and unsharp, a couch-sitter. But her eyes bespeak trustworthiness, laughing hidden laughter even while brusquely taking orders.

'There's this bed and breakfast further in town,' she says, 'but I don't think you want to stay there. It's more of a gay place. And kind of pricey.'

'Oh.'

She leans forward on the counter. 'I'll be the asshole and ask who you are.'

'David.'

'And what you're doing here.'

'I'm sort of … I'm in between things. Between places.'

He smiles sheepishly. She laughs, then heads off to serve a table. People are beginning to shuffle in as the day stirs awake: old couples, a quintet of men in matching polyester jackets commanding a corner table.

She returns. 'I'll tell you my name. I'm Trixie.'

He notices another pair of men in matching jackets. There is a buzz of anticipation, something amiss.

'What's with the uniforms, with the matching jackets, on all these guys?' he asks. 'Is there something happening?'

'The Speedway's just around the corner on this road, by the bridge.'

David nods. Identifying his non-recognition, Trixie explains.

'Stock cars. You know, races. NASCAR-style. These guys are all in crews. The racetrack is just down the road, just over there. You really just wandered in, huh. You seem sort of dazed.'

By now the day has blossomed to fullness, sun streaming unrestrained through the diner's windows, its cold brightness somehow complementary to the sizzle and spackle of the fryer, the clinking dishes. David doesn't know where he'll go next. In last night's punishing storms he'd lost his way, the direction of his hunt. Even the beckoning hum of his teethy prey has subsided, leaving him no choice but to settle and wait for it to re-emerge.

'What time are the races?' he asks Trixie.

Stock cars, hitched to 4x4s, parade through a chain-link fence into the crowded Speedway parking lot. Their frames are motley, gaudily multicoloured, bedecked in logos: STP, Valvoline, 7-Up. Others, less familiar: Pro Plus Auto Detailing, Daughney's Kwik-Pik.

There are men with protruding bellies and impressive belt buckles, smoking, jawing on plug, tilted against their cars, sizing up today's competition. Men, betraying nerves and excitement through tinted glasses. Men – dads – gleeful in anticipation. Who are these men. Heroes of their own plots. Men who turn wrenches and tick off invoices. Men in offices and garages, men who drive pickups, men who argue with their brothers-in-law about catalytic converters and brake lines and premium versus ultra; they pursue knowledge practical and tactile, balding scholars divining the secrets of unprying or redoing or applying a new coat. They build sheds. These are men David has never known, and in their midst he is a weakling, a soft touch, a wuss. David doesn't fix stubborn sinks or Polyfilla suspect dings in his walls. He doesn't possess the knowledge. In war's drama he would be an early casualty, sobbing in the muddy blackness of a tripwire's crater. He would be tragic in his death, but more importantly, he would be admonitory, a cautionary tale against unpragmatic dreaminess. He would be unheroic. The Father would call him a *fruit* or a *fifty-fifty*.

Once, in his childhood, he had been invited on a fishing trip with a pair of boyhood pals and one of their fathers, an overnight jaunt down a river to a pond where they snagged a few minuscule lake trout, then paddled back to a campsite where they pitched tent and fried up their catch. The boys hooted and flung sticks at each other while the attendant dad sat quietly thumbing through a Lee Iacocca biography, then went to bed at dusk. The boys stayed up gnawing licorice and laughing at farts and looking at the starlit river slithering by. The next day they returned home, and David had found The Father sourly mowing grass. David was sunburned and exploding. He wanted to tell. How they had. The fish's eyes were wide and surprised. It was *this* big, not that big. And all along The Father looked at him with unimpressed eyes, without a glimmer of concession. When David had run out of things to say, The Father simply palmed a sweaty trickle from his cheek and revved the lawn mower back into action. *Enough,* he had clearly said, without stooping to utter actual words.

Enough.

But in later times, when David was the only one keeping contact with The Father, there was no impatience to be detected. The Father never interrupted or blocked him from speaking; there had been few words, yes, but there was a cessation in hostility. The Father, rubbing the scratchy under-ridge of his lower lip, a phantom beard of reddened flesh, fixed on the television as David opened his mail for him. Nodding and sipping a can of Moosehead. His neck was already in the rope.

Tyrants become zombies. The zeal of the charge, once furious, ebbs.

When David spots Trixie, accompanied by others, heading across the lot to the entrance where he waits, he immediately regrets agreeing to her invitation. This strange scene is making him feel jumpy and exposed. This is nowhere he knows.

Nonetheless, he greets them as warmly as he can manage. Trixie introduces her sister Donna, who pushes a stroller holding her daughter, Charisma, salivating contentedly. David is also introduced to Trixie's boyfriend. Lars: red-faced and hefty, hair pomaded, arms tattooed, babyish cheeks detailed with a winding shave. His T-shirted stomach swells hugely with a screaming Harley Davidson logo; he shakes David's hand in an elephantine grip, his gum-clacking smile baring yellow teeth.

'Do you drive?' David asks him.

'No, man. My brother Eric, though, that's what he's all about. He's got a nasty little scoot. Full-on kitted Chevelle. It's a screamer. You?'

'Me? Um … '

'Are you into engines and shit?'

David rubs his nose. 'Oh, me, no. My licence expired. I'm not really what you would call a big car guy.'

'What does *that* mean?' Donna asks.

'Uh. I don't know. I guess I sort of put myself and the whole thing of cars in, sort of, two different … situations … '

Inside the stadium, noise reigns unchallenged. Deafening thunder, metal-on-metal mayhem – the noise is a growling revolt accumulating from the track's bowl, heightening to a rusty pained scream. Belches from the abyss.

David winces, bewildered in the bedlam. The cars are enraged rhinos, their skeletal frames shuddering, armoured with roll bars quaking for the ensuing slaughter. The track is a plain, a blanched vista; the spectators are sagebrush, dusty and thicketed and thorny. The packed bleachers stink with a groiny warmth. Everything is plastic and almost broken.

Lars nudges him. 'Beer? I'm going up.'

David nods and hands him a fistful of money. 'Get me two.'

A loudspeaker declares this Hobby Stock Division B Heat 1, and the race begins, not with a gunshot but with a hooting bullhorn. The cars buckle for an instant as rubber grates against blacktop, hovering, then they spurt forward in a confusion of decaled roofs and tire squeals – the battle begins. Trixie leans and says something into David's ear that gets lost in the din. He nods weakly.

Watching the cars skid circles around the track, chasing each other in heated pursuit, the cheering fans captured in a sort of mute helplessness, he feels suddenly sick: sick with dislocation, sick with disorientation, sick with not knowing. He is moving further backward in time. Each step he takes, every move, transports him further from reality. This world is populated with misfortune and desertion. Killers, suicides, dreams. Knives with light-trapping blades. Skeletons, golden duck beaks. The unfathomable stuff, washing over him and wasting into drains below. Engines howl rebellion against placid afternoon, burping and wheezing and dying, wielding speed like weaponry, like snowmobiles slicing through flung snow, everything racing for the flagged finale.

A word emerges in the billboarded horizon, like epiphany, like result, like truth: BUDWEISER.

Their house is flanked by dumps. On one side, separated by a buffer of tar-veined concrete and weedy growth, is a dilapidated recycling plant clinking of heaped bottles and thumping with sheaves of soiled cardboard, even at a distance reeking of stale beer bottles and the constant exhaust of delivery trucks; on the other side, across a trench of grassy muck, runs a minor rivulet of the town's river, a large pipe pumping frothy waste into a murky reeded pool at the base of its trickle.

Between these two damnations sits the house Trixie shares with Lars, Donna, Charisma and their cat, Dracula. It is large and unkempt, its slapdash exterior patched and blemished with peeling paint. Dandelions form a dusty wig-like mass on the lawn, where a spent Econoline van sleepily rusts. Yet out here, sheltered from the highway by the river and its rocky shore, their house assumes a stately honour. It stands, it lasts.

As Trixie explains, the house had last belonged to their uncle Ricky. Ricky had been a lifelong residential pest-control agent, and stuck with procedures and pesticides that were, though effective, perhaps outdated; unfortunately, he also rolled his own cigarettes, Drum in E-Z Wider papers, and after years of touching his mouth with unsanitized fingers, steadily ingesting PCB toxins, Ricky had apparently contracted a vicious cancer that spread rapidly, ultimately to his respiratory system. This was the price of being a scrupulous worker, a diligent specialist.

'At least that was his rationale,' Trixie says. 'He stuck to it, up to the end.'

The house had sat empty until their mother died, just two years ago. Cancer again. David expresses sympathy, but Trixie waves it away with a cigarette. Shortly after the death Donna found herself pregnant; David doesn't dig for details. The sisters gave up the apartment they had been renting and moved out here. Here among the heaps. It became home for this new version of their family, despite ongoing conflicts, Trixie says, with *those vindictive cocksuckers* who run the recycling depot.

Trixie's eyes narrow as she recounts these details. She and David are in the living room, seated at either end of a battered loveseat. The television is tuned to a newscast, sound lowered. There are scenes of soldiers in desert camouflage, toting rifles and binoculars, among African civilians. In the next room, David can hear Donna baby-talking to Charisma, coaxing her to sleep.

'I lost my father last year,' David says.

'That must be terrible.'

'I'm not saying this to, in any way … diminish your … '

Trixie nods, smoking. Here everyone smokes incessantly. Ashtrays, stolen from the diner, rest on every surface, spilling butts.

'How did you handle it?' she asks.

He wants to say *I didn't   I will never* – that it's all still shifting, still coagulating. Still ripping abdomens, still incalculable.

'Slowly,' he answers. 'Not easily. It's gradual … it's, um, coming to terms.'

'Undoubtedly.'

The TV cuts to weather reports, foretelling more rain tonight. Showers continuing until morning. High winds expected. Cloudy tomorrow with chance of heavy precipitation throughout the afternoon.

Then Lars storms in, hoisting a towering stack of pizza cartons.

'Dig fucking in,' he cries.

A staggering number of cigarettes smoked. Litres of Pepsi, flowing steadily.

'Ever been up to the Arctic?' Lars asks David, dunking a floppy mozzarella stick into a cup of orange-red goop.

'Me?' David answers. 'Oh, no. Never that far north.'

Lars: 'My bro Eric just did hit the detachment up there. Military hardship pay. Work a base up in Yellowknife or Fort Norman or some shit, check it *out*. That's potential dollars. Sweat it out, do some clipboard bullcrap, come back with a sunburn and a fresh perspective and cash in pocket. Fuck.'

'But there are … drawbacks,' David says. 'You might have to shoot people.'

Lars shrugs. 'Whatever. There's no real wars anymore. You just sit at a computer and look at lists and type reports and whatever. This isn't like Nam or whatever, with the Agent Orange or any of that action.'

'You'd go to the Middle East,' Donna says. 'You'd see the deserts.'

Lars: 'Now *that* is cool.'

'It just sounds a bit … *harsh* to me,' David says.

Lars looks at him blankly, then abruptly reaches into his pocket and produces a lighter, a stainless-steel Zippo.

'Hey,' Lars says. 'Check *this* out.'

He hands it over. David turns it in his hands. It is heavy and firm, Japanese characters etched into its metal.

'This means what?' David asks.

'*Death before dishonour*,' Lars says, 'loosely translated. Try to light it.'

Its wheel turns under David's thumb, catching a spark and producing a butane odour and a blue-orange flame.

Lars: 'I've had that lighter nine years. Nine years. Guess how many times I've refilled it.'

His nic-stained fingers, his pocked eye pouches.

'I don't know,' David says. 'A lot. A hundred.'

Lars's grin expands. 'No sir. *None.* Zero. Filled it when I got it, never again. It's been empty for years, but it lights every time. It's fucking *magic*, man. It's magic.'

'Wow,' David says.

Trixie tries to steer the conversation in another direction. 'David, you never really said where you're going. Are you in a ... '

David: 'Oh. Jeesh. I really appreciate you having me. Thanks so much. But tomorrow I'm going. I'm gone. I'm a memory.'

Everyone, girls and boys and babies, chomping pizza, present and accounted for.

This house is almost too big, too spacious, for their odd little family. It surrounds them, containing them in a way that is almost parental. Here: Lars glancing at a TV cop show while thumbing through a Future Shop flyer, Donna and Charisma squeezed on the couch, Trixie in the kitchen crunching pizza boxes and running water over plates. David sits nearby, watching the tap flow.

Finishing the last of the dishes, Trixie turns to David, as if to say something. Her face is pale, porcelain. Her dark brows and severe bangs frame her features into a bundled order.

'I'm just thinking about what we were saying,' she says. 'Coming to terms.'

'Oh.'

'It's a process. But I think I can be content. Donna still gets upset, but for the most part it's case closed. We've laid Mom to rest. It's in the past. We can't keep knocking our heads.'

'No.'

'Leave them in their graves.'

She lights a cigarette, looking at him through smoke. 'I think of Rilke.'

'What?'

Trixie closes her eyes. '*I have my dead   and I have let them go
and was amazed to see them so contented   so soon at home in being
dead   so cheerful   so unlike their reputation   only you return
brush past me   loiter   try to knock against something   so that the
sound reveals your presence.*'

She reopens her eyes. 'Though I wonder,' she says.

So cheerful   unlike their reputation. David has his own dead, but
the disclosure of their presence is blades against flesh, letted blood.

Trixie: 'Do you believe in ghosts?'

'For a long time I didn't. But now … I think I do.'

She nods. 'Me too. But I don't really have room for them
anymore.'

She waves a hand, indicating the room, the house, everything.

Dream of hills. Falling through hills. Dream of fates rushing
upward, of violent ends. Fate churning like a milkshake. Like frosting in an electric mixer. Like turning cement. Dream of endless
heights, endless depths, chasms – land like oceans. Doubt your
powers against the tides. Fall through rifts into Hell – or into the
spindly fibres of coarse shag carpet, the floor of a downstairs den.
There is a fire blazing and there is a smoky odour, a stink of cigars
and Lemon Pledge; this is the basement of your childhood, a dark
underworld of shut windows and ancient musty furniture and a
television with a blown tube and a pair of collapsible bridge tables
leaning against the wall behind the stairs. Here. Immersed in a
wilderness of shag, a dim underworld of threaded stalks. Here you
meet a shape, a beaming small body. A girl. She is hiding with you
in the carpet jungle, holding you, cupping your face in tiny hands.
She is singing to you: *baby hold on to me   whatever will be will be.*
Eddie Money. Her eyes are disembodied spheres in lightlessness,
pearled mysteries. Yet even in their cool light there is helplessness
– eyes scanning your identity like streaming figures, like code. Eyes
probing, deciphering you. It is clear: what understands you best also
bears the most dangerous knowledge; what knows you closest also
best understands your destruction. The enemy has agents. They are
taking pictures with hidden laser-lensed cameras, worming their
way into the darkest core. He who smiles most warmly has the cold-

est heart. She who sings most sweetly knows the foulest curses. Its song is delirious venom. It is the echo of death, the endless song: *hold on to me. Baby, hold on. Whatever will be will be.*

The moon bobbing outside the window is unfamiliar. It's a poke-hole. A porthole.

The head swims. Where is. *Where am.*

For an anxious instant David is utterly lost. He sits up quickly, his heart fluttering, his stomach leading the rest of his body in revolt: shaky hands, his position unsteady. These ratty covers, the couch's groaning springs. The room is an ashtray. He is sleeping in an ashtray. Dreams are aquariums, decompression chambers. He is moving and static. The *basement*. The highway is the truth, the room a lie. Lies are decades. It is the 1970s. The 1940s. The skies are crisp with bursting shells. Bodies flung everywhere. Credits floating in the sky. Names of unknown soldiers and executive producers. End credits. Finale. Terminus.

A hand on his shoulder. He bolts.

A sharp whisper: '*David?*'

Falling through hills. Cast to tumbling suicides.

'Are you okay?'

Clouds part. The hallway light is on, producing a backlit figure standing over him: Donna, eyeing him with concern. 'You were shaking.'

'I was dreaming. It was this really ... vivid ... I was falling, and then I was ... '

But trying to describe dreams is, inevitably, futile; it's an incompatible marriage of abstraction and vocabulary. Donna kneels on the floor near him, bound in her terrycloth bathrobe. Her movements are pragmatic, undreamy. Though still young, she seems somehow old. She's a mother, while David is still a son.

'Do you want anything?' she whispers.

'No, no,' he says, slightly too loudly.

Donna winces. '*Sh.* Charisma finally conked out.'

She is drinking from a big bottle of whisky. She offers it to David. He accepts it, swigs, then hands it back.

Donna: 'I wonder where you're heading next.'

'I don't know. Where my inclinations take me, I suppose … '

'Your *inclinations*?'

David shrugs. Donna lights a cigarette.

'I'm a little anxious,' she says. 'Apparently one of the recycling dudes said something to Lars yesterday about the crops.'

'The crops.'

'We grow pot. Well, Lars grows it. In that little shed out back. The crop gets bigger every month. I'm worried that the recycling guys'll rat on us. They hate Lars.'

They pass the bottle back and forth. David's head swells, still reeling from his dream. Burbles of infinitesimal realizations, darting panoramas, the dream girl's heart-weakening eyes.

'Charisma,' Donna says. 'What if I went to jail?'

This is the first time David has seen her without child at hand.

'She seems like a good kid,' David says. 'Not a lot of crying. Blonde curls. She's got a future.'

'Think so? Honestly?'

'Sure. Why not.'

'Because you worry all the time. There's so much you can't do. There's so many things you have to think about. One step forward two steps back, all day all night. You get to where you just want to melt the fuck down.'

Back and forth with the bottle. David stares at the fuzzy hint of moon at the window. He tries to pinpoint his focus, confirm its apparent importance, but he finds himself too befuddled and disassociated to work out its parameters.

'I haven't had sex in fourteen months,' Donna says.

David drinks and rubs his eyes. He is dreaming again. He is dreaming that he is far from home, in the pizza-heated midst of strangers, with no one in this world wondering where he is and what he does. Dreaming: just him and that moon.

Perhaps we will be swept under by the magnitude of a greater assumption, squashed by greater truths. Perhaps we will suffocate in wild hallucinations.

'Fourteen months. That's a long time. That's a long long time. It's just sad. It's so messed up when you have a child. Not so that … it just doesn't even *happen*.'

David sinks back into his bedding.

Donna: 'You're not even listening.'

'No. I'm listening. What's the, I'm sorry.'

Flurries of children continuing all night, clear by morning, precipitation of tears and poop, breaking to sunny patches. Ruins like structured breakfasts, dead-end storms vigilant over highways.

'But you can see.'

'Maybe.'

Lost in the honking truckyards of the night, in the cold. Being nowhere with nobody. Stock-car racers yowling dirges. Cars grumbling, dinosaurs displaced from a sleek future. Drivers clinging to the past, aligning themselves with bygone eras when engines were marvels. Before cars were disappointments.

'I've seen ghosts around this house,' Donna says. 'Sometimes, early in the morning, when the fog is still on the lawn, I see them hanging around. But they're not romantic pretty ghosts like in movies, like women in old frilly dresses with oil lamps or anything like that. They're ugly. They're disgusting. They're totally repulsive. And they make these gross whining sounds.'

'I … '

But before David can manage any response, there is a sharp cry from the nursery. Charisma, cooing, waking. Donna stubs out her cigarette and hurries away.

David collapses back on the couch, paralytic. His head swims.

The future is so far away.

In the morning Trixie heads to work, leaving the others quietly breakfasting in the kitchen. Lars buries his face in a comic book and a bowl of Shreddies, while David sips coffee. He watches as Donna spoons puréed yams into Charisma's mouth, waving it in aerial loop-de-loops, a barnstorming airplane wailing – *neeeerr* – before smoothly sliding into the baby's gleeful gulp.

'My mother used to do that,' David says.

Lars looks up from his cereal. 'Your mother's doing what?'

David indicates Donna's spooning technique. 'Play airplane.'

Lars doesn't follow.

'You know, flying the airplane. Feeding the baby. To make it fun.'

Lars returns to his comic. 'That's just sick and retarded.'

Steam and water to purify. Heat in ceramic. Scouring wetness. Jets of water like points of light, stars streaming. The bathroom suffocates in haze.

His body has grown tired and weak, wasting without the gym's mechanical rigours. He is untreadmilled, repless, his muscles unburning. He is starved for routine, direction, schedule. Fifteen on the StepMill, five down, ten on the StairMaster, ten on the Spinnaker bike. Hydrate, rethink, huff and puff. He razes his cheeks with a Lars-borrowed Gillette, skimming away the accumulated grit. His body has grown soft but his face has grown hard. Molly shaped this face, tore away its sling and made him new. This new guy – this blameless hunter.

He masturbates and thinks about Lydia, Junior Accounts Manager. He imagines her narrow salon-tanned face, her glistening face like an adulterous tropical vacation.

So much time has passed. Divides widen.

Lars is unwrapping rubber gloves from a plastic package. David asks what. Lars explains how last autumn's leaves have clumped up the roof's gutters, and last night's rainfall and melt have rendered their re-emergent mass a gunky decayed blockage. Now he has to climb up and unclog. David offers to help.

'Go right ahead,' Lars says, thrusting the gloves at him. 'I hate that shit. Being up there freaks me out like a son of a gun.'

The ladder is wobbly and the angle is precipitous, but up he nevertheless proceeds – *step* – Lars, on the ground, observing through silver Ray-Bans – *step* – morning sun, morning now empty of rain – *step* – wobbling – *step* – ladder unsteady – *step* – gutters at hand. These are the immediate fears: failure and falling, a broken collarbone. So much possibility for damage. But David persists, the empty pail looped to his belt a mere distraction, perspective a momentary befuddlement; he reaches the ladder's peak, skewing location and gravity. Then, casting caution aside, he thrusts a leg upward and asserts a foothold on the roof. The rest of his body follows.

Here. High.

'Over on the front side,' Lars directs from the ground with a cupped-mouth shout.

David climbs hesitantly, foot by foot up the roof's steep grade. Move up. The roof is a sloppy grid of shingles battered down by rusty tacks, dying out in gluey hunks at its ends. He reaches the front gutters and secures his seating, heels braced and ass squared. He slides on the rubber gloves, all the way up to mid-forearm, and steadies himself into a crouch.

Here he is, high above, separated from everything. Rough shingles under his knees and hands. Lars's voice, barking in the background: *you have to get right to the edge.*

David looks down, across the house's lawn. Beyond: trucks spill loads of bottles and paper into massive metal bins; a huge logoed sign reads *ReCyclorama*. The world is green and clouded. The world is uncoloured. The horizon is wide, too wide, too uncertain. Rooftops and dead trees, uncoloured snow along zippers of road. The horizon buckles in disorientation. Where is he. How high. How far down.

He edges over the roof's peak and inches toward the front of the house. The gutters are indeed full of a fecal mess of water and decayed leaves from nearby trees, the remnants of a spent autumn and a wet winter, stopping the flow. David places the pail to one side and probes the muck with a gloved hand. The smell is horrid, digestive, the purge of some malfunctioning stomach.

Lars: *are you gonna need another bucket?*

David clenches and withdraws a fistful of muck. Muzz: *reaching through blades of glass and coming up with a fistful of gold.* The muck is warm and soupy, glopping through his fingers; it is red and brown and black, stained, splashed on the carpets and on the bedcovers, knifed in slashes, spilling from pale unscarred skin, young and free, untamed and unbound, no sickness and no death. Blood in rivers down through rice-field countrysides with helicopters like pterodactyls, bundles of flesh in their jaws, hung from ceiling fans spinning like suns over pyramids, like swastikas staked in cinders and ruins, glaciers of glutted years, devils like ducks, screams soiling computer screens in analytic spectrums, calling from the grave. The world is up, the sky huge. *Which way is the.* Down or. Dripping through the. Where did. The sky is. Huge, up, back.

This is where the shit begins, junior. All your sarsaparilla and sassafras won't mean squat when you're staring into the eyes of the enemy. I look at all this moisturizer and lip balm and I don't see a man, I see a lily-hearted *boy*. I see cowardice. Get your hands out of your pockets, kid. Pulling on it all day won't make it any longer. I want to see the fullback line charging up the field. The second the ball passes the goal line I want you moving. Comb the field. Don't hesitate. You hesitate, you *die*. No farting around. I want to see each wave move up over these trenches and straight ahead into the battlefield. Keep up with those tanks. Cuddle up to the tanks. I want you to feel engines in your balls. Keep advancing, don't hold position. The only thing we are holding is the enemy. We're going to hold on to him by the nose and kick him in the ass. We'll go through them like crap through a goose. If you hesitate that means you are thinking, and if you think you will *die*. This is a war. Feed your fear. Make it your ammo. Fear is the way you live against death. Fear lets you see through the *flashes of light and the clouds and the bleeding fingernails and the curtains.* You can't be a fifty-fifty rinky-dink. *You have to be able to bend to the caprice of the universe the tranquility in disorder.* Death is waiting for you. All you have to do is decide – are you a killer or a corpse? Come on, you pantywaist. Keep up with the tanks. Do you want to live forever?

David awakens with warmth on his nose. The first thing he sees is Trixie, her hand clapped to her face.

The eye. Is it. Blood on his cheeks: *evisceration.*

He blinks through the haze to find the kitchen, the table, the counters and cupboards. Unflat, true.

'Tanks,' David says.

Lars is there, smoking. 'You're welcome.'

'Lars, please,' Trixie says. 'David, are you okay? I think he's coming around.'

Another chair, another room. Here he is.

'I'm. Where am I?'

'You fell off the fucking roof,' Lars laughs.

Off the roof. He puts his hand to his forehead and finds it wet. His fingers return to his vision coloured red.

'You fell into the tree,' Trixie says. 'Luckily, the branches and bushes stopped your fall. But that slice on your forehead is pretty nasty. We should clean that out.'

Lars: 'Why'd you fall, you klutz?'

'I've been having this tendency to ... conk out ... '

'Shit. Dude.'

Trixie: 'You blacked out?'

Donna enters, also smoking, Charisma cradled in her arms. 'I checked on the Internet – we should get him checked for concussion. David, do you feel sick?'

'Always.'

The three of them eye him, filling the room with smoke, inspecting him like a specimen. Yes – he is a relic, an artifact. This is how he vaults forward into the future, disappointed with the future.

'We have to take him to the hospital,' Trixie says.

Donna: 'The Catholic hospital or the normal hospital?'

'Not the Catholic hospital,' Lars says. 'No way he's going to that fuckhole.'

'I'm really fine … ' David tries, to no avail.

The car rumbles down the driveway's gravel, coiling to the cres-cented road. To their right is the brick building of the recycling plant, its huge green garage doors gaped for the perpetual trucks dumping off their loads and roaring back out by the plant's broadly paved spread. The place is noisy, stinky, obnoxious. Severe lights flood its parking lot, lit all night.

'Put on your seat belt,' Lars says, shifting into Reverse.

At the front window, Trixie watches them leave. She is a pale outline, smoking and clutching a bottle of Pepsi. David presses a crumpled Kleenex to his forehead and dabs away a bleeding spot.

'Maybe we can get some wings at the KFC while we're down there,' Lars says.

Family Bucket.

Then there is a violent jolt. His neck snaps forward, back – Lars grunts *ugh* – and a noise, a strident *skreek*.

'*Fucker*,' Lars howls, hitting the brakes and violently shifting back to Park. 'That fucker. *Again.*'

David twists and looks. The rear bumper of a cargo van, white with the massive ReCyclorama logo on its side, is jammed into the back end of Lars's Mazda. Lars throws open the door and leaps from the car, approaching the van with a raised finger of indigna-tion. The van's driver jumps from the van. Lars says something loudly. The driver also raises a finger. There are shouts. Lars's finger becomes a fist, laying into the driver's face. David can hear the collision, a crumpling sound. Knuckle to nose, pulverizing, liquefying.

Trixie is already racing down the lawn, screaming, as David apprehensively leaves the car. Lars strikes again, and the driver falls. Lars's face bites down, hardens – the generosity of his size becomes a force, a pressure, as drool dislodges from his scowled lips. He delivers staccato kicks, unrestrained. The driver brings his arms up to protect his face.

Trixie blasts past David and snatches Lars by the shoulders. He snarls at her and shakes away her grip, walloping her to the gravelled ground with a thick arm.

'Fucking time after time after time,' Lars growls over the van's moaning engine. 'He pulls this shit every time.'

The driver scrambles to his feet, readjusting his jacket, palming his face. 'I think you broke my nose, you bloated jerkoff.'

'I hope so, fucko,' Lars says. 'I honestly hope so.'

Trixie, climbing to her feet: 'Just keep your crap off our property.'

Lars: 'And tell Mister Hank ReCyclofuckingfaggot he can kiss all our white asses.'

The driver wobbles back to the van. 'I hope you all have insurance. And a lawyer.'

The van backs up and manoeuvres around the dented Mazda. Lars swears, hawks and spits, projectile-snotting onto the van's windshield.

The van brakes and a window rolls down. The driver leans out. 'I'm sure the cops'll be right interested in the *horticulture* cropping up back in that shed of yours.'

Lars freaks out. He scoops up the nearest armament, a clump of gravel, and pitches it at the van as it speeds away. Stones spatter its glass; the van does not slow.

Nightfall. The house is filled with screaming. The monster, it seems, is everywhere, shifting and reshaping. The monster sidles up, appearing harmless and familiar, disguised; it reflects *you*. Just when you place trust, it is right next door. Offering, generous. You dine with the enemy. You are its plaything.

David is examining a map unfolded on the living room floor, trying to decide which way to go next. Dracula keeps trying to lie down on the map, and David keeps shoving him away as gently as he can, tcching him quietly. But Dracula persists, rubbing his sleek black fur against the map. Fur against counties and highways. Dracula lazing across sweeping tracts of land.

In the kitchen Trixie shrieks: *you never ever ever EVER.*

David looks at the map with regret. Kilometres and kilometres, and what for it. Here are lakes and rivers. Cities and islands.

Everything, so fluid, slipping away. Distance is making gaps, substanceless. It is all here, flattened. This unrecognizable world.

Lars: *if you weren't so tight-assed about everything   this wouldn't even be a fucking issue   but   no.*

David would be knelt over mountains and B-52s, Crayolaing construction paper, while in the next room his mother said *if you could just help me comprehend* and The Father quietly mumbled *I think I like the kind without pulp better   it's less gritty and less irritating on the stomach.* Perpetually thwarted, David's mother would softly cry, then begin to stack magazines.

Where once there had been heated arguments, clattering glasses, thumping footfalls, eventually they rarely shared a room. They became a mutual alter ego, a binary cleaved in tension. Words degenerating to mere irritated grunts and sighs, The Father retiring into a shield of silence and non sequiturs. Wound so tight, the house would quake: the rafters shuddering, the foundations quivering with pressure, the air choked with huffed breath. Conflict and friction – soon the house was non-existent, a collapsed memory. David's mother packed her husband's belongings into three measly trunks. And still, The Father remained unresponsive.

Lars's fists had flown with too-familiar trajectory. Warrior rage, striking blows, aiming. David hears Lars calling Trixie a *fat cunt.*

Trixie told David *it's in the past   we can't keep knocking our heads.* But in another room, she wails remorse in deep sobs unlike herself. Like wistful Muzz, like thirsty Bill, like post-agoraphobic cokehead Sarah Promise, she has traded a portion of herself for freedom from prior shackles.

Dracula turns over onto his back, exposing his belly, hoping to be stroked. David obliges.

Maybe someday   you'll rise from the dead too   kitty cat.

Half sleeping on the couch. Dracula purring at his feet. Murmurs of television from Donna's bedroom. In the rafters: lively thumps and rustles that might be sex.

David longs for deep sleep, temporary death, the peace of Sloth. Rest is not rest, unthinking is not rest, only unsleeping is rest, zones beyond dozing. Sleep is a hunger. Demons never dream.

The Father hisses *we've been dilly-dallying for too long*.

He sits up. Dracula shifts, raising his shimmering head.

You can talk about battles   and killing   and triumph all you want.

Whispers, just outside the door, on the front step. Voices, wicked.

Ungrateful asshead   son of Jesse   foolhardy emissary   child this is no fucking picnic   you can blame and blame but   do you carry arms   will you finish the job   behead the Philistine   are you listening to me.

The enemy is at the doorstep.

He is frightened, but must see. He locates his pants, yanks them on and goes to the window. Spreading curtains, he peers out – everything is dark and indistinct. Dracula, licking paws nearby, emits a questioning noise of dissent: *rowr?*

Is it killing. Is it sharpening.

On the map laid out on the floor, he has markered an X on the spot where he had met Trixie, along with arrows marking coming routes. The joke is how the very idea of place has become another, more sinister, useless fragment. Signs inform: he is not himself, not anymore.

Time traveller. Wayward hero. Wherever it's going, find it and kill it.

Ike said: *frankly   the stink of death is too strong right now for me to even think otherwise.*

The knife is in his hand; he'd picked it up unconsciously. Its blade gleams electric in the dimness, seeking something to cut.

Let's see some goddamn hustle.

David throws open the door, wielding his weapon – but all he finds is the empty doorstep and an ominous mist eddying across the lawn. Beyond the trees, trucks clatter toward the highway.

Dracula motions for the outside, but balks at the cold night, hovering at the entrance.

Find it and kill it.

Love becomes fear. Fear becomes pity. Pity becomes confusion. The Father sits mute, beer in hand, befuddled by all the blood and wreckage escorting his resurrection; maybe he changes channels in

Hell, nibbling at sandwiches while laying waste to the world, slashing and maiming in a reign of remorseless destruction, while the progeny mops up the squashed brains and lies in sleepless waiting, trailing an enemy he could never hate.

Tomorrow he will head west.

Everywhere there are lingering hints and passing remnants of The Father's presence: stray spots of blood on a pile of papers bound in cord and plopped next to a supermarket's doorway; a half-eaten hamburger, still in its wrapper, bundled with a paper napkin, crushed and balled in a particular way David intuitively recognizes as the work of The Father's nervous twitching hands. Everywhere, as days wobble by with distance measured only in sunrise and sunfall – time prehistoric, pretechnological. Everywhere he looks there are allusions encoded in the landscape. Chomping a cheeseburger in a roadside café atop a rocky riverbank, watching geese rise like sneezed pepper over ash-coloured water, he thinks that this is a moment assigned to him, a mandate issued via memory; he glances across the aisle to discover a thin Korean woman with her nose buried in a thick book titled *L'anti-Oedipide*. Son slays Father. Riding a bus through a town's outskirts, he glances up from half-slumbers to find a billboard for a classic rock station bearing a giant rendering of the Rolling Stones lips-and-tongue, marred by a violent scar of rusty spray paint, the bleeding mouth, ghastly bold red lips – this is The Father's mouth, oozing Bedel's blood.

Clues, everywhere. A whiff of a cigarette he knows to be The Father's brand: Matinée Extra Mild. The smudged headline of a leaflet pasted by rain to a bus shelter bench: *Know Thy Father*. David suppresses a laugh; these days he knows nothing else.

A Super 8 motel, a standard-issue single room replete with an unresponsive television, drab wallpaper, cigarette-burnt carpet frayed at the edges. Everything yellowed and ungleaming, washed out in overuse. Haven for salesmen and adulterers. Normal, ordinary.

Yet something is wrong. David stands in the middle of the room, listening to his own laboured breath. He is wary of touching anything. Of laying hands. He senses something, right here in the room. In the walls, in the bureau. In the room's lifelessness. The same icy sensation he'd had in the truck-stop bathroom.

He takes a cautious step back, locates the doorknob, twists. He backs up and opens the door a crack. A car alarm boops from the nearby parking lot.

Yes. Something is amiss. David retreats.

At the front desk, an effeminate man, whose hairline is forcibly abandoning his pinkish dome, is licking his thumb, leafing through a stack of yellow registration slips. 'Mm?'

David rubs his nose. 'I'm in 202.'

'Right. You need towels?'

'No. Everything's fine.'

'Peachy.'

David tries his most tactful smile. 'I was just wondering if there was anything that I should know about the room. Like did someone a bit, maybe, *strange* stay there, or if there was anything ... '

The clerk crinkles his nose. 'Is there an odour?'

'No, no. Well, maybe. Maybe an odour, to tell the truth. But I'm sort of wondering ... '

'Because I noticed that the man in it last had a bit of an odour, I hate to say. I'll be glad to set you up in another room, if you'd like.'

'What kind of ... He had an odour. What was his name, this man?'

The clerk's eyes dart side to side. 'Oh. We don't give out information like that. It's just a policy. Some guests wish to retain a certain degree of confidentiality. You understand.'

'Right.'

'In the hospitality industry, everything is strictly governed by policy,' he confides.

The man's sleeves expose unrippled forearms sprouting golden, weirdly delicate hairs. His hands squirm, gnashing a ballpoint.

'It was kind of a charcoal odour,' he says. 'Sort of methane. This odour was very powerful. As soon as I saw him I was on edge. The whole situation was very disconcerting.'

'At least tell me what he looked like. A little bit.'

'Well. I can only go so far. There's a line I can't cross. It's an issue of ethics.'

David maintains his forced smile as the clerk picks at his lower lip, recollecting. 'I don't think I'd be able to nail much down,' he says. 'This guy was just a guy. His hair was mostly grey but not all grey. He was skinny, or at least for a middle-aged guy, you know how most guys when they're getting up there get big guts, but he was pretty small. He looked tired, mostly. Mostly tired. Bags under his eyes, his face was all gaunt and, you know, what's the word, not *swallow* ... '

'Sallow?' David suggests.

'Right. Sallow and tired. He was wearing this crappy jacket and Levi's and dirty sneakers. Very K-Mart.'

'But you can't tell me his name.'

'Sorry.'

David considers this. No way of knowing for sure. Thanking the clerk, he heads for the door, then turns back. 'Can you tell me, when did he check out?'

The clerk nods. 'Just a couple of hours ago. I think he left on foot. He didn't have any bags or anything.'

Sallow. Thin. Poorly dressed.

Recall: a party, a birthday. The havoc of reunited family, smushed together. Picture The Father among other men, other fathers, men in rows like crows on a wire, cawing challenges at one another, their eyes agog with stimulation and early beer-buzz. Men discussing hockey scores, commenting on surrounding goings-on, impotently offering help to wives preparing dips and spooning vegetables and gravy into pots on hot plates. Voices rise and mingle into incomprehensibility. The Father would be the most drifting, the most remote, of the men; he'd dart in and out of conversations, never at ease; eyes always searching, attentions always meandering, gesturing here and handshaking there, taking regular leave of social duties to escape; he'd be clutching a tumbler of Dewar's or a beer, his focus unsteady, ordering David over and over: *go help your mother with the dishes.* Before dinner had even been served.

The Father, always the misfit. Did other fathers, confident in portfolios and tee times, chide him behind his back? Were they irritated? Pitying? Did The Father not ably enough hike the cuffs of his sweatshirt to just below the elbow, as other fathers did?

Greying hair. Methane. Charcoal. Burning. This is brimstone, the conflagration of mortal flesh. The by-product of his process. Travel back in time to the point of conception, dig down, deliver destruction unto your creator.

Everything is strictly governed by policy.

Back in the room, David regathers his thoughts. He toes off his sneakers and kicks them into the corner. The room lies still, cryptal. A vague *bzz* emanates from the baseboards. David closes the blinds on the only window and drops his room key on the nightstand.

The Father would loaf in a doorway, palming his plate of roast lamb with mint jelly and boiled carrots and spinach salad, a serviette folded underneath. Detached from everyone – the family, his wife's family. Forgetting where he was. David would watch him trying to cram an overambitious fork of spinach into his mouth, and compare this man to other fathers. Was he smaller. Older. Smarter. Wiser. Who was this man he had been assigned. Could he run faster?

David sits on the bed. Uncomfortably. He can't shake the sensation: it was just here. He *knows* it.

But even more disturbing is that this store of data might confirm his deepest suspicion: that genetics have reared their bullying weight, that fate has proven inexorable and freighted, that he has wound up exactly like The Father. David, skulking on the sidelines, condemned to disengagement. David, fidgety. David, wishing he had a few cans of beer to kill the loneliness of watching TV alone in this desolate room. The cookie-cutter offspring, the mirror held in crude light. Following: literally, figuratively.

The television, brought to life, introduces country videos and reruns of *Family Ties*. Click, flip through television's varied scope.

Channel 42. A man in uniform, trapped in black and white, his moustache neatly waxed to angled flips, speaking soberly: *you've spoiled the keenness of your mind by wallowing in sentimentality.* The camera is steady, laboured; the screen is a vacuum, drawing history and tragedy into its greedy craw – *we're fighting a war,* the man, a general in uniform, says, *a war that we've got to win*. A man stands on trial: Kirk Douglas as Colonel Dax, square-jawed and magnificent, wrings his hands as the general asks *wherein have I done wrong*, to which Kirk/Dax answers *because you don't know the answer to that question I pity you*. This is the loss, the negation, the absolute zero – *Paths of Glory* from 1957, David hasn't seen it in years – in which every man has responsibility and a cause, and our lives' purpose is fulfilling these responsibilities, no matter how meagre they seem against a backdrop of disarray. There is damage to be dealt with and ground to cover, and even in the darkest most trying days of this sad era, a man can stand and declare himself to be what he is – that is, a man without regret, a soldier serving sensitively. We have nothing but our souls. We are not cockroaches to be squished to underline points issued by highers-up. And, maybe: there is indeed a way to die honourably. Not for all, but for some. Death is not necessarily glory, nor is wrath.

But death, at least, is true.

Long after the movie has reached its conclusion, David is lying back on the bed watching a clip of Dan Rather interviewing Colin Powell when the phone rings. His initial reaction is paralysis – *who the?* – but a peculiar sense of obligation compels him to pick up.

It's the desk clerk. A woman is calling. *Who.* Anyone, no one. Can he put her through – keeping with policy, he has to ask. David says sure.

A voice, out of nothing: 'Hello, David.'

David practically gasps. 'Molly. Wow. How did you … '

'Are you all right?' she asks.

'Um. Fine. I'm good. For the most part.'

'You're not injured, or in bodily distress. You haven't been wounded. You're whole.'

'Pretty much … How did you find me, here?'

'I knew where to look. Location, locating – these things are clear if you know how to look in the correct way. You're watching television.'

'A little bit. I was dozing off. Where … are you still at Chaos?'

'I'm still here. But things have been in serious disarray since you left. The mood is uncertain. We've been watching a lot of pay-per-view. Everyone's quite shaken.'

Chaos continues without him, as it did before him. David wants to ask questions, find things out – to be there again, if only in telecommunication. But he is exiled, no longer welcome.

'How is … is Muzz still there? Is he … '

Molly: 'He's still here. On crutches, but here. David, there is a deep and dark vacancy. I don't even want to call it remorse, or grief. We're all at a tenuous point, understand. We don't want to live under oppression of the external. We're talking a lot about blood types and hunger and the infectious realm. Ike isn't doing well. He's still in shock.'

There is a sound, a pause, voices in the background, and an audible dampening as she cups the receiver with her hand.

'Molly,' he says.

She returns to the line. 'David. I want you to know that I'm with you. Out on the highway, wherever you are. No matter what, I'm with you. You need to know that.'

'Okay … '

'How is your eye?'

'It's fine, it's perfectly … But you've got to understand. Ike gave me this knife, and I don't think I can do what everyone is, you know, expecting me to … '

'You have to listen to what I tell you. If you want to succeed, you have to be ruthless. You can't complain. Don't wallow. Self-pity will destroy you. Have no pity. You have to be able to give up compassion or consideration in what you've begun. Do you see what I mean? You have to be *unlike yourself*.'

'I'm not a hundred percent sure … '

'I mean you have to be prepared to accept things. You saw what happened that night. Do you doubt what we conjured?'

'No.' He does not doubt.

'Well. If you accept that, then you have to embrace other possibilities. You have to accept that what is going to happen might be hard to accept. Have you seen it since Chaos?'

'*It*, meaning … '

'You know what I mean. Have you seen it?'

'I'm not sure.'

'But you know it's out there.'

'I can practically feel it here, in the room with me. It's close. I've seen what it's done.'

He's not sure if he can describe to Molly what occurred at the truck stop. Graffiti of strewn blood, like a logo, his own name mangled into a trademark of doom.

'Do you know anything about *seppuku*?' he asks her.

'As in ritual suicide?'

'Isn't there a thing … in the process, after the incision with the knife and … where the apprentice, or whatever, is supposed to step in and put the … *seppuk*-er, out of his, whoever's, misery?'

Pause. 'I don't see what you're driving at.'

'Ike gave me your advice,' he says. 'To stay away from small dark places.'

Another pause. 'He told you.'

'Yeah. Do you have any … '

'I think you should definitely listen. And check your e-mail.'

'Why?'

'An intuition.'

'Molly. Do you know something I don't?'

She sighs. 'I know *tons* of things you don't. But nothing you couldn't learn.'

With this, their conversation is essentially over. Molly inquires about David's sleep patterns and his diet, her disappointment apparent as he describes a steady diet of road food: coffee and chips and chocolate bars, mountains of french fries. She wishes him well and again says that she is with him. *No matter what.*

This is how they bid farewell to one another.

The TV fades from a red-white-blue montage to a public service announcement for Mothers Against Drunk Drivers.

Loneliness swells in the core of David's throat. Like a cyst, inflating.

Pain is torment, nagging. Pain is the rawness with which true regret and guilt cling, affixed like industrial adhesive. Pain is severance, or scraping. Pain is sheets of sleet and hail assaulting your unshielded face. Pain is forgetting, then remembering.

But: just as cataclysm can be sudden, an unexpected jolt, pain can be temporarily eased.

So, accepting this, consider: the wan visage of our hero, hunched over a foaming beer, somewhere on the outskirts of another forgettable town.

Outside, a bluster of freezing rain rages, scouring the earth. After another highwayed night without progress he is exhausted, and all he seeks now is escape from the journey, mercy and rest, for now. A place to sit and let his aching shoulders relax. Beery comfort. The bar is warm and familiarly stocked: a waitress with a flabby bicep, signs beaming GUINNESS and BODDINGTONS and 50, tables of students splitting pitchers.

A jukebox sings: *does your mother know you scratch like that.*

Pain. Pain prompts a jolt. Pain as nemesis to ecstasy, to glee. Pain as freedom. Pain reminds.

Somebody brushes against him, stumbling to the can. *Oof sorry man.*

David: *hgh.*

Working at the end of the bar is a girl who may or may not be gorgeous. A waitress, or manager, penning figures in a ledger. Auburn locks braced in a high ponytail flow from her markedly round head, her skimpy T-shirt revealing the small of her back as a pale fleckless skin, a ribbon of spine, and at its base, a glimpse of red waistband.

Yikes, David thinks, trying to avert his eyes.

This is weakness, impossibility. But the thump of insurgent blood denies common sense. Opportunity is a half-second, a millisecond. Visions of girls, in tennis shoes and tank tops, sadness in the hazy eyes of lonely afternoons. Elusive universes. Uncommandability. Lisa's lips, seeking smoke and escape; Lisa pronouncing *ping-pong* like a twist of archaic verses, a riddle for years. *Where oh where now.*

Molly, peeping into his future, tried to make him understand. *You have to be unlike yourself.* You see with both eyes, but you can never own what you see.

It's not love; it can't be – it's losing, it's *succumbing*.

The girl at the bar bundles her hair atop her head with a barrette. Her head is astonishingly round, her hairline shiny and clear; it is a sculpted marvel, proportions taut and neat. David finds opportunity hovering, waiting for him: if he is ever going to speak, speak to her now. Now or never.

The girl looks up, teeth gnawing pen tip, and catches him looking. Her eyes are unforgiving.

David quickly orders another pint.

Outside, wind whips snow into a bleached tempest. This is winter's last hurrah, razing the earth one last time before seceding to spring's fuckery, loping off to hibernate and plot next year's punishments. But in here, with warmth and waistband and beer, there is no pain. For now.

As was written: *the ultimate in good times is just an exit away!!!*

Three exclamation marks. Total disregard for responsible syntax to be interpreted by the art department in vectored outlines. *Pow pow POW.* In his months spent in faked labours, pumping out ad copy, David learned to be quiet and complacent. To nod and process directive without scruple. No matter how unsightly the typefaces with which they glossied up his copy, how obscenely generic the campaign, he never griped. His duty was to conjure a range of catchphrases for a local furniture store, something wicker-oriented. There was lengthy discussion about *positioning*, a term that meant nothing but which everyone understood. *Your home is. Embrace the. It's about.* Lunch at the food court: kabab Sushi Combo Jumbo Fries falafel McChicken pepperoni Caesar Salad Cold Cut Combo. Decisions. Caesar-like decisions. Return to find the obligatory Post-it smacked onto his computer's keyboard, questioning: *is 'good times' an is or an are?* Its underlined conclusion: *See Me!* So David spent twenty minutes – reinterpreted for his time sheets as 2.5 hrs – trying to convince Helen that, in this case, *the ultimate* was to be considered the sentence's complete subject, with the modifying phrase *in good times*, despite its particular plurality of meaning, advising the singularity of the verb. Helen nodded blankly, a plastic fork of rigatoni hovering at her chin, and told him *irregardless of everything   let's get moving on some other options.*

Irregardless.

When a project was about to be completed, Shan the Man would wiggle his mouse in the air, saying *do we have liftoff* and somebody, Owen maybe, would respond: *yessir.*

In the beginning, David suffered stinging disappointment when his copy was rejected, taking it as a personal affront to his aptitude. He'd resolve to tune more finely, to adjust, to strive. But as he settled into the job's dismal truth, beyond the agency's policy of meticulous redundancy, he discovered that there was to be less and less space in which one motored subject could indulge in any syntactical arbitration, in any leeway, in anything beyond calculable value. He learned that any affirmation of actual *working* was very much secondary to the general attitude toward working – what counted most was *hours logged.* So, gradually, he learned to fake with the rest of them. Message to Helen, *cc* to Deb. Mark it on the time sheet, cross-referenced to client and invoicing period. The machine was a sham. The work was a joke. And David, he was a fraud, a glugger of coffee, a nobody e-mailing and faxing and photocopying, duplicating unoriginal ideas to be rejected or ignored, repackaging it all into the chugging ad nauseam. He was no battlefield poet; he was another minion. A pawn. A record-keeper. He'd visit Tower 1's ATM weekly to trace the rise and fall of the digitized figures accounting his finances. Bills piled up. He lived in credit.

Undo.

But as he peered out the window at the city below, the hulking buildings like fortresses, like joyless monuments, the view from this towering position didn't make him feel superior. It made him sad. He wondered how many souls out there wallowed like he wallowed. Wasting, faking. An entire city of fakes, the elevators revving falsehood against altitude, the hopes of thousands laser-printed on dejected slips. Photocopies of photocopies. People tallying days.

The snow does not touch him. Snowfall is only a distraction, nothing but stray mists in wetness. His body strides light and free, possessed and untouched. Snow falling on pavement and power lines and peaked roofs, the scraggly crotches of vacant lots, snow everywhere like the shaken tousle of something invisible and stratospheric. David is drunk and lost and in love with all of it, with none of it; he is impervious, stunned euphoric by cloudy moon – he is excavating romance from headlights, extracting metaphor from slush. Live, die, whatever. He has his dead, and he will let them go, just as Trixie said. He'll let them go, set them free, give up the ghosts. Sure. Any second now.

Moving through the empty nighttime streets of this bleak town, he passes trailers and duplexes, a boarded-up laundromat still adorned in grotesque Christmas trimmings, a ghostly pizza place where kids in chiselled denim peer out from behind streaked glass. This is the world in its miseries. But he was born different, he is quarantined – the snow that litters other bootfalls doesn't even touch him. David, untouchable vanquisher of the Philistine aggressor. David, bringer of death. Here there are hurricanes. Here there is bloodshed. Battles rage, and all else is merely distraction. David has moved beyond. He is untouchable, heavy-headed in new glories, drunk. His training has proven potent result – he is becoming a soldier. Learning to outthink, outfox, outkill. Where once there was fear, now there are high-pressure systems, sturdy new realms. In the studio Sarah Promise's voice had bellowed *ye a servant of Saul battle me I defy you why are ye come out to set your battle in array you will fall like sheared wheat.* Fall how, where. The future is so far away. The future is a dirge wafting in potential – here, in the least expected place, at the ridge of looseness, he finds honking cars streaming into a huge packed lot, a coruscating marquee, a banging drum loop spiralling out of a dance club, muted bass. Here, in the brutal margin, the party rages. As if nothing has happened. As if you are standing in line. As if you are passing under spastic light. As if you are grinning with anticipation, where you are so brutalized, slave to Saul, slave to momentum.

Now. He passes through doors and a curt once-over of doormen demanding IDs, into the path of a whizzing steamroller. Music. Squeals over music. Music over squeals.

The girl who still may or may not be gorgeous left the bar around one; David overheard her mentioning to co-workers she was meeting *the girls* at this place, further down the road, so here he ventures. Fuzzily weaving through the club, he is presented with a damning unfamiliarity of faces. Drinks, cigarettes. Bared shoulders. Light bursting and diminishing against a zillion surfaces, like the heavens repackaged in neon and glass. Somebody tears off their shirt. Nothing is forgiving.

This is a battleground.

Eventually David is successful in obtaining a beer, then is jostled sharply back into the crush. He wades through the crowd – *untouched untouchable* – deeper into the darkness. Even here, he is no one. The crazed light avoids him. No one sees him. Clots of red and orange and blue ignite above a churning dance floor, bouncers in matching yellow windbreakers hulking at each corner. Bodies jerk and twist in worship of a steady kick drum: *duj duj duj duj*, beckoning all. David finds himself nodding to its despotic meter, sucked into the traction.

What is pain. Pain is confronting mortality's forward surge. Pain is cold present complicated by laboured past. Pain is isolation among many, standing alone as red-faced young hotshots in Hawaiian shirts mosey up to agonizingly beautiful girls huddled, giggling.

There are hints of danger here, a feeling of lawlessness. At any instigation this mob could flare into violence, like Lars pouncing on the unsuspecting driver, like truncheons felling hapless protesters, like teeth tearing Bedel in sections. Combatting tides of bodies amid collisions of thrown light, derailings of drunk heat – there is too much of everything.

He sights the girl: on the dance floor, wiggling to the music, encircled by close bodies. Her face stutters in strobe light, her eyes dreamily closed, her narrow hips swivelling in low denim; she is lost, her body unwracked, flawless, faultless. Dancing innocence. No suicides in her dreams. David's chest swells as he pushes closer, manoeuvring around the dance floor's perimeter, dodging the tides. He keeps her in his sight: her body is a whip of licorice, a blowtorch, a pinwheel, a flambé.

David wobbles, bracing himself against the wall with an out-stretched arm.

His head swims. He continues forward.

It was Christmas and Lisa couldn't stop saying *this beak is blinkin' like a blinkin' beacon*. Constantly: *beak blinkin' blinkin' beacon*. Then, at breakfast, this bacon is blinkin' like a blinkin' beacon. Or, at night, my blanket's blinkin' like a blinkin' beacon. At first, it was funny, then it was very unfunny; but then, when it became so nonsensical and bastardized and relentless, it was again funny. Sitting in the living room, by the Christmas tree – lovingly decorated by Jo-Beth and Lisa in a dazzle of tinsel and ornaments and multicoloured lights, indeed blinking like a beacon – David couldn't help but laugh at her dumb joke. The line was from *Rudolph the Red-Nosed Reindeer*, the stop-motion puppet play that aired on TV every year, Burl Ives its puppetized narrator. They'd watched Lisa's tape of it for the millionth time that year – *when was that three years ago* – and Lisa had gone ballistic for it all over again, especially when one of the beady-eyed elves, upon first seeing young Rudolph's stop-light of a nose, delivers the line. His beak is blinkin'. Like a blinkin' beacon. The funniest part being the second *blinkin'*, which stood in for *fuckin'* or something. As the afternoon lazed into evening, Lisa in front of the TV in her pyjamas, rewinding and rewinding, and Santa's North Pole Winter Wonderland froze and thrived and revived and relived. Elves. David sat nearby, watching Lisa watch the TV.

Christmases. Pancakes drowned in syrup. Sausage links. Coffee percolating. A complex architecture of toast, buttered and browned. Orange juice, freshly squeezed from a chrome juicer. Thanksgivings. A turkey the size of a sedan, stuffed overflowing. A colossus of turnip. July barbecues. Sauce-slathered chicken breasts. Thick patties and crusty buns. A cooler of imported beers.

Gary would say *in my humble opinion this widespread breakdown in the family unit could largely be attributed to the lack of this sort of thing everybody gathered together around a communal meal.* And Jo-Beth would say *I don't see what's so communal about me doing all the cooking.* And Gary would shred something in his small nubby teeth and say *well okay ha ha but what I mean is that the coming together* – long pause, eyes merrily narrowed – *that is what makes people strong as a family.*

David, nodding. The Father hadn't been there; no, he'd shrunk from his ex-wife's family like a cat recoiling from a spritz of water. And David's mother had already fled to parts wider and worthier. And yet David would be telephoned, invited, called to the table. He had remained attached to the family. Nervous and evasive, he nevertheless always showed.

Why.

It was Lisa. *Of course.* Lisa, bright buoyant luminous, laughing louder and fuller than anyone. Young and beautiful and braless, T-shirted. Against the drab domestic background, brighter than any angel mounted on the family's enormous Christmas tree. After *Rudolph* she put on her new slippers and, sleepy from eating too much turkey, curled herself into a ball on the couch next to David. Everyone else had gone to bed or home, Jo-Beth and Gary, Lisa's aloof older sister, Jenny, home from nursing school, cousins, all the family's ranks. They were alone, David and Lisa, with the tree and the dimmed lights and the couch and the slippers and the weight of the moment.

Lisa, half-awake and sighing, packaged in slumbers, slid over and encircled his arm in her own, squeezing gently. David sipped at a glass of eggnog and apprehensively looked as she rested her head against his outer thigh – her eyes shut, her face lowered, snoozing.

Radiant in the tree's lights, the cheek her lazing head offered seemed the most impossibly soft and pure thing in the world. A cake coated in whipped frosting, something cushiony and sweet, something unknowable. Description or correlation, he thought, would only taint the cheek's wonder, make it into something sloganed or catchphrased. David had carefully brushed the outer ridge of an index against her cheek, and for a fleeting second, just a second, her arm tightened around his arm in response.

Death, despite all consequence. The wrongness of love. With her. His teenage cousin. There is no higher love. No wispiness more wispy than love's whited clouds, no purer maelstrom. In the plummet of meteors, in the tangy smoke of napalm, in the gloves of The General. Love in the wasted bin of mortality. Love borne aloft as the wrongest. Self-sacrifice, *hiri-kiri*. The invitation. Welcome reaper. Welcome ruin. Lisa died alone, like every casualty. Killed not by chance. Self-slain. Every single person, alone, in different degrees.

Think: does *everyone*, in a way, invite their own demise.

You think, and you are thinking you are thinking. Thinking and thinking, and your brain is bleatin' like a fuckin' beacon.

In the squish of bodies, David is a minor aberration, an ancillary element, unnoticed. Time freezes and implodes, everything is unsteady – the music downshifts into a less malignant pulse, a disco thump, and the floor goes wild. People raise cigarettes like spikes, like burning crosses. David keeps going, wavering but determined, fixed on the girl's dancing. Fleshy armpits revealed in upward gesticulations. Eyes cast downward, then upward. Yes, she is in fact gorgeous; she too is pure.

A bouncer with arms like glazed hams eyes him judiciously.

She shakes, hips upward. Ass wiggling. Every move an incision against surrounding air. Air hacked to pieces.

Further still within the dance floor's churning glut, David, or someone like him, wobbles through this assembled mass. It is not David, it is a flimsy transparency wielding beer like baton, bobbing his head, banging into bodies, rowdy, disjointed. Heading for the girl. This girl is not dead. The girl is just there – nearby, facing away from him. This is a corpse-littered trench. This is the slogging camp where Patton scrapes Sicilian mud from his boots. This is the scorch of bombs. Her jeans are within yank. A cymbal swells. Perhaps we will perish in sweet flooding floods. His face and head are wrapped in bandages doused in thin blood. He is staring into the flat lifeless ceiling. Snipers are in the periphery, their scopes honing in. Die here or elsewhere; this is the moment of truth.

Children of forgotten destinies, like the meek soldiers in *Paths of Glory*, condemned to the firing squad as hapless example. Resistance, children smoking against reunions and Thanksgivings.

Boogieing forward, finding a crevice, he reaches –

As was written: *I have my dead and I have let them go.*

His hands find her hips, the material of her tank top. There is the brief availability of her feel, her waist. A whirlwind, a cyclone, rolling. She twists, and her face expresses outrage and shock. Appalled. Her hands fling aside his grip and she shoves him away, hard, shouting something indiscernible against the music's thump. David's balance fails; he falls back against something ticklish, a net of hands that buckles, then rejects him. He lurches forward, scattered like spent ammunition – *what but I just but but* – as his reach finds the surprised shoulders of a fattish redhead. She yelps as her drink spills. David yo-yos back.

Are you interested in chaos?

Firm hands seize him, bouncers' arms flexed. He sinks helplessly into their hold. His knees are gone and his vision is useless. The advance has been thwarted. The girl is now lost, vanished in retreat.

He is being moved, away, outside. Fresh air like ice. Pavement. Transparent snow.

A bouncer roars *get your fucking ass home*. If only he could.

In the parking lot there is a hot-dog cart, steaming against the cold night. Guys, beered up and perspiring, stand exposed to the heavens, hoisting dogs piled with relish and sauerkraut, postponing heading home. The vendor, a dim-lidded Jamaican sporting a Rams cap, grins widely as David orders a jumbo dog. His sign reads *Docta Frankfurta.*

'Looks like you had a rough night, my man.'

David nods and hands the man a fistful of change.

'Tough times with the ladies?'

'Mm … '

The guy nudges the grill with massive tongs. 'The thing with the women is that you always gotta remember who's lighting your fire, understand?'

'Huh?'

'An ancient mythological thing. It's Orpheus looking back, down into Hell. You know that story, right?'

'Sort of … Eurydice and Orpheus.'

'Goddamn right, Eurydice. My girl. The one who sang and danced and goddamn. He scooped her up and led her from the underworld, up to the light. And you know what that light is, right?'

'Um. The world?'

Docta Frankfurta laughs, shaking his head, 'It's not just that. It's everything. It's love and hate and killing and shit. Because, you know, at the last minute he looked back to see if she was still with him, he couldn't help it, right, and that was it – *zap* – she was back down in the shit. Because he didn't trust she was there with him.'

'Right.'

'But you know what? Fuck that. I think she wanted to stay in the underworld. People create their own little personal hells, and they love them like fucking children. They need it like they need the Vitamin D, and that's D for *Docta*. Eurydice was like anyone, she craved the hurt. You ever wonder why good-looking, intelligent brothers like you and me don't get the poont? I don't even think I need to tell you this, but, my man, it's because women don't want the good stuff. They want hell and hate. Eurydice *wanted* Orpheus to turn around and look and lose her. Look over your shoulder, doubting that shit. Because women don't want to be trusted, they want to whip off their shoes and throw them at you. They want to make you feel like the droopy-balled mutt you are, my man.'

David piles onions and relish onto his dog. He squirts ketchup.

'Eurydice knew that hell was safe. Orpheus was just going to sing to her all day. Take it low-key. But in hell she was purest. No dude on earth was as pure as hell.'

Sauerkraut. Hot peppers.

'Hell is for slaves and rapists. You and me, my man, we don't belong in hell. We belong in this world. These are days of plenty, my man. We're princes, driving around in Cadillacs and smoking Cuban cigars. This shit is paradise. I eat breakfast in the same restaurant every day, and I clean my plate. I pile my eggs on my waffles and get grease all over my face and I wipe it off like who gives a fuck. I look at these billionaire Bill Gates sons of guns and I feel sorry for them, because my paradise is here. Right here.'

Pointing with tong to the grill, the ground, the earth. David bites into his hot dog. It is warm and good.

Docta Frankfurta leans forward. 'You want to hear something sick?'

'Maybe.'

'I seen the devil once. I was sitting on the roof of my building. They were shooting off fireworks for Canada Day down at the waterfront, and I was sitting on my roof and I was just having a few Coronas and watching fucking fireworks – and then I felt something next to me, or maybe it was above me, I didn't know. And what do I see, just shimmying up the drainpipe like a fucking squirrel or something, it was this *monster*. It came right down next to me and said *hey*. This was the devil. Motherfuck stunk like farts and ... sulphur, you know. I'm practically shitting my pants, but I just kept watching the fireworks and drinking my beer. I didn't know what to think, you know. Then, once the fireworks were done, the thing just hopped back up and said *see you later* and cut out.'

'How did you know it was the devil?' David asks, his mouth full.

Docta Frankfurta: 'My man. When it's he himself, you just *know*.'

'Did he have fangs? Did he have a big mouth?'

'Hard to say. I didn't see.'

He moves to the next in line, a little guy with a calligraphic tattoo on his neck. 'Evil is everywhere,' he says. 'Evil is like glue, and the devil speaks in a lot of different sticky voices. It's up to everybody to keep that fire outta his lungs. That's crack, you know what I'm saying – that's the devil's toejam. I smoked it. I got hooked just like every nigger in my neighbourhood. But I pulled myself out of Hell. I survived, and I'm here, and all the white kids look at me, the funny hot-dog guy, but I'll take their fucking money, who gives a fuck. I live this blessed life in paradise, my man.'

Some guy back in line says *good on ya dude.*

He looks back at David. 'Good is right. Crack and pussy, they're the devil's best weapons. It's Eurydice, it's everything. I can tell you're an intelligent brother, but I can see you don't see. You need to look deeper into the thick stuff.'

More guys, swearing and laughing, produce wallets from back pockets. Everybody's hungry. Hunger for everyone. Hot dogs for everyone.

Here he is. These outlying streets, disassociated spaces, the dreamy terrain of the frozen automotive night. The trail of The Father has grown cold; right now, coldness abides in everything. The snow and ice have recognized him. He jams his hands in his pockets and tries to restore feeling. His toes are on fire. His hunt is at a standstill and he is many miles from anything he knows. Morning is hours away, and all he can do is keep walking. All ties are cut. There is nowhere for him to go.

He is homeless.

Good day, Leo!

Here is your daily horoscope, courtesy of serious-horoscopes.net:

Leo (July 21–August 21): Let life's little setbacks dampen your spirits and you'll miss sight of something much more important. A task that seems at first glance impossible is much simpler than you think. Use your natural wisdom and roar like the king you are, Leo!

And, next:

Subject: Absence

David,

We've left countless messages on your phone, to no reply. It's been over three weeks since you've been to work, with absolutely no word as to your whereabouts. This is to let you know that we've begun interviewing applicants to fill your position. If we don't hear from you by tomorrow, consider your position terminated. We'll set aside your desk's contents in the meantime.

Deb

So there it is. The words on the screen lie raw, like crude oil burbling angrily in a vat. David has been away from work for weeks. Jim would be shaking his head, rubbing his beak with mounting agitation, eyeing his watch. Or he would be eyeing takeout menus, springing for lunch. He would be getting peeved about computer servers: *when they say automatic upgrades are they actually claiming to be automatic.* But David is now beyond Jim's jurisdiction. He closes the mail window.

There are a few more new messages in his inbox, mostly junk, but one subject heading glares: FROM CHAOS.

Double-click.

David. We are still in a shift. David – Chaos is not new. Bedel was our son, and you murdered him. And his ancestors. But your heart is soft. Kill or be killed, that is the only wisdom I can readily offer. Everything else I leave to you.

Last night I sat by moonlight on the roof of the western cottage and studied some maps a friend from the U.S. Geological Survey Library archives had scanned for me. I tried to sit upright in cobbler pose with the printouts held in my left hand and right arm over my head as my dear friend Xiang once recommended. But my latent hernia proved too painful. And though the moon was brilliant and suspenseful, the light was too dim to sop up the topography. I was about to admit defeat but then the miraculous occurred. The sky was clear. And then rain came gushing. Like a faucet turning on. It gushed. Lightning began to strike the forest. And then lightning began to hit the farm. Over and over the lightning struck. I was too frightened to move. I felt electricity in my arteries and psychic fire in my spine. My back hair stood on end. But then, as suddenly as it began, the lightning ceased and the sky was clear. And the moon returned. It was bright and huge and it seemed to laugh. The clouds sank.

Based on this, I beseech: believe in nothing but the moon. The moon is ready. Be in with its pink layers, its congested tissue, understand? Believe in your most hurting instincts. Follow the moon. Look there for insight, ignore everything else. Be hard-hearted.

I'll never forgive you but that doesn't mean I can't exist alongside you. Find the thing and wreak havoc against its own persistence. Be true and fierce and elongated, or unruly. Remember everything about me, because if you die, we die with you.

    Only,

    Ike

David sits numb. Recall the smells of French toast, snow-driven winds, pot smoke – the interplay of Chaos atmospheres.

Around him, others peer into similar screens. The library is overheated and stuffy, windowless and largely empty.

Stride through the aisles, the corridors lined with the spines of books. Pass through a barrage of availability. The library is populated by a scant few souls, loners seated by windows, noses in books and magazines – a huge fellow thumbing through computer magazines, researching hardware; a short man with a messy beard and a shabby raincoat, thumbing through a battered GQ; a tall woman in tight tiger-striped pants wiggling to her Walkman while leafing through sci-fi hardbacks. The middle of the afternoon on a cold slushy day.

David scans the spines of books, bored in the mid-afternoon glaze. He picks out a Pauline Kael anthology, thumbs its pages, reshelves. Books to be considered, scrutinized, then dismissed. Pages in hand flutter like a derelict moth's wings fighting tough breezes. He is wondering about seeking out breakfast when he spots a book called *Les Chants de Maldoror*. This is the book Ike had been reading. *O austere mathematics*. Entrails, et cetera.

Plucking the book from the shelf, he opens it to a random page. The first words he reads are *But courage! In you there is an uncommon spirit   I love you   and do not despair of your complete deliverance provided you absorb certain medications which will surely hasten the disappearance of the last symptoms of sickness.* Yes, David is sick, but his sickness is penetrable; there is a contagion in his life he must expurgate. He holds the book in his hands, questioning. There is an entire world encoded in the gaps others miss. The hernia and psychic fire.

He crams the book in his pants and continues on.

In *Patton*, George C. Scott as Patton defeated Rommel in their first encounter because he had stubbornly learned from him, reading the German's own book on tank warfare. The two adversaries shared more than military status, more than just aggression – they were two interpretations of the same components. The wise warrior is one who understands that strength can be gained only from the assumption of his enemy's repertoire, from knowing the enemy. Keep him close. Study. Fixate. Patton smelt the truth in the air, its chalky stink a reminder of his past-life glories. He rubbed dirt through his gloved fingers with both respect and contempt for the past.

Muzz once said: *you die owning nothing but your past.*

As he nears the library exit, he halts, checks the room behind him, then darts out the exit, the magnetic strip embedded in the book's spine triggering an alarm: *boop boop boop.*

Excuse me, someone calls out.

But David is already gone.

Back in time.

They say Hitler liked well-lit rooms. Roosevelt had a fondness for sweets. Mussolini wept at the opera. Churchill needed naps, in his pyjamas.

David, he feels a connection with ducks. This is true. And when he gazes from the bus's window at the landscape hurtling past, the cement and slush and gnarled trees and unwelcoming slabs of buildings, his heart is lifted from melancholy by the sight of a team of ducks lifting off from a boggy patch between overpasses, their brown and black bodies like shot scattered from a blunderbuss. Taking to flight. Maybe these are relatives of those Chaos ducks, as grounded to the earth as Ike is inextricably fixed to his nightmares. Ducks, chasing the sun just as he chases the monster.

Perhaps.

The bus bounces along. David slouches in his seat and shudders against the bus's faulty heat. At least the seats are relatively clean; with his musty clothes and unbrushed teeth, he is decidedly not.

The doors *vooosh* open and shut. Bodies are expunged, others are ingested.

Into the elsewhere, back in time. Grain silos overlooking truck yards. Red-brick buildings displaying worn dry-goods logos, acres of unpaved emptiness. In and out of old tired towns, nickel towns, steel towns, coal towns, travelling back in time, the world as a chopping block. Peer out the window at the passing world, time stretched out tight, tendon-like and fibrous, time subject to its own self-perpetuating centrifugal force. The road gets bumpier under the bus's aggrieved shocks, and all he can do is hang on, relying only on instinct, nothing else. His only guide is hope. The battle plan is fuzzy at best.

Back in time. The kitchen was lightless, grey. The dishwasher lay open, its dishy mouth gaping. Long afternoon, a moment emptied and drained. Unopened envelopes lay scattered on the table. Tread lightly with bated breath, move through this room, expectant and hidden with the secrets embedded in this wallpaper, this coffee machine, these countertops ringed with mug stains, covered with bread crumbs. A decomposition of domesticity has set in. The floor is unvacuumed; a lightbulb has burnt out. The ashtrays overflow.

From another room, there is the regular sound of a newspaper's pages being turned.

And still time trudges backward. The bus races past towns like a pavement-scouring whale, consuming hours as kilometres. And the further it rumbles, the more years wear away. Further – defeating time's momentum, drawing it back in and reversing its flow. The rain rises from earth to the stratosphere. The sun arcs toward the east. The world turns ancient, prehistoric – let all these modern trappings dwindle away, machines and networks husked to dry piles. Further back in time, down the tunnel toward the darkened end. Think of Bill: *to return to that original state in the gulley with the fluid and the shut eyes where it was safe and calm and you didn't even have to breathe for yourself.*

David thumbs through the book he snatched from the library. He opens to a random page: *the soprano voice of a woman gives out its vibrant and melodious tones my eyes as I listen to this human harmony are filled with a latent flame and throw forth painful sparks while my ears seem to resound with the crash of cannon fire.*

David's head is heavy.

And then. There is a sudden lurch, and the bus seems to leave the ground, shirking gravity. David is roughly jostled in his seat and there is a horrific *skreeee*.

What.

The bus driver throws his arms around the wheel, hugging it desperately for control. The bus skids sideways, slanted sickly against the road. A woman at the back of the bus yelps like a puppy. David grips the back of the bench in front of him, bracing as inertia shoves him and the other passengers forward. The brakes howl. He almost slides out of his seat as he is thrown to the left, then forward.

It was a caramel Dairy Queen Peanut Buster Parfait that exploded onto his thighs. Horrors – the chemical tar re-engineered as caramel, peanut shards embedded in the gooey sauce. And when the car, the beigeish Aries station wagon, took a reckless wide left at the intersection against the red, burning left into the outer lane, disregarding approaching traffic, the oncoming minivan veered as hard left as it could manage to avoid contact, but failed; and when impact occurred in an abrupt jolt and a horrendous metallic squeal, the youthful sundae-eater remained – even until after the Aries braked and swerved into a proximal BiWay parking lot – fully unaware of what had happened. What *had* in fact occurred was that the driver of the car, the same who had purchased the sundae for the kid and steered the wagon so poorly while lightly twisted on several fingers of Dewar's with a couple of beers, had fucked up. Fucked up badly. This driver wheezed and dug his fingers into the steering wheel. Almost immediately, there were sirens. You said nothing, feeling ill as ice cream trickled into your shorts. Nothing, even as The Father was cuffed and crammed rudely by junior officers into the back seat of the police cruiser; even as a nose-breathing cop led you to a police van while a tow truck hauled the station wagon to the pound, you maintained disbelief. Engulfed in this strangeness, you simply didn't understand. The siren's woop meant nothing. You were still in shin pads and mud-spattered soccer jersey, having just been destroyed on the field, trumped by swifter, sturdier opponents, and you were dying to just get home and bang the cracked clumps of dried mud from your cleats, hoping for and expecting nothing – and then out of nowhere. Impact, there. You rolled down the window and inhaled the finished air of early summer, and you were almost calm. Caramel is the thickest of sauces. Ruining your new Umbros.

This cop asked *are you okay* because you hugged your arms, but you were unhurt. You were simply puzzled. Tears didn't come, not then.

Perhaps we will go swiftly and unstoppably tearing into apocalypse, hurtling into a violent gear-grinding end.

Look: cars rushing at all angles, the view spun, all direction in chaos. Headlights enlarge through blots of rain, hurtling closer.

Somebody says *but*.

Collision.

Policemen escorted The Father home, but they removed his handcuffs before he got to the door – perhaps out of respect, perhaps to spare the family the shock of seeing the patriarch in shackles, or maybe just out of procedure. His chin was bruised and bloody and his eyes never left the floor. David's mother, aghast, wept and shook with anger.

The ambulances arrive quickly, wailing in waves, crashing through rainfall. Paramedics burst from their doors and quickly begin to assess the situation. Traffic is blocked to paralysis. The bus is several yards ahead, its internal lights still burning and its engine wheezing. On the other side of the road a small Civic sits demolished against the median. Its frame is folded and shredded. Against its shattered windshield is a boy's head, pressed face first into the hood, attached to a strangely bent body. The body does not move.

The paramedics swarm the car. Apparatus is produced. They are a well-oiled machine, working in collaboration, getting the job done. Jim would approve; he'd clap his hands together and smack his lips and declare *now this is HAPPENING!*

The Civic's width lies halved. Shock pervades. A woman with a sloppy dye job, blackish roots showing, lolls limply as the paramedics extract her from the car, glitters of glass caught in her hair. In her head.

Policemen in emergency-orange raincoats approach, sniffing for details. A pair of them question the bus driver; the short tubby man bawls through his moustache and tinted glasses, as shocked as anyone. How could. This. Have happened.

Jim would say *don't tell me anything I don't need to take home with me and agonize about until four in the morning.*

The clammy grip of death is everywhere, clinging like a foul stink. Gore and smashed skulls, hacked limbs. People dying in the rain. Look: the shards of glass and the skidmarks on the pavement. Listen: shrieked sobs and honking horns and the cry of more sirens, more ambulances and police cruisers approaching from the rain-swept road – David stands on the road's shoulder with the other passengers, getting soaked, eyewitness to this carnage, and thinks that, somehow, this is his doing. The blood. The mess. Somehow the monster must be implicated in this hellacious shit.

The police. A tallish Mountie, thin and Indian, advances on David, asking if he is hurt. David says no. The cop demands his name and checks his ID, taking notes.

'You're headed where?' he asks.

David: 'West.'

'West where.'

'Um. West...*erly*. Western. West.'

The cop squints needles at him. 'What the hell are these words you're saying?'

David winces. Fortunately, the cop is then summoned away as a man bursts hollering from the increasing blockage of cars, irate at the pair of cops clumsily halting traffic.

An old woman appears before him in visible distress. She cradles a dirty blue blanket in her arms, shivering with worry.

'Do you think they'll take us somewhere?' she croaks. 'They won't leave us here, will they?'

'I don't know,' David replies.

'But they won't just leave us stranded here. They won't just leave us without hot chocolate or anything. Will they?'

David glances around, then makes for the bus, using the escalating activity to shield any detection. Cars are backed up into the distance, honks sounding, engines revving, radios playing. David flees down the road, past police cars, past the lengthening stall of traffic, the snaking dotted chain of brake lights. No one notices his departure.

Goliath deserved to die because he was boastful and swollen with pride, she said. And David was the only one able to slay him, to knock him on his ass with the pull of a sling, because David's heart was pure, and he was endowed with the spirit of the Lord. The most fearsome and foreboding people, David's mother explained, are not always necessarily the most *powerful.* In the storybook Goliath stood *six cubits and a span* and wore heavy plates of brass armour and had a chiselled jaw that drooped as he lay on the ground, felled by David's expertly cast stones. *I will smite thee.* His dead face spoke of shocked disappointment, empty Xs for eyes. Humiliated, ridiculed, shame of the fleeing Philistines. The book had a golden spine and thick pages, watercoloured illustrations, ornate text simplifying Old Testament stories. Noah gazing upon the curled waves. Baby Moses among the reeds.

Sitting on the couch in his pyjamas, David listened intently as his mother read of David's victory over the giant thug. Her words were sharply enunciated and direct. The story felt significant. In the years after this battle, she told him, David took to flight, escaping the jealous ire of Saul, whom he was destined to succeed as King of Israel. David in the hills, in villages, in the wilderness near Engedi. Even the conquering truth had to hit the road. David's mother pointed to a painted rendering of the young hero, the future King with his hands worn and rugged from tending sheep and working his father Jesse's farm, his jawline expanding to manhood, and she would say *that's you   David   pure of heart.* There are generals wearing badges and medals. There are saviours wandering hillsides. Circumnavigating destinies, like the sneakered treading of treadmills. His mother, heading off for Sunday services.

Goliath's sin was Pride; Saul's was Envy. David himself bore no prevailing sin because he was attuned to the voice of the Lord, the Lord who was drunk on the loneliness of ultimate power, his face happily blotchily illustrated, smiling into a crystalline sun. After he slew Goliath with his sling of stones, David decapitated him with the Philistine's own sword, then carried the mammoth head with him to Jerusalem as a voucher of his vanquishment. Yes. The square jaw, the flattened nose. The deadness of the face, and the glee of the killer. That's you, pure of heart. It is you. It isn't anyone else but you. It's you, killer.

Still the rain, washing away crusted snow.

David finds refuge under a bridge near enfolding train tracks. Seated on a concrete slab, the sheltered slope safely dry, he gazes into the unappetizing folds of a plastic-wrapped ham sandwich. The mayonnaise seems off. He sighs, then digs in.

Buried in snow, way back when. He'd tramped and seethed. But now those frozen days are mere memories, too fuzzy to recapture. Chaos Farm, somewhere. His lonely home, gone. It once seemed unendurable. Now he'd kill for his bed.

Patchworked eroded graffiti adorns all nearby surfaces. TRX LUV 98. DB POSSE. TRISH ♥ EVAN.

And: something sloppy and gangly-lettered he can only interpret as B E HEL N DEL.

Like Bedel. Like Hell. Like, maybe: *Bedel in Hell.*

Lingering hints, passing remnants of The Father. Sandwiches as collisions of experiences.

Rain patters metal above and behind him. He finishes the sandwich, scrunches its wrapper and cracks open a tallboy of Beck's.

Weeks in pursuit, and still no closer to fulfilling his mandate. Still, he nonetheless senses that he is vaguely on the right track; whatever doubtful consensus drives this quest, its crawling force compels him further. His course unfolds in glinted clues, in the persistence of woe. Screeching buses. A trailer park on fire. Police cruisers with angry lights ablaze. A highway construction site flooded with reddish mud. Funeral processions in strip-mall parking lots. A sign outside a church – by all appearances long forsaken – that spelled out in badly spaced letters: EM BRAC E THY FA THE R BEFO RE AL L.

Yet no matter how quickly or competently – how recklessly driven – he moves, his target remains just beyond sight.

This morning he'd checked his messages from a payphone, revisiting by proxy. Poked keys, a few messages: Deb from work, reiterating his forthcoming dismissal; a recording from the power company warning him of a temporary blackout in his area; a couple of hang-ups.

And *you better phone   gah   gahdamn   David you phone us now   now   now.*

Gary, collapsing. He'd forgotten this message had been saved. The telephone's dispassionate voice warns him *this message will be erased.*

David re-archives it. It is important, integral.

The push. Urgency, an itch. The future, an itch. He watches a train approach, its momentum of ancient rotors tunnelling into the future. It passes, gone to wherever.

Clank clank clank.

Worlds splashed in destruction. Murders in stalled decisions.

After checking his messages, David strolled into a section of forest to find it closed to the public by some recent action of ecological containment; a huge sign hung on its wrought-iron fence: QUAR-ANTINE   BY ORDER OF MUNICIPALITY. Everywhere there is putrefaction masked as progress. Buildings crumble alongside gleaming new freeways. Ambulances patrol the streets, scooping up derelicts, the fallen wounded, from filth-smeared sidewalks. This is the path leading him to his objective. This is the way to the end.

He is running out of money. His pockets humiliate themselves with pennies.

The attendant investigator, an impatient man in unflattering glasses, claimed the rope for examination. After the paramedics cut the old man down and stretchered the body away, they dutifully bagged it away as evidence. A twinge of regret resonated in David's gut; a part of him wanted to keep the rope as a souvenir.

Maybe there can be new frontiers, new leaders. This is war. This is dogged need, emptiness as combat, life in peril. Things are tough and they're getting tougher. Under relentless sun the bodies bake. Strange cinders breathe toxic smoke into the air. In seamed distances oil fields burn, split arteries gushing black fire for blood. Soldiers squint into the distance, waiting for Jeeps and Humvees to arrive for patrol – Baghdad, la Drang Valley, raccoon-swarmed woodlands. Vultures circle overhead. Battles transcribe deaths into the databases of heroics.

Now we need guides to rile the troops, to gleam through the muck. To stand tall with cheekbones like sanctuaries and chests like continents. Hearts of unyielding meat. Arms to hold us in their powerful grip. We need fathers, if we are to locate victorious sons. Our aspirations can be only as noble as those we are shown.

Sandwiches as fates. Beer-can-cracking as ceremonial rite.

David imagines he could stay here forever, under this bridge, in no man's land. Nothing but shelter, no demand but the dead earth and the wet air and the waning sun. From his pocket, David produces the knife Ike gave him – its blade shines, refracts, redepicts, confirming its own aims. Its grip is solid.

He finds himself beginning to weep.

He will do it. Soon. Battles will rage. Huns, helmets, soldiers, sandwiches – a frontier of fire, just ahead.

The knife writhes in its sheath, aching for something to cut.

Across the bridge, the view expands into a vast pudding of concrete and light. To the right: the slow-moving waves of a pale harbour. To the left: ruined blocks, fled streets, motels.

A monstrous billboard screams NISSAN   NEW THINKING AHEAD.

He is riding with a skinny French woman who, like Sarah Promise, doesn't talk much while driving. The radio fills the silence between them, playing the Best Hits of the Eighties, Nineties and Today. It sings: *she's got eyes of the bluest skies   and if they thought of rain   I'd hate to look into those eyes   and see an ounce of pain.*

Cars weave rowdily through lanes, braking hard and accelerating harder. A large cargo van bursts through a gap into a narrow space in front of them, forcing the woman to lay on the brakes.

'Jeesh,' David exhales.

The woman steers briskly into the next lane, then sends David an annoyed look.

He gazes out, up at the sky, searching it for clues, data, answers. Navigate by the stars, or the clouds. Negotiate with the peppered swirls of clouds, worry against the rain, stomp on the snow. Question the sun trying to slip through.

The woman lights a cigarette, her millionth. David cringes, feeling ill from the persistent smoke and traffic nerves. Recall: glass-cut, bloodied blonde. Bodies in the rain. But he remains quiet. Unaffected – *unlike himself.*

She drops him off near a strip of motels and speeds away without farewell.

Look at him, plunked on the corner: bag slung over shoulder, cheeks unshaven, clothes grubby and stale-smelling.

He finds a room at a shabby motel next to a Pizza Hut and a computer parts warehouse. His heart sinks as he enters the lobby.

The place stinks with sad familiarity: battered linoleum and yellowed ceilings, whining ceiling fans, antiseptic atmospheres, eroded gummy carpets. Lumpy mattress and cranky heater.

He falls on the bed, kicks off his shoes and clicks on the television. The glitchy image of a woman, bent over a podium, appears. She slowly reads from a list into a microphone: *Lipitor   Atenolol   Amoxicillin   Hydrochlorothiazide   Paxil   Zocor   Prozac   Cyclobenzaprine.* No explanation, no context. The words ring like poetry, like incantations. Ike similarly uttered the names of deities: Adonai and Phaa, Sadday and Abrage, chaos cherubim and golden beacons, calling upon the holy name of Sacamia, or Salamia, David never knew. Wrestling with names from occult texts. Circe and Jebefuckingdiah.

In a hopeful moment, he wonders if Molly will call again. Does she still follow him, overseeing his movement. Does she still care.

The phone is silent.

He sinks into sleep, half-dreaming his own name announced with these cryptic prescriptions, bound with the televised ranks.

Your body was insignificant against the immensity of ocean. The persistence of waves, rising and falling. Salt gritting lips. The tang of the ocean and the coughing dryness of the yellow beach, the chalky sandy rocks, the whistling salty bone-dry moment, bronzed forever in recall. Smells like life, real and potential life, forgotten life.

Adrift in the sea, you conjure fantasies of floating this inner tube to the end of the earth. Think about escape. Ecstatic loss. The ocean. Poised at the brink of freedom. But you saw: a tanned figure in a yellow swimsuit, hailing. This shirtless authority called you back to shore. Commanding. Forbidding Europe, the South Seas. *Back in   get back in.* But the ocean, the waves. All so great and unbowed. Above, endless blue. The man called you back from watery adventure. Why retreat. Why.

Now he sits, satiated amidst antiseptic decor – pale blues, mauves, mild-hued trash receptacles, in the Burger King next to the motel, wolfing down a Whopper. He is removed, beyond. He is nobody but everybody, everything. Untouched. The fluorescent light doesn't touch him. He engages the burger's squishy goo, its smushed bun. Whopper meat and bready pith. Whoppers as emblems of delirium. Sandwiches as melancholy.

Everything he has gathered over these years – the flow of films, hours buried in slugfests and scenarios and sourness, guilt and preoccupation – have only made him less of a person. Now he has a purpose, this mission forcibly thrust: *kill or be killed.*

Tonight, in this weird plot's wane, where the gruelling whirr of the videotape wobbles with foreknowledge, he will seize that thing – that hideous whatever – by the throat and gouge out its innards. He will exorcise this sucking spirit from the world. He's sick of this shit.

The final fight will have to be fought tonight. Crushing the Whopper's greasy paper in a determined fist, David vows it.

Wyatt would tell him his weariness is *the malaise of spoiled youth.* Lisa would tell him to loosen up.

The Father would say *the lawn isn't going to mow itself.*

Ike advised him to follow the moon. Look at the moon. At the ungraspable moon, bobbing in space. The dead moon, its fuzzy light, its exhausted craters, its dried shores. Follow the quivering moon through streets long expired, past beaten men crawling in doorways and peering into sewer grates. Past refuse and ancient stink. Led by the moon toward water.

Picture The Father staring at the television, searching for answers.

The sky is darkening and the wind is rising as David reaches the dockyards. It's a dispiriting and gloomy landscape: piers jutting out into the dirty river on rusty legs, boarded storefronts and anonymous warehouses, a hulking cannery. Knowing gulls cawing at heaps of trash, plastic bottles bobbing on the water. Unidentifiable foam lapping against the goo-crusted wharf, everything rotten and disintegrating. Time has moved on, left this place behind as refuse. This is it: end of the road. Like battlefields in cinders, bathing in wreckage of upturned Jeeps after a hail of shells.

Moving along the edge of the pier, David is reminded of the twin office towers back home, overseeing the harbour and waterfront. Those docks were for smoothie-slurping tourists and restaurant busboys in fish-stained aprons, suit-and-tied Jims on expense-account lunches, bored grandfathers sporting binoculars. These foreboding wharfs, austere rusts, slimy broken waters – they exude menace. The ocean is a million miles away; he is the shell-shocked soldier, barely budging along muddy tracts but moving nevertheless; he is sinking down down down into a gassy bowel. The gulls observe in cruel inspection. They are buzzards, vultures. They are pterodactyls.

Across the water, buoys blink, twinkling cheerily like Christmas lights, like a puppet reindeer's nose: *blinkblink blinkblink.*

Then: he halts and freezes. In an instant, he knows. *Yes.* The demon is close, watching with gooey eyes, licking blood-cracked chops.

Taking position under a lamppost, he considers his surroundings. No one and nothing but the shoreline unfurling into the distance, empty water, the occasional truck passing. The wind increases, howling between buildings, clanging chains against piers. Wind whipping and howling, rising and parrying. In unseen distances, tires squeal.

He pats his jacket pocket – the knife is there, attendant.

General Patton recommended using the guts of the enemy to grease the treads of the tanks. This is the decisive scene. *Take one.* Speed. Rolling. Action. Dialogue, burbling up like vomit.

Cautiously, he heads back from the pier and crosses the street toward a compound of container buildings, dormant and dark. Chain-link fences guard the lot, shipping containers within stacked into a dense shadowy maze. Nothing is happening.

Then: *ssss.*

From around a corner, a jutting alley: a snaky hiss. Serpentile, enticing.

David's breath fails. His heart clamours in his ribcage. His head swims. He presses himself against the wall at his back, eyes in paroxysms, hoping against hope. He's not ready. He's not able.

Against all thought, all better judgment, he swallows hard and rounds the corner. And, *yes* – there is a glimpse of a shadowed shape, trailing smoke, escaping into a garbage-strewn lane at a restaurant's sealed back doors. Its movement is impossibly light, unrestricted by gravity. Limbs quick and clinging, creepily simian.

David powers himself to follow. He is in pursuit, an assassin.

Or: is he the one being stalked?

Tailing the figure, David hurries down the brick-sheltered alley, weaving around trash cans, kicking up puddles of dirty sludge. Past a row of overflowing dumpsters the alley splits, left and right. The decision presses, urgent.

Sssssss. Where.

To his right, scrambling nimbly over a chain-link barrier. Follow. *Hurry*. Reaching the fence, David throws his hands up and hoists himself forward, his arms straining against his weight. For a moment, he hangs, unable – he is working the chin-up-dip machine at the gym, battling the burn of pecs, the fatigue of lats.

Pain as motivation. Pain as castigation. Pain as absurdity.

He hikes a leg over the fence, casting himself forward, then downward. On the other side his feet hit the pavement at an angle – his ankle crumples in a spiky jolt of pain.

Faaghk.

Stars assail his vision. He bites his lower lip. But he manages to haul himself upright and limp forward, grimacing against the throb. The monster is out of sight, faster and nimbler. He hobbles from the close alleys into a paved expanse, a truckyard lit with floodlights and crammed with sleeping rigs, then weaves cautiously through the grid of trucks, searching. Breath comes hard and heavy.

Where the fuck.

He spies a cigarette stub crushed on the ground, its heater still aglow, still tufting smoke.

And from somewhere close: *sssssss*.

I have to I have to do what they when they, no matter what the. Look at the moon. The moon is not the moon.

David drops to his knees and shuffles forward. His ankle moans twisted dissent. He peers through the trucks' underbellies, scanning the ground ahead, around, back.

There: in a peek of light, a pair of sneakers, mud-grimy Reeboks, up ahead, a few trucks over.

David removes the knife from its sheath, wielding it gingerly.

Ike said *go and get rid of this thing you have unleashed find it and kill it.*

I hear you, Ike. Molly. Jim. Lisa. I won't let you down.

Carefully, cautiously, he inches forward. His palm is sweaty around the knife's handle. The only sounds are the incessant buzz of floodlights, the steady whoosh of distant traffic, the raging frenzied pulse of his terror-wracked mind. The night's air is sharp and watery. The moon dies in the sky. The sky is full of flames, probable flames or authentic flames or unconscious flames. The sky burns, announcing apocalypse. It is happening *now*.

He creeps past a truck, rounding its grill. He rises slightly to peek over the hood. From the other side, he hears a rough clearing of throat. An uneasy grunt.

If I could just be where once I was when all of but there is nothing now but. This is too real. This is too unreal.

Now – he springs from his crouch, coming face to face with the horrible hideous thing.

The mouth. The rotten gums. The cracked bloody lips, leaching a lazy trickle of fluid. The yellowish eyes, crazed like a rabid mutt. The stink of beer, the ancient, peeling NY ISL ND RS sweatshirt. The rope burns on the razor-raw neck.

'David,' it grunts wearily, 'either shit or get off the pot.'

David's head swims. Terror. Terror compounded with disbelief and paralysis. Disbelief at the paralysis.

The monster squeals its horrific metal-shredding whine, an ear-splitting roar, its noxious mouth spreads wide, exposing its cavernous gullet, its pharynx engorged and glossy with blood-thirsty saliva, its uvula dangling like a speedbag. As its gnarled claws clench angrily, clacking together with agitation, its wiry frame lowers into a hunch of preparation.

'I had it in my hands,' The Father says, 'but it was hard to get a solid grip on, the way it was just there. I burnt my hands on the burner. I didn't know it was on. They kept sending my employment cheques late. I hear myself talking on the answering machine and I don't recognize the voice. Some days the humidity gets to me, and I can't do anything but lie on the couch.'

Witness the weaving shamble of the drunken Father. Witness the reeling of The Father, witness the bleary gaze. Witness the drained fury apparent in his unsteady perusal of his son. Look at them, these men. Witness their glee, stained with dread. They have both travelled miles, years, to stand like this: soldiers of armies, unarmoured.

'I remember nights at the cottage when the tide was high and the jellyfish would come up close to the shore,' The Father says, 'and then in the morning they'd be all laid out dried up on the sand.'

David senses that this assault, these words, this poking, are not even necessarily meant only for him, maybe; they are for some unseen opponent, they are a function of The Father's dense fervour of anger, they are pokes against everything. You bawl like a baby as your Father attacks you with words that *don't even make fucking sense* – this is not real. Why. Why should he have to. Why shouldn't he just. How come.

'You're putting too much of your upper body into it. It's more of a whipping motion – just lean back and whip the ball forward with your arm. More of a whip than a push. Put your fingers on the stitches. Don't hang your wrist limp like that. Come on. You have to *try*, dammit. Don't be such a goddamn girl. Just do it. Come on. Put it here. Just bring it right in.'

David raises the knife. His slick palms almost lose grip. Yet he maintains.

'If you can't handle the responsibility then maybe you don't deserve the privilege. I sat up until five last night looking at my reflection in the toaster. They say raccoons won't get in your garbage if you keep the outside light on, but last night I looked out at the back porch and caught one of the little buggers tearing like crazy into the trash. He had a steak bone in his paws – his hands were like little human hands, little hands like an old person's. I flicked the lights on and off but he didn't flinch. The little bastard was bold. Dammit, he was bold. I opened the door and he ran away, but before he went he turned and gave me this look. With his little black bullet eyes. That little critter gave me this look like *who do you think you are*. He had me pegged. He knew me. I told you to put the bags in the metal can, don't just leave the bags sitting there so the raccoons can get into them. Jesus, I told you a thousand hundred times, for christ's sakes.'

The pallid skin, blemished and suffocated. The bloodiness, the caked guts, the entrails for a halo. Infernal damnation in parted lips, gums trickling uncertain stuff. Skin translucent, a mask of scraggled tissue, dangling and shredded. Still hungry.

The Father is wearing the same faded jeans he'd been wearing when David had found him, dangling.

Now might be a good time to think about getting away from it all!

'Check the oil on that thing,' The Father wheezes. 'This is the second time I'm going to have to bring it into Sears this summer, for god's ... just unscrew that little cap there and squirt a few dribbles of 10w30 ...'

David never saw The Father cry, but, now, there seem to be glimmers forming in the crooks of his eyes. If David could summon the strength, he would step forward and do – *something* – but he stands disabled. He is breathing the flowery air of their house, the vacuum cleaner's sterile exhaust and the potpourri-scented carpet powder, the dishwasher leaking, the heavy toxic cleanness of Bounce dryer sheets – everything is fluffy and fabric-softened. Open the windows, take a whiff of freshly mown grass. Listen to the mower's engine growl. Scan the crescented horizon, the invisible suburban horizon.

Memory, here: parental figures exchanging coarse words, assuming oppositions in the kitchen; David, nearby, digging crayoned trenches into construction paper, understanding nothing. Back in time. *Undo.* Everything undone. There is no blood and there are no messages on his phone. There is no ocean of unpaid bills. No loneliness, no lack of love. He is empty, invisible; the snow does not touch him, the air does not breathe on his dirty cheeks. There is no one left on the planet but these two men – this family.

Yet one of them is also a killer of men, a beast conjured from the abyss.

Recall, announced in Chaos's barn: HUMILITY BEFORE THE SLAUGHTER.

'I've been trying to find you,' David tells The Father.

The creature's yellow eyes widen to enlarged discs. The monster shrieks again, a shrill machine-like yawp, the purplish veins in its neck enraged and bloated, its taut body readied.

Then, the headlights of a nearby truck suddenly ignite, splashing high beams in their direction. The present wipes away the past. The monster recoils at the guttural rumble of the truck's engine turning over. The standoff is thrown asunder.

This is the chance.

Patricide. He can't. When it comes down to it, he can't. The wielded knife droops and whiffles like a bent pipe cleaner. They say Oedipus was condemned by fate, by irony's gnashed machinery. Men with their chins and their fortitude. Their virtues, or lack thereof. Oedipus poses as a caricature against crimson clots. Storybooks show Moses holding tablets; by penned order of the accounts department, he is compelled to edit, merge, converge: *honour and do not kill thy mom and dad.*

In the stall, the letters smeared in fluid.

Oh Bedel   oh slick-haired stranger   oh Lisa   I'm sorry.

The truck starts toward the exit, its beams training across the lot in strobed stutters, backlit shadows rendering all indistinguishable. David blinks, trying to cast away the interference; he strafes evasively to his right, only to be met with – *fghaaak* – a hot wet gush of pain in the meat of his shoulder.

A bite. It's *bitten* him.

Dizzy with disbelief, David falls to the pavement, and the beast is upon him. Lissome limbs and searching jaws – screaming warm rancid breath in David's face. The sound: *skreeee.* The smell: aftershave and Dewar's and embalming fluid. Brimstone and antiperspirant. Cigarettes on bloodstained lips.

The world is afire in panic and pressure. Against the creature's assault, David rams the knife upward – it meets something and digs in.

The knife is embedded into The Father's shoulder. The monster's body collapses onto him, its weight pressing hard.

He'd asked Lisa *what do you need a sword for.*

Summoning all his strength, David wrenches himself from its pressure, scrambling away on all fours. David feels warmth on his arm; he looks to discover a dark blotch dilating on his shirt. Pain, pulsating. Steadying himself with the door handle of the closest truck, he manages to haul himself back to his feet.

The monster tears the knife from its flesh in one decisive move and pitches it aside. Screeching screeching screeching with fury – like needles to David's scrambled sanity, like the cawed outrage of some demonic parrot.

The Father: 'Are you listening to me. Are you even *listening to me.*'

Where is the knife. *There*: on the ground, just behind a truck's wheel, beckoning in bladed glints. David lunges for it, only to be again intercepted, foiled by the monster's nimble reflexes; its outstretched arms encircle him in a vicious hug, grappling him. David squirms against its grip.

The Father whispers in his ear: 'In the morning I hear the trucks going by on the overpass and when their brakes release they whine like a dying dog. And I don't even know where I am.'

David jabs an elbow back, hard, into its bony abdomen – it howls, rank spittle spraying David's cheeks, and momentarily weakens its hold. David flings away its arms and wheels around, diving, nabbing the knife.

The blood *sprayed* – she turned herself inside out.

Lisa: *my wakizashi is so sharp   I could slice you into skewers without trying.*

The monster buckles, shocked at this insurgence, then recomposes itself. Again, they stand in opposition. There is no one around; they quiver here alone. Within David's inner workings, in his *self*, he feels everything going haywire, his heart ready to explode – but he also thinks that maybe, *maybe*, he can actually do this.

The Father lifts his face to the sky. 'Looking at the moon, I never … '

There is no more moon overhead, no stars. The moon has sunk into the night's black congested sea and the sad smoulder of floodlights.

'I've been considerate … ' David says.

The creature scowls and makes sounds resembling laughter – a sick wail coming unscrewed or unsealed, the release of internal bedlam, laughing away sense and sanity. Death songs, chaos songs. Songs of suburban evenings, with trees sputtering shadows across the facades of split-level houses and dogs woofing and bikes dropped on lawns, the slamming of a car door and the torturous trudge up the front steps and the re-entrance into a life, a family, you had never, actually, really wanted. How *that* kills. Defeat, misery, unemployment.

Then, just as it fled so abruptly from Chaos Farm, the monster scurries away in a sudden leap, racing through the rows of trucks into dark distances.

David watches, dazed, clutching his shoulder. He had thought it could end here. But he was wrong again.

The Father, fleeing. The Father, constant. David curses and follows.

Cardiovascular stamina is achieved through rigorous and regular exercise, repetition and exertion prolonged through patterns and phases of strenuous motion at varying duration. Strength requires dedication. The battle is to be waged in the tendons and muscles, in the heart, in the shallow labours of the lungs. Endless hours battling the treadmill, countless sessions with the AbRoller, the LifeCycle, the EFX machine, the myriad appurtenances of pained fitness.

David has been negligent; his sin, that of Sloth.

In pursuit, he races back out of the truck lot into the vacant street, crossing utility lanes past gravelled yards, over a stretch of dead pavemented routes. Ahead, the monster bounces effortlessly over curbs and bounding obstacles, while David's atrophied muscles whimper and struggle. His feet slap against the ground in hapless *fwaps*. His ankle aches and his shoulder bleeds. And yet he continues. He sights his prey in a splash of light from a closed muffler shop only to watch it again break away, slithering into another narrow slit of alley.

Chasing through these dark trenches, into the burnt welter of the waking world, racing over the tank-treaded countryside of France, over snowy pastures and along muddy roads, pushing the drive further and harder toward stiff-spined Deutschland, to Providence and the final butchery. He is soldier and warrior, dupe and marauder. He is a sniper, targeting his scope. He is a wolf sniffing for prey.

He slips on a smear of dogshit and wipes out into a pile of crunched cardboard boxes.

Molly would warn caution. He thinks of crippled Samantha and the sumptuous cooking of Chaos Farm: there would be antipasto, truffles, a kettle brewing. There would be an oven's warmth and discussion of forgotten histories. Blankets to cushion the persistent tingle of sex and dread and magnetism. Chaos Farm is another mystery, another realm in the weirdness. Chaos schedules and Chaos dialogue.

All of that has been left behind. The chase is the dream; the dream is pursuit of deeper waking. You are tearing down the field, back along the left wing, sidestepping the approaching opponent; your sweat-heavy forehead drips. Coach implores *easy easy easy* as you shift to defend access to the goal. You are racking digits as time spent, energy expended and offered to the treadmill and its timer-caloric trappings; you are burning and wasting, reducing in the name of greater betterment, the greater lesser. The chase is kilometres refused. Conquering highways, destroying time. You are drinking coffee and nodding politely; you are replacing reality with jingles, catchphrases, alliterative sequences of words. You are remaking your quest into a campaign.

He can run and hurt and sweat, but David is still only a foolish dreamer: dream of water, of dense fog rising on water, wafting over slow ashen waves. Dream of concrete plains like oceans, rivers like highways, skies like forests. Dream because the dream has come true. Dream of lives lived in failures. Dream of apocalypse. Dream of a pinprick, a beacon, a pulsing light visible through the murk.

The monster ahead. Keep going. Move. Hideous laughter ringing, just out of sight. No choice but to continue.

David finds himself back at water's edge, breath heaving and energies near exhausted. At the edge of the facing pier an uncertain cloud of activity circulates around a streetlight. As David nears, he realizes that the cloud is a colony of bats, circling in the queasy light.

And, bathing in the light, The Father is again waiting for him, gawking up at the bats with a rapt gape. His lungs heavy with breath, David approaches cautiously. The monster faces him with a glistening grin, and in a subsonic gargle, says *I have murdered and murdered laid weaklings to waste and won't let up until my glorious havoc is exhausted.*

'If you don't shovel it right away,' The Father says, 'it just freezes and hardens, and then you're out there for hours breaking it up with the edge of the shovel. Do you want to be doing that? You *like* being out there for hours? Go ahead and freeze your balls off, if you're so smart.'

David remembers this. January. An overnight snowstorm.

'If you can't just sit and hold still for a second, then get the hell out of here. Act your age for once. When we buy these chairs, it's not like we're just standing here like idiots. When I tell you I'm *telling* you.'

David winces and squishes his eyes with his knuckles.

'I'm here to kill you,' he says.

'Kill *who*?' The Father scoffs. 'Death is painted all over us, guy. We drive Death like a station wagon.'

And in an abrupt motion, the monster leaps over the side of the pier, disappearing into the shadows. David hurries to the edge and looks over: it has vanished, coaxing him further.

A set of crumbling steps leads under the pier. David staggers down, tired eyes peeled for the monster. The dark underbelly is musty and polluted, stinking of decay. Indolent waves foam against sludge-coated rocks, dirty harbour water broken by jutting topples of gravel and garbage, cardboard slices, pop bottles, condoms riding the surface.

He moves up the shoreline, taking guarded steps over the slimy rocks. Above, the clouded night skies briefly part – for an instant, the moon slinks back into view, like a hinted hazy image transmitted by fax to flimsy paper, steeping this grim scene with light. And in this brief glimpse, David detects motion ahead on the shoreline: something slithering around the opening of a fat iron drainage pipe. Something jerky and hunched – the monster, burrowing further.

Tiptoeing over the intermediary ground of rocks and slimy shoreline, David heads for the pipe. His target has vanished; the pipe's hinged lid has been unfastened and pried back, opened to inner shadows.

David bends and peers inside. He hears something shuffling, somewhere in the darkness.

Reluctantly, he crouches to his knees. His hands find thick water, putrid syrups.

As he crawls forward, the pipe surrounds him like a throat, like a dream of a throat, for this whole chase is a dream of a chase, a fabrication of flashbacks and false rememberings. He can barely fit; the darkness holds him, brings him deeper.

Back in time. Ahead there is nothing but the eroded past.

'You,' he calls, unable to think of anything else. The word careens through the echoing insular space.

He crawls deeper into the throat. Hands and knees. The pipe stinks. The cold shallow trickle of water resting in its basin is unmoving. A confusion of smells: chemical exhaust, fishy waters, Windex, feces. Deadness.

Keep. Going.

All through this hunt, he has been digging deeper and deeper into the past. World and history have crumbled, surrendered. And now he remounts the passage back into the dark, crawling toward deliverance. Deliverance runs backward. Sewage and slippage. Sliding into the throat, into the bile. He is Martin Sheen in *Apocalypse Now*, gliding through reeded waters; he is Luke Skywalker in *The Empire Strikes Back*, hunting Darth Vader through foreboding Imperial chambers. Enduring tests, wrestling challenges, waging defiance. Dejected wreaker of havoc sculpting maps into sloganed Chaos, like Oedipus polishing Eurydice, another uninspired depository, another Saul. To be the knife or be the killing, to be reunited with the dearly departed. To be true, even as truth crumbles.

Back in time.

Ahead, there is no light, no discernible opening. David halts. *Wait a sec.* He reaches out into the oncoming darkness with a wary hand, finding something contoured and rough.

The pipe is sealed, a dead end.

Then, from behind, he senses an inkling of rising heat. He peers back between his legs: at the opening of the pipe there is a quick flash of movement, a swift shadowed move.

Fire. At the opening from where he entered, there are sparks, hints of emanating fire. David freezes with fear. Somehow, it has doubled back on him, impossibly manoeuvred its way behind him. He's been double-backed, fooled, led into a trap. He's in trouble.

There is laughter ringing, the monster's laugh, amplified in the echoing squelch. Hellfire and damnation, out there, out where.

The pipe closes around him, constricting, swallowing. Light narrows, the iris closes. The cover creaks shut.

Perhaps we will be burnt up in the bleak-white fruition of our own self-determination, blown to bits in the charred swelter, skin melted and flesh wrung, the whole mess remade into a puddle of destruction. Even against our fiercest resistance.

The thing is once again free to kill at whim in the world. And David, once again, is fucked. He squirms his body in the tight space and tries the lid's handle. It's firm, locked. He bangs his fists against the steel lid. Nothing but echoes.

He's trapped.

Fuck fuck fuck.

In *Maldoror*, the book he swiped from the library, he read: *happy is he who slumbers peacefully in a bed of feathers torn from the breast of the eider   without being aware that he is betraying himself.* The back cover told how the author, Ducasse AKA Lautréamont, wrote only the one book and some poetry, and died mysteriously at twenty-four.

If you choose to accept this, then you must accept other absurdities.

You've been waiting your whole life for something, but you don't know what it is. Maybe you'll never know. Maybe this is the point.

David once ate a Whopper while standing at The Father's grave. He balled up the wrapper and tossed it in a trash can at the cemetery's gates.

Here. He does not slumber on feathers. But he has betrayed himself.

There is no sound except a steady hum of toiling mechanisms ringing in the pipe's core and his own breath escaping, seething. It is coffin-like, not only in its confinement but in its isolation. Perhaps even in its sentence. He lies like the dead.

He hammers the iron panel with his fists. He calls out: *halp halp   hey.*

There is no one to hear.

From the other side of the pipe's cover he can hear harbour wind rising, whooshing in whispers. Somebody has to come along, any second now. If he can just remain calm in the meantime. Stay cool. Don't lose it.

Don't. Lose. It.

Lying still in uninterrupted dark, one conjures death fantasies, death plays, the invisible anti-theatre of bodily rest. This is how the dead feel, prone and cold. When David was younger he was wracked with constant thoughts about death, his own death. To consider his own demise, to jump into that black abyss of thought, sent his mind reeling. After lights out, bedtime was haunted with the constricted terror of mortality, the trying to comprehend, the trying to get a grip. Contending with the understanding that death – *his* death – wouldn't be a explosion – *BOOF!* – in a Marvel comic, or a fantasy *Magnum P. I.* episode; there would be no pearly gates or shining knives of light, no wings, no plateaus to wander happily, forever and ever. It was swift finality. His bedroom in that old house was always too warm, and he would shuck the covers and lie in his tiny bed in only underwear, exposed, his skull battered with panicked extrapolations. Staring up at the stucco ceiling and the play of headlights skimming across the *Incredible Hulk* posters on his walls, the dreadful tempestuous scope of it all coalesced in his mind. So much thunder. Soon enough there would be no him. In the future, when people vacation on Venus and robots mow lawns and days unfold under filtered suns, he won't be there to partake in these marvels. The world will continue without him – this realization came hard. One becomes dust, flimsy, a memory. If even that. Familiarity with the irrevocability of it all was, he grievously accepted, the only truth. All else was misguided hope.

Boof.

Now that has all changed. The scales have been reset. The Father has risen from the dead. Memory collides with the present. Blood spills. The understanding is reconsidered. Icy mortal truth is interwoven with the recurring vision of Bedel's hacked body. Death walks with fiery life.

How does he move so fast, David thinks. *He hasn't jogged in years.*

Molly warned him to *beware of small enclosed spaces.* Again he has overlooked a sign, misinterpreted plain information. Wedged in this dark cranny, he fights panic with every ounce of determination he can summon; if he allows himself to lose it, serious difficulty lies ahead. Summoning every fibre of his being, he forces himself to not spaz. To summon another focus, a distraction from his present quandary.

Sushi. The restaurant with the cartoon fish, where they named every combo after a sport. Basketball, Football, Tennis Box Menu Meal. She radiated. Whenever they spoke their conversations began with bold statements, lofty claims, stumbling with distractions and giggles, then collapsing into nervous happy laughter. The waiter brought complimentary sake, and David knew Lisa was seventeen, maybe only sixteen, but they clinked tiny cups nonetheless, toasting the spontaneity and wonder of the moment. Lisa's eyes were blue, oceanic; her eyes were a vision of the world he was waiting to find. *Eyes of the bluest skies as if they thought of rain I'd hate to look into those eyes and see an ounce of pain.* She wowed him with stories of high school soap operas, crushes and rivalries playing out like epic tragedies. And he never knew. *Ask David:* all he knew was ringlets coiled around sharp ears, freckles, a soapy scrubbed scent. A shudder of pleasure while chopsticking agedashi tofu. When was this. Past lives. Chronology fails him. Memory: adversary of narrative, rebel of flow.

Flow. The water under him stinks like shit and mould. He looks for drips, gaps in the structure, without luck. This jail is sealed. Just him and his memories.

If you accept *this*, then you must accept *that*.

If you accept Molly's intimacy with strange arcane forces, if you accept that Molly can raise the dead, that she can know where exiled David hides, locating him haplessly bunkered in some shit motel room; if there can be showers of blood imagined in snowy sidewalks and versions of the eternal raised in hot dogs, or glittering clouds of smoke huffed in the bongs of teenage girls – deaths that tramp only as half-deaths, memories jogging again in dream and violence – if all of this pandemonium can be accepted into the unsteady fold, then you must accept just about anything.

If you accept that death is not the end, then a dizzying range of potential conclusions emerges. The temples in the sky and the werewolves in the forests, partings of seas, Smurfs frolicking in mushrooms – all manner of weirdnesses are possible. Think of Bill, born-again atheist trucker, ploughing through the solitary highwayed night, his eyes steeled on the rushing road, his heart sinless and dry-tongued. What would he say, staring into those pits for eyes, those ravenous spewing jaws? Would he hawk and spit, sprinkle pepper on his eggs and dismiss the whole heap of shit?

He thinks he hears something on the other side.

'Hello?' he tries. 'Hello hello *hello*. Anybody? I'm trapped.'

Nothing. His voice rings so emptily, so fruitlessly, it's almost funny.

Here there is no measure of time's passage. Hours indistinguishable from instants, time unknowable. A deep numbness from prolonged immobility is beginning to settle into his shoulders. He is in exile, extricated from time. No light, no stars, no earthly rotation. His quest has been a shift back in time; now he has reached the end, where time is rendered nil.

Perhaps we will be ingested by buildings, sucked down into the beetle-flecked gum-dabbed sidewalks, our futures spat out in broken dreams, forgotten like erased files. Perhaps our doomsday will be a reunion with dour routine, and we will scream curses while hacking this bullshit to ribbons with huge fucking swords.

If you accept these apocalypse imaginings, the plural glut of damnation, then you may as well accept that Sarah Promise spoke in the croak of the dead. The lazy voice, like a mournful bassoon wooting in a freight elevator, cross-faded with the *ssttt* of an unattended cigarette burning through a tablecloth. Heartbreak and horny anticipation. Her lips were smeared in lipstick, her tongue sharp, her breath stinky with cigarettes, but the voice emitted had rung clearly: *what're you up to dude* – unmistakably Lisa's.

Sarah Promise had a body like a wedding cake. Her skin was soft and full of creamy possibility, fluffy, sectional. Her weight fell upon him with dreamy urgency. Tides of Promise. Her smell was something refined and processed – freshly minted money, or aspirin, or juice crystals. With her body at his hands, everything was available. Opportunity shook in his guarded touch. Cushiony tissue and downy softness, wedding cake squishing, whipped and iced and lovingly frosted, everything carefully angled and situated.

If you accept the blood smeared upon the wall, then you accept the possibility for its further spillage; you accept the ritual and the repetition. Fathers and sons. Fears. Declines. Sons following fathers. There is the dream of Abraham with his blade set before Isaac's chest, though this dream is far-flung. But if you accept the dream, you accept the blood.

If you accept that The Father has risen again, then you accept that others might follow suit; for no reward would celestial justice afford a wretch like him resurrection and deny it to Lisa. Lisa of truth and seriousness. Lisa, angelic.

She would say *if you only knew dude if you only knew*.

A hero can't be denied heroics. And David can't prevent this killer from killing. Still so much vengeance to wreak, and whimpering in Chaos Farm cottages, snowmobiling, filling time sheets, biding time while Europe goes to shit in a sheep house in an Allied push, or whatever, solves nothing. Cigars are smoked, decrees are sealed in wax. Large-throated men make deals.

If you accept these challenges as compatible with death's parameters, then all subsequent bets are off. You consider death as a program, a system, a result; but now, here in resurrection, death is a window. Souls passing in, passing out.

The mind reels. The head swims.

Here. Accept this, accept that.

There might be rats, bugs, vermin. Here in the darkened crevices, the pipeline sealed on all sides by plating and concrete. If you accept everything that has led to this place, then you accept the possibility of any gruesomeness. Creatures of the night, vampires, *Maldoror*'s moon-blessed monsters. Grinning, biting skulls. Concrete or no concrete. Humming in the walls: an insurrection of insects or mice or maggots, things squirming out of the decay. The wind outside sings lonely failure; mourning our forgotten sons, for babies thrown to piranhas, to gulping, gilled octopi lurking in the walls. Winding fears. Battlefields smouldering in time.

His mother opened the picture book and showed him the water-coloured picture of baby Jesus, lying among curious lambs and cattle in the hay-lined manger, bearded men gazing upon the new child; Jesus' blankets were blue and his cheeks were rosy. Cherubic cheeks. His eyes beamed gladness into the candlelit barn, gladness and hope. The men's bearded faces, etched in sharp profile, were identical, but the colour of their robes varied: green, beige, violet-blue. Jesus had a curl, just a wisp, of reddish hair on his newborn dome. And in a fuzzy arc behind his head, a slight glimmer shone. A halo, gleaming from the page in soft brushstrokes. His mother turned the page and kept reading and explaining, but it was the halo that held David's attention. Unlike the Frisbee halos he'd seen angels sporting for Hallmark cards, this was a cranial *glow*, a golden brilliance emanating from the baby's head.

This boy, this birth, David's mother explained, was what everyone had been waiting for. A son; everyone had been waiting for the son.

The muscles of his right shoulder begin to spasm, rousing him from a shrouded taper of thought. With a cold shudder he realizes that he'd fallen asleep.

Sleeping like the dead.

His body is disintegrating. His lungs wheeze with airless vapours. Cold sweat gathers in his armpits and crotch, glazes on his forehead. His parched throat clacks as he swallows.

He has to get out of here. *Now.*

He drives fists of frustration against the metal, pounding its cold surface, achieving nothing. But even though he knows how weak and pointless this expenditure may be, he can't help it. He is *trapped*, and growing very scared. He digs his knuckles against the metal above him and bites his lip, hard. He is buried alive here.

And here he will surely die.

The stretch of time is a battle plan demarcated in Magic Markered Xs and Os, regions rectangled into points beyond. Think of Muzz, itchy and restless in his suffering. Think of his unflabby frame and wrinkled forehead. Though his addictions still hummed in his veins, he'd shake away these pains in hopes of a purer way, something simpler. The singing of songs, strumming his banjo. Muzz was peculiar but strong, and he sang his songs with unbounded conviction. There was sadness in his eyes, but there wasn't fear. At Chaos Farm, David learned to understand something, a smidgen of something, things only now forcing decisions. The sands of this journey are perpetually shifting, the landscape forever mutating. Battles rage: scouring acids from enraged clouds, firefights over beleaguered outposts, cartoon cannibals chowing on the ill-fated. Collarbones jutting from sweaters like solar systems. Lisa's skin, its secrets wedged into a platform of allure – David hugged Lisa's forgiving frame against the crushing impossibility of it all. You look into the shadowed dip of a young girl's throat and locate a galactic problem, and shrouded forms of negative matter burble up in bluish video interference, plutonium rain clobbering the world in torrents of waste, and everything makes sense. Thrown into this downward crest, you travel down into dense jungles and lagoons of snakes, woozily spun into the full rift of this hurly-burly with every leaf jutting as a bone or a vein, the dip creating a rhythm, the rhythm creating a depression, the depression a cavern, the cavern formed in stalactites and stalagmites dripping incisors petrified in darkness, disembodied, historic.

If you accept that creatures with knives for teeth and gassy moons for eyes materialize in the living rooms of the idle rich, then you admit that this creature is a symptom of seeing *life as one endless fantasy*. To accept this is to swallow suicide notes: stomach as file cabinet, intestine as e-mail inbox. These are wretched thoughts. These are condemning thoughts. This is the end of thought. This is to desire to die. This is to let the trash mount up, to seal the windows shut against the world.

In the dream's atmosphere there are messages from freaked satellites, prophecy like weather messages. The sands shift like pyramids of half-melted sherbet, engulfing all in their path: highways and cityscapes, corpses and teenagers. Above, the sky fumes in ripples, the clouds dotted like a face blotted with broken blood vessels, the hide of a man living past his prime. The sky full of flame, weeping requiem, mourning time.

David wakes to find his cheeks sticky with tears. States of sleep and waking are fading into one another, coalescing into panic. Here. Time here is expendable and infirm. Everything is clammy and unsure and horrible.

Struggling to not conk out again, he consciously forces data through his mind. He begins weighing outcomes, wagering deals with fate. If he is somehow let out of this place, by whatever forces wield the power, he will make amends. To himself. To anyone, everyone. He will improve. He will be better, try harder. He will be gracious and helpful and honest. He will increase reps and tread-mill sessions. He will exact a purer way. He will make it up to Gary and Jo-Beth. If he could only be let out of this fucking coffin.

It's been hours now, prone in the dark. Days. Lifetimes. He can't feel his toes.

A deathly freeze has fallen upon the troops. Rations are few and supplies are low. The men advance slowly, heads lowered against punishing wind, their boots solid bricks of ice and their cheeks dirty with frost-flecked stubble. The hills of Switzerland, Mycenae, Afghanistan lie ahead, as ominous and perilous as the enemy itself, as unyielding as the maelstrom of death. The wind scathes. Battle is at a pause, paralyzed in its progress.

Switzerland. He's failed. Fucked up. Blown it. *Fifty-fifty*. Not enough hustle.

And somewhere the monster shrieks laughter.

Late August. Guests hovering around mosquito coils on the back deck overlooking the pool. Hot dogs warming in rows, mountains of processed cheese and vats of relish, overstuffed coolers of beer and boxes of white wine. David had sat poolside, nursing a Heineken and avoiding conversation. Gary heaved a huge foil-wrapped catfish on the grill. The sun blazed. Then Lisa emerged from the house in a bikini and flip-flops, her hair in a lazy ponytail. Her introduction had been a welcome affront to the whole vacuous mustard-squirting afternoon; her presence defied everything. David sat on a pool chair and watched as Lisa sauntered up to the Hawaiian-shirted asshole manning the barbecue, some associate of Gary's, and swiped a burger. Topping it with a generous gloop of ketchup, she crammed a huge chomp into her mouth. Her lips, gory with sauce. Her slight thighs. Her tiny feet padding over deck tiles. The elastic band of her bikini hugging fatless flesh. The sun smothering all, chlorinated water splashed everywhere by cannonballing kids. And David, skin red and peeling, watched as Lisa leaned against the pool's fence to polish off her burger. Her skin drank sunlight, stealing glimmer from everything that surrounded, refashioning it as her own inner radiance, the most sparkling sparkle. Someone nearby said *if David needs another beer he'll say so* in a burping chuckle. Lisa lolled over to where David sat on his deck lounger, meekly sipping his beer in wet shorts and an Oakland A's T-shirt. She stood boldly before him, tiny but huge, playfully cocking her eyes and saying *well well well what do we have here.* They hadn't seen one another since Christmas; in the interim she had transformed, full pubescence had taken over, and it came as a befuddlement, a choking arrest. David tried to avoid staring, fixing his gaze on his bottle's half-unpeeled label, until Lisa placed her hands on her hips in a thoughtful pose, frowning, then hoisted her left leg and propped it up on a nearby lounge chair, then began to coat her shins with a squeeze of sunscreen, moving up to her thigh. And in this scarce moment, in the moment's heart-vexing availability, her bikini unknowingly revealed an unanticipated view; in barely a glance, barely even *that*, David spotted something precise and distinct and bewildering between her legs. A glimpse of pube. Combed back by her bikini's brevity, a stray hair, peeking from the lower lip of her bathing suit. This errant bristle would bring apocalypses, squashed worlds, suns imploding – but, *this*. This defied everything. So perfect, so poked, so accidental, this deviant hair, obtruding as scandalously as a dirty joke in a hymnal, a perfect black curl against the cavity of her pelvis. This is perfection. Shame and loathing overpowered him. This is death, completion, this shame. All other instinct lies beyond this. Die and live in this impossibility. Curled against thigh, perfection, preserved forever, untainted. Perfect perfect *perf* –

Wait a sec.

From the other side of the pipe's cover, there is an audible thump. David starts, jarred back to attention. Something rattles or rustles, just beyond. Then, over the muffled containment, a throaty voice. And another in response.

David licks his lips, his skin tingling perspiration. He thrashes his fists against metal.

Hey, he tries. *Hey   hey hey.*

Hoarse, warbled whispers. The mind is still in the sun and the skin and the sweat. Half in the past and half in present peril.

He hears clearly: *no reason this outlet should be shut.*

More noise, more fists, more cries. His breath is unavailable, slow in coming. This is the ocean, bearing down upon you like a defensive line, the salt of your throat forced up – like lava eructed from tectonic guts, hot and hard. This is the rocky sand beneath as waves slam you pitilessly, your hands flailing as gravity vomits and gives up, the audio of the world filtered into sounds of death, cold sound screaming pressure against your eardrums, all swelling and pushing: panic. All fear compounded into panic, urgency, escape.

Oh – it's now or never, or nowhere because to die, not now then –

Shrieking: *help   help   help   help.*

Nothing could conceivably be more important than the opening of this coffin, the gush of pressure as he is *risen from the dead.* David is Lazarus, hiked upward by strong arms, the blood gushing back to his extremities in pained spikes. Nothing more important than freedom and its blessings, and even with his rescuers' confusion and questioning, and even though he's failed in his mission, there is minor success in crumpling back on the shoreline, his muck-stained hands raised to the sky, because life in chaos – *finally* – is better than death in the dark.

The airport smells of burnt coffee and disinfectant. All around, glum travellers shuffle in questioning anticipation, inflated with hope, or dread, the terminal guiding them via its propulsion of signage and arrowed stretches toward gates, seats, flight. At the office there had been lengthy discussion of momentum. Jim stood and smacked the back of one hand against the palm of another, emphasizing the impact generated by *momentum* and movement and direction. At the agency they had emphasized determination. Jim had pleaded, begged, for genuine drive, *determination*.

So long ago. Eons. Ages. Mouthfuls.

After an eternity, David reaches the ticket counter. Against everything and anything, he wants to move, flee, get home *now*. Everything here is an impediment.

But when he attempts to purchase a ticket for the next flight home, there is disaster. The clerk at the desk shakes her head, showing him the result of his MasterCard's swipe: *Transaction Denied*. He wants to argue, to plead, but knows it's futile. His account is long maxed out and he's months behind in payments. The ride is over.

He is Napoleon, suffering ferocious storms of wind and snow in hastened retreat from the Russian interior. He is the bedevilled young actress Mackenzie Phillips on page 121 of TV *Babylon*, coked into Hollywood oblivion, a spectre fading out of the limelight.

He has failed. He is a failure. Delusions of grandeur dissolve.
STOP. EJECT.
The clerk says *better luck next time.*

Then the PA squawks, clipping in with terse and measured tones: *due to extreme weather conditions all eastbound flights have been rescheduled   expect significant delays   consult the terminal monitors for estimated departure times.*

With this news, the terminal bristles with tested patience and short tempers. A woman behind him groans *for fuck's sakes*. Mobs congregate at every information desk and terminal gate, incensed travellers demanding answers.

David gazes outside from the arrivals lounge, miserably wondering what to do. The sky darkens, pissing down heavy wind-crazed sheets of freezing rain. There are calls he should make, difficult calls. Nothing appealing lies ahead.

Another public restroom, another sterilized space. In the mirror, a puffy mug confronts him. He is aged, a hundred years old, ancient, timeless. Time enwreathes him and extricates him from its laws; he is Methuselah, Rip Van Winkle, Dick Clark. He selects a urinal, unzips and sighs. So long in these clothes. So long since a long bath, trimming his toenails, degunking his ears.

Someone steps up next to him. David shifts to the left and condenses his width accordingly. He stares ahead, into the grungy cracks between the wall's tiles. Then he realizes that it is not one but two people positioned beside him: a small person, *very* small, accompanied by a less small person. The smaller person loosens his pants and shoves his pelvis into the urinal, guided from behind by the larger.

The person at the rear instructs *go ahead do it*.

The smaller person says *I can't*.

Unable to do otherwise, David glances over: a tiny boy, in a baggy chocolate-smeared sweatshirt, backed by a gangly dad, trying to help him. The dad is bucktoothed and minute, a nerdy dad, coaxing *don't with your shirt   all   there   all right   okay* and the kid, trying to whiz, is pleading *but*. The dad reaches around the kid's narrow waist and gruffly clutches the child's vulnerable penis with rough, pragmatic hands. This little helpless hairless unit, griefless and unbesmirched – he grasps this tiny flap between his fingers and aims its spout, trying to persuade action.

A fatherly gesture. Fathers, pushing. Fathers, pleading.

The kid sniffs snot back into his throat and says nothing. He says *but I don't want to*, then begins to cry: soft and forlorn tears.

David stares hard into the worn yellow tile facing him, feeling his own flow tighten. He understands how the kid feels: there is too much pressure, too much anticipation. Even those you trust most dearly anticipate too hastily. There is so much to distrust. And as you get older, the pressure only builds and builds; no matter how hard you try to keep things balanced, gauges creep unremittingly upward – barometers rise, pressure intensifies.

And in this frame, this penis – at the furthest reach and desperation of all that has brought him here – this penis, despite its tiny stature, acts as a probe. Like a wand waving revelatory magic, like a key freeing locked chambers from secrecy. In a fleeting moment, as he stands there in sympathetic awe, David is granted a vision.

In the future, the citizens of the world will dance on rooftops, waving cups of champagne and draught beer, singing joyously. They will tear off their soiled sweatshirts and bathe in the goose-bumpy evening without chagrin, without inhibition. They will congregate atop the city's towers and be drunk on steamrollering greatness. They will spit rainstorms down onto pitiless sidewalks and clogged parkades, hugging and kissing merrily. The citizens of the world, feasting and stomping with a kick drum's pulse, clapping together on the two and the four, sailors and soldiers and bankers and burglars and singers and lovers and killers, all collapsing together into a giant ridiculous pile-on. The world will shrug itself silly. In the future the world's topography will curl and reintegrate itself as one huge toiling machine of glittering joy, like a colossal disco ball twinkling in a whirlwind of glee as the universe busily expands.

David sees through The Father's eyes. All that stood in his way was David, delivering beer and chicken and sympathy. The Father was asking permission to sink away. In the end he was unselfish, he wanted David to live so he could die. Now he needs David to let him go.

In this there is truth. In the interaction between fathers and sons there is a basic something that he, as a son, can't avoid. A genetic playing field. A stubborn and ill-fitting puzzle. George Patton's father was fond of invoking the *Intimations* ode: *the soul that rises has elsewhere its setting and cometh from afar,* or something like that. So to our sons rise broad lessons: to thine own self, thine own genetics, be true. Be, if not virtuous, at least consistent. Be rigorous. Drink from fountains of beer and accept responsibility. Fathers, teaching sons basics of capability. David has never fished or hunted or fired a gun, but he has been taught knots: how to tie one around your own neck without chickening out. There was no one capable to advise him on his earliest steps toward manhood, but now, maybe, he's figured it out: manhood is trembling and clumsiness. Blame everything on the resignation of The Father, who worshipped solitude and television and drink in the same way David's mother worshipped the God supplied to her by the vinyl-sided church: out of convenience and lassitude. You see young mothers in stretchpants and sweatshirts, chunky and tired and cigarette-face glum, pushing strollers to the Green Gables for scratch tickets, and you think *there is nothing bleaker and more miserable than parenthood.* You watch tearful reunions between abandoned children and the biological parents who long to know them on afternoon chat shows, and you think *there is nothing more selfish than self-perpetuation as procreation.* People have children in hopes of eternal life, that strangest and most ancient of lies. A bigger lie than love: evade death by plunging unsuspecting zygotes into this shit.

Donna said *there's so much you can't do   it's that whole one step forward two steps back.* Donna: a nurturer, a provider, a mother. Patton cast his gaze across plains erupting in poofing cannon fire and was affirmed in his duty. This was his quarter, his sanction; he was both authentic and fictional. Along dusty ditches men fell randomly; act fast, lest you fall easy pecking for buzzards. Casualties. Here lie victims. Modern myths aspire to ambiguity; rugged gut-wrenching heroism assumes otherwise. Weakness wriggles in homogeny and standards. Weakness is fashion and silence. But heroism is savage; heroes are by definition ruthless, principled, iconoclastic. Truth clutches at ideals. Truth knows no limits. Truth is ambitious. Today there are no heroes, only examples. We crave models, examples, when in truth we need *heroes.* But none are left; they disappeared and sailed out to sea.

The citizens of the world will cry tears for the slain, but they will raise their faces, optimistically, hopefully, to the misty skies. They will shed grudges. They will let their most grievous weakness be their greatest strength. They will invite you into their mania, welcoming you into the fray like a long-lost half-brother. In the young boy's penis there is a plot of the future, destinies spilled into a urinal's drain. Manipulated, soft. Malleable and shrunken against the crush of coming prospects. But the citizens of the future will not cry for the fallen; they will embalm the dead with champagne and music, singing oldies radio like swirling arias. They will ring in the emergence of new generations with hoots and hollers and hearty belches. Yet, the future will be hard-fought and unromantic; it will flourish only by tireless fists and resolute aims, and there will be no room for pantywaists and melancholics. And David, having proven himself in battle, will laugh with the citizens of the future, looking down from dizzying heights at the world spread before him; below is an ocean of gentle tides, and above it is clear, bluer than blue, free of rage. In the empty unbroken unirritated heavens, ducks flap fervent wings and find flight, achievement, climbing up and away.

Look: our hero, standing at the urinal with the kid next to him trying to relieve himself, his dad reaching from behind to pinch his nostrils between fingers, removing a tendril of booger. This kid, innocent, sniffing hard sniffs. Tonight he sleeps in a bed, curled in pyjamas.

Slight and spare through the bathroom's plumbing noises and echoes, through the wheeze of hand dryers and the gush of running taps, barely detectable beginnings are heard: a humiliated trickle into the urinal's base.

A moment passes, then his Dad says *now zip up your zipper okey-dokey*.

They step back from the urinal and move to the sink to wash hands, yet David remains frozen. Suddenly, this entire endeavour is defrauded. Evidence: genetics or powerlessness or shrouded inheritance, that heavy, unavoidable stuff – this is denied. The Father wasn't evading death, and he wasn't fleeing David's pursuit.

The Father was beckoning. The Father was inviting him. Look, see: this fragment of rope is an opportunity, this way of unliving is preferable to suffering. Isolate. Internalize. The TV barked. The heating clacked. David sat across from The Father as he shrunk, visibly shrunk, and finally disappeared to a tight knot of. Nada. *Poof.* The Father was dragged down to a hell of disappointment; this was his curse, and all he desired was to be finally freed of this charge. His ash-speckled moustache, the constant clearing of his throat. The pocket-jangle of change. All of these signs, these transgressions, David now understood to be merely signals of deeper aims.

The Father begged for his own demise. He sat staring into his television and stewed in its shallow rule. He peered into sunnier ways of being – sculptures of heads, sitcom wives running manicured fingers through the compressed hair of sitcom husbands – and offered no resistance. Living in a Chaos Farm of his own, replete with mysteries and terrors, he questioned nothing, only whether or not to greet another day. He stood shell-shocked against it all, unable to face another tour of duty. And fear is a foe more deadly than any German tank division, any vandal punk or nightclub bouncer, any knife-toothed demon. And *that*, maybe, is the secret, or a fragment of the secret – do you face your fear? Do you resist? Fathers, by their very identity, are also only sons. He is no higher power. He is still a servant of the universe, a soldier. Confucius, whose quotations the temp receptionist Claudine saw fit to clip, said *let the ruler be a ruler minister be a minister father be a father son be a son.*

The Father once enjoyed beaches and Len Deighton novels and fried chicken and ice-cold beer, but in the last few years of his life he expressed no fondness for anything. His eyes, half-shut. His shaky hands, cupped like pincers around knife and fork, slicing a pork chop. His body thinning, his moustache greying.

His apocalypse arrived with the exhaustion of hope. All that stood in his way was David, delivering beer and chicken and sympathy.

The young boy heaves a heavy sigh unbefitting his age. He rinses his hands, then dries them under the automatic hand dryer as told.

His Dad says *all right way ta go champ.*

Driven by an overwhelming inclination, David finds the nearest exit and sheds the airport's harsh climate and rising tumult of frustrated passengers. Automatic doors reintroduce him to dark night as overhead planes fall to earth and lightning crackles in the clefts of clouds. Thunder rumbles, its heaved draw like labouring machinery. A steady rain pounds, but its touch goes unfelt. Nothing affects him now. His hair drips and his shirt sticks to his body. Who cares. He wants *more*. More rain, more grief. All the punishment the world can send him. Typhoons, lava, torrents of hail, frogs, plague, all the pestilence and shit of heaven and earth. He invites it all.

Bring it on. Give it all you've got. Owen, wiggling mouse, singing giddily to himself: *keep on with the force   don't stop 'til you get enough.*

He follows the road's gravel elbow, passing hangars, rental kiosks, darkened looming bunkers. Next to the highway there is a darkened patch littered with lumber. He stares out into this unoccupied field, a barren splotch of land framed by guardrail and dormant petroleum pumps and crumpled barbed wire. Dead land. A portentous battlefield, a wilted expanse, aching with tire treads and aphid-holed grasses poking, shrubs overgrown to tangles.

It's in the furthest reaches, in the lost compartments, where we find what we've been seeking for so long.

The Father is waiting for him out there. Shrouded in fog, he stands motionless, surrounded by strewn trash, soiled cardboard and papers, pared sections of tubing. The garbage encircling the old man forms a filthy makeshift ceremonial ground. Rite and ritual, nostalgia for past days and past ways – tonight, all this will be laid to waste.

The rain flattens his wiry hair and drips from his moustache, condemning him as a living weakness, an attractor, a speck in Chaos's spiral.

David approaches the monster. It is noticeably drained, its ammunition of fire and violence now depleted. Goliath, sluggish. Like Trixie quoted: *so soon at home in being dead.* So cheerful. So unlike his reputation.

The monster hoists itself into a *ten hut*, a thwacking together of heels, a mock salute.

'They left me here,' The Father says.

David: 'Who?'

The Father gazes upward, squinting as rain patters his face. 'There are deeper things than you'll ever know, chief,' he says.

'Tell me,' David pleads. 'I've been chasing … all the … Just give me *something*.'

The dead eyes of The Father, his rope-burned neck burning in broken lines. 'I see that knife. You've got it in your pocket. Let's see that thing.'

Yes. David had almost forgotten, almost been able to forget. He produces the knife. Its weeping blade.

'You were going to try and get on a *plane* with that?' The Father scoffs.

David winces. 'I guess I didn't think … '

'There's no point in receiving an education,' The Father says, 'without putting it to use.'

He'd said the same thing before, once, long ago. Something he'd remembered from an ER episode, maybe.

Thunder explodes again and again. This battle will be fought under the heavens in gooey plains, duked out in mythological wars.

'I can't keep this going,' David says, 'this whole … This is it. It's fucking *over*.'

'Hey now,' The Father says. 'Watch your language there, mister flappy lips.'

David shakes his head. 'Dad. The sky in Barcelona was so beautiful I couldn't believe it. But … thinking about how it was left, when you. I still have … everything beautiful makes me faint. I feel so sick I want to die.'

'You should take something. Take a Gravol.'

Sloping eyes, always so much more expressive than his words. Crow's feet and laugh-lines, the wasted pallor. His arms are sinewy and veined, muscly but quick. Here is a man who once finished his laps, who lifted what you wanted lifted. But there is a waste and a stiffness, a trace of *rigor mortis*.

Suicide: so fierce, so true. You want to ask *why*.

David says, 'There was this ridge, up in the hills where Muzz took me, where you could look across and see the whole countryside. Everything was coated with snow and it was this blanket ... by now it's all thawed, I guess. But they say seasons are flexible there, at Chaos Farm. Remember we went to that place near Sunday River, just that once? And it snowed like crazy. And we had that crappy little room.'

'I caught you smoking.'

'Holy ... I can't believe you remember that. That was, what. I was fourteen, fifteen, and ... I remember. That ski lodge. I was eating onion rings and then I bummed a cigarette from that guy with the hat. And you came in right at that moment. I can't believe you remember that. Uncanny.'

'My death has become your responsibility.'

Yes. This flimsy apparition, this phantom, finally says it. In a confused split-second, David feels an impulse to embrace the old man, but no. No gestures, no sympathy.

'The moon tonight is like the moon when ... I waited until morning, and lunch, and when the rope was properly tied I did it,' The Father says.

He smiles, tired and waiting.

'When the moon was ... By the afternoon the rope was secure.'

David says, 'I will smite thee.'

The Father says, 'I've been looking forward to finally speaking with you, like this.'

The knife finds the pit of his throat, just below his Adam's apple, targeted squarely in the soft cords above his collarbone. A clean break. A confident incision. The forgiving sponginess of the throat allows for unresisted insertion and an inspired jiggle of the blade, fixing it firmly in place.

So sorry oh deliver me.

Initially there is no blood, only sound: the residual motoring whirr of the dishwasher, the ripcording of lawnmower. Somebody somewhere, complaining. A beer can cracking open. David holds the knife fast. The knife is the avenue. The knife is the connector. The monster offers no resistance, just draws hands to its neck. As David drives the knife deeper it crumples. Yes, initially there is no blood – but then thick crimson goo spurts from its throat, staining the golf shirt and denims and the puddled ground beneath. The blood is the debt, now paid. *The blood sprayed David the blood sprayed.* The knife's blade separates something tough inside, and the neck twists, and the monster's eyes loll backward, skyward, then close.

The Father says something like *gh*.

Blood spews by moonlight. There is no moon. There is no blood.

Perhaps we will be only as happy as history allows us to be, through its fictions and storied streams. Perhaps everything will be viciously okay, eerily *okay*, until in the end we meet ourselves on some strange road to duel ourselves for the last time. Perhaps we create epic fictions as attempts to grapple with not-quite-dead truths, to ensnare hellfire in scenes, to write sentences that sing elegies. Perhaps we will slay our foes to discover what lies beyond, to remake impending futures.

The hero seeks destruction, atrocity, full-blown mayhem, but there is only a shrug and a slump. In the end, the demon gives up with a whimper.

Planes are poised to fly overhead in the cutting fog, but storms hold them to the earth. And across the dead land, beyond the road, the control tower is blinkin' like a blinkin' beacon.

IV

The setting sun bobs huge and bloated in the western range. Men march. Their bodies sag, withered by another campaign, every mile along this tough road a year sapped from their young souls. Their rifles are slung around their backs, ammo expended, muzzles emptied. Sunburned skin flakes their noses. The feeling among the troop is of accomplishment, but the outcome of their exploit remains unclear; the consequence of their efforts is still unformed. They have seen action. They have slashed miles of trenches into fields of flesh, wardened the unspeakable: figures halved and maimed and disassembled by swift machines. Brash guns ablaze. Ballets of butchery. They have ploughed endless stretches of dense jungle, vistas defying understanding, sprawls of vines shredded to slaw. They saw these things, and now they walk as blind men. Die with your eyes, like Cyclops thumbing the backs of sheep. The soldiers march in single file up the hill. Hills are coordinates. Survive a hill. Die for a hill. But now they withdraw. There are no rifle calls across the rice fields. The vanquishment of the territory is complete. No more roars in the night. The troops walk numbly.

There is no lip balm, no e-mail, no frothy milk, no angst.

Shift to a long circling helicopter shot, slow-mo into hypnosis. Scenes: cut and splice. Dry wind flushes into the valley. And at all sides, mud. Focus the frame on the mud. Mud, spoots of dirt, are in everything, trickling down the land soldiers tirelessly boot.

Winter has receded. Winter was cold, then colder, but now spring arrives in warm breezes and new life.

Post-apocalypse: silence.

Undo.

The most serene, yet eerie, scene in *Patton* is near its conclusion, after the decisive battles of Patton's cinematic redemption have been fought. With war won, the general sits atop his trusted steed, executing circles in his stable as reporters clamour nearby, casting excited questions his way; they want to know about suspicious Russian allies, about America's post-war prospects, about the future. But already Patton is elsewhere; he is shaping his own retirement, his fade-out – he is already over the next ridge, ready for the next battle. He is laughing in the face of expectations. Patton, the man, would die soon after the war in a car accident.

Credits. The screen goes black.

This is familiar rust, time's passing. David's apartment has shrunk in his absence. Unfamiliar light streams from windows, new dust adrift in the air.

He should be able to re-occupy this place, to fit back in. Things appear as always: the lifeless furniture and dreary walls, the mail slot spilling envelopes and MasterCard statements. Videotapes on top of the VCR, unreturned, long overdue: *Rocky II*, *The Thing*, *The Killing Fields*, *Patton*.

Empires persist, unfallen. The Earth hasn't brittled in revolt. The system perseveres, feeding back recursively – yet, eventually, this graph, this Chaos map, returns to its prime. X here Y there, make it your own. Days generate days, hours slice hours, hours compound into days. Stasis is resumed.

Yet, in this familiarity, he finds himself unfamiliar. He twists faucets, inspects the refrigerator. Jars and tubes and tubs. He picks up a rubber spatula, then returns it to its drawer. He swipes a thumb of dust from the top of his digital cable receiver. All these things are artifacts. All these things he has purchased, for which he endured Jim and Jeff and the Shan-Man and Naoko's irksome time sheets – he wants to chuck them all into snowy nethers.

It's the rebirth of time's passing. The park opens for the season. Mother ducks lead new ducklings, tight formations of yellow fluff, across the pond's surface to bushy nestles. Little kids coo in glee, tossing fistfuls of crumbs and seeds, attracting ducks and pigeons and the occasional seagull. Birth is a spectacle. Kids marvel at the ducks like they marvel at robots and cartoon flames.

The ducks have little to say. David wishes he could discuss things with the ducks. Where he's been, what he's seen. But their language, to him, is prohibited.

They might say: *yo David   long time no see.*

Or, perhaps: *quack.*

It's the conveyor belt of time's passing. Indolent days, back in the sludge of routine. Days. Laundry. The bank, the video store. Subjects introduced, processed, added and subtracted. Residual paperwork from the insurance company surrounding a death in the family, still unfiled. A policy, unattended. Treadmills, kilometres endured without transport. Racing nowhere as fast as possible, as hard as possible.

These are false missions.

It's the mechanism of time's passing. David cranes his neck, squints up into the clouded wash framing the twinned office buildings, Towers 1 and 2. Sun ignites the windows, the tiles of refractive windows, into refractive spikes.

He almost goes up to the office. He would stroll in with a cool demeanour, say *hi* and maybe negotiate his way back into his job. He pictures his former co-workers seated at their desks, eyes buried in computer screens. Filling out time sheets, collating pages, photocopying.

Jim, somewhere, saying *I gotta deal with these yo-yos while coddling those complete fucking space cadets.*

A woman pulls up next to him in a wheelchair and asks, 'Are you waiting for someone?'

'Yes,' he says.

She smiles generously. Her glasses twinkle.

He flees.

It's the continuous bout of time's passing. David watches movies: the contender's gruelling regimen, the systematic definition. Rocky against time sheets. Rocky against managers in braided belts and yellow ties. Rocky atop roofs, hopping fences, avoiding debt. Rocky punching his way through a maze of fax paper and Post-it notes. The Undisputed Heavyweight Champion of the World, bleeding from the head, in the throes of rapture.

Rocky, running up the steps in the freezing Philadelphia morning. Triumphant.

Occasionally, David finds himself startled by worried thoughts of Muzz. Sometimes it seemed Muzz was barely holding on. Muzz slept on gossamer supports, a fragile canopy, wobbling around the stark reality of his addictions.

Muzz had, for a short period, manned a taxi in Portland. Maybe David could become a cab driver too. Anything's possible.

It's the insomnia of time's passing. He dreams he is eighty years old, an old grey-haired man. He is standing on the back deck of some huge country estate, gazing out on a tumbling backyard, the inlet of a glistening lake at its foot. In ripened age, dreamt passage, he is satisfied and serene.

On waking, David realizes that in his dream he had been Ike Hamdaber, in the future, decades from now.

Then: one morning, as he is eating toast while consulting his itinerary for the upcoming trip to Spain, the doorbell rings. He rises slowly, still in sleep's groggy daze, still clad in undershirt and sweatpants.

Sarah Promise is at the door. 'David,' she groans.

He is flabbergasted.

They embrace. He notices how her smell has changed; its gummy fragrance has become darker, more weathered and beaten, like the decomposition of a meadow into an overrun plot of weeds and vines. Wilder and rawer.

Flustered, he invites her in. As he guides her through his mess, he tries to draw her attention from the stained floors, scooping away wadded Kleenexes and kicking away clumps of dust, straightening things, wiping away morning's gunk from his lip crooks and eye corners, trying to hide the dishevelment: strewn papers and videotapes exposed in their cases, clumps of papers and clothes in every corner, sauce-streaked dishes left out and attracting flies.

They sit at the kitchen table. She tells him things about the last few months: Honolulu, with Paul Hirota and his brother Alvin on their palatial estate; gambling in Buenos Aires with a millionaire manufacturer of specialized hinges; shopping in London; recording overdubs for a prominent Hong Kong director, whom she used to love passionately but now considers a *vile babyish beast.*

'But,' David says, interrupting her travelogue, 'when did you leave Chaos? Why did you leave?'

Her lips twist. She crushes her cigarette. 'I split once Sam stopped making the trout. It just wasn't there. The whole thing. The *vibe* just wasn't there. So I split.'

'After I ... '

'The whole thing.'

'Sarah,' David says. 'We brought hellfire. We raised the dead. We invoked the wrath of ... '

Her eyes are impatient. 'Oh. I don't think so.'

'I travelled back in time.'

Again: 'I don't think so.'

'Don't fuck with me. I stood for hours in the rain. I slept under bridges. And all the while I was ... Tell me, where's Ike?'

Sarah Promise looks at him, then shakes her head.

'I told you there would be visions,' she says. 'They can be quite elaborate, these visions. What you think you saw was simply one of these manifestations. You have to regard this as less than reality, while also greater. Like Ike says, self-deception can be an avenue to a new path. You have to be able to give it up.'

What she says isn't true. It is a violation of truth. This is horseshit.

'Sarah, ' he says, 'Look at me. Am I a vision? Am I blind? Look at my eyes. Do I look like I've been sleeping? I was healed – I lived, I was repaired, while Bedel died. His body fell in halves. Tell me why. I went so far ... I just sit here and try to remember everything, but it's all slipping away. I was keeping notes, on those little yellow Post-its, but I keep forgetting where I stuck them ... '

'I used to keep diaries,' Sarah Promise interrupts. 'I had a whole shelf of them in my bedroom. But eventually I grew to think of them as a failure of experience. And a waste of good hours to boot.

I started with people. I learned their voices – or more truthfully, I *took* their voices. '

David: 'You take truth and make it into a cartoon.'

She glowers. 'Fuck you, David.'

'Cartoon whales.'

'Cartoon heroes. Cartoon fathers. Blah blah *blah*. What does it matter?'

David leans closer. He focuses all his powers forward, at Sarah.

'Do Lisa,' he says.

'Who's Lisa?'

'At the Midtown. The first night we … met. You did a voice, a young girl. A teenage girl. You asked me for a voice to do and you did it. Remember?'

'Vaguely.'

'And later, at Chaos Farm, you did it too. It's the voice of my … '

Sarah raises a hand. 'David, I'm just an actress. I play roles. I do routines and voices.'

'But you don't. You do it. You did her.'

'You had a vision. That's what happens.'

'Do it. Do her. Do it.'

'David. Give it up.'

He can't argue. No. He bites into his toast. His hands tremble. Any second now he will tear away and throw himself back into the forgetfulness of bed.

From a huge leather shoulder bag, Sarah Promise produces a small squarish package wrapped in scrunched paper and plops it on the table before him.

'Molly wanted me to give you this.'

He unwraps it to find a photograph in a simple burgundy wooden frame. David and Muzz, in the farmhouse solarium, seated in opposing wicker chairs. They face out the window at snowy land slathered below, snow-clumped trees against pale blue, frost on the sills. In profile, they both smile widely, trapped in laughter.

David picks up the picture, turns it over. On the back of the frame there is an inscription in blue pencil: NOT BAD *Love Molly.*

'She gave this to you for me?'

She nods. 'It's a pretty good snap.'

The two of them had shared many hours together, shooting the proverbial shit, and at some point Molly had captured them in her frame. Muzz yapping about Aboriginal digeridoo technique. David peering complacently out, the eyepatched side of his face hidden to the camera. The two of them, photographed in three-quarter angle, lit in stark contrast, laughing, momentarily free. David smiles.

It feels like the whole thing was one long fucked-up dream.

'Where is he these days?'

'Who, Muzz? I don't know, David. I just don't know. I lose touch with all of it. Maybe next year.'

Sarah Promise is the harbinger of wreckage and loss and confusion, and yet she departs with zero fanfare. She coughs and slaps him on the meat of his shoulder, an impartial gesture, then exits. David closes the door behind her and slides the bolt into its hinge.

Not bad.

It's the torture of time's passing. Life as a grid, a blank time sheet, ready for data and lies. They say *true life is lacking*. They say *life is suffering*. They say *life is but a dream*.

The next morning, he wakes to find his vision halved, his left eye again rendered useless, its flesh again pulverized. But he blinks, and waits, then wakes – this too is but a dream.

It's the tactical momentum of time's passing. But there is no plan, no strategy in his mind as David hops the bus, anxious as he gazes out at the passing city, riding southward into gleaming neighbourhoods, into the sparkling thick. Uncertainty grips his stomach and clenches. In transit, he reoccupies dead space, the purgatorial province of in-between.

The last time he'd been on a bus, things had gone badly.

When he arrives at the house, Jo-Beth greets him with a cautious hug. She leads him to the living room and they sit, he on the couch and she in a chair. The curtains are drawn wide, filling the room with solemn light. On the coffee table before him is an empty candy dish and a leafed stack of magazines: *People* and *Maclean's* and *InStyle*.

'You need something to drink,' Jo-Beth says.

'That's all right.'

'I'll get you a Sprite.'

She heads for the kitchen. The TV chatters in the next room, a baseball game. He won't come out. Gary. He can't lay eyes, can't bear to confront the transgressor, the usurper, the nephew.

Ask David, Gary spat. *I'm asking you   you piece of shit   I'm asking you.*

David sits with every muscle clenched. He picks up a magazine with Jennifer Aniston on the cover and flips its pages. The TV's play-by-play – *zero for four this afternoon* – battles the house's restrained quiet. Regret moans in the walls, across the immaculate lawn, in the dustless surfaces.

This house is a crypt.

Jo-Beth returns with a can of Sprite and a tall glass clinking with ice, setting both on coasters. 'I didn't know if you wanted ice or what.'

'Thanks,' David says. 'Thanks. That's great.'

She sits, attentive as he cracks the warm can and pours the soda into the glass to bubble over the ice. He sips, swallows, then sets the glass down, nodding appreciatively. Jo-Beth nods back. Her face is taut.

'It's still raining,' she asks. 'That's all you wore?'

'It's easing off.'

'I meant to spend all day in the garden, but looks like that won't happen. Everything's soaked out back.'

'Are you growing tomatoes again? I still remember that salad with the plum tomatoes. Those tomatoes were legendary.'

She grimaces. 'Truth be told, David, I was surprised you called.'

'Well. I guess … '

'I was taken aback.'

'I wanted you to know that … '

He fails to explain. He is staring at Jennifer Aniston. Her hair shimmers impossibly, like some laboratory-fashioned composite.

'Where have you been, David?'

'I just. I had to get away. I had to get out of here.'

'But you went *where*.'

'I was … called away.'

Jo-Beth: 'Things have not exactly been a walk in the park around here. Every day I wake up and all there's this lingering … sometimes I think I'm. I fall into this *state.*'

David's throat is tight.

'She was just a girl, David. In her … *God.*'

She presses a palm against her forehead and begins to sob.

The TV says *and that's three up three down   and we'll be right back for the top of the sixth.*

David, powerless: 'It's not that I don't … understand. I wasn't only, you can't … '

'She was just a child. She was your *cousin.*'

Yes. She was. 'What are you trying to say?'

'You … you tell *me* what it is that I'm trying to say.'

'But I don't know what that *is.*'

Jo-Beth rises to her feet, shaking her head, her eyes spouting tears. She is a small cautious woman, a hand-wringer, a dishtowel-folder.

Her voice breaks. 'If you knew how hard we tried … '

The dismal afternoon is reflected in her destroyed posture, the room wounded in her mourning. Sniffing, she spins and hurries to the den. Toward the baseball game, and Gary reclining in his recliner. Voices whisper sharply above the TV's squelch.

Should he leave now. *No.* He stays and braces himself. David stares at Jennifer Aniston and her otherworldly tresses, her compact torso, the inextravagant mounds of her boobs.

Jo-Beth re-emerges with Gary in tow. Gary has aged years in months; brownish tinges ring the lower folds of his eyes and his posture has fallen to a demoralized stoop. He stands shorn of his command. His future has been assassinated, his domestic pride befouled. His mouth hangs slack. He removes his glasses.

Something passes between the two of them, Gary and David. A stirring of knowledge.

Then Gary turns dejectedly to his wife. 'This is pointless,' he says.

Jo-Beth again smushes her hand into her temple. 'I wish we'd talked before.'

David tries to speak. 'But … '

Gary faces him with pained, oblique reluctance. '*Listen*. Did she call you? Were you talking to her?'

Did she. Even in her absence, David still wants to preserve Lisa's confidence. Maintain her intentions in memorial. Her facade. He alone witnessed. She saw and spoke. She relayed intentions. Conclusions beyond her teenage scope. He longed only to hold her tightly in his reach, unexposed to danger. Just to hold her, to hide her away. So she couldn't be ruined by the terrible world beyond, as others had. To hold. Momentarily. To hide. But in this too he failed.

'We spoke the night before,' David says. 'Briefly. She was a bit indecipherable. I don't know if there was any hint of any ... I can't really say for certain.'

Jo-Beth: 'Did she talk to you about anything ... anything about the. The sword.'

They are all afraid to say it. Death. Suicide. *Seppuku*. The tomorrowlessness. Gary and Jo-Beth: together against the gory reality, yet both isolated. They can't evade it. Blood and tragedy: too resonant, too immediate. They move like robots, powered by pulse of sorrow and outrage.

Gary: 'I told you. The thing, the note, said to ask you. Yet you still won't say what's what. Though you know. This whole thing, you *know*. Now, you tell me, you son of a ... damn you. What did you do to my daughter, because I am ready to, I'm thinking about doing something serious. I could be calling the cops.'

Things are suddenly, awfully, plain. 'Wait a sec,' David says. 'Don't tell me you think there's something ... *sinister* you're implying here about me and ... if you think that. No. *No*. Gary. You guys, listen. We talked on the phone. I was just waiting by the falafel stand ... '

Gary shakes his head. His body quakes. 'What the shit are you *talking* about?'

David recognizes the signs of Gary's retreat, the weather of his storms; he's stared into tired eyes, broken with unweeping hours, blood vessels broken into a scrawl of veins. The dry mouth, exhausted, curled around a cigarette. The pit of the throat. David has witnessed this withdrawal, the process of slow retreat shaped in fear and regret. Eventually – it just takes the right arrangement of stars, humidity trapped in a room, certain noises – the moment makes itself clear, and an escape route opens. Refusal is impossible, and unreasonable. *Hiri-kiri*, self-extirpation, terminus. An act of protest, maybe. Or a rite of self-definition.

'I loved her,' David says.

Now he's crying too. They're all crying; they're a bunch of crybabies.

Jo-Beth: 'Love. What do you know about love?'

There are deeper things than you'll ever know, chief.

'I ... I know enough.'

Lisa's parents stand together. They are losers. They have lost. David wipes his nose against the ridge of his palm.

Gary: 'I still can't. I'll never. Do you ... All the ... When they came to take her away, I had to stand there like an asshole ... '

Struggling through spasms.

'Her blood *flew*. It was everywhere.'

He collapses into the chair. The man as puddled heap. His wife gathers herself around his sunken shoulders. His bushy brows twitch. 'She called you *why*.'

David: 'Maybe she found ... '

'What.'

'Maybe she felt that we, she and I, had some sort of ... that, when no one else was ... '

Jo-Beth breaks in. 'If you're implying we weren't *there*. Because we were there. We reached and reached. And she never said anything indicating anything remotely in the realm of ... '

Gary places a hand on Jo-Beth's arm, halting her.

'I want to know,' he says. 'I want to hear the answer.'

Zeroing in.

David: 'The answer.'

'*Ask David*. So here I am, asking. Like the note. Here's David. I'm asking.'

Everything is weighted toward him. Testify. Speak. David clears his throat. Then, steadying himself for the reaction, he tells them the answer.

In the final scenes, the killers come home to roost, the aims of their missions extended beyond the plan and the path, fears still fiery in their bellies. The trenches are narrow. The fissures holding the heaped bodies are never large enough. You can still hear them stiffening, still shivering in the ground. Mere inches, mere decades.

You want to dig deeper into the soil. Bury them in deeper graves, further apart.

The past seems so far away, distant and dim like meteors dotting Chaos Farm's blue-black night sky. Everything is misty reminiscence, a likeness of truth pitted in nostalgia.

And yet: despite the past's decline and the oncoming hurtle of the future, despite the heaviness and the depth, things never quite wrap up in neat finales.

David ambles through the cemetery gates, up the slope toward The Father's grave. His shirt sticks to his back and his forehead leaks an annoyance of sweat. Around him headstones tile along the coiling paths under huge grasping trees, marking the buried remains of these countless souls and their passage into the great whatever. Memorial wreaths fry in the sun.

An ancient groundskeeper putts past atop a grumbling John Deere, grinning a huge shit-eating grin. He hoists a sunburned forearm and offers David an indistinct salute, blinking *hello*. David nods back, but finds himself irked by such leisure, in this place. This scene should be serious and sombre. *Grave*. Frivolity is for toga parties and baseball games, not visitations to the lost.

But. This guy, this old doofus eking out his days plopping sod atop coffins amid the wails of grieving widows, is surely better acquainted with the process of mourning than David; perhaps his obliviousness is the sanest reaction in the face of this decomposition, this uncrazy craziness, the huge transparent mystery. Better goofy than tortured, maybe.

Maybe it's all right to eat hamburgers at The Father's grave.

The heat is livid. It's determined. It's aimed squarely at him, microwaving his brain. The sun hates him. It loves to see him sweat.

Standing at the grave site, he feels exhausted, spent of all feeling. Under the ground it would be cool. Locked in a sealed box, crumbling to dust. In the cushioned coffin the reprieve of rest achieves honour, sullied in ease, thwarted and shredded – you lose weight in battle. The brain weighs about three pounds. Give or take. The creature ran hard and far, but eventually lost steam; with enough time any inertia dwindles. Years of mulling over dim-lamped scenes, stairwells encased in dimness. It dwindles. We enslave ourselves to recollection.

The emphasis was on *hustle*, whether the fullback line could outpace the attacking forward line – those finessing sprinters who moved like spat lightning. Both teams sallied forth with victorious aims, yet neither managed a crushing win. Final score: 2-2. On the sidelines, the sharp whiff of springtime grass heavy in their lungs and the mud clumping in their cleats, there is time to think. Tie as success, tie as failure. Tie game as worse than loss – tie game as ineffectiveness. Tie game. Even Steven.

Heaven is a young girl's dreaminess. A young girl cries out in anguish. Skirts swirl in misplaced avenues, swirls of spilt blood. Share death with the glorious dead. Here, sombre survivors lay flowers. Today we drape our heroes with honourable tidings where weird myth is sucked of middling aims and reshaped in elevated spheres. Heavenly virtues guide us to the hereafter and our hungry stomachs bind us to the earth. Kill the brain and the body surrenders. Kill the man and the memory lingers; but, in time, that too passes. He had schemes to avoid paying his parking tickets. Success, always so distant in the stony temples of his eyes. Like a caged rat in a lab. That's you, David, pure of heart, alone, dreaming of deserts and ice plains and craters on the moon. His mother smelt of lipstick and aerosol deodorant. A funeral hearse eases across the cross-crested horizon. The Father's epitaph reads only IN MEMORIAM. He would stare at the road, gripping the wheel, peeved, shamed, while David sank in the shotgun seat with turf scrapes on his legs, shin pads in his sweat-sticky socks. A tie is as good as a loss in the standings, now you need to win every single frigging game left in the season to make playoffs. The Father, his mind already trudging to a new scrapyard of thought. Success was never a possibility; this battle was a losing game, a sucker's bet, a disaster. It was Napoleon's Leipzig, Yamamoto's Midway; it was a Sicilian Expedition, a Gettysburg, a Bay of Pigs.

The odds were stacked. The layout of surrender is incalculable, too mysterious.

In Barcelona the boats sat on the water like contented cartoon whales, and over dinner his mother seemed to grow younger with every giggle; with every unbearable generalization she made she aged another year in reverse. Tomorrow, after a long, surely exasperating flight, she will welcome him with open arms, envelop him, naturalize him, remake him for the sleepy old world with the currents of progress at her feet – someday she too will go down that sad road to crumble to dust, but not on this soil. Not on this parking-lotted new world; this is land reserved for fathers, for Adam and Jesse and Ra and Kronos and the countless infernally flawed – famed in infamy – fathers writhing in the slime of history and myth; this is the domain of wide forearms, of manhood stretched out in flame-broken capture, of punishing tests. Armwrestles. The police asked questions, hastening through procedure, jotting in pads, taking stock in identification. The paramedics were stony and respectful and wore orange vests. You stand and answer dutifully as they wheel out the body, obliging, frozen in a monstrous block of ice called disbelief.

Here, stain-tinged grave markers crack and etched letters erode into illegibility, years hammered into stone retranslated as indecipherable glyphs. The sun's stabbing heat bears down like a punishment, or a test of who can make it through *this* to the next, who can survive Now to graduate to Later. This is the battle. Peer through the brush, rifles mounted on shoulders beleaguered with pack-welts. Squint to find the enemy crouched in their lairs. Aim, fire. Muzzles spew blazes into the heart-hammering night. Soldiers in foreign lands, saluting imagined flags with chesty joy, stabbing at glory like jewellers pricking stones, gleaning proof and heroism from the raw stuff of the world. People create situations. They sleepwalk through mayhem, like Sarah Promise, performing in the drama of her own life, aiming for gratification by way of imitation. She blows smoke into the Carnegie Hall of her own skull and whispers dialogue into a microphone, and in her performance she might assume the mantle of a queen. Ike forever seeks what he can never find, the dreamer never rousing, always in the cosmos and never of the earth, choked on arcane texts and oversaturated with versions of the divine, studying and experimenting his way deeper and deeper into the oblivion of unknowing. His mind, fraught with neurosis, can't convince itself of another way; like the drunk driver who veered the Aries wagon left despite the facing red, his only basis of knowledge was what sat immediately before him. He was an impudent general. Like the crumpled station wagon slowing into the parking lot, Ike's trajectory would continue, unhappy and unsatisfied. So they all continue, all spectres of past episodes. Now they are all lovable and human.

Patton died a mere nine months after his final battle in the spring of 1945. A freak automobile accident. But the man had already given up – *the great tragedy of my life was that I survived the last battle,* he said. Neither poetry nor history could satisfy his thirst for combat.

Sadness isn't awareness of grim impending future – that's *dread.* Sadness is a function of the past. The past is what kills. The past sneaks up coldly, exactly. The past knows which buttons to push. The only thing hiding is the unopened future.

So what do you say, with your father's grave at your feet, his rank demoted to a servitude of grass and dirt? There are no zombies or vampires in this graveyard, only memories terrible and terribler. Recall: a mother's humiliated raging tears as David stepped into the doorway with cop escort. Looking back, David could see that this was the moment where his parents separated; the detachment had begun years previous, but in that moment everything disconnected. *Bam.* Survey the wreckage on the road, scraped in blackened tire squeals.

Death is everywhere; death is everything. Eddie Money sang *baby hold on to me   whatever will be will be* as protesters cast hazardous glass on the ground. Eddie Money as the voice of the innocent. *Whatever will be will be* – all this heavy shit going down, however all this shit might turn out, well, *fuck it,* whatever will be will just *be,* whether you invest your soul or not, so just accept it and fuck the consequences. The battle will be waged in countrysides, in suburbs, on car-congested freeways, in the elevators of office towers, in conclusions and biases. The battle will define its terms through the assumption that life, this growling life, is *hard*. All soldiers will be provided graves, even the nameless hunks of riddled flesh and body chunks left behind. All will receive a hero's remembrance, even the left-behind.

But The Father, unheroic and unimportant – what does he leave? The Father never changed, and the world wouldn't stay fixed. Tomorrow David will fly across the sea, and in the night's depths he might shed a few cold tears for everything that he's lost, but in his core he will be happy. A tough version of nauseated worried anticipating happy. No more will he fear the sad old man, and no more will he pity him – all these sentimental battles are finished. Here adolescence crumbles into dispirited manhood; there are no margaritas or bongs, no free janglings of chance or loose change. Judgment will be unsympathetic. The Father's ambition for self-annihilation is fulfilled, his impact skimmed away like a footprint in wet sand, washed away by lapping tides. No more threatened by the frenzy of traffic, of buses, of squealing brakes, he will stand prepared against the surging speed; he will laugh heroically like a child in cradling arms. No more will he be paralyzed. Ike insisted that *freedom is infinity trapped in whorls of mayhem locked in a matrix of disarray spooned into the cauldron of chaos*. But David knows – freedom isn't infinite; it's pushing, suffering. It's continuing, against. And he will continue. He will sleep with his memories of highwayed nights and Chaos valleys and clicking phone calls.

And he will dream of his father. The Father, now forgotten, his barren ways leaving no mark on the world. In the end, it seems no one will carry on with the man held in their mind or kept close in their heart. No one will associate. No one will daydream. No one will survive the apocalypse.

No one but David.

The elevator was again on the fritz. The stairwell's concrete amplified his echoing footfalls as he footed it up up up to the fourth floor, and then into the hallway: mildewed carpet, dim ceiling bulbs. David lugged a large bag containing a bucket of Kentucky Fried Chicken and an eight-pack of Moosehead. The bag was spotted with rain. He proceeded down the hallway, listening to voices behind doors, TVs blasting, taps gushing. Reaching the second-last door on the left, he knocked twice, then let himself in. The place was too dark and stiflingly hot. As always, the windows and drapes were shut. He went to the kitchen. Plastic cups floating butts in blackened soda sat on the counter. Wads of paper towel lay demolished to smears among spills of coffee. He plopped the sack on the table next to a cluster of department-store flyers glued together with some ketchup-like sealant, then proceeded to the den. Television: *Entertainment Tonight* on the set of. The faint mosquito *bzz* of the dimmer switch. David said *how you doing* to the room's only resident and the old man answered *nuh bad*. The old man scratched his temple, burrowing upward to an eczema-wracked scalp. Thumps from a nearby apartment resonated in the floorboards. The TV presented a sweep of blue skies over Nevada's picturesque deserts, estates, arid ridges rippling like sandy potato chips. The old man's heavy eyes accepted Nevada, the drooping folds wearying every blink. *Hungry?* David asked him. *Sure.* David returned to the kitchen, on the way lowering the thermostat. He removed the contents from the bag and placed them on the counter, a sweaty bucket of chicken and fries, containers of gravy and coleslaw, an arsenal of vinegar and ketchup and salt and plastic forks. He then located a pair of plates and allotted even portions of food to both, carefully forming arrangements: a sprinkle of salt on the fries, as he knew his father to like, spoonfuls of coleslaw evenly spread, a genial base for breast and drumstick. Throughout this apartment there was stark focus. No candour, no joy, no frivolity. There was negative order. David separated a pair of cans from the ring, then brought the plates and beers to the den. The TV said *you'll never guess what she told ET insiders*. David delivered a plate and a can to The Father, who accepted both without a word. Even with just the two of them, they were family enough for a Family Size Bucket. David sat in the other, less comfortable, chair, with his plate in his lap. They dug into chicken and television. They were in studio, in Burbank. Live before a studio audience. All else was unnecessary; TV noise enamoured them with emptiness. They watched the last few minutes of an episode of *M*A*S*H*. They were in Korea.

Shells fell and dust fell from the ceilings. Radar O'Reilly clutched his hat. David tore open a packet of ketchup and squeezed it onto his fries. The Father, as was his way, eschewed the packets of condiments, taking his portions dry. By the murky bluish glow that provided the room's only light, David watched The Father work on a drumstick. Then David switched channels, and the TV exploded with *Hollywood Squares*, Whoopi Goldberg waving hideously at the camera amid blinding glitter. The beer was cold, but not quite cold enough. Outside, the rain began to peter out, but inside the room was stuffy and stinky with chicken. The Father dropped a wad of greasy skin in his lap, saying *aw fuck me*. He pinched the skin back onto his plate, then proceeded to dab a serviette at his pants, battling the stain. His mouth worked phrases, cursing his pants. David handed him a moist towelette, assuring *that'll wash out*, but The Father was persistent. He struggled against the stain. He wanted to attack it alone. He rubbed and rubbed and dabbed and dabbed until he paused, and took a look, and the stain was actually defeated, gone; the pant leg was wet but clean, and he was done.

Typeset in Aldus and Alphaville
Printed and bound at the Coach House on bpNichol Lane, 2004.

Edited and designed by Alana Wilcox
Top cover image and author photo by Catherine Stockhausen

Coach House Books
401 Huron Street (rear) on bpNichol Lane
Toronto, Ontario
M5S 2G5

416 979 2217
800 367 6360

mail@chbooks.com
www.chbooks.com